**"All of th[...]re hormonal?"**

"No, you idiot! I'v[...]

The words rippled through the air and she immediately pressed a hand to her mouth. She hadn't meant to say it. Especially not like that. Coop's face went white and he looked like he needed to sit down to digest what she'd just said.

"You've been… With who?"

He turned his face toward her. Heat rose to her cheeks in embarrassment. For years she'd ignored the fact that once upon a time she'd have done anything to have his hands and lips on her like they'd been only moments ago. Now that they had been…it took her back to those days of desperately trying to get his attention. To make him see her as more than just a friend. And now he thought she was involved with someone. At any other time it would be comical. In light of the situation, it was just plain awkward.

"It's none of your business."

He looked up at her from beneath his sooty lashes and said ominously, "From the way you were kissing me a moment ago, I'd say it is very much my business."

# A COWBOY TO
# COME HOME TO

BY
DONNA ALWARD

First published in Great Britain 2013
by Mills & Boon, an imprint of Harlequin (UK) Limited,
Eton House, 18-24 Paradise Road, Richmond, Surrey TW9 1SR

© Donna Alward 2013

ISBN: 978 0 263 90134 4
ebook ISBN: 978 1 472 00517 5

23-0813

Harlequin (UK) policy is to use papers that are natural, renewable and recyclable products and made from wood grown in sustainable forests. The logging and manufacturing processes conform to the legal environmental regulations of the country of origin.

Printed and bound in Spain
by Blackprint CPI, Barcelona

A busy wife and mother of three (two daughters and the family dog), **Donna Alward** believes hers is the best job in the world: a combination of stay-at-home mum and romance novelist. An avid reader since childhood, Donna always made up her own stories. She completed her arts degree in English literature in 1994, but it wasn't until 2001 that she penned her first full-length novel and found herself hooked on writing romance. In 2006 she sold her first manuscript, and now writes warm, emotional stories for Mills & Boon® Cherish™.

In her new home office in Nova Scotia, Donna loves being back on the east coast of Canada after nearly twelve years in Alberta, where her career began, writing about cowboys and the West. Donna's debut romance, *Hired by the Cowboy*, was awarded the Bookseller's Best Award in 2008 for Best Traditional Romance.

With the Atlantic Ocean only minutes from her doorstep, Donna has found a fresh take on life and promises even more great romances in the near future!

Donna loves to hear from readers. You can contact her through her website, www.donnaalward.com or her page at www.myspace.com/dalward.

To my girlie girls, who have grown into an awesome
pair of brainstorming partners. I'd still be stuck
at the words "Chapter One" if it weren't for you!

# CHAPTER ONE

COOPER FORD WAS six foot two of faded denim and plaid cotton, accessorized by an insufferable ego.

The smile slid off of Melissa Stone's face as Coop pulled the door to the flower shop closed behind him, the little brass bell dinging annoyingly as he reached up and took off his hat. Oh, wasn't he all charm and politeness. Melissa's replacement smile was plastic and somewhat forced. Just what she needed at five o'clock on a Friday afternoon. To be face-to-face with the one man left in Cadence Creek who she wished would simply dry up and blow away.

"Afternoon, Melissa."

She gritted her teeth at the sound of his deep voice, somehow musical even when saying the most mundane things. "Cooper."

She refused to call him Coop like everyone else in town. Like she had years ago when they'd all hung out together, having a few beers around a campfire after a Sunday-night softball game. When he'd been the sort of guy she'd been proud to call *friend.* Now he was Cooper. If she thought he'd let her get away with it, she'd call him Mr. Ford. He deserved it.

But that would be a little *too* obvious. A very stiff "Cooper" sent the same message with a touch more subtlety—even if he did remain Coop in her head. The old days were gone. They weren't friends any longer. To her recollection, this was the first time he'd ever deigned to darken the flower shop door.

He smiled at her. "Nice day out there. Cool, but sunny."

Oh, this was positively painful. The weather? Seriously? She blinked, trying to ignore Coop's big frame, which fit perfectly into his dusty jeans and the worn denim jacket that looked as if he'd had it for at least a decade. The edges of the collar and cuffs were white and slightly frayed. The jacket gaped open, revealing an old plaid shirt with a streak of dirt smeared across his chest.

One positive thing she could say about Coop: he wasn't lazy. From the look of him he was straight off the ranch. From the smell of him, too—the pungent but not unpleasant scent of horses clung to his clothing.

"Forecast says frost maybe tonight." She resisted the urge to tap her nails on the counter. The weather, she realized, was a safe topic. "What can I do for you, Cooper?"

He bumped his hat on the side of his leg. "I need some flowers."

His gaze dropped to the green apron she wore when she was in her shop. The words Foothills Floral Design were embroidered on the left breast. Pockets lined the bottom, where she could keep her scissors and pocket knife and anything else she needed as she worked around the store.

Her cheeks heated. No big surprise that Cooper was staring at her breasts. He liked women, did Cooper Ford. When she'd been married, Coop had a new girl hanging off his arm every other month, it seemed.

A real love-'em-and-leave-'em kind of guy. She took a deep breath. "What kind of flowers?"

His gaze lifted to meet hers and she found herself drawn to the golden flecks in the hazel depths. He had lashes that were too long to be decent for any self-respecting man, which made his eyes quite pretty.

Pretty enough for him to get away with just about anything in this town, she reminded herself with disgust. Except with her. She knew exactly what kind of guy Cooper was. He'd definitely shown his true colors the day he'd betrayed their friendship.

"I don't know," he confessed with a sheepish grin. "Something big. Something that says I'm really, really sorry."

Acid soured her stomach. Ugh. Apology flowers. And she could just imagine what the combo of Coop and a big bouquet would do to some silly doe-eyed girl who didn't know any better. "Who'd you do wrong now, Coop?"

The words were out before she could think better of them and she couldn't take them back.

His gaze sharpened, but he merely raised one eyebrow. It made her feel small, as she always did when she was reminded of what a fool she'd been three years ago.

Walking in on her husband, Scott, and his girlfriend had been the most humiliating moment of her life. It had made her one big cliché.

She'd thought it couldn't get any worse, but then she'd discovered that Coop had known all along. He'd been aware that her husband—his best buddy—was having an affair. And he hadn't said a single, blessed word to her about it. No heads-up. No...nothing.

The joke had totally been on her, and she'd never forgotten it. Even now, as she took the steps to truly move on—alone—his betrayal stung. There was sticking by your friend and there was doing what was right. Cooper didn't choose right.

"I missed my mother's birthday," he replied, putting his weight on one hip and hooking a thumb in his jeans pocket. "I was out of town all week. But it was her sixtieth and so now I'm trying to make it up to her."

Once more Melissa felt foolish. She didn't like Cooper. Actually, the truth was more that she didn't trust him. She didn't respect him. She should just let it go, like water off a duck's back, as the old saying went. She definitely should not let him get to her, especially after all this time.

"Oh," she answered. "Then I'm sure I can help. Do you want it in a vase or paper?"

"Paper," he answered. "She's got a million vases around the house. And no roses. They're too formal and old-ladyish. Something mixed."

Melissa tended to agree. Not that roses weren't great, and they were definitely a classic—elegant and timeless. But she secretly preferred something simpler, more wildflowerish and whimsical. "Colors?"

"Yellows. Maybe with some red and blue in it? Colorful and, well, large. It's a big apology."

He smiled down at Melissa and she nearly smiled back before catching herself. "Give me fifteen minutes or so," she replied, jotting the order on her notepad. "You can come back and pick it up, yeah?"

He nodded. "It'll give me time to go to the pharmacy and get a nice card."

"Gee, nothing says 'Happy Birthday, Mom' like a last-minute card," she replied drily.

He didn't answer.

"Okay," she said, putting down her pen. "Fifteen minutes."

"Thanks, Mel," he said, putting his hat back on his head.

Mel.

No one had called her that in ages. Certainly not Cooper, who she avoided as often as possible, which took some creativity in a town the size of Cadence Creek. Thankfully, he felt the same way, and even if they ended up at the same functions, they steered well clear of each other. Opposite ends of the room sort of thing. Definitely no eye contact or chitchat.

But hearing the shortened version of her name—Mel—took her back to the old days. The days when she'd thought she was happy, and she'd really been living in a fantasy world.

The bell chimed as he left, a cheerful sound that was out of key with her current dismal mood, a good portion of which had nothing to do with Cooper at all. She was getting tired of taking her temperature every darn day. Of getting her hopes up, only to be faced with disappointment. Of spending her savings on trying to get pregnant the nontraditional way. She was going to give it one more try, but she wasn't holding out a lot of hope. Maybe she'd be better off filling out the paperwork for the adoption registry.

But deep down, she wasn't ready to give up. The end of her marriage had also marked the end of her plans for a brilliant life. Plans that had included starting a family. Why should she give that up just because circumstances had changed? She'd done so many things on her own since the divorce, like start her own successful business. She was absolutely certain she could manage this, too.

She would be a good mom if given the chance.

But first she had to look after Cooper's order. She was just getting out the red gerbera daisies when Penny arrived for her Friday-night shift. Penny was in eleventh grade at the high school and was the best worker Melissa had on staff. Most of the time she wished she could have her for more shifts, but Penny and her parents were firm on the eight-hours-a-week rule. Melissa got her Friday from five to nine and Saturday morning from nine to one and that was it.

Melissa hoped that if the planets aligned and things finally went right, she could offer Penny a lot more hours next summer—especially if Melissa was spending more time at home with a baby. Between Penny and Amy Wilkins, who covered a lot of the day shifts, Melissa had some breathing room in the schedule.

Penny's arrival meant Melissa wouldn't have to wait on Cooper when he returned. All she had to do was finish making up the arrangement before he came back.

Her fingers plucked bright yellow yarrow a little quicker at the prospect. Cooper Ford had nothing to do with her current life.

She made her own way now, and that was exactly how it was going to stay.

Cooper let out a breath when he was out on the sidewalk again. He'd finally gathered up the courage to go into her shop. This nonsense of avoiding each other had gone on long enough. Surely after three years she might have mellowed where he was concerned.

But nothing had changed, had it? Melissa still looked at him as if he were dirt beneath her heel. It had been a long time since she and Scott had split. But the truth was she still hated Scott, and she still hated Cooper's guts because he'd known about the affair and hadn't said a word.

He walked away from the flower shop, his long legs eating up the concrete as he made his way to the drugstore. The problem with Melissa was that she didn't know the whole story. She thought Cooper had kept his mouth shut because he'd been looking out for his best buddy. "Their little club," she'd called it. And she'd called him a lot more than that, too, words he would never have imagined coming out of that sweet little mouth. He'd taken all the verbal slings because she'd been right. Not in her interpretation of how it all went down, and definitely not right about his motives. But she'd been right that he should have had the guts to say something. God knows he wanted to. He'd come close so many times....

But all his life he'd been a coward where Melissa was concerned, and the day she'd walked in on Scott with another woman hadn't changed anything. Cooper had had no right to her friendship after that. He'd failed her, and she would never know how badly he felt about it.

At the drugstore, he headed for the greeting card aisle. Without too much trouble he picked out a birthday card for his mother, but he paused as he passed by a smaller section of cards. Close to the thank-you notes were half a dozen with I'm Sorry messages on the fronts. They sported sappy pictures of flowers and cute puppies and kittens. He gave a dry chuckle as he picked one up and opened the flap. There were no words on the inside, just a blank space to write in a personal message.

He imagined what he'd write to Melissa. "I'm sorry for keeping the truth from you all those years ago," maybe? It was true. But it wouldn't be enough. Not for her. And there was no way in hell he was going to write "I'm sorry I didn't tell you about your husband's infidelity, but I was in love with you and didn't want to hurt you."

Even if he were stupid enough to confess such a thing, it didn't even scrape the surface of what had really happened.

He'd been between a rock and a hard place and it had marked the end of his lifelong friendship with Scott. Not that that mattered one bit to Melissa, he thought bitterly. Not once had she considered how he might be caught in the middle, between his two best friends.

He put the card back in the slot and went to the cash register. Once outside, he headed back to the flower shop, gearing himself up for another few minutes of pretending they didn't have any past history at all.

But when he went back inside Foothills Floral, there was no sign of Melissa. Instead, a teenager with braces smiled at him and rang up his purchase.

He left and got into his truck, a crease forming between his brows.

It appeared he wasn't the only coward.

The early September sky was the clear, deep blue that Melissa particularly loved, and it seemed to go on forever. As she got out of her car and shut the door, she took a deep, restorative breath. How she loved this time of year. Everything was warm and mellow after the brash heat of summer. The prairie was green and golden, the air crisp and the leaves on the poplars and birches were turning a stunning golden yellow. It reminded her of back-to-school days and how she'd loved filling up her new backpack and lunch bag and getting on the school bus as a girl. It reminded her of sitting on the bleachers during football season, cheering on the Cadence Creek Cougars and, in particular, Scott.

Well, that memory was a little tainted now, but she still remembered what it had been like to be nearly seventeen and in love with the handsome star of the team.

These days the fall weather made her want to do all sorts of nesting things, like baking and freezing and canning and knitting. It was silly, because why would she bother freezing and canning for herself? Maybe if she had a family, a few kids running around…

She shook her head and focused on the house in front of her. She had a good life. Maybe it hadn't turned out exactly as she'd planned, but she had a thriving business and a nice, if small, home. She had good friends and a lot to be thankful for.

She looked up at the unfinished structure before her. Things could definitely be worse. Take, for instance, Stu Dickinson and his family. They were going to own this house when it was finished. The Dickinsons had been living in a cheap duplex rental in town when it had burned and they'd lost everything. With his wife suffering from multiple sclerosis and unable to work, Stu was the sole breadwinner for them and their two kids. Tenant's insurance had made it possible for them to replace necessities, but they were struggling to make ends meet.

Which was where a local charity organization came in.

Melissa wasn't that great with power tools, but she'd signed up to volunteer now that the house was framed. She had no idea what she'd be doing today, but the coordinator had assured her that she'd be fine and that someone would show her exactly what to do.

When she stepped inside the house, the racket was

unbelievable. The shrill whine of a saw rang in her ears, followed by a bang and the sound of male voices.

"Hello?" she called out in a brief moment of silence, putting her purse by the door. The room on her left had been finished with Sheetrock and had had its cracks filled, but not painted. The one on the right was still only framed and the wiring was visible, including electrical outlets and dangling wires for an overhead light fixture.

Boots sounded at the back of the house and she wiped her hands on her jeans. "Hello?" a voice returned.

A strange feeling slithered through her stomach in the instant before the man appeared.

"You!" she exclaimed. Oh, wasn't this just her luck! Twice in one week, no less.

Cooper halted in the doorway to the hall. "Oh," he answered, his face going completely blank for the space of a second. "You're volunteering today?"

She nodded. He sounded as pleased about it as she was. "And I take it you are, too?"

He nodded in turn.

She couldn't back out now. For one, she'd committed to volunteering. And two, if she did withdraw, Cooper would know it was all because of him. She wouldn't give him the satisfaction.

At some point it might be good if they could be in the same room together without her wanting to spit in his eye.

He took off his gloves. "Stu works for me. Least I can do is help out, you know?"

Melissa blinked. "I would have thought things were too busy out at your place." Cooper's ranch was profitable and his reputation for breeding great stock horses was growing. Ranchers from all over the prairies and northern states came to the Double C for their cutting and working horses.

"Sure it's busy. But I don't run it alone. I have good men working for me. They know what they're doing and I trust them. You know what it's like. You must have someone working the shop this morning."

She did. Against her better judgment she'd hired Amy Wilkins on a part-time basis. Amy's reputation around town wasn't always the greatest, but Melissa had taken a chance and given the vivacious blonde a try. So far she'd worked out well. She was a fast learner and was good with the customers. The only thing she couldn't do was arrange flowers, so Melissa had gone in early to do up the day's orders and make sure the cooler was filled with prearranged bouquets for walk-in sales.

"So, is there someone here to tell me what I need to do?"

Cooper grinned. "Yep. Me, for now. The bedrooms are all painted, and we've just finished laying the floor in the master. How are you with a brad nailer? We've got the baseboard and crown molding ready to go."

Melissa hesitated. Couldn't he install the trim while she worked with someone else? The last thing she wanted was to spend the next four hours in the same room with Coop.

"Melissa."

His rough voice pulled her back. "What?"

"Is it so bad? Really?"

She met his gaze. He wasn't smiling, wasn't making fun or trying to be charming—for once. He was dead serious. He shifted his gloves from one hand to the other—was he nervous? He hadn't aged, other than a few lines in the corners of his eyes that were more likely from the sun and wind than time passing. He still looked so much like the boy she'd laughed with over the years. Though she wouldn't admit it out loud in a thousand years, she missed that guy. Once upon a time she'd called him her best friend.

"You remind me," she said coolly. "You remind me, okay? Of how stupid and naive I once was."

"I'm sorry about that." He took a step forward. "But I can't change it. We're grown-ups. Surely we can manage to work together for a few hours without killing each other."

He was right. "Yeah, well, this place isn't about you or me, so we just have to suck it up, right? Besides, I don't know much about construction, so it appears I get to swallow my pride and let you boss me around."

He smiled then, a crooked upturn of his lips that reached his eyes. "Like I could ever tell you what to do."

The air hummed between them for a few minutes. Briefly, Melissa missed the way things used to be, the easy rapport they had shared. Cooper had been a tease, though she'd always known that his flirting meant nothing. It had been safe to banter back and forth because he was Scott's best friend as well as hers. He'd given the toast at their wedding, for Pete's sake.

She ignored his last statement and checked her watch. "Shouldn't we get started? I only have until one o'clock, when I have to be back at the shop."

He led the way to the master bedroom, pausing briefly to introduce her to the other people working there, installing oak hardwood in the other bedrooms. To her surprise she saw Callum Shepard, a local dairy farmer and newcomer to town, and Rhys Bullock, Martha Bullock's son and one of the hands over at Diamondback Ranch. The big surprise was that they were being bossed around by Chelsea Smith, whose father owned the hardware store.

After the hellos, Melissa followed Cooper to the back bedroom, pausing in the doorway to admire what had already been done. The walls were the shade of her favorite vanilla latte, and the rich color of the hardwood looked lovely against it. There were windows in two walls, providing a view of the distant Rockies in one direction and a view of the creek valley that ran to the north in the other.

"This is nice," she said, stepping in and hearing her boots echo on the wood floor.

"Stu deserves it. They were already struggling to make ends meet, and then to lose all their belongings... Sometimes life just isn't fair. I'm glad they were able to get this going and I'm happy to help. He's a good man and a good worker. He deserved a break."

It was easier to dismiss Coop when he was being deliberately charming. When he was sincere it was hard to remember why she resented him so much.

Lengths of baseboard were stretched across the floor, and a saw was set up on a heavy drop cloth. A loud drone filled the room as the air compressor fired up.

Cooper saw to filling the air nailer and then reached for his measuring tape. "Hold this here," he commanded, leaving her with one end. Together they measured the wall, then measured the baseboard—twice—and Cooper marked it with a carpenter's pencil.

She held the end while he made the first cut, then angled the other side with the miter saw so the next piece would match up in the corner.

Together they moved the piece to the wall, putting it flush against the end cap of the woodwork in the doorway. "Okay, now you're on. I'll hold it in place and you nail it."

"Me?"

"Sure, you. Take the nailer and press it against that hollow part there." He pointed to the curve in the baseboard design. "Is it pressed all the way in? Okay, now squeeze the trigger."

With a loud snap, the nailer jerked in her hand. "Is that right?"

"Looks good to me. Keep going."

The tool felt odd in her hand, and the noise was loud, especially when the compressor kicked in again. But it was kind of fun, nailing the molding into place. They had to adjust a cut when working their way around the doorway for the walk-in closet, but for the moment Melissa forgot about how much she disliked Cooper, and simply focused on the job.

They worked in relative silence as they finished the baseboard, and then moved on to the crown molding. This was harder, getting the angle just right. It took a few tries with each piece, and nailing it in place was awkward when Melissa had to hold the nailer above her head.

It was after twelve when they finished. She stood back as Cooper took a tube of wood filler and touched up the corner seams where there were inevitable tiny gaps. He took his time and she watched him on the stepladder, the way his jeans fit and how his customary cotton plaid shirt spread across broad, muscled shoulders. Scott hadn't been the only one on the football and hockey teams. Cooper had been a bit of a jock, too. But unlike Scott, he'd never had a girl watching from the stands.

Nope, he'd had about ten girls, all gazing at him with

love-struck expressions, sighing blissfully if he ever turned his attention to them. Which he did. Just never for too long. And never at Melissa.

"Once this is dry, it'll just need to be touched up with a bit of paint. What do you think?"

Melissa looked away so he wouldn't know she'd been staring at him, and made a point of sweeping her gaze around the room. "It looks finished," she said, realizing it truly did. "The crown molding was a nice touch."

"We didn't do that in the kids' rooms," Cooper said, screwing the cap back on the tube. "It's expensive. It's a nice addition in here, though."

Melissa checked her watch. "My time's just about up. Are you done here, too?"

Cooper nodded. "For today. I come out most mornings for a couple of hours and lend a hand. Bring the guys coffee. It won't be long now until it's ready. The drywall guy is coming back tomorrow to finish the den, and then it's just painting the front rooms, putting down the flooring and installing the kitchen cupboards. You coming back another day?"

He rolled up the hose from the compressor as he spoke. Melissa paused. It hadn't been so bad, being with Cooper. Awkward and at times uncomfortable, but they'd been civil, which was more than they'd accomplished in years.

Now that she'd seen the house and helped it take shape, even just a little, she wanted to come back and help out again. "I'll have to check the work schedule at the shop and call the coordinator. Amy's fine with running the store, but I'm the only floral designer."

"Well, there's always stuff to be done. I'm sure your help would be welcomed."

On the way out of the house Melissa stopped and

picked up her purse. Cooper had put the compressor in the hall by the other bedrooms and she heard his voice as he spoke to some workers. She was walking to her car when he called out her name.

She turned and saw him jogging her way. "Hey," he said, slowing as he approached. "I'm going to pick up the lunch order from the Wagon Wheel and bring it back. You want to grab a sandwich or something?"

With him? There was letting bygones be bygones and then there was…what? Lunch for two at the busiest spot in town? They'd been civil this week, but the idea of sitting down and making pleasant conversation was unfathomable. They weren't *friends*. Adults, maybe, but the time for friendship and hanging out together was long gone. It was far too late to rewrite the past.

"I have to get back to the shop, sorry," she stated, reaching into her purse for her keys.

Cooper stood back. "Sure. Maybe another time," he suggested, though they both knew it wasn't really an invitation.

"Maybe," she agreed, but it was an empty agreement.

"See you around, Mel."

"Yeah. Bye, Coop."

She reached for the door handle and scooted behind the wheel before he could see the color rise in her cheeks.

She'd called him Coop. After staring at his behind and being asked out to lunch.

This was exactly why she had said no. The last thing she needed in her life was a complication like Cooper Ford. They'd done a good job of avoiding each other in the past, and she could take care to do it again.

# CHAPTER TWO

SHE MANAGED TO AVOID HIM for almost two weeks.

Melissa yawned and locked the door to the shop. Saturdays and most weeknights she closed at six, except for Fridays, when she stayed open until nine. Last night had been crazy busy with walk-in traffic, which had been unusual but good. And today she'd had to interrupt her design time to help Penny cover the front. People were purchasing fall arrangements, particularly sunflowers and warm-colored mums and zinnias. Premade silk wreaths for front doors were disappearing like hotcakes and so were decorative sheaves of wheat.

To top it off, she'd barely finished the weekly standing order of flowers for the church when the president of the Ladies' Circle had come to pick it up. And Melissa had moved directly from that to working on the arrangement for a funeral happening on Monday.

Now orders were flooding in for the funeral home, and instead of taking a day off on Sunday, she knew she was going to be spending her one lazy day a week here at work, rather than at home vacuuming and doing laundry.

She loved the store and owning her own business, but there were downsides, too.

She'd walked to work this morning, taking the extra

precious minutes to enjoy the cool air and fall sunshine. Now she wished she'd brought her car. All she really wanted was a quick dinner and a hot bath before falling into bed.

She'd take care of the quick dinner by stopping at the diner, she decided. The sunlight was fading as she made her way down Main Street and around the corner to the busy restaurant. The parking lot was full and she nearly considered just going home and ordering a pizza. But the great thing about the diner was the convenience of a restaurant with the advantage of good home cooking. When she stepped inside and saw that the special was meat loaf and mashed potatoes, she was sold. Total comfort food.

She placed her order and waited just beyond the counter.

The noise was deafening and she closed her eyes, reminding herself that it was only a few minutes and she could find peace and quiet at home.

And then there was a warm hand on her shoulder and a deep voice said, "Mel, are you okay?"

She opened her eyes to find Cooper's worried ones staring down at her. For a split second something exciting leaped at the recognition of his fingers gripping her shoulder. Embarrassed, she nodded quickly, slipping away from his touch. "Fine. I'm just waiting for my order."

"With your eyes closed?"

She shrugged, even though she felt ridiculous. "I'm tired and it's loud. That's all."

"Melissa? Your order's up," Martha Bullock called out from behind the counter, holding up a white paper bag.

Relieved, Melissa stepped forward to collect it, only

to hear Martha announce, "Yours, too, Coop. Extra cheese and a side order of onion rings, just like you wanted."

He took the bag from Martha and handed her a twenty, then leaned forward and kissed the older woman's cheek. "You sure know how to look after a man," he teased, sending her a wink.

"Oh, go on with you," she answered, flapping a hand at him but grinning widely. "Your charm's wasted on me."

"Did you put in extra ketchup?"

"Sure I did."

"Then it's not wasted. Have a good night, Martha."

Melissa restrained herself from rolling her eyes. The thing about Cooper was that the teasing truly was genuine. He was a charmer, but there wasn't anything fake about it. If there had been, people would see clear through it. Maybe that was what had hurt so much. Coop had been the most honest, genuine man she'd ever known. Until, of course, he'd lied.

It was quieter outside. Melissa expelled a huge breath. "Well, good night." She started walking across the parking lot to the sidewalk.

Cooper's voice stopped her. "Hey, Mel, you want a lift? Getting dark for you to be walking home alone."

"I'll be fine. I like the air."

"But my truck's right here. I can drop you off, no trouble."

She halted and turned back, pasting on a smile. She did not want Cooper Ford driving her home or anywhere else. "Really," she said firmly. "I'll be fine."

He frowned. He was wearing the same battered jean jacket as he had that day in her shop, and she marveled once more at how broad his shoulders were. She should not be noticing these things. She wasn't exactly blind, she reminded herself, but the real problem was they shouldn't matter. She couldn't honestly say they were simple detached observations. She noticed, and then she got this odd feeling. Kind of tingly and warm.

"If you won't take a drive, I'll walk you home."

Suddenly he didn't seem so attractive. Why did he have to be all up in her business lately? Hadn't they managed to avoid each other quite successfully the past three years? It had been an unspoken agreement, and suddenly he was breaking it left, right and center.

She decided to ask. While the smell of meat loaf wafted up and teased her nostrils, she squared her shoulders and faced him. "Why now, Cooper? For three years we've barely said two words to each other. Now all of a sudden you're making conversation and offering to walk me home—in Cadence Creek, and on a route I've walked a million times."

He stepped closer. "How long did you think we could each pretend that the other didn't exist? I guess I thought three years was enough time for you to stop hating me quite so much. That we could stop avoiding each other in a town this small. It's gotten to be quite a challenge, you know. Trying to stay out of your way."

"I don't hate you."

"Really?"

He raised his eyebrow again, and she could practically hear what he was silently saying. *Riiight.*

She sighed. "You're not going to just let me go home, are you?"

"Not walking alone. Cadence Creek is a nice town, but it's not totally crime free, you know. Stuff happens."

"Fine. But I'm still walking. I need the fresh air. It's been a long day."

He caught up to her and fell into step beside her on the sidewalk. "I haven't seen you at the house this week."

"I was there one afternoon and did some painting in the living room. You were gone already when I arrived."

"I'm sure you planned it that way."

She kept walking. It was kind of surreal, strolling through town in the semidark with Cooper. "I ended up being swamped this week," she confessed. "If this keeps up, I'm going to have to hire a part-time designer."

She bit down on her lip. She'd also made a trip to Edmonton, to the clinic, when conditions were "right." A few weeks from now she'd know whether or not she needed to pee on a stick. She kept telling herself not to get her hopes up, but each morning when she woke, the first thing she thought of was that this time next year she could be a mother.

They were passing by the Creekside Park and Playground when Cooper reached out and put his hand on her arm. "Hey, why don't we stop and eat? There are a few picnic tables here, and our food's getting cold."

"You want to eat in the dark? Are you crazy?"

"By the time I walk you home and get back to my truck, my stuff will be cold."

"You didn't have to walk me," she pointed out.

"Yes, I did."

She recognized that tone. Cooper was charm itself, but he was also incredibly stubborn. Not only that, but she was so hungry her stomach was actually hurting, and the food smelled unbelievable. "Fine. You're going to pester me until you get your way, anyway."

They crossed the grass to a picnic table and Melissa spread out the paper bag as a place mat. Cooper took the spot across from her and began pulling take-out containers from his own bag. She gaped as she counted three: an extra-large one holding his burger and fries, a medium-sized one with onion rings that smelled fantastic and a smaller one with the Wagon Wheel's special recipe coleslaw.

"You're going to eat all of that? Yourself?"

"I'm a growing boy." He patted his flat belly and opened the container holding his burger.

She shook her head. "It's a wonder you're not the size of a barn."

She picked up her plastic fork and dipped it into the mashed potatoes and gravy. The food wasn't piping-hot any longer, but was still quite warm, and as she tasted the first bite she was struck by a pang so bittersweet it made her heart ache.

This was something they might have done in the old days: a bunch of them together, some takeout, hanging out on a Saturday night. Only it wasn't a bunch anymore, but just she and Cooper. Some of their circle of friends had drifted away, some had left Cadence Creek and gone to work in bigger towns and cities. So little of the past remained. In some ways it was good, but in other ways, Melissa missed it. Up until things had blown apart, there'd been a lot of good times.

"You okay?" Cooper asked, pausing to look at her while holding a French fry.

"Yeah, I'm fine. Just thinking about when we were kids, and some of the stuff we used to do on a Saturday night. It sure wasn't picking up takeout because we were too tired from dealing with 'real life' to cook."

He chuckled. "We all have to grow up sometime. At least mostly."

He held out the box of onion rings. "Have one. You know you want to."

She wasn't sure if she was glad that he remembered her fondness for onion rings or not. It was too much to resist as he waved them under her nose. She reached into the package and took out a round battered ring. When she bit into it, her teeth caught the onion and it came out of the batter. She pulled it into her mouth like a piece of spaghetti.

Cooper laughed. "Good, right?"

"So good," she admitted.

He put the box between them on the table, an unspoken invitation to share. A peace offering? Was he hoping that the deep-fried treat would accomplish what time had not? It was a big thing to ask from a carton of onion rings.

For the moment, she chose to cut into her meat loaf and peas and carrots.

They were quiet for a few minutes, eating and listening to the breeze whisper through the leaves that still remained on the poplars lining the creek. She didn't know what to say to him. Talking about the past would only bring up the painful way her marriage had broken apart. And anything else seemed…contrived. Awkward. He ate his burger in silence as she finished her meal, then he handed her another onion ring before taking one for himself and dipping it in ketchup.

"You still like doing that?" she commented.

"Yeah. Ketchup should be a food group all by itself." He put his empty containers in his bag. She did the same with hers and they left the picnic table, stopping at the garbage cans to deposit their waste.

"Feel better?" he asked quietly.

She did, surprisingly. It wasn't just the food, either, although she'd been very hungry. She'd had a few moments to breathe, to unwind. Funny how he'd seemed to know she'd needed that. Or maybe she was reading too much into his motives. Maybe it truly was all about eating his dinner while it was hot.

"I do feel better," she admitted. "I was pretty spooled up after my day."

"Give me five more minutes, okay? Come with me."

She frowned but followed. He led her over to the swings. "Sit down."

"Okay, now you're being silly. I just want to go home and get off my feet."

In response, he sat on the swing beside hers. It was set low for kids, and his long legs folded up like a frog's, but he pushed off anyway and put it in motion. "This gets you off your feet. Look." He held his booted feet up in the air. He looked ridiculous.

She felt foolish, but sat down and scuffed one shoe in the dirt, making the swing rock a little.

"Hold on to the chains and lean back."

"Cooper, you're crazy."

"Do it, Mel. Lean back and then open your eyes."

She pushed with her foot a little harder, then gripped the chains between her fingers and leaned back. The breeze from the motion ruffled her hair, making bits of it feather across her cheeks. Slowly, she opened her eyes and looked up.

There were stars. Not too many, but a handful that seemed to rock in the sky as she swayed back and forth. When had they come out? Sometime between leaving the restaurant and eating her dinner in the twilight.

The sky was so big, so endless. She heard a loud sigh and realized it had come from herself. As she watched, more stars appeared out of nowhere. One second vast emptiness, then the next time she looked, *pop*. There they were, twinkling down at her from the infinite blackness.

"Make a wish," Cooper suggested.

Her throat tightened. What in the world was she doing, sitting on the swings in the dark with Cooper Ford? "I'm too old for that nonsense. Besides, that's for the first star you see, and there are at least two dozen right now."

His voice was low and warm beside her. "Then make two dozen wishes. Wish on every one."

"Cooper…"

She knew it was stupid and juvenile, but she couldn't resist. She closed her eyes and made a wish.

*Let this time be the one.*

All she really wanted was to be a mom. She'd wanted it when she was married to Scott, and they'd supposedly been trying when she'd caught him cheating. The divorce had killed not only their marriage but her dream of a family, too. And she wasn't interested in getting married again.

But the longing for a family, for a child of her own, hadn't abated. If she could survive starting her own business and her marriage blowing up, she could handle being a single mom. She certainly didn't want to marry someone she didn't love just to make that happen. That made less sense than doing it alone.

She really wanted the pregnancy to take this time. If not, she could look into adoption, but she truly wanted to experience the joy of carrying her baby inside her. There was just something so…complete about it.

"You still here, or are you on another planet?"

Coop's voice intruded. Her swing had stopped swaying and her arms were twined around the chains, while her face remained tilted toward the sky. She swallowed and opened her eyes. "I'm still here. It takes a while to make twenty-four wishes."

He chuckled in the darkness. That funny curling sensation wound its way through her stomach again.

She jumped off the swing and brushed her hands down her trousers. "I really do need to get home. I've got to be back to work tomorrow to do up all the arrangements for the Madison funeral."

"All work and no play makes Mel a dull girl."

She shrugged and reached for her purse. "It happens when you own your own business. You know how it is. There's no real time clock to punch."

"Yeah, I know. I'm going to be locked up in my office tomorrow going over paperwork."

They made their way back to the sidewalk and on toward Melissa's house. "We really did grow up, didn't we, Cooper?"

His boots sounded on the concrete, steady thumps that seemed slightly out of place and yet reassuring. "Yes, we did. And some of it was painful."

Melissa had hoped he wasn't going to bring it up. She shivered in the rapidly cooling air. Without saying a word, Coop took off his jean jacket and slid it over her shoulders.

"Live and learn." She injected some lightness into her voice, as if it was no big deal.

Her house was just a few blocks away now. She had to put him off for only a minute or so and she'd be home and he'd be gone.

"Live and learn?" Coop stopped and put a hand on her arm, halting her, too. His voice was harsh. "You don't talk to me for three years and then come out with a flippant 'live and learn'?"

She pulled her arm away from his fingers. That was

twice tonight he'd taken the liberty of touching her. "Maybe you should take the hint that I don't want to talk about it."

They carried on for a few minutes, the silence growing increasingly awkward between them. Twenty more steps and she'd be at her front walk. She was nearly there when she realized she couldn't hear his boots just behind her anymore. For some weird reason her heart was pounding, but she made herself keep going. She took five more steps before his voice stopped her.

"I was wrong."

She slowed, paused for just a breath of a moment, but kept walking. They weren't going to do this. Not tonight and not on the sidewalk outside her house.

The memory of their argument was still fresh in her mind—as if it had happened yesterday—and nearly as painful. She'd been so angry at Scott. Angry and hurt with the vitriolic bitterness of a wife betrayed. But with Coop, it had been different. It had been a trust of a different kind that he'd broken. She'd been hurt by that, too. Hurt and disappointed that the one person she'd turned to when everything blew up had already known. He'd betrayed her, too.

"So you said already," she replied, wondering why the last twenty steps felt like a hundred.

"I thought maybe you'd be willing to accept my apology after all this time."

His longer legs caught up with her by the time she reached the first row of interlocking patio blocks that wound their way to her front door.

"Melissa. Please. Hasn't this gone on long enough?"

"What, our hating each other?"

She looked up into his face. In the glow of the streetlamp, he actually looked hurt. That was preposterous. She'd been the person wronged in all of this and they both knew it.

"I *never* hated you."

"Well, you sure never cared about me. That was clear enough."

A muscle ticked in his jaw and his gaze slid away for a moment. He took a deep breath and let it out before looking down into her eyes again.

She really wished he wouldn't do that. It was so hard to stay angry when he gazed at her that way, all wide eyes and long eyelashes. *"Bedroom eyes,"* her mother had said once. Eyes that were used to getting him what he wanted.

Melissa also knew she was entitled to her anger. Coop had told her once that he would always be there for her. And when push came to shove, he hadn't been. There was no way he could deny it.

"I never hated you," he insisted softly. "Not ever. It was complicated, but you are completely right in that I should have told you. I was wrong, Melissa, and I'm sorry. You have no idea how sorry."

She did not want to believe him or be touched by his apology. It was a real struggle, because he was looking at her so earnestly that she knew he wasn't lying. Nor was he trying to charm or joke his way out of anything.

But one thing stuck in her mind from that whole speech, and it wasn't that he'd admitted he was in the wrong, or that he was swallowing his pride to apologize.

It was that he'd said it was complicated.

"How complicated could it have been, Coop?" She kept her voice down—there were neighbors to consider—but her words were still crystal clear in the cool night. "Scott was cheating on me and you knew about it."

"Scott was my best friend."

"So was I. You said you'd always look out for me. You were like my big brother, do you know that?" She lifted her chin and finally said what she'd wanted to for ages. "You knew he was with her in the afternoon and coming home to me at night. Do you know how sick that is?" Tears pricked Melissa's eyes. "How dirty I felt for months afterward? All it would have taken was a few words from you. I trusted you, Coop."

He ran his hand over his hair. "Mel."

Her name sounded ragged coming from his lips. So he wasn't completely unaffected, either. Good.

"I trusted you," she repeated, softer now, and a sadness took over where her anger had lived. Sadness and acceptance.

"I was friends with both of you. Have you even considered for one moment how caught in the middle I was? I swear, as soon as I found out I confronted him about it. I begged him to put a stop to it. I *demanded*."

"Did you threaten to tell me?"

"Yes."

"And yet you didn't."

He swallowed and looked away. "No."

"And why is that?"

He didn't answer, but they'd come this far and she wanted to know. He'd been the one to open the can of worms, and now he would have to deal with her questions. "Why didn't you tell me, if you told him you would?"

Cooper took a few moments to respond, and when he did his words seemed measured. "Scott said he would deny it, and that you'd believe him."

She frowned, puzzled. "Maybe I would *want* to believe him, but don't you think I'd ask why you would tell me such a thing if it wasn't true? Come on, Coop."

He shoved his hands into his pockets. "Look, my intention wasn't to relive this thing from start to finish, okay? I just wanted to say I was wrong, and that I'm sorry. Isn't it time we moved on?"

It bothered her that he was probably right. It had gone on a long time. She'd picked herself up and dusted herself off, made a good life for herself. The one thing she hadn't done was let go of her resentment for Cooper. Funny how she'd been able to put Scott in the past and not miss him a bit, but not Cooper. She supposed it came from staying in the same town and being faced with seeing him on a regular basis, even from a distance.

"I forgave you a long time ago, Coop."

"You could've fooled me."

"Forgiving isn't the same as forgetting. You're right. It's over and done. But you know the old saying, *'Fool me once, shame on you, fool me twice...'"*

"'Shame on me'," he finished.

"Our friendship as it used to be is over, Cooper. We can't go back. It's how I'm built. Once someone hurts me, they don't get a chance to do it again. Once I learn a lesson, I don't forget it. So maybe we can just call a truce, okay? I can live with that. If you're expecting more..."

She didn't finish the sentence, but she didn't really need to, did she?

Cooper took a step back, out of the circle of lamplight. "You should go in. It's getting late."

She didn't like how they were leaving this, but knew there was no other way. "Thank you for the walk home."

She'd turned and taken two steps along her walkway when his voice stopped her once again. "Mel?"

Her heart quaked. Why did this feel like goodbye? Why did it feel final? Final had been three years ago when she'd said she never wanted to speak to him again.

The words had been extreme, but that had been an extreme period in her life.

"I lost two best friends, you know. You might think I sided with Scott, but I didn't. I hated what he was up to and begged him to do the right thing. It was the end of our friendship. I did not condone or support his behavior in any way. You need to know that."

Sadness swept over her. "You didn't stop it," she whispered. "To me, you condoned it by doing nothing."

Silence spun between them, until finally Cooper gave a curt nod and turned, walking away. She watched until the sound of his boots faded and his tall form turned the corner, out of her line of vision.

Only then did she realize that she was still wearing his jacket. She curled her fingers around the edges and pulled it close, drawing in the scents of hay and fresh air and the cologne he'd worn for as long as she could remember. The smell of it was imprinted on her brain, bringing a wealth of memories and emotions. It took her back more years than she cared to count.

She'd worked so hard to put the past behind her, but as the scent of him wrapped around her, she grieved just a little bit for the life she'd nearly had and the dreams she'd lost.

# CHAPTER THREE

COOPER SAT IN HIS TRUCK a half block from her flower shop, trying to muster the courage to go in. The other night he had come *this* close to telling her the truth. It had all been going so well. Not quite like old times, but at least they'd been talking. He'd gotten the impression that she'd be open to his apology, so he'd made it.

Only it hadn't gone quite according to plan. She'd pushed. He'd thought for a long time that she hadn't spoken to him for years because of simple pride. The longer the impasse, the harder it was to swallow pride and end it, right? It was difficult to take the first step. But he'd miscalculated. It wasn't just pride with Melissa. He had truly, honestly hurt her.

He'd never intended for things to get so intense the other night. With any other woman he could try flowers to ease his way back into her good graces. Considering Melissa owned the flower shop, he'd had to come up with something else. Besides, she'd see right through that sort of thing.

So a plastic container of his mother's peanut butter chocolate chip cookies sat on the seat beside him as a peace offering. She'd always had a weak spot for those.

He was still trying to figure out what he hoped to achieve by mending fences. Was it simply a need to put the transgressions of his past behind him? To receive absolution from his guilt for the part he'd played in the breakup of her marriage?

Then there was the problem of his feelings for Melissa. They'd been good friends since junior high school. By the time he'd figured out he wanted more, she'd only had eyes for Scott. What was worse, Scott had known how Coop felt, but had never said anything to him. It had been an unspoken rule—that they didn't talk about it. To Scott's credit, he had never rubbed Coop's nose in it. Not until Coop backed him into a corner. Then Scott had shown what sort of man he truly was. And what sort of man Cooper was, too. The kind of guy who would choose to save his own skin rather than do the right thing.

So what did he really want? Coop drummed his fingers on the steering wheel. He considered the idea that maybe he should let her go. Until he did, he couldn't move on. And he really should at some point.

He was twenty-seven years old and he'd never had a serious relationship. All because of Melissa Stone. It went beyond his mom and dad asking when he was going to settle down and give them grandbabies. He wanted that, too. He loved his business, but he wanted a wife and a few kids running around his big empty house. He wanted to teach them to ride and coach their hockey team. More than that, he wanted a partner to share things with. A meal at the end of the day. A beer while watching the football game. A woman he loved waking up beside him in the morning.

It was just that it seemed impossible to make the connection from his life as it was right now to his vision of the future. Melissa—and their unfinished business—was in his way.

So he'd go in there and give her the cookies and get his jacket back and wish her well, and finally, *finally,* move on.

Resolutely, he shut the door to his truck and gripped the dish in sweaty hands. This was stupid, wasn't it? A grown man going home and asking his mother to bake special cookies, of all things. She'd even remembered Melissa's fondness for them. His pulse beat at his wrist and the muscles in his chest tightened with nervousness as he reached for the door. Dammit, he felt about fifteen years old and not anything like a man preparing to let someone go.

Amy Wilkins stood behind the counter, a cordless phone pressed to her ear when he walked in. She looked up and smiled, and his pulse jumped again—not because he was particularly fond of Amy but because she was a notorious flirt and gossip. The last thing he needed was her overhearing anything he'd come to say.

"Cooper?"

He turned to his right and there stood Mel, dressed in a soft sweater the color of red wine and a pair of gray trousers. The sweater draped over her body like some sort of shawl, and it was utterly feminine and flattering. She held a finished bouquet in her hands, an arrangement of red roses, white carnations and baby's breath. Her brown hair was caught up in some sort of clip that left little pieces sticking out. It was one of those casual, purposefully messy looks, and it suited her perfectly.

"Hi," he said, so struck by the sight of her that he lost the few words he'd put together in his mind. Instinctively, he reached for his hat, then remembered he'd left it in the truck.

"Something I can do for you?"

"Um…"

She smiled, but he saw lines of tension around her mouth as her gaze strayed to the front counter. "Let me put this in the cooler."

Amy hung up the phone and tore a piece of paper off a pad. "An order for a get-well arrangement, any color, no more than fifty," she said. "For between five and six."

"I can do that." Melissa pushed open the sliding door to the cooler and put the roses inside. "The Carson arrangement is ready. Joe said he'd be in around three for it."

Cooper shifted his feet as Amy's gaze slid to him. "Something we can do for you, Coop?"

"I, uh…"

He felt Melissa's eyes on him and wondered if he was blushing, because his cheeks suddenly felt on fire. "Sure. I'll take…" Panicking, he scanned the fridge. "Sunflowers. One of those silver buckets with the sunflowers in it."

"Sure thing."

Amy moved to take it out of the cooler, but Melissa's voice stopped her. "I'll get it, Amy. You're already late for your lunch break."

"Oh, I can eat here, I've brought a sand—"

"You wouldn't pick me up a coffee from the Wagon Wheel, would you? I'm not sure I'm going to make it through the afternoon without an extra shot of caffeine."

Amy's gaze slid between Melissa and Cooper. "Oh, sure. Just let me get my purse." She retrieved her bag from beneath the counter. "See you in a bit."

The bell jingled behind her.

"That was probably stupid. It'll be all over the diner, within five minutes of her arrival, that you're in here."

Coop grinned. Amy wasn't a bad sort. She tended

to be unlucky in love and a bit vocal about it, but she wasn't intentionally mean or vindictive. "Well, it's probably better than having her eavesdrop."

"Is there something to eavesdrop about?"

He held out the plastic container. "It's a peace offering. For upsetting you the other night."

She came forward and took it from his hands. "Is this what I think it is?" She peeled back the cover and he watched, fascinated, as she closed her eyes and took a deep sniff. "Peanut butter. These are your mom's cookies, aren't they?"

"I remembered they were always your favorites, and begged her to make a batch." He grinned. "You only got half. Sorry."

"I should have had Amy bring me milk instead of coffee." Melissa smiled at him in a genuine, easy way. "Thank you, Cooper."

The warm smile hit him right in the solar plexus, robbing him of breath. "You're welcome. I was thinking about what you said and…I can't change anything that happened. I just want to offer a truce, like you suggested."

"Bygones be bygones, that sort of thing?"

He nodded. "I know you were affected so much more than me, Mel. I'm not disputing that. But the whole thing has hung over me like a black cloud. I know I can't make things right, but will you please accept that I wish I could?"

She put the lid back on the cookies. "Oh Coop," she sighed. "If it were only that easy."

The door jingled and they were interrupted by Callum Shepard. Cooper stood back as the local farmer stepped up to the counter, a wide smile stretched across his face. Cooper was pretty sure he had never seen the normally reticent Callum look quite so happy.

"What can I do for you today, Callum?" Melissa tucked the dish discreetly beneath the counter. "You look like you're in a good mood. Anything to do with the cupcake joint opening up down the street?"

For Pete's sake, the man was practically bouncing in his boots, Cooper thought irritably.

"You heard about that?" Callum asked. "Avery Spencer's opening it. She and Nell are moving here for good."

The latest bombshell in town was finding out that newcomer and all around keep-to-himself kind of guy Callum Shepard had a baby daughter no one knew about.

"That's great," Melissa replied.

"We're getting married," he blurted out, and Cooper nearly choked on a laugh. The guy sounded both thrilled and scared to death.

"Congratulations," Melissa said, smiling. "Have you already done the asking? Or is this wishful thinking?"

Callum finally seemed to chill out and he chuckled. "Sorry. It's still so new. I asked her yesterday and she said yes. But it wasn't planned, so today I'm surprising her with a ring. I thought flowers might be nice to go with it…."

"Absolutely."

Callum seemed to just realize that Cooper was standing there. "Oh, gee. Sorry. You were here first, Cooper."

Coop grinned and held out his hand. "I'm in no rush. Congrats, man."

"Thanks." Callum gripped Cooper's hand and he gave a shake of his head. "You just never know. A year ago the last thing I planned on was getting married and having a kid. Funny how things work out."

"Isn't it?"

Mel interrupted. "What were you thinking, Callum? Something simple, or a grand gesture sort of thing?"

He grinned. "Grand gesture. Roses?"

"Perfect," she decreed. "A dozen, long-stemmed? Maybe in red and white. You can tell her it stands for love and unity."

"That'd be wonderful. Thanks, Melissa."

"It won't take but a minute."

Cooper watched as she deftly selected half a dozen of each color from buckets of roses in the cooler, then arranged them on a huge sheet of green-and-gold floral paper. In no time flat she'd added a touch of greenery and sprig or two of baby's breath and had the bouquet wrapped up and taped and ready to go.

Cooper studied her as she worked. Melissa was good at what she did, and she truly loved the business she'd built. No matter how her life had derailed, she'd landed on her feet and with a smile. She was a strong woman, no doubt about it.

The register dinged as the cash drawer opened and she shut it again, then handed Callum the arrangement and receipt.

"There you go," she said cheerfully. "Good luck."

Cooper wished Callum would hurry up. Before long Amy would be back and any chance to finish his conversation with Mel privately would be gone. But the farmer had other ideas.

"One more thing…I picked out this ring today, but I'm not sure she'll like it. Would you mind…?"

Callum reached into his pocket and pulled out a box. He handed it across the counter and Melissa flipped open the lid. It creaked, as all jewelry boxes did, and she looked down at what nestled inside.

Cooper couldn't see what the ring looked like, but he could see the way Melissa's face softened as she gazed upon it with a mix of wistfulness and tenderness, pain and happiness.

"It's beautiful, Callum. Just gorgeous."

She closed the box and handed it back. "Avery's a lucky woman. I know you'll be very happy together."

"Thanks," he replied. "And thanks for the flowers."

"You're welcome."

"Go get 'em, tiger," Coop said, lifting a hand as Callum made for the exit.

"He's excited," Melissa observed as the door clicked shut.

"He's marrying the woman he loves. Of course he's excited." Cooper surprised himself with his sentimental observation. Seeing Melissa look at that engagement ring had affected him more than he cared to admit. She deserved something like that. Happiness. She certainly deserved better than what she'd gotten the first time around.

"Well, I hope it all works out for them," she replied, tidying up her countertop.

"Why shouldn't it? Just because your marriage didn't work doesn't mean every couple is doomed to unhappiness."

"I know that." She looked hurt at his observation.

He stepped closer to the counter. "I didn't mean that the way it sounded. I just meant…you can't stop believing in love just because it didn't work out once before."

"Did I say I had stopped believing?" Her hands paused on the tape dispenser.

"No."

She fussed about, but he could tell she was just trying to keep busy.

"So, have you considered giving it another try?" he asked.

"No."

"Why not?"

She looked up at him sharply. "Just because it exists doesn't mean it exists for *me,* okay? Why the sudden interest? Boy, you've been all up in my business lately. Thanks for the cookies, Coop, and we can shake hands and let bygones be bygones like you wanted. But let's just leave it at that, okay?"

He looked out the display window and saw Amy turning the corner, coming down the block. He frowned. "You mean that? About letting bygones be bygones?"

"Sure."

"Then shake on it, like you said."

He held out his hand and waited. Silently counted the seconds. Amy would be back at any moment, curse her busybody self.

Slowly Mel's hand stretched out. Met his. Her fingers curled around his palm.

Her skin was warm, her fingers slightly callused from working with flowers and chemicals all day long. He turned her hand over in his, looked at the close-clipped, unpolished fingernails that were part of the profession she'd chosen. Years ago she'd grown them long and always had them painted.

Mel wasn't the same girl he remembered, and perhaps it was time he accepted that.

She slid her fingers from his while a strange silence filled the shop. "There," she finally said, her voice oddly tight. "Truce."

"Truce."

The word seemed hollow somehow, and left him wanting more. So much more it left him floundering.

"Mel…"

Amy came back inside, rosy-cheeked and bringing a rush of fall wind with her. "One coffee, cream and sugar, just as ordered," she announced brightly.

It was time Cooper got out of there. He'd done what he'd set out to do—given her the cookies and made peace between them. More than that, he'd realized that all this time he'd been holding on to a vision of the girl he'd once known and loved, rather than the woman she'd become.

"I'll see you around, Mel," he said quietly. "Amy."

"See you around," Melissa replied, while her assistant merely smiled and gave a waggle of her fingers.

Outside the shop the air had turned suddenly cold. Coop shivered as he realized two very annoying things.

First of all, he'd forgotten to ask for his jacket back.

And second, his whole plan had backfired. Instead of letting go so he could move forward, he was starting to realize that the woman Melissa had become could be even more of a threat to his heart than the girl she'd once been.

Melissa watched Coop walk down the street, and tried hard to ignore the shocking way her stomach seemed to be tangling in knots. Her pulse still raced, beating at the hollow of her wrist where his fingers had rested only moments ago. That had been no ordinary handshake. Things had *tingled*. In a way they hadn't since she'd been sixteen and had finally given up on him ever looking at her as if she was a girl. Scott had kissed her one night after a school dance and that had been the end of any crushes on Coop. She'd accepted that they'd only just be friends. It had been fine while she'd dated Scott, and after, when she'd married him. Coop had ended up being more like a brother.

And when the divorce happened, there certainly hadn't been any romantic feelings. She'd despised him too much for any tingling or shortness of breath.

So why was she feeling it today, after all these years?

"You okay, Melissa?" Amy's voice cut through the clutter of her thoughts and drew her eyes from Cooper, who was now getting into the cab of his truck.

"Oh, sure! Thanks for bringing the coffee."

"Cooper never took his flowers," Amy commented, her perfectly plucked brows crinkling. "Should I go after him?"

Mel shook her head quickly. "Oh, he changed his mind." She reached under the counter and brought out the plastic dish. "Want a cookie?"

"Cooper Ford brought you cookies?"

She shrugged. "I know you're a few years younger than we are, but Coop and a bunch of us were friends in school. We all used to hang out." She scrambled to cover, to make it no big deal, because she knew Amy would definitely make something out of it. "Ask anyone in our group and they'd remember Jean Ford's peanut butter chocolate chip cookies."

Amy reached into the container and took one. "Coop's kind of funny. He used to date a lot, but the last few years I've hardly seen him with anyone." She scowled. "I asked him out once, you know. He turned me down. Said I was too young for him. Shoot, he was twenty-five and I was twenty-two. Not that much of a difference."

Melissa felt as if she were walking in a field of land mines. Amy's disastrous love life was nearly a thing of legend in Cadence Creek. It was a shame, really, because Amy was a nice girl. She had a generous heart and would do anything for someone in need. For a while it looked as though she and Sam Diamond would become an item, but that had gone south. In Mel's opinion, if Amy had one fault, it was that she had difficulty hiding her feelings—and she did tend to get hurt quite easily. When she did, everyone in the county ended up hearing about it.

"Well," Melissa said carefully, "if he hasn't been dating, then you know it wasn't just about you."

But the news that Coop hadn't been dating made her curious. Why not? Had someone broken his heart? She'd been so wrapped up in her own relationship failure, she knew nothing about his love life.

Not that it mattered. It was no less than he deserved, after years of playing the field with such enthusiasm. Perhaps everyone else had clued in to the kind of man he was, the way she had.

*That's not fair,* a voice inside her head protested. Melissa tried to quiet that voice, but it persisted. *Cooper Ford is a good man. A good man who made a bad choice.*

"Huh." She gave a huff of disbelief that sounded overly loud in the little shop.

"What?" Amy asked, nibbling on a cookie.

"Oh." Melissa's cheeks heated and she hid behind her coffee cup, taking a sip that nearly scalded the inside of her mouth. She swallowed painfully and blinked. "Nothing, really. I was just thinking about something." Like how she suddenly seemed to be forgetting all the reasons she had for disliking Cooper. He'd basically condoned Scott's affair by doing nothing. That was a pretty good indication of his view of how to treat a woman.

Amy grinned. "Yeah, thinking about Cooper Ford, I bet. Just because he turned me down doesn't mean I don't have eyes in my head. I bet you could bounce quarters off that butt."

Melissa figured Amy was right. There was absolutely nothing wrong with Cooper's looks. That had never been an issue.

She dropped what was left of her cookie in the trash can and brushed her hands. "Maybe, but you don't have a relationship with a guy's butt, Amy. It's about a lot more than that. Believe me, I wouldn't go near Cooper Ford in *that* way with a ten-foot pole."

She moved off to the workroom to get started on the get-well arrangement, but could still feel Amy's gaze on her as she moved around, gathering materials.

It was a good thing Amy hadn't seen Mel and Cooper on Saturday night, then. Because she'd come very close to going after Cooper Ford in exactly that way. Looking at the stars while swinging in the park? Come on.

It had been a momentary lapse, and that was all. Because Mel was smarter now. She had no plans to enter any relationship, but if she did?

It would sure as shootin' be with someone more trustworthy than Coop.

# CHAPTER FOUR

MEL SIGNED UP to volunteer at the construction site a few more times. Stu and his family would be able to move in within a week or so, and now it was down to the finishing touches. Bifold doors were being hung for the bedroom closets. The appliances arrived, and on a particularly warm afternoon in late September, the washer and dryer were installed while heavy equipment worked outside, leveling what would be the front yard. It was too late to seed or sod, but come next spring, the ground would be ready.

By choosing afternoon time slots, Melissa had figured she'd miss seeing Coop. He tended to quit by lunchtime so he could get back and look after things at the Double C. It was just easier if they kept their distance from each other. The last thing she needed was to be getting ideas. A truce was one thing, but she wasn't stupid. She knew what that tingly, breathless sensation meant, and it would only mean trouble—for both of them.

In another week she should know for sure if the last attempt at the clinic had been a success. Until then, she was simply keeping herself busy to make the time go faster. She made sure she was eating right, just in case, and that she got a good seven to eight hours' sleep every night. If by some miracle she'd conceived, she was determined to do everything right from the start. She'd even cut back on her caffeine consumption, drinking only half-caf in the mornings.

She was just taking a pot of bronze mums out of the trunk of her car when she saw the familiar brown half-ton pull into the yard.

She inhaled and exhaled deeply. Okay. Just because Coop and she were both here didn't mean they had to work on the same thing. She'd done a good job of avoiding him for years. She could manage to be in the same general area and not speak a word to him. She'd done it tons of times in the past.

Except there was one problem. Coop had always made a point of avoiding her, too, and now he wasn't. It was way harder to ignore someone who didn't ignore you in return.

"Hey, Mel."

His voice came from behind her, warm and smooth. She tried very hard not to sigh. Instead, she picked up the huge pot and turned around, half hiding behind the greenery and rusty-orange blossoms.

"Cooper. Excuse me, please."

He reached out. "Let me take that for you."

"It's fine. I've got it."

She started off toward the porch. The mums would look great flanking the front steps, out of the way of the wheelchair ramp that had been built in anticipation of Cheryl's declining health. Mel put the pot down and spun it so the blooms showed to best advantage. When she turned to go back to her car for the second pot, she nearly ran smack into Coop, who was right behind her, carrying the partner arrangement.

"Thought I'd bring the other one."

She gritted her teeth. "Fine. Put it on the other side." She darted away to grab her supplies and shut her trunk.

He'd put the pot in the precise spot she'd wanted, and was waiting as she approached the steps. "What else have you got?" he asked pleasantly.

She wrinkled her brow. "Don't you have something to hammer or nail or screw or something?"

He burst out laughing. She blushed. She could feel it flood her cheeks and neck, and her tone grew even more irritated. "Oh, you know what I mean! What are you, twelve?"

It only made him laugh harder. "What is so damned funny?" she demanded.

"You!" He paused and wiped his eyes. "Some truce," he commented. "You're meaner than ever."

"Having a truce does not make us besties all of a sudden," she said acidly, moving past him and up the steps.

"Clearly," he answered, following her.

She had more going on in her life than he could imagine, certainly more than worrying about what he thought of her. She tried to envision his face if she told him she was possibly pregnant by a sperm donor. He'd swallow his tongue. She nearly did tell him, just for the shock value.

But she kept silent, knowing this was too important to joke about. She frowned. A lot of people in this town would talk behind their hands if they knew what she'd been planning. She'd thought about that a lot while making her decision. She had a business here. Family. It was a very small town. Not everyone was that forward thinking. They still thought the correct order of things was to meet someone, get married and then start a family.

Truth was, she tended to agree with that assessment

in most cases. But real life wasn't always that neat and tidy, and in her world, a girl had to do what she had to do. Melissa was responsible for her own happiness, and damn public opinion.

She reached into her canvas bag and pulled out a wooden pole and bracket, a small cordless drill and a flat packet that contained a rectangle of brightly colored nylon. She liked the homey touch of a decorative flag. This one was in autumn hues, a collage of fall leaves in yellows, oranges, reds and browns, with the word Welcome across the bottom.

"What's that?"

She took the pole and bracket out of the plastic sheathing. "It's a flag. I'll mount the bracket here, on the porch pillar, and then put the flag up."

"Need a hand with that?"

"Not really." She took out the screws, set the bracket against the post and held it there with her forearm while she placed a screw on the drill bit. It wobbled and she shifted, which made the bracket slip so that it was off center.

"Pride goes before the fall," Coop noted.

She refused to look at him. "I'm hardly in danger of falling."

He chuckled. "The saying isn't literal, you know. Here, let me hold the bracket while you set the screw."

She could refuse, but if the stupid thing slipped again she was going to look like an idiot. And she did appreciate the fact that he was offering to help rather than do it for her, the way most men would. "Fine. Just make sure it's centered."

He held it and she put in the first screw, then the second.

"Thanks," she said quietly. "It won't move now. I can put the last ones in just fine."

He didn't leave as she finished fastening the bracket. Instead he opened the package and unfolded the flag. "This is nice," he said, spreading out the nylon.

"I know Cheryl tires so easily with her MS. She's going to want to pick stuff out herself, but a few touches here and there might make this seem homey right away."

Melissa took the flag from his hand and threaded the pole through the pocket. Then she slid the stick into the bracket, tightened the screw to hold it in place, and it was done. The flag rippled gently in the warm westerly breeze. *Welcome*.

"There," she said, standing back and putting her hands on her hips. "I should see what else there is to do."

She left Coop standing on the porch while she went inside to find the coordinator and get her assignment.

It turned out that the big project of the day was constructing the deck, so Melissa made her way to the back of the house. Six-by-six posts were stuck in concrete blocks, and a group of men, Cooper included, were finishing the construction of all the support pieces. A pile of decking sat to one side, waiting to be cut into the appropriate lengths and screwed down. A makeshift table of sawhorses and plywood held a box of coffee from the shop out on the highway, as well as two brown boxes half depleted of doughnuts.

When Cooper saw her standing to the side, he tilted back his hat. "Hey, George," he called out. "Melissa there is pretty handy with a drill. You should get her set up with a belt and a pouch of screws."

George Grant, a retired farmer, pushed back his own cap. "That true, Miss Stone?"

She lifted her arm as if she were holding a pistol. "I

brought my own." And she knew how to use it. Maybe she wasn't up to speed on brad nailers and miter saws and everything else, but she did most of the upkeep on her property herself. Having a drill, a set of screwdrivers and pliers had come in very handy over the years.

George laughed, a good-natured wheeze. "Of course you did. Well, give us a few minutes and we'll be ready to put you to work. Gonna start cutting the decking real soon."

Cooper threw her a wink that she ignored. Just as she ignored his dusty boots, snug jeans and the way his chest filled out a plaid shirt and fleece vest. The Double C brand decorated the left breast, one *C* nestled within the other.

She understood that he was sorry for what had happened. She was even willing to call a truce. But there was a long way to go to reestablish trust, or even respect. She could forgive him for making a bad judgment call. That didn't mean she was naive enough to let him close enough to have an impact on her life again. Throw her own surprising reaction into the midst and she'd prefer to stay as far away from Coop as possible.

There were enough people around that she was spared having to engage in much conversation. Instead she worked steadily, lining up the decking and screwing it down to the supports. It wasn't an overly large deck, but the Dickinsons would be able to put a barbecue on it, along with a set of patio furniture for enjoying warm summer days. Since it was south facing, it would get a lot of sun, and as the structure took shape Mel could envision pots of flowers and herbs blooming there. The afternoon waned, the floor of the deck was done, and as a group they began working on the railing. It was past five, then past six, but everyone silently agreed that they'd come this close to finishing and may as well carry on.

At quarter to seven they were finally done, and spent another ten minutes picking up wood scraps and storing everything in the garage. As Mel walked to her car, Cooper fell in step beside her. "That was good work today," he said. "Long, but good."

"It's all pretty much done now, isn't it?" she asked, reaching her car door and opening it. She threw her purse inside and then bent to carefully place the drill on the seat.

"The official unveiling is next Saturday. Are you coming?"

"Oh." She straightened, resting one arm on the top of the open door. "I hadn't actually heard about it."

"We're doing a spit roast. Side of beef, half a pig, baked beans, you know the drill. Make it a real housewarming for them."

"That's nice."

He gave a small shrug. "Like I said, Stu's one of my guys. I'm happy to help. Mom's organizing the food stuff, but I think we're just asking people who are coming to bring some sort of dessert. You should try to make it."

"We'll see." It did sound like fun, and it was going to be a community event so they wouldn't be in each other's face the whole time. It wasn't like this was a date or anything.

"I'd better go. I was gone a long time today," Coop said. "I need to check on things at the barns and grab some dinner. I'll see you around, Mel."

He walked away. She watched the movement of his shoulders as he reached into his pocket for his keys, and then admired the length of his legs as he put one foot in his truck and swung himself up into the seat. Amy had commented that he hadn't dated much in the last few years. Again Melissa wondered why, because during the years she and Scott had been married, he'd gone through a bunch of girlfriends, none of them lasting more than a few months. Cooper had broken his share of hearts.

Dust flew up from his tires as he backed up, turned around and headed out the driveway toward the road.

She'd thought he played the field a little too enthusiastically, but she realized now that Amy was right. The last few years Melissa hadn't seen him with anyone on his arm. He'd said that he'd been really angry with Scott about the affair. Had that event made Coop take a look in the mirror?

Maybe she really hadn't been the only one affected by the situation. After all, Scott had left town. She hadn't realized that Coop's friendship with him had ended so completely, as well. She'd kind of figured they'd stayed in touch.

She got behind the wheel of her car and sighed. Tonight he hadn't made the slightest suggestion that they go for coffee or a bite to eat. Not that she'd wanted him to, but their last few encounters he'd been pressing his case.

Apparently he'd finally gotten the message. There was no earthly reason why she should be feeling let down about that, but she was. As she turned in the opposite direction from Coop, she laughed a little. Maybe all this indecision was just hormones.

A girl could hope, after all.


Mel went right from the shop to the housewarming, carrying her favorite caramel bread pudding in a covered glass dish. She'd dressed for the weather, which had turned quite cool at the end of September. There was a frost warning for tonight, and even though there were rumors of a bonfire happening later, she knew it would get chilly. She wore skinny jeans and her favorite black boots that came to just below the knee, a raspberry-colored tailored shirt and a multicolored scarf twisted around her neck. Over that she had on a charcoal sweater-coat.

Cars lined the lane when she arrived, and she had to park nearly out at the road and walk in. Country music came from a stereo somewhere, getting louder as she approached the house. From a hundred yards she could make out the sign draped over the eaves of the front porch: Welcome Home.

Melissa smiled and felt a lump rise in her throat. It was a good thing they'd done here, and so typical of Cadence Creek. Despite the lack of privacy, and the fact that everyone was aware of her history, she knew she didn't want to live anywhere else. It was home. She just hoped they'd be as welcoming to her if and when she showed up expecting a baby.

She should know anytime. Her period had been due a few days ago and she'd done a home pregnancy test right away. It had been negative, but she wasn't giving up hope. The fact that she hadn't started yet was a good sign. False negatives happened.

But for tonight she was not going to think about it. Instead she was going to focus on enjoying herself.

She went straight to the open garage and put her dessert on a table along with the rest—a staggering array of cakes, pies and pans of unnamed things that generally started out with a graham-cracker crust and ended with whipped cream on top. There was a carousel of gorgeous-looking cupcakes, too, which had probably come from Callum and Avery.

Mel said hello to the Diamond family couples—Sam and Angela, and Tyson and Clara—before moving on to their hired hand, Rhys Bullock, and then Callum and Avery. Amy had come with a date that Melissa didn't recognize, and she gave a wave across the yard. Finally she reached Stu and Cheryl, both of whom were beaming.

Mel reached up and hugged Stu. "Happy housewarming."

He squeezed her back. "Thanks. This community..." He just shook his head, overcome with emotion.

"I know," she replied. "And Stu, don't think we all don't realize that you'd do the same for any of us." She turned her attention to Cheryl. In her early forties, his wife was an attractive woman with a few gray strands in her hair and a little extra weight around her middle from bearing her children. She had a rough time of it with her MS, but tonight her wheelchair was tucked away and she was making do with just a cane as she enjoyed the party.

"Cheryl," Melissa said warmly, reaching out and squeezing her arm. "How do you like your new house?"

Cheryl smiled. "It's beautiful. The kids already have their rooms picked out. And everything on the main floor makes it so much easier for me." She leaned against Stu, who put his arm around her. "We've got furniture coming on Monday. I haven't been this excited since we got married and moved into our first apartment."

Mel's heart gave a little pang as she watched the two of them. The couple personified wedding vows, in particular the loving and cherishing part, and in the sickness and in health. She hoped they knew how lucky they were. In one way it was reassuring to know that sort of love truly did exist. In another it was a letdown to know that at one time she'd made those promises and meant them, and it still hadn't been enough.

Stu gave a nod at something behind her and she turned around. Cooper was standing before a huge metal grill, laughing at something Rhys was saying.

"I don't know how I'll ever repay Coop, though," Stu mused. "He's a good boss. And a better friend. I know how much he had to do with this project, and I know he's responsible for tonight."

Melissa's eyes were drawn to the sight of Coop laughing as he shut the lid on the grill. As if he'd known she was watching, his gaze lifted and met hers, and he gave an almost imperceptible nod and touched the brim of his hat.

It was utterly unfair that her heart pattered.

"Excuse me," she murmured, moving away and out of Coop's line of vision. "I think I'm going to get a drink."

She meandered over to the folding tables set up with paper plates, cutlery and cups, and coolers underneath. Instead of taking a cup, she popped the top on a can of soda and took a drink.

"Melissa, dear, how are you?"

She spun to find Molly Diamond behind her, wearing a broad grin.

"Molly. I'm fine, how are you?" She went forward and gave the older woman a hug.

"Oh, I'm right as rain. Got a couple of grandbabies and another on the way, and Callum and Avery are around a lot with Nell. They keep me busy. Keep me young."

"At least you have grandkids," another voice grumbled.

Melissa laughed and turned. "Oh my goodness. Hello, Mrs. Ford." Cooper's mother. Mel had spent hours in her kitchen when she and her gang had been kids, hanging out after school or getting together for movies on a Friday night. They'd been partial to horror flicks, Mel recalled, and Jean had always provided popcorn and potato chips.

"Call me Jean, like you used to," Coop's mother ordered. "Haven't seen you around much, Melissa. You keeping busy?"

She nodded. "The store takes up most of my time."

"The flowers Cooper bought for my birthday were lovely. How'd you like the cookies?"

"Cookies?" Molly asked.

"Cooper got me to whip up a special batch," Jean confided. "Peanut butter chocolate chip. He hasn't asked for those in years, and I remembered they were Melissa's favorites." She looked at her with a twinkle in her eye. "Did you share?"

Melissa didn't quite know what to say. It would probably be best to make a joke out of it, dispel any matchmaking inklings Molly and Jean might come up with if they put their heads together. Mel and Coop were both single, and in a town this size, pairing people up was a popular pastime. "Of course I didn't share. I made Coop eat crow pie."

Molly and Jean laughed. "Good girl. Coop needs someone to keep him on his toes."

"Oh, it's definitely not like that."

"Too bad," Jean observed. "I always liked having you around." She put a hand on Mel's shoulder. "I know you and Coop had a blowup when you and Scott split. I hope you've worked it out now. You were always such good friends. He needs that."

So Jean didn't know what had caused their rift? Interesting.

"The past is in the past," Mel said, trying to sound breezy. "Sometimes you have to stand on your own two feet and get on with it, you know?"

"Atta girl," Molly praised.

"I just wish Coop would get on with settling down. I could use a grandbaby or two of my own to spoil."

Someone started clanging a triangle, calling everyone to dinner, which was convenient, since Mel's palm had absently strayed to her flat tummy at Jean's words. She'd never been mad at Jean, and in fact she'd missed Coop's parents almost as much as she'd missed him.

If she was pregnant, it might be nice to have someone like Jean to give her baby cuddles. She rather hoped her own parents would fill that role, but last spring she'd let them in on her plans and they'd expressed dismay rather than support. Like most people, they thought she should just wait, maybe see if she was going to get married again.

Things had been tense in their relationship ever since. Normally they'd be front and center at an event like this, but since taking early retirement a few months before, the Stones were on a long-overdue vacation. New England in the fall. There'd only been one email since their departure, letting Melissa know they'd arrived safely. No updates or pictures sent. She didn't much like being out of favor with them, but she had a right to make her own decisions.

For the next half hour, the throng settled in lawn chairs and on steps to eat the tender beef, succulent roast pork, baked beans, fresh rolls and coleslaw. It got dark, and patio lanterns were turned on and the bonfire lit. When the main meal was over, everyone wandered into the garage for dessert and a cup of coffee that was brewing in the big urns borrowed from the church. Mel left the coffee alone, but wasn't so disciplined when it came to dessert. She helped herself to a small piece of carrot cake with cream cheese frosting, a sliver of apple pie and a piece of something that could only be described as a mound of dark chocolate sin. There were at least a dozen other gorgeous-looking desserts, but she had only so much room.

She found a quiet corner where she could stand back and watch. Now that the fire had burned awhile, she saw Coop and Sam Diamond set up the kids with sticks and marshmallows for roasting. The stereo was turned off when someone got out a guitar and started taking requests. She sighed, letting the day's fatigue and her full belly lull her into a mellow state of mind. She loved Cadence Creek. Always had. She'd never lived anywhere else nor did she want to. Maybe that was why the acceptance was so important.

When her marriage had hit the skids, there'd been a lot of long faces and sympathy to go around. On one level it had driven her bonkers—both the continual "so sorry" sentiments and the knowledge that she was gossip fodder. But on another, it had felt good knowing people cared. And they'd certainly supported her business when she'd opened her doors short months later.

A cramp slid across her belly. Boy, she'd overdone it with the cake, hadn't she? That and beans and so much meat were bound to give her some indigestion. She frowned. Except it didn't feel like indigestion. It felt heavy and...

She swallowed. She knew that feeling. Not now. Not here. Dammit, not again.

With a wooden smile, she made her way through the garage and into the house. She knew exactly where the half bath was, and made a beeline for it, clutching her purse handle with tight fingers.

And when she saw that she'd been right—not indigestion at all—she fought to keep from crying. She'd wanted this time to be the one, so very badly. She'd been so *sure.* But wanting something desperately did not make it so, and for a second she bit down on her lip as two hot tears slid out of the corners of her eyes.

She brushed them away immediately. She had to go back out there. People were going to see her. She did not want them to notice red eyes and blotchy cheeks and a wobbly lip. A wobbly lip that quivered despite her best attempts to stop it…

She gasped, bracing her hands on the edge of the sink, trying to catch her breath as the truth settled, hard and uncompromising. She'd let herself hope again. She'd done everything right—paid the money, had the procedure, watched what she ate and drank and how much she slept, how much she lifted at the store, and still…

Words scrolled across her brain like a profane ticker tape of frustration.

At the same time, her heart was breaking. She only wanted this one thing. Hadn't she earned it? She'd been hurt and humiliated and abandoned, and she'd picked herself up, brushed herself off, and got on with it. She'd planned everything so carefully, so why wasn't it working?

Melissa jumped as a knock sounded on the door. "Anyone in there?"

She inhaled and straightened. "Be right out!" she

called with false brightness, then turned on the water in the sink.

She dried her hands, pressed them to her face and willed herself to hold it together.

Clara Diamond was on the other side of the door—pregnant, beautiful Clara Diamond with glowing, rosy cheeks. "Oh, hi, Melissa," she chirped. "Sorry to rush you. My bladder seems to hold only a teaspoon right now."

The words stabbed into her. She smiled. "It's all yours," she said, making her way to the garage door, down the aisle between the tables and straight out the driveway to the parked cars. She loved Clara, she really did, but seeing her at that precise moment was salt in the wound, and it stung.

Mel held it all in, every last bit of emotion, until she was past the crowd and flanked only by the shadows of parked vehicles. As soon as she was certain no one would hear her, she tried gulping in some air. The air went in just fine, but shocked her when it came out on a sob. She frantically tried to reel it back in, but it was too late. First there was one, then another, and the next thing she knew she was stumbling her way to her car, hiccuping and half crying.

"Mel!"

Oh crap. She knew that voice. It was the voice of a man who suddenly couldn't seem to let well enough alone, and he was the last person she wanted to talk to right now. She shoved her hand into her purse, desperately searching for keys. She could get inside her car and lock the door. He wouldn't see her face then. She hooked her finger on the key ring. She could hear his boots on the dirt and he called her name again. "Mel! What's going on?"

She scrambled to hit the button to unlock the doors—and dropped the keys.

She was not going to be able to hold herself together for very long.

There was no light this far from the house and she crouched, frantically feeling for her key ring. It was too late. Cooper reached her and knelt down. "Mel, what's wrong?"

"I dropped my keys." She tried to sound normal, but her voice was thick.

"That's not what's wrong. You were running and crying. What the hell happened?"

A spurt of anger rushed through her. "Oh, what do you care, Cooper Ford?"

"I care," he said simply.

She found the keys and stood up, though her fingers shook. "You don't have a right to care!"

It felt good to be angry. To lash out. She had a sinking feeling that it wasn't really Cooper she was mad at, but it didn't matter. He made a great target.

He gave an impatient sound. "News flash, Melissa. You don't, and have never had, the right to tell me who I can or can't care about! So if I want to care, I'll damn well care, all right?"

She stared at him in stunned silence for a breath.

And then completely embarrassed herself by bursting into tears and throwing herself into his arms.

# CHAPTER FIVE

MELISSA CAME BARRELING at his chest, forcing Coop to take a step backward as his arms instinctively came around her.

He hadn't meant to yell at her. He especially hadn't meant to make her cry, or at least cry more than she already had been. His throat tightened. She was in all-out sobbing mode now. Thank goodness they were sheltered from any light from the fire, and far enough away that no one would hear. He knew Mel well enough to know that she would want to keep a meltdown private. What he didn't understand was what had set her off in the first place.

Her sweater was bulky and the crazy scarf she wore tangled with her hair. Cooper pressed his hand to the back of her head and, unsure of what else to say, murmured, "It's okay. Whatever it is, Mel, it'll be fine."

"It won't be fine," she replied, half wailing. "You don't know, Coop! It hasn't been *fine* for three years now!"

Three years. Ever since Scott left. Cooper had figured that as the months passed he'd be less angry about it. But seeing how it tore Mel apart—after all this time—brought those feelings back again. She had deserved so much better. The fact that she still seemed to carry a torch for the guy made Coop want to hit something.

But he kept a lid on it, forcing gentleness into his voice. "What don't I know?"

*"You don't know anything!"*

Coop figured the best thing to do now was let her cry and get it out of her system. He'd seen her upset before; they'd known each other for two decades, after all. And he'd seen her angry. Angry at him. Definitely angry at Scott. But even in the anger there'd been an underlying layer of hurt. She'd been betrayed. And she'd loved Scott. Coop knew that without a doubt.

"I don't know anything," he confirmed softly, holding her close, his heart contracting at the sad sounds muffled against his coat. Knowing she was hurting so much only made him feel worse about himself. He'd always been the sort of guy whose creed was that honesty was the best policy even when it meant taking your lumps. He hadn't been honest with her. He'd hidden the truth from his best friend for the very worst of reasons: to protect himself.

He didn't like what that said about the kind of man he'd become. Hadn't Scott done the exact same thing? Lied to cover his own butt? Coop was no better than Scott had been in the end.

"You don't know," she continued. "All our plans. My plans." She hiccuped a sob. "And I've tried so hard to do it all alone, but this one thing…I keep failing and it hurts. Oh, it hurts, Coop."

He just held her tighter.

Finally, he pulled back a little, keeping his hands on her upper arms. "Let me take you home. I don't want you driving like this."

"I'm fine…."

He cursed. "You are not fine. You're not even in the same postal code as fine. You're tired and upset. Give me your keys, Mel."

"What will you do? You can't walk home…."

He was relieved she was capitulating. "I've got my cell. I'll call Mom or Dad. One of them will come get me in the truck."

"And have them know what just happened? No, thank you. I promise I'm fine to drive."

My, she was obstinate. "And I say you're not. Look at you. You're shaking."

She slid the keys into his palm. "You're so stubborn."

He tried to smile. Yeah, weren't they just peas in a pod? "Glad you remember."

He held the door for her and she slid into the passenger seat. As he got behind the wheel, he found his knees pressed against it. He reached for the lever to adjust the seat, mercifully sliding it back into a more comfortable position. Her compact was so much smaller than his truck, but it was economical and suited her purposes, didn't it? He turned the car around and stopped only briefly at the corner where the driveway met the road.

"You want to tell me what's got you so upset?" he asked quietly. "You kind of lost it back there."

"It's nothing."

He looked over. She was staring out the window, her jaw set in a mulish way he recognized. "I think we both know that you crying in my arms is not nothing."

She sighed, a tremulous sound that proved to him she wasn't quite put back together yet.

"If I tell you, you'll either laugh or tell me I'm crazy, and I'd rather save myself the trouble."

He slowed down as they entered the main part of town. "I promise I won't laugh or tell you you're crazy."

When Mel still didn't spill, Coop tightened his grip on the steering wheel. More and more he'd been wondering about her feelings for Scott. He'd hoped she didn't still love him. She needed to get over him and move on, with someone who would treat her right.

His fingers tightened on the steering wheel. Someone like him?

Right. He'd blown that chance twice already.

In a matter of seconds they were pulling up in front of her house. He turned into the driveway and killed the engine. Still Mel said nothing. She simply gathered up her purse and opened her door.

With a put-upon sigh, Coop got out, too. If she wasn't going to say anything, he'd call his dad and get him to bring the truck. He was just reaching into his pocket when the motion light at her front steps came on, illuminating her face.

Her lower lip was still wobbling. Just a little, but he got the feeling that she'd step inside her house, shut the door and start crying again.

He should let her go, and not get in the middle of whatever it was that had her so upset. One minute she'd been fine at the party, and the next…had someone said something to her? And then there was the knowledge that he'd failed her once before when she was in trouble. If she needed help, he couldn't walk away again.

"Mel…" He reached out and took her hand. It was meant to be a gesture of consolation, of comfort. But the moment he felt her soft skin against his, the familiar feelings kicked in.

He knew he shouldn't, but it tore him up to see her so upset. When she lifted her gaze to his, for a split second it felt as if all the oxygen had left his body. Moisture clung to her lower lashes. Her hair curled around her face, so similar to how it used to when they were teenagers and he'd longed to tell her how he felt, only he couldn't, because she was Scott's girl.

He'd waited long enough to find out, hadn't he? Over ten long, torturous years.

Before she could respond, he leaned forward and kissed her.

There was a brief moment of surprise when she froze beneath him and his lips hovered, barely touching hers. And then she moved her mouth, the tiniest little nibble on his lower lip, shyly inviting him in.

His whole body vibrated as he forced himself to go slowly, slowly. He still held her hand, but his right arm went around her waist, pulling her closer until her soft sweater was pressed against his fleece. He angled his head a little and gave a small nudge, urging her to open her mouth wider. Oh God—she tasted like chocolate and spice and woman. So much better than he'd ever dreamed.

"Mel," he whispered, awed. "Mel."

A little of the fragile control he held snapped, and he kissed her again, more urgently this time. Her arms slipped around his neck and she made a little sound in her throat, the soft vibration of it rippling through his entire body. Her front door was just behind them, and he reached for her hips, settling her against the painted steel, pressing his body closer to hers.

He slid his lips off her mouth and tasted the skin where the graceful column of her neck met her ear. Her pelvis rubbed against his and he started to lose his ability to be rational.

Panic threaded its way through Mel's veins. This couldn't be happening. For heaven's sake, she'd given up hoping for anything physical with Coop when she was sixteen. She'd fallen for Scott. There'd never been any...anything between her and Coop after that. She'd outgrown her crush, right?

Clearly not, because he was sliding his tongue down her neck and she loved every second of it. And this could not happen. It could *not*.

"Stop. Coop...please stop."

Slowly he relaxed his body, putting a few inches between them. The column of her neck was cool where the air touched the damp skin. The sound of their heavy breathing was loud in the dark silence. "Oh my God," she whispered. On top of everything else that had scrambled her emotions today, necking with Coop only made matters worse. "We're standing right in the middle of the light. How could you do this?" She turned her head and scanned the neighbors' yards. Had anyone seen?

Her body was still humming from the feel of him pressed against her, and when she challenged him with her eyes, he glared back. With a grunt of frustration, he tugged on her wrist and pulled her away from the door and the circle of light.

"What the hell is going on with you?" he demanded. "First you throw yourself in my arms, then you won't say a thing. Then you wrap your arms around my neck and kiss me, and then accuse me of...what are you accusing me of again? Mel, make up your damned mind!"

She ran an agitated hand through her hair. This was going all wrong. She was supposed to come home, go inside and fall apart. She wasn't supposed to be skulking in dark corners with Cooper! But his question brought her back to the present with a thud. The truth was, she was a mess. She didn't know what she was feeling. So when he gave her arm a little shake, she snapped her head up and blurted out, "Look, I got my period, okay?"

His hands dropped to his sides. He groaned. "That's a little TMI, isn't it? All of this is because you're hormonal?"

This time she drew back and punched him in the arm. "No, you idiot! I've been trying to have a baby!"

The words rippled through the air and she immediately pressed a hand to her mouth. She hadn't meant to say it. Especially not like *that*.

Coop's face went white and he looked as if he needed to sit down to digest what she'd just said. Stunned, he made his way to the stoop, motion light and all, and dropped his weight on the third step. "You've been... holy hell. With who?"

He turned his face toward her. Heat rose to her cheeks in embarrassment. For years she'd ignored the fact that once upon a time she'd have done anything to have his hands and lips on her like they'd been only moments ago. Now that they had been...it took her back to those days of desperately trying to get his attention. To make him see her as more than just a friend. And now he thought she was sexually involved with someone. At any other time it would be comical. In light of the situation, it was just plain awkward. "It's none of your business."

He swallowed, then turned those cursed bedroom eyes on her. He looked up at her from beneath those sooty lashes and said ominously, "From the way you were kissing me a moment ago, I'd say it is very much my business."

"I was not kissing you! I mean, I was, but it was just

that I'm such a mess and, oh Coop, you always complicate everything!"

Complicate was an understatement. It wasn't just
the past feelings making it awkward. She'd *liked* kissing him. A lot. After months and months of wishing
he'd just disappear!

A rueful grin flickered over his face. "I don't mean
to."

She sighed, then came over and sat beside him on the
step, careful not to let her leg touch his. "Don't say anything to anyone, please? No one knows. And it doesn't
matter now, anyway. This was my last chance." She
fiddled with a nub of denim on the knee of her jeans.

"What do you mean, your last chance? One, who
have you been seeing? He can't be from Cadence Creek,
and you're always working, so when have you had time
to date? And two, you're not even thirty. You have lots
of time to have babies. You'll probably get married
again, you know?"

"I don't want to get married again. Ever."

Her voice was flat and definite.

"Aw, come on. Forever is a long time."

She angled him a sideways look. "Yeah, well, I don't
have any burning desire to put myself in a position to be
hurt and mocked and lied to again. No, thanks."

"You know not every marriage is like that," he rea-
soned.

"Well, I've been burned once. I don't think I'm willing to chance it again."

"Maybe you just haven't met the right guy."

The words shouldn't have stung, but they did. They
brought back every broken teenage dream she'd had,
along with the sledgehammer of painful memories from
the divorce. Add to that kissing Coop tonight. Clearly,

he didn't categorize himself as "the right guy"—he never had. And as such he never should have kissed her at all.

"I plan on doing this all on my own," she explained, her tone a little sharp. "I haven't been seeing anyone besides the lovely people at the clinic in Edmonton. Flying solo."

He sat back. "Are you saying you've been going to a sperm bank?"

She nodded. "It's called intrauterine insemination. This was my third try. I was really hoping it would take this time. I don't have much in savings and I won't borrow against the shop."

He let out a huge breath. "So the crying and running from the party…"

"I was a few days late. I got hopeful that this time was it. I even wished on that stupid star the night you walked me home. And…"

She let the rest of that sentence hang. They'd worked through a bunch of stuff that night. Now she half wished he'd just left her alone. Of course, the other half was still sighing blissfully, remembering the magic of his lips just now.

"But why? Why now?"

She tucked her hands between her knees. "I always wanted kids. When my marriage broke up, we'd been trying, with no luck." She looked over at Coop. "You probably knew that."

"No, no I didn't." His gaze met hers. "I didn't know you'd started trying."

"Looking back, I think it was probably more me trying. Or maybe Scott trying and thinking he wouldn't get caught dipping his nib in the company ink. He was more about himself than I ever realized. Oh, what a stupid cliché we were."

Coop sighed. "I always knew he had a good ego. I didn't think it had developed into such a big sense of entitlement. Not until…"

He didn't have to finish the rest. She sighed. "Scott took everything from me, at least for a while. My marriage, my dream of a family, my self-respect…" She lifted her chin. "I got back my self-respect, and I found a way to support myself. Unfortunately, humans have yet to find a way to reproduce on their own. And the last thing I want to do is marry someone just to have a child. That's ridiculous. So I did what I've been doing since the day I threw his stuff in the front yard. I did it myself."

She sniffed. "At least I tried to. Didn't turn out so great."

Cooper didn't say anything for a long time. She knew it probably sounded crazy to a guy like him. Heck, he was right, they weren't even thirty yet. But he'd never been married, and there were days where she felt about fifty, not twenty-seven.

He dropped his forehead on his hand. "I should have found a way to make Scott see reason," he mumbled. "To make him do the right thing. You should never have been put in this position."

"Do you really think that's accurate? Yes, Coop, I wish you'd told me. But would I want Scott back? I've had lots of time to think about it and the answer is no. Even if you had convinced him to break things off with her, I realize now that he probably would have done it again. He didn't love me enough. I'd rather he was gone than settle for what he was prepared to give."

"So you're not still in love with him?"

She nearly choked. Almost laughed, but saw that Coop was dead serious. She folded her hands together. "Did you really think that? That I was still in love with him?"

"I'm not sure you ever get over someone you really love."

She hesitated. Coop was hovering too close to a truth she'd suspected for quite some time. "Scott can't hurt me anymore," she whispered. "I promise."

"I'm glad to hear you say that. No one should have to settle, you know?"

"I'd rather be alone than be the woman everyone talks about behind their hands. To be a laughingstock or worse…pitied. Poor Melissa, so oblivious that her husband is sleeping around. I'm well rid of him."

Cooper reached over and took her hand. "For what it's worth, he's the one who should be pitied. Look what he threw away."

Something warm curled within her. This was the Coop she remembered. Not the physical touching; he'd been careful not to cross that line. But he always knew what to say when things went sideways. He might tease her incessantly, but when the chips were down, he'd been around, and he'd say something to make her feel better.

It was a shame that he had also thrown that away, though by inaction, not by being a sleazebag. At least she could say that for him.

She let him in on a little piece of insight she'd never shared with anyone. "Yeah, well, I know that love-for-a-lifetime thing happens, but I'm not sure it's meant to happen *to me*. Hence, me doing this on my own."

"You're a strong woman, Mel. Stronger than a lot of people give you credit for."

She was surprised and pleased that after the initial shock, he wasn't judging. "I don't know about that. I'm sad, Coop. I really thought this time was it. I pictured putting together a nursery and buying cute baby things and thinking about next summer and the two of us taking walks in the summer sun. I wanted it so much. Now that's not going to happen. I'm just so…disappointed."

"You can't try again?"

She shrugged. "When do you say enough is enough? Four tries? Five? When you start going into debt? There are other options. I'm just not ready to think about them quite yet."

She knew very well that she could start the adoption process. But there was that little part of her that desperately wanted to experience everything about motherhood, including pregnancy. She wanted that rounded belly and the chance to feel her baby kick. She wanted to hear the heartbeat and see the ultrasound picture. She wasn't sure she was ready to let go of that dream yet. She was going to have to let the dust settle and then think about a next step.

"I'm sorry. What are you going to do now?"

"You mean tonight? Or after that? Because I'm not exactly thinking long-term right now. I won't be pursuing the idea for a little while, until I can think things through."

He nodded. "And how about tonight? Are you going to be okay?"

She nodded. "I am now. I'll go inside and uncork the bottle of wine I've been avoiding, you know, just in case. Then I'll get up tomorrow and clean my house and probably go to the shop and get a jump start on Monday's arranging. I've got a shipment coming Monday afternoon, and that'll keep me busy." She truly was feeling better, and she knew Coop was to thank for that. "It helped just to talk about it, you know? Anyway, do you want me to drive you home? Now you're stranded here without a vehicle."

"I can call my parents. One of them will run into town to get me."

"That's silly. It's the least I can do after you talked me off my ledge. I'm fine now." She held up two fingers, like a "scout's honor" sign.

"Then that'd be great," he replied.

This time she slid behind the wheel and moved the seat ahead while he got in the passenger side. The radio provided some sound in the car on the drive out to the Double C.

When Melissa turned off the road and through the iron gates, she sighed. She'd forgotten how impressive the ranch property was. The lane led straight up to a majestic house, flanked by the dark, hulking shapes of barns. Rolling fields extended for acres and acres. When she'd spent time here, she'd always felt as if she had room to breathe. It was wide-open spaces and serenity.

"I haven't been out here for a long time," she remarked. "I kind of forgot how big and beautiful it is."

"I took over the running of it four years ago," Cooper explained. "Though Dad still has a hand in decisions and works around the place whenever he wants."

"No friction between you two?"

He laughed a little. "Not much. We think a lot alike, and I value his wisdom. He's been doing this a long time."

The headlights touched on the main house. It was large and impressive, but the shrubs and garden around it— his mother's handiwork—kept it from seeming cold and impersonal. The front was lit with floodlights, illuminating the beige stucco, white trim and heavy wood door.

"Turn left," he said, pointing to a drive leading away to a smaller structure tucked slightly behind the house. "I'm over there."

She obediently turned. "When did you stop living in the main house?"

He chuckled. "Shortly after I took over and decided it was a bit lame to be living with Mom and Dad at my age. It's not as big, but it's big enough. Couple thousand square feet, four bedrooms."

She stopped the car in front of the two-bay garage. "For that family you haven't started yet?"

Cooper felt a strange mix of feelings at her question. He'd built the house at the same time that she was starting her business. It was his attempt at moving on and starting a new phase after something so painful. And it was strange talking to her about it, considering he'd held a torch for her for so long. Had he really had the asinine thought that this would be about letting go and moving on? The more time he spent with her, the more complicated his thoughts became. Especially after tonight, and finally kissing her the way he'd wanted to for years. It didn't feel like an ending. It felt like a beginning. A beginning where he was walking on a tightrope.

"I do want that someday," he admitted. "I always have."

"Well, I hope you choose better than I did," she answered, putting the car in Park.

She said it so easily, this suggestion about him finding a wife. What clearer indication did he need that she wasn't interested in him? He should get that through his head by now. She only wanted to be friends. Any crush she'd had on him had died when they were sixteen, and the kiss tonight had simply been the result of high emotion. He needed to accept that. She was never going to love him in that way. No, instead she was in love with the idea of being a single mom. Doing it all herself.

So what was he doing, torturing himself by bringing up old history? She didn't want him. Not anymore. And he had enough male pride to be a little put out that she felt better after *talking*. Wasn't that just awesome.

"Thanks for the lift. Drive carefully, okay?"

"I'm fine now."

"You're sure?"

"I'm sure. Thanks for the talk, Coop. I know I've been harsh but…it was almost like old times, you know? I always felt better after talking to you."

Yeah. Just like old times. He'd done a lot of listening about how much she loved Scott. He was one patient, caring SOB.

But he didn't say that. What he said was, "Anytime, Mel. I'm here for you anytime."

He got out and shut the door, then stood in the dark watching her turn around and drive away. Her taillights disappeared down the road and he kicked at the dirt in the driveway.

Damned if he hadn't meant every word. And he knew exactly where that left him.

Screwed. Because right now he was considering something so crazy, so impossible… It was the one way he might be able to finally make up for all the things he'd done wrong. And in order to give her the one thing she wanted most, he would have to let go of any lingering hopes of them ever being together.

# CHAPTER SIX

MELISSA DID EXACTLY what she said she would. She went home, uncorked the bottle of wine, unearthed the emergency stash of chocolate and felt sorry for herself. Then she fell into bed, exhausted, and got up the next morning feeling even worse. She swallowed pain relievers with her orange juice to help with the ache in her head and her back, and then cleaned her house until it was spotless. She wanted to forget that the humiliation of last night had ever happened. But to do that, she'd have to forget kissing Coop, and that event was branded into her brain. Every sound, every touch, every taste.

She just had to try harder to put him out of her mind. She went into the shop to do some arranging. It never failed to divert her thoughts as she worked with the different blooms and color combinations. Fall hues were in and she liked working with the asters and mums and carnations, all in cozy orangey-rusts. But after the second cheerful bouquet—this one set in a very traditional cornucopia—went all wrong she knew she might as well give up. Her head wasn't in it today. Neither was her heart.

She knew exactly where it was. It was at the Double C.

She'd been surprised at how she'd opened up to Coop

last night. Granted, he'd pressed her into it, but it had come as such a relief to finally just *tell* someone. And he hadn't judged. At least, not much. Maybe because he'd been there when her whole life had gone into the toilet, and he understood the why behind her decision.

Now she was reminded of the friendship they'd shared before. Maybe he'd made a mistake. No, not maybe; he had. But he had also been caught in the middle, trying to do what was right.

Hmm. Was she forgiving him? She thought she had before, but now she wasn't so sure. All she knew was that she wasn't as angry. And that had come with the words she'd uttered last night about not wanting Scott back. She wished she'd found out about her ex-husband's indiscretion a different way, but it would have been far worse to not know and spend years in a sham of a marriage. Her spidey senses told her that his affair wasn't his first and probably wouldn't have been his last. She'd been so wrong…about so many things.

Cooper could never know how affected she'd been by that kiss. How everything had seemed to fade away until all that was left was the sensation of finally being in his arms. Finally knowing exactly what he tasted like, and even more disturbing, realizing that it was somehow familiar, even though it had never happened before. All the hopped-up, tingly sensations today made it feel as if someone had reached in and turned the clock back to age fifteen.

But they weren't love-struck kids anymore. They were adults. They'd been through stuff a lot more serious than not having homework done or losing a football game. More than ever, right now, Mel longed to be somewhere that felt familiar. Someplace like home, a touchstone to a past she'd once known and loved. The iron gates and majestic house at the Double C had sent a flood of familiarity through her last night, even in the dark. Maybe she'd take a drive out there today.

Or not. That was a bit obvious, wasn't it? Resolutely she got out a pumpkin-shaped bowl and inserted a foam core in the center. For several minutes she worked on adding orange lilies, yellow daisies and poms, peachy-orange roses and crimson-veined carnations into a Thanksgiving arrangement. Frowning, she reached for a few spears of wheat and bunches of artificial cranberries just for a teensy pop of color.

She tapped her fingers on the work counter. She liked this one. And yet her mind kept straying to the Double C and Coop. What was he thinking in the clear light of day? People became single parents all the time, but normally because they got caught or their marriage had split. This kind of thing—intrauterine insemination—simply wasn't done in a town the size of Cadence Creek.

Melissa wanted to believe Cooper would keep the information to himself, but what if something like this got out? She had to make sure he understood. She'd been prepared to deal with questions after the fact, but now, when it looked as if pregnancy was a moot point, she'd really rather keep it hush-hush. No sense overturning the apple cart.

And then it hit her—the perfect excuse. She'd never given Coop back his jacket, or Jean back her cookie dish. Mel could drop both off and say thank you for last night. And remind him—very nicely, of course—that he'd promised to keep her secret to himself.

Before she could change her mind, she locked up the shop and stopped by her house for his jacket and the dish.

The autumn afternoon was gilded in warm sunlight. When Melissa pulled up to the gate, she caught her breath. She hadn't been able to see things quite so clearly last night in the dark, but she'd truly forgotten how stunning the Double C was. What had been dark shapes then were in full, vibrant color today. The house looked like a country club with its white pillars and creamy-beige stucco. Coop's place was smaller but equally as beautiful, with a similar, downscaled design. To the right and beyond lay the immaculately kept stables and fields where the Fords made their fortune breeding stock horses.

The Double C appeared to be doing even better than before. As she pulled into Coop's yard she paused to watch a pair of chestnuts gallop along a pasture fence, manes and tails streaming. She sighed, watching as one gave a sassy little buck. Coop must love it out here, with all the space and freedom. She felt a bit of pride, knowing her friend was such a success. He'd always been focused and driven. Now he put that attention into the family business, and it was clearly thriving.

She went to the door and knocked. His truck was in the yard, but there was no answer. Mel was heading back to her car when her cell phone vibrated in her pocket. She pulled it out and saw a new text message on her screen.

Watching football at the big house. Come on up.

Her gaze swerved to Jean and Bob's place. A figure stood in a big window facing her way, and as she squinted she saw him wave. With a laugh she tucked the phone back in her pocket, got in her car and drove the short distance to the mansion.

Coop met her at the door. "Hey. This is a surprise."

She held up the jacket and container. "I was at loose ends. I thought I'd finally return your jacket. I forgot last night."

"You're doing okay?"

She shrugged. "Yeah. I guess." It was nice of him to ask. Was she still bummed? Very. But she was giving herself time to settle, not make any rash decisions.

"I thought you were going to go into the shop today."

"I did for a while. I got restless."

He seemed to accept that and stood aside. "Well, you might as well come in. We're just starting the second quarter and there's a rumor that Mom is making nachos at halftime."

"Are you sure? I don't want to intrude."

"I'm sure."

Stepping inside felt familiar, even though she hadn't visited in years. Despite their obvious affluence, the Fords had made their house warm and welcoming, with no pretense or airs. She followed Coop into the den, where his parents sat together on a leather love seat, eyes glued to the screen as the Edmonton Eskimos hit first down and ten.

"Hey, look who I found," Coop said, stepping into the room.

Jean popped up from the love seat immediately. "Melissa! This is a lovely surprise."

"I brought back your dish," she said, holding it out. "I know it's the real deal and figured you'd want it back."

"Are you feeling better? Coop said he drove you home early last night."

Mel smiled, warmed by the concern. And feeling a little let down that she wasn't spending the afternoon with her own parents. She hadn't talked to them in a couple of weeks. "Much better, thank you. A good night's sleep was just what the doctor ordered. I don't mean to intrude on your afternoon, though."

"Don't be silly," Bob said, tearing his eyes from the screen. "It's good to have you around again. Have a seat. We're getting our butts kicked, but there's still time to turn it around."

She sat on the sofa, a different one than she remembered. It really had been a long time since she'd been here. Cooper sat, too, but left the middle cushion between them. She let herself get absorbed in the game for a while, cheering when the quarterback made a great pass, only to have it incomplete. When the kicker missed the next field goal, everyone sat back in disgust.

"I can't watch. I'm going to put those nachos in the oven," Jean said.

"I'm going to grab another beer," Bob added, putting his hands on his knees and getting up. "You want another, Coop? Melissa? Get you anything?"

"I'm fine, thank you," she said, and Coop waved his dad off. As the halftime whistle sounded, they found themselves alone.

"Why'd you really come today, Mel?"

She tucked one ankle beneath her other leg and turned a little on the sofa so she was half facing him. Leave it to Coop to get right to the heart of the matter. "I was trying to put together some arrangements for tomorrow and I couldn't focus. I just needed to get away, get some space, you know? These days my life is going from home to the shop, maybe to the Wagon Wheel or grocery store or post office, and back home again. I needed some room to breathe, I think. Especially if..." She paused. "Well, I can't go on this way indefinitely. I need to figure out what comes next."

"So you came here. To me."

She frowned and looked away. "Gee, don't make it sound like that."

"Like what?"

"Like *that*."

He persisted. "Like someone who kissed you silly last night?"

Her gaze snapped to his. She didn't want it to, but it was a reflexive response to his question. For a moment tension snapped between them and she remembered his fingers digging into her bottom as he moved into a full-body press last night.

"That shouldn't have happened."

"Why?"

He was undeterred. Mel stole a glance at the archway, but only heard muffled sounds of Bob and Jean talking and the creak of an oven door. No chance of being interrupted yet.

"Because we're barely even friends again. It just confuses everything. And I wanted to make sure you weren't going to say anything about…you know."

He gave a snort of disbelief. "You mean about you trying to get knocked up by some anonymous donor with a turkey baster? Don't worry, my lips are sealed."

She pursed her lips. "That's exactly the reaction I'm trying to avoid. Thanks a lot."

He let out a breath. "Sorry. That wasn't fair. What you do is your business, Mel. I'm more annoyed that you think I'd shout it to the rooftops or something. You should know me better than that."

She swallowed. "Fair enough." She looked down at her hands, which she'd twisted together. "Coop, about three years ago… I need to get over that. After all, it wasn't you who cheated on me. When Scott left, I had to have a place to put my resentment. I guess I chose you, because I felt betrayed by you, too."

"I know, and I'm—"

She cut him off. "I know you're sorry. And the truth is we can't change it now. In some ways I wouldn't even want to. The last few weeks reminded me of the kind of friends we were before. I've missed that. I guess I'm kind of hoping you'll forgive me for holding a grudge for so long. And I'll forgive you for being so snippy just now."

She looked into his eyes. They seemed almost green in the afternoon light, the color brought out by the green in the Eskimos sweatshirt he wore. Coop was so good-looking. He was a good guy deep down, he was successful, and she couldn't imagine why some woman hadn't snapped him up yet.

And he'd kissed her last night.

Remembering caused her to shift her gaze away, back to the television screen. There were ads on, but she didn't register them.

"So you're not interested in me that way," he said, more of a confirmation than a question.

"I'm not interested in anyone that way," she replied. "And besides, it would be a quick way to ruin a friendship."

"Food's up!" Jean called from the kitchen.

For a second Coop looked as if he was going to say something else, but he finally gave a crooked smile and relaxed his shoulders. "What do you think? You up for nachos?"

Mel grinned, relieved he hadn't pressed the issue. "Of course."

They made their way to the kitchen, where Jean had the platter set on the island counter, surrounded by bowls of salsa, sour cream and guacamole. Coop's eyes widened when Melissa pulled several cheese-encrusted chips onto her plate, all topped with jalapeño peppers. For the next several minutes they chatted and laughed, and Melissa helped herself to a can of pop to counter the heat from the peppers and salsa.

The game came back on, but the score got worse when a turnover resulted in a touchdown by the opposing team. When Coop asked if she wanted to go for a walk to stretch their legs, Melissa agreed—especially after eating that many chips and guacamole. The afternoon was warm, so they made do with what they were wearing as they wandered outside, gravitating toward the ranch buildings.

"We've expanded some since you were here last," he said, leading her past the main barn. "Business is good." He pointed at a new structure. "We built an indoor ring, and use it for a lot of training. It's quiet now, because it's Sunday, but it's usually pretty busy, working the horses, training them up. Stu's good around the barns, but I've got a couple of first-class guys who really know what they're doing."

The passion and pride in his voice was unmistakable. "You've got a good reputation," she said, ambling beside him, feeling the warmth of the sun soak into her. "I mean...in business."

He barked out a laugh. "Not so good with the ladies?"

She kept step with him as they made their way down a dirt lane toward a small pasture. "Rumor has it you haven't been too active in the love department lately. Which is funny, because I seem to remember you enjoying female company quite a bit."

He was quiet for several beats, and she turned her head to look up at him, questioning.

"I dated to put in time," he confessed. "So that I wouldn't be the single guy when everyone was pairing up. But I wasn't looking for anything serious."

"So you changed girls like you changed your socks?"

His lips twitched. "It was hardly that often."

"You never dated anyone more than a month or two," she pointed out.

"No, I didn't."

"So why the sudden drop into celibacy?" They'd reached a fence and Mel stepped forward to rest her arms on the white painted rail. "Amy said she asked you out and you turned her down. I think you hurt her pride."

He did laugh then. "Amy seems to manage all right. One of these days she's going to find someone and get her claws in good and tight. I sure didn't want to be that guy."

"She thinks that someone broke your heart."

Coop's gaze pierced Mel. "Since when did I become a hot topic of conversation around Foothills Floral Design?"

"Since you brought me cookies," she confessed.

Instead of responding, he bent forward and gave a low whistle. About a half-dozen heads popped up, ears twitching, and then, as a group, the animals trotted over to the fence, all long legs and soft noses and wide eyes.

"Oh, babies!" Mel smiled widely as the colts and fillies approached the railings. "Oh my goodness, Coop, they're adorable!"

"Aren't they?" He reached through the gap and scratched between the ears of one buckskin colt. "I love them at this age. They're full of oats, you know? All energy and cuteness. And all except for one is spoken for."

"Which one?"

He pointed to a sorrel filly with a white star. "Her. She's from Ford's Firebrand and Morning Mist."

"Misty! Oh my gosh, you still have her?"

He grinned. "Yeah, we still do. I remember she was your favorite. She's fourteen now and has a number of offspring. I wanted one of hers here, you know?"

"You sentimental, Coop?"

He smiled. "Maybe a little." The filly came over to the fence and Mel reached out and rubbed her soft jaw.

"You really love this place, huh."

He nodded. "Always have. It's my heart and soul. The only thing I ever wanted to do was work with Dad and take over the reins when the time came. I learned at his elbow. It's not a job. This is my life, you know?"

"I think I do. It's rare, your connection. I love the flower shop, love what I do and how I've built it. But this…this goes deeper. This is right down to your boots, isn't it?"

"It is. The land, the horses, breeding them, training them…I can't imagine doing anything else."

She was quiet for a moment as the horses drifted away, and then she sighed. "Can I make a confession, Coop?"

He chuckled. "Why not? Hate for you to stop now."

She gripped the fence and stared at the fields beyond the small pasture. "How you feel about this place? That's how I feel about having a family. It's like there's a part of me that's missing. I'm proud of how I got back on my feet after the divorce. I love that I've made a go of my own business and I enjoy the business I chose. It's not that I'm unhappy. But there's a part of me that wants—needs—to be a mother. I can feel it in the deepest part of me, you know?"

She looked at him and raised her eyebrows, asking the question that had bugged her more than anything the last months. "Does that make me less of an independent woman, do you think?"

Coop reached over and put his hand on top of hers. "Of course not. What makes you strong and independent is making choices that are right for you no matter what anyone else thinks. Following your heart and doing what it takes to make your dreams a reality. And you know this, right? Believe me, Mel, having a career and being a mom are not mutually exclusive events. I know people don't realize it, because she was always here, but my mom was—is—a fantastic parent, yet she also put in countless hours on the ranch. She's always kept all the books and records, and wasn't afraid to get her boots dirty, either."

"So you don't think less of me for what I've been trying to do?"

Coop chuckled and slid his hand away. Melissa missed the feel of it, warm and reassuring, on top of hers. Just weeks ago she couldn't stand the sight of him. But maybe the time had been right to let go of old grudges.

"Was I surprised at last night's revelation? You bet. Who wouldn't be? I can just imagine what the women in town would say if they knew."

"Probably something very similar to what you said inside," Mel admitted.

"It's just not how we do it here in the Creek. But I don't think less of you, of course not. I'm a little in awe, to be honest. It's a brave thing to step outside a comfort zone and take a chance, especially knowing what people will say."

The backs of her eyes stung a little. "Thank you for that."

"You're welcome." He grinned. "For the record? You were fierce when you caught Scott with his hand in the proverbial cookie jar. When you put your mind to something, you don't mess around. If this is what you want, you'll find a way."

A flock of magpies chattered in the barnyard, the cacophony filling the silence. Finally, Coop spoke again. "So what's the plan now?"

She knew he was referring to her plans for motherhood. "I'm taking a bit of time to think. I'm probably going to look into getting on the adoption registry. It wasn't my first choice. I wanted to experience carrying a baby, you know? Feeling the first kicks, buying maternity clothes, going through childbirth classes…"

"Morning sickness, weight gain, labor?"

She laughed. "Those, too. They come with the package." Suddenly the emotion that she'd managed to keep at bay all day came flooding back. "I want to feel my baby stick its toes in my ribs. To go to the doctor and hear the heartbeat, see the ultrasound picture. I want that experience, Coop. If I can't have it, so be it. Like I said, I can't afford to go through IUI attempts indefinitely. And I absolutely refuse to take my mother's advice."

"Which is?"

Mel made a disgusted sound. "Get married. I don't plan on doing that again, but if I did, I would have to be in love with that person, utterly and completely. I couldn't marry someone just to have a baby. I'd far rather my child be brought up by a single mom than in a home where the parents didn't truly love each other."

Which was why, though she hadn't breathed a word of it to anyone, she'd been secretly relieved when she'd gotten her period after Scott had left. If there'd been a baby on the way it might have changed things. It definitely would have complicated them. She would have been tied to him forever, with a child between them. He might have tried to convince her to give their marriage another go. Sometimes in the back of her mind she wondered if that feeling of relief had jinxed her from future success. But then she dismissed it. Wishing on stars was fine but people made their own luck.

"You're going to be a great mom, no question. And who knows? Maybe someday you'll find the right guy."

She swallowed. She'd found him already, when she was fourteen. That ship had sailed. She already knew what it was like to be caught in a marriage that wasn't built on the real thing. Oh, she'd done a good job of lying to herself, but she knew the truth. She'd never loved Scott the way she should have. Maybe that's why she hadn't fought harder to keep him.

And he hadn't loved her completely, either. Otherwise he would have been faithful.

She swallowed against a thick lump in her throat. Together, she and Scott had made a mess of everything, hadn't they? They'd been too young, too foolish.

"Mel?"

"Hmm?" Coop's voice pulled her out of her musings.

"I've been doing a lot of thinking since last night. What would you say if I told you I have a solution to your problem?"

"A solution? I don't follow."

He turned away from the fence and faced her with

an intense gaze. His whole demeanor was sober, telling her that whatever was coming next was really important. She didn't know why, but a heaviness that felt like a warning began a slow slide through her body, landing in her stomach.

He picked up her hand. "What if *I* helped you have a baby?"

# CHAPTER SEVEN

MEL STARED AT HIM, wondering if she'd heard him correctly. What he was suggesting was preposterous. And yet the steely look in his eye told her he meant every syllable.

"Cooper, that's ridiculous." She felt as if the blood rushed out of her body as she ripped her hand away. Oh, she never should have confided in him last night! She'd grieved a little and then told herself she simply had to move ahead with the next plan. The last thing she needed was Coop breathing life into the old dream again.

Not to mention this was *Coop*. The whole idea was fraught with so many problems she wasn't sure she could count them all.

"It's not ridiculous. For heaven's sake, Mel, who knows you better than I do? Look, I feel partially responsible for your life blowing up in the first place. This could make things right. I know you'll be a fantastic mom."

She drew back, and her gaze shifted from surprise to suspicion. "Is that what this is? Redemption for you? A way to make you feel better? Because if that's the case, I don't want it."

His brow wrinkled. "Don't call it redemption. What

I did was wrong, and I've regretted it every day since. Maybe this is a way to make amends. You want to be a mom. Why shouldn't I help if I'm able? Isn't that what friends do? Help each other?"

Help? She was almost scared to ask the next question, but knew she had to. Cautiously, she looked up at him. "What exactly are you offering, Coop? Because this sounds a little above and beyond the requirements of *friends*."

"To be the father of your baby."

She needed to sit down. The blood rushed out of her head and she felt strangely light. In the absence of any place to sit she held on to the fence rail, gripping the wood with white knuckles.

For a split second she had thought that perhaps he was just going to offer her money to continue trying the treatments. But no, he'd actually said the word *father*.

"Before you freak out, just listen to me," he pressed. "I thought about this all last night. Wouldn't it be better to know who the father of your child is? I mean, you know me, my family, where I come from. Heck, you'd have my genetic history, for that matter. Isn't that better than some stranger from a lab?"

She had to admit that she'd had qualms about not really knowing the donor. There were benefits to that sort of anonymity and there were drawbacks. Any details she saw on paper told her nothing about the man behind the profile. What was he like? Was he a hard worker, funny, kind? Did he like to read or go to movies, did he like the outdoors or was he more of an urban jungle type? And here was Coop. Hardworking, handsome, healthy Coop. Offering to be her baby daddy.

Not in a million years had she seen this coming. The very idea seemed to suck the air clean out of her lungs.

"You haven't really thought about this," she began cautiously. This was a disaster in the making and she knew it. Yet a part of her hummed with hope. What he was offering was a chance. A way to not give up the idea of having her own child.

But with Coop… She gazed up at him. He shouldn't look different than he had only moments before, but he did. She suddenly noticed the way his chest and shoulders filled out his Edmonton Eskimos sweatshirt. The narrowness of his hips and long legs, and the way his jeans seemed to show off his assets to best advantage. She saw his strong, sexy jaw, smoldering eyes and thick, dark hair. And she wasn't just cataloging his features in genetic terms. It was a deep down, visceral acknowledgment that Coop was incredibly good-looking, rugged and fit.

Cooper was gorgeous. And oh, she could just imagine that he'd make gorgeous babies.

On the heels of her assessment came a lightning strike of images so intense that she bit down on her lip. Making a baby with Coop, the traditional way…

She cleared her throat. "Um, how exactly did you see this happening?" she asked. She heard the wobble of nerves in her voice and felt like an idiot. But really, how was one *supposed* to talk about this kind of thing? It was the strangest conversation, with a plethora of land mines to sidestep. "I mean, did you think we… or would you…"

She was so embarrassed. She half hoped the ground would open up and swallow her.

"Would we—" God, his voice was soft as silk "—go about it the usual way?"

She looked up and nodded.

His expression stayed exactly the same—unreadable—as he answered her query with one of his own. "Would you want to?"

*Let me die right now.*

Again with the images. She was not thinking about sleeping with Coop. She was not.

Only she was. At fifteen she'd dreamed about kissing him. It had been angsty and innocent. At twenty-seven, it was completely different. And that was exactly why it couldn't happen.

"No," she replied, though she suspected she didn't sound very convincing.

"I could be your donor," he said quietly.

Melissa tried to make sense of all the thoughts running through her brain. When she'd thought about coming out here today it had been to escape the noise in her head. To let go of what had been, and to clear a space for thinking about the next step. This was all too much.

She looked around. The sun was still shining, though dropping a little lower in the sky as the afternoon waned. The birds still chattered, the horses grazed, foals frolicked in the pasture—nothing had changed. And yet everything had changed. It had all shifted with his crazy offer to give her the one thing she wanted most.

"And what about the baby?" Her heart lodged in her throat as she asked. "You're prepared to be a sperm donor? Because I'm not looking for any personal entanglements, Coop. How do you see your role in this… after?"

My word, was she actually considering it?

"The baby would be yours, of course," he said calmly, coming forward and taking her hands. "I want to do this for you, Mel. One…friend to another."

As he held her hands she was reminded of how he'd kissed her last night, and the brief flare of passion that had erupted between them. She'd been unable to stop the rush of desire at the touch of his lips on hers. Whether they admitted it or not, there was now this *thing* between them, muddying the waters.

Besides, she knew Coop. She knew him probably better than anyone else on the planet. He would never be satisfied with fathering a child and then stepping back as if it had never happened. Especially in a town this size, where their presence would be front and center every day. He wouldn't be one to stand on the sidelines while his son or daughter grew up, started school, learned to ride a bike.... It simply wasn't in Cooper's DNA and she knew it.

She tried to imagine what a child of theirs might look like, and her heart lurched. Hazel eyes like Coop. Maybe her hair, her nose. She closed her eyes. Coop's smile.

"Don't answer now," he said, letting go of her hands. "Take some time to think about it. It's a big decision. Just know that I'm here, and I'll help you any way I can."

She couldn't speak past the lump in her throat, so she nodded. The fact that he'd even offered...

"Listen, I don't know what your parents have planned, but we're doing our Thanksgiving dinner next Monday. Why don't you join us? Dad's going to try deep-frying the turkey this year. And Mom's guaranteed to have pumpkin pie."

"My parents are still going to be on their New England trip," Melissa admitted. "I don't have plans."

"Then you should definitely come. Maybe we can saddle up Misty for you and we can go for a ride after dinner. And you can tell me what you've decided."

She couldn't deny that there was a part of her that

understood the logic behind his offer. And he was right about one thing—she should take time to think it over before she made a final decision. "That might be nice," she answered weakly.

They turned from the pasture and began walking back to the house. They passed the barn, where a couple of the hired hands were doing evening chores. The sound of laughter and shuffling hooves echoed through the open doors, and Coop lifted a hand in greeting to one worker as they passed.

They finally paused by Melissa's car. Coop shifted his weight as she put her hand on the door handle, knowing she should open it, but not quite wanting the afternoon to end. It had been so great—being included in the game and snacks, seeing the babies in the pasture, the warm afternoon. Even Coop's unorthodox suggestion didn't take away from the fact that she'd felt very welcomed and included. Maybe too included.

But it wasn't just that. She didn't want to leave him. It wasn't a new sensation, but it was one she hadn't felt in a very long time. Not since she was a twitterpated teenager and she'd hoped, prayed every night, that one day Cooper would see her as a girl and not just a buddy. She'd spent hours daydreaming about a moment when he'd reach over and twine his fingers with hers, or slide forward that little bit and kiss her like a boy was supposed to kiss a girl. She'd wanted to be his—to wear his jacket and hold his hand and be the one to sit next to him in a booth at the Wagon Wheel, sharing a milkshake after a football game.

She'd waited…and waited…and waited. And then Scott had come along and offered her all the things that Coop had not.

That weightless, nervous anticipation was swirling

within her right now, though. And all it had taken was one kiss, followed by a not-so-simple suggestion about making babies, to put it back in her head.

"I need to think," she whispered, tugging on the door handle. "There's a lot to think about."

"You do that," he answered. "I'll be here. I'm not going anywhere."

For some reason she felt a flicker of anger at the words. No, Cooper wasn't going anywhere. He was as solid as the day was long. He was practically a saint in this town—a good boss, generous with his time, good-looking and affluent. He was damned near perfect.

And it had only taken him all these years to kiss her, and just because she was an emotional wreck. And now he was suggesting something incredibly amazing—but only as her friend, not as her lover.

"Why can't I shake the feeling that you're trying to buy your way back into my life?"

He shoved his hands in his pockets, but his brows puckered as if he was annoyed. "I'm not proud of what my past actions say about me. Maybe I *am* trying to make up for that. If that's looking for redemption, so be it. Is it so wrong for me to want you to be happy?"

"It's just such an abrupt change.…"

"Guilt kept me away for a long time. That and the way you looked at me with daggers in your eyes. I figured it had gone on long enough."

She blinked, out of responses. Got behind the wheel and turned the key in the ignition. "See you at Thanksgiving," she said through the open window, and he lifted a hand and waved as she drove off.

It wasn't until she hit the main road that she felt the urge to cry. She didn't, though. She forced herself to remain dry-eyed and steely jawed the entire time. But inside, the feelings were there. It was so obvious and hurtful.

It was the reason why she was so sure she would never marry. The one man who should have loved her hadn't, and the one man she'd always wanted to love her never would.

Having Coop's baby was out of the question. Because being in his life was not at all the same as sharing it, and only a foolish woman would put herself in that position.

Coop plopped his hat back on his head, grabbed his oilskin from the peg and shoved his arms in the sleeves as he made his way out the door. A cold front over the mountains had dropped a mere half inch of snow on the ground, and it had already disappeared as the precipitation turned to rain. But the rain was cold, and he still had hours of work to get through yet. The farrier was here, and one of the trainers, Luke, was down with the flu. Stu was helping work the horses today, but Coop knew that in just a few days a client would be making his way up from Montana expecting to pick up four horses. They were damned well going to be ready and worthy of coming out of Double C.

He turned up the collar of his jacket against the bitter rain and lowered his chin as he made his way to the barn.

No doubt about it, the rain wasn't helping his mood any. But then, he'd been a bit grouchy ever since he'd offered to be the father of Mel's baby.

It had seemed like a good idea at the time. He understood her reasoning, even if he did think she was being a bit hasty. It also killed him to see her hurting, especially after all she'd been through. If she truly was determined to go through with this—and he could see that she was—he wanted to help.

And that was the problem, wasn't it? He sidestepped a puddle and cursed under his breath. He would go to the moon for her. The only reason he'd stayed away so long was because he knew she had a right to be angry with him, and he'd wanted to give her space.

It had all changed when he'd kissed her. He'd lost his edge, the upper hand. It had made him weak. Willing to accept her friendship on whatever terms she offered. And wasn't that a sure way to get hurt.

Light glowed from the barn windows and he pulled on the sliding door, anxious to get out of the wet. Yes, kissing her had been a mistake. And so had asking her if she wanted to go about things the "usual" way. Because while Scott had been wrong about Coop trying to split them up, he was dead right about Coop's feelings.

If he told her everything about the night he'd confronted Scott, she'd finally understand the real reason he'd acted the way he had. But she would also wonder if his offer to be her donor was his way of making his move, insinuating himself into her life.

And while that hadn't been his initial intent, he wondered that himself. Spilling his guts would take the tenuous trust they'd built lately and crush it to dust. And yet going on without telling her the truth was unthinkable. If nothing else, they had to reestablish their friendship with total honesty. Lack of honesty had been what had driven them apart in the first place.

He shut the door behind him and shook the water off his hat and shoulders. Maybe it was time he stopped letting his feelings for Mel make him look like a fool. But if he hadn't figured out how to do that in ten years, he wasn't too confident in his chances now, either.

* * *

Thanksgiving Monday came smack in the middle of a Chinook. The cloud arch formed to the west, cutting the sky in a precise arc, and the westerly wind was mild, bringing back an echo of summer. Mel was surprised to see extra cars already parked at the Ford house. For a moment she considered scooting away and then calling and making her apologies.

Instead she reached back into her car for the flower arrangement she'd brought, as well as a long, rectangular gift bag containing a bottle of wine. Why should she be alone today? The idea of roasting a single turkey breast and making boxed stuffing for herself sounded horrible. Especially when she had a perfectly good invitation.

She rang the bell and wished she had a free hand to run over her hair. She'd put it up in a simple twist, but was sure the blustery Chinook wind was ripping it to shreds. A piece flew free and stuck to her lipstick. Perfect. She was already unspeakably nervous about today, about seeing Coop again. To let him know her decision. She'd done nothing but think about it since the last time they spoke.

The door opened and Cooper stood there, dressed in jeans and a starchy-looking red plaid shirt, the front of his body covered by a cotton apron with the words Mr. Good-Lookin' Is Cookin' emblazoned on the front.

"You came."

"You thought I wouldn't?"

He grinned. It made the corners of his eyes crinkle and chased away some of her nerves, filling her with warmth and gladness. "I wondered if you'd turn coward."

"Shows what you know," she retorted, but she was smiling. "Do you suppose I could come in?"

"Oh, sure. Sorry."

He stood aside and she stepped into the foyer. Voices echoed from the kitchen and then there was loud laughter. "Uncle Jason is here with Aunt Sheila, and so is Aunt Rae. It won't be a quiet dinner."

Mel was thinking that was just fine. It would save awkward conversations and she could melt into the background a little. But then she stepped into the kitchen and was immediately pounced on by Bob, who was feeling rather jovial—perhaps after a predinner cocktail.

"Look who's here! I don't know what's prettier, those flowers or the roses in your cheeks."

So much for blending in.

She put the flowers down on the end of the island and couldn't help but chuckle. Bob was dressed similarly to Coop, only his apron boasted a picture of a bull and the message Aged to Perfection.

"Nice," she commented. "But if you two are cooking, I'm not sure I want to stay."

Coop pressed a hand to his heart. "Oh, you wound me!"

Jean came from the pantry with a jar of pickles in her hand. "They're under my direct supervision, Melissa. Don't you worry." She came forward and kissed Mel's cheek. "Glad you could make it. Coop will be on his best behavior."

"I highly doubt that."

Like Coop and Bob, Jean had on an apron, too. It seemed this was a family tradition. And in typical rodeo queen fashion, the former barrel racing champ had on a pink apron with the caption Barrel Racer, Cowboy Chaser.

The aunts and uncle were out on the back deck enjoying a drink. Mel handed over the bottle of wine and asked Jean, "Is there anything I can do to help?"

"Not at the moment. Oh, Melissa, did you bring those flowers? Of course you did. They're gorgeous!" She fussed over the arrangement, a bigger version of the one Mel had created just over a week ago at her shop.

"It was no trouble."

"You've got such a talent." Jean moved the flowers to the dining room, putting them in the center of the table and moving the candles to either side. "You were a real smart cookie, starting up that business."

"Thanks."

Jean paused in the doorway to the dining room, close to Melissa. She reached out and put her fingers lightly on Mel's arm. "We were so sorry when…well, when things weren't going so great for you. But you picked yourself up again and got back in the saddle, and we're real proud of you. We probably should have said it before, but we knew you and Coop…" She colored a little. "Well. You know."

"It's okay. I'm glad you told me now."

"We're just glad you and Coop are…well." She laughed. "I'm usually not so bad at putting words together. Anyway, you were always good friends and it's nice to see you bury the hatchet. And not in his back. Not that he didn't deserve it. He should have told you what was going on."

"You knew he knew?" All this time Melissa had been under the impression that they'd been in the dark about Coop's involvement.

"Oh, not at the time. He told us one day ages ago

when we asked why you weren't friends anymore. Anyway, water under the bridge and all that. How about I fix you a drink? Pumpkin lattes are the warm-up beverage of the day."

"That sounds lovely," Mel replied, already warmed by Jean's awkward but welcoming speech.

The drink was delicious, blending coffee, pumpkin, spice and cream with a dash of toffee liqueur that made it taste more like a dessert than a cocktail. The kitchen smelled of roasting turkey and savory and sage from the stuffing. Everyone sat in the sun on the deck for a little while until Jean went inside to put on the vegetables. Mel offered to help and Coop's mother insisted she wear an apron so she didn't get anything on her good clothing.

She slid the loop over her neck and tied the strings behind her back, then looked down and burst out laughing.

"It's mine," Jean said with a grin.

It said Cowgirls Ride the Hide.

"Let me guess, you collect them?"

"I have a whole drawer full. It's kind of a tradition now. They usually show up in Christmas stockings."

Together they turned the burners on beneath the vegetables, took the turkey out of the oven to rest before carving, and put the brussels sprouts in to roast.

While Jean uncorked a bottle of wine, Mel spooned cranberry sauce and pickles into bowls and placed them on the table. She sliced and buttered fresh buns and arranged them in a wicker basket, and filled water glasses while Jean went to work whipping cream for the pumpkin and pecan pies. The sprouts came out of the oven, the carrots were drained and the potatoes mashed. Bob came in and carved the turkey, and the aunts poured wine and carried bowls to the table while Coop got a lighter and lit the candles flanking Mel's flowers.

And then they all finally sat down at the table, Bob at one end and Coop at the other, Jean at Bob's right elbow and Mel on Coop's, with the aunts and uncle rounding out the sides. Mel tried not to notice that she was seated in the mirror position of Jean and Bob, though she and Coop were not a couple. And yet, as they took their seats, her knee bumped his beneath the table and something exciting shot up her leg. Oh boy.

"Cooper, won't you give a toast?" Jean asked.

Coop raised his glass, then waited until all the glasses were lifted before he said, "To family, to friends, being together and our many blessings. Happy Thanksgiving."

The sound of tinkling crystal echoed in the dining room, and Coop leaned slightly sideways and touched his glass to Melissa's. "Happy Thanksgiving," he said quietly, meeting her gaze.

She was so used to him teasing, to seeing the twinkle in his eyes, that she was quite mesmerized by the soft, serious quality she found there. "To you, too," she replied, and that swirly feeling intensified as they each took a sip of their wine with their gazes locked.

Coop's suggestion echoed in her mind: *The usual way? Would you want to?*

Yes, she thought. Oh yes, she would. And wasn't that a huge surprise. Because ever since Scott left she hadn't felt any burning desire to get caught up in someone that way. Especially Coop. She dropped her eyes to her plate, hoping her thoughts weren't reflected in her gaze. Something her mother always said kept nagging at her, too. She'd always claimed that hate was as passionate an emotion as love. And Melissa had hated Coop for a long time, until it became a habit. Now she was beginning to realize that she hadn't really hated him. She'd had a whole bunch of other emotions where Coop was concerned, hurt and betrayal that had been devastating. She'd called it hate because that had been easier than dealing with her true feelings.

"Mel? Potatoes are to you." Coop nudged her hand with the bowl and she wondered how long he'd been holding them, waiting for her.

"Oh. Thanks."

She made a point of filling her plate and eating, always aware of Coop on her left. He laughed and smiled a lot, teasing his family and getting as good as he got. He'd taken off the silly apron and had rolled up his sleeves. She noticed he wore a watch but no other jewelry, no rings, no nothing.

Coop, she realized, hadn't changed that much at all. He was still a no-fuss kind of guy who didn't feel the need to put on a show. But then, he didn't need to, did he? He was the kind of man who seemed to command attention without even trying.

"More wine, Mel?"

She looked up at him. He was holding the bottle and waiting for her response. She shook her head. "I probably shouldn't. Not after that dessert masked as a cocktail earlier. I have to drive later."

He put down the bottle. "We still on for that ride?"

The meal was delicious, but at his question her appetite started to fade. So far this afternoon she'd ignored the fact that later on they were going to have an uncomfortable conversation.

"Why not? I haven't ridden for a long time. It's a good day for it."

"Give us a chance to work off dinner," he added.

"No kidding. I haven't had a turkey dinner with all

the trimmings since last Christmas at Mom's. I almost had to roll myself home. I can't eat like I could when I was sixteen anymore. I look at a meal like this and gain five pounds."

His gaze swept over her. "Naw, I doubt it. You look as good as you always did, Mel."

Her cheeks warmed and his leg brushed hers again. Whether it was intentional or by accident, the ripples still felt the same. Oh, she'd definitely made the right decision. Finding the right way to tell him, though— that was going to be a real challenge.

When the main meal was over, Mel joined the women in clearing the table of plates and then serving pie and coffee. She was slicing into the pecan pie when Coop stepped up behind her and put his hand over hers on the knife, sliding it farther to the right to make the piece bigger. "That's about right," he said.

His breath was warm on her ear, his body close behind her so that if she backed up even an inch, her spine would be pressed against his broad chest. She swallowed and told herself to breathe normally. "Are you sure you don't want a smaller one so you can have a piece of each?"

He leaned in closer. "I'll let you in on a little secret." His lips brushed her ear. "There's a second pumpkin pie hidden in the fridge for later."

She shivered. And she knew he knew, because she felt his lips curve in a smile against her ear.

She shrugged him away. "Oh, stop pestering me and let me cut the pie, or else you won't get any!"

"You tell him, Mel!" Bob cheered her on and Aunt Rae laughed beside her.

"Get on with you, Cooper," Aunt Rae chided. "You always were a torment. I'm with Melissa on this one."

He took his piece of pie and got a scoop of whipped cream for the top from his mother, then left the kitchen for the comfort of the dining room again.

But Melissa couldn't help feeling as if the family was pairing them up today, and Cooper's actions did nothing to deter that line of thinking. And that simply couldn't happen. A guy like Cooper flirted without even realizing it. It was second nature to him; she'd seen him turn that smile on girls for as long as she'd known him. It annoyed her a lot that she wasn't any more immune than those other girls had been.

But it ended here. He didn't really mean it. He never did. And it was why there couldn't be anything between them, and exactly the reason he could never be the father of her child. In the end she'd be the one to pay. She'd start to care too much and she'd be the one hurt.

Once was enough for that, thank you very much.

# CHAPTER EIGHT

SHE NEARLY BACKED OUT of the plans to go riding, but doing so would put her in an awkward position. Granted, she hadn't had a lot to drink at dinner, but she'd had the latte and then a full glass of wine, and wasn't quite sure she should drive yet. The dishes had been put in the dishwasher and the aunts had insisted on washing up the rest as Mel and Jean finished clearing the table. When Cooper said they planned to go riding, they'd practically been shooed out the door.

Now Melissa was astride Misty and finding it hard to be sorry. When they'd been kids, they'd gone riding a lot. Misty had been younger then and full of beans, as Bob used to say. But he'd trusted Mel with her, and while Melissa's equestrian skills were rusty now, it all felt very familiar as she relaxed in the saddle and held the reins easily in her hands.

"Where to?" Coop asked. He was astride Sergeant, a ten-year-old sorrel stallion with strong hindquarters and a wide, muscled chest. The horse tossed his head a little, his mane shivering in the wind, and danced a bit to the side. Without breaking his gaze from Mel, Coop settled the animal with barely a movement of his body or hands.

"Up to you," she replied. There were tons of places

on the ranch. They could head east and wind their way along the creek to the butte, or north past the pastures and on to the slough, where there was shelter in the trees. Or they could follow the creek the other way, down into the gulley.

"Let's go west," he suggested. "Then we'll have the wind at our back on the way home."

He led the way and she couldn't help but admire the figure he made in the saddle. He was all long legs and lean hips, with a perfectly straight back and relaxed, wide shoulders. He'd put on his jean jacket again and when he turned his head to follow the path of a flock of geese, the brim of his hat nearly touched the collar. Once they were out of the yard, Coop looked back and grinned, and then nudged Sergeant into a canter. The speed was nothing Mel couldn't handle, and she settled into the rocking gait easily. He was letting the horses get some exercise, and it was fun, too. She caught up to him and moved alongside, then gave Misty a nudge and opened her up to a gallop. She heard Coop's laugh behind her, but only for a short while. In no time he'd brought the stallion forward and they rode neck and neck, heading nowhere fast and loving every minute.

Before long they reached the narrow, snaking creek and slowed to a trot, then a walk. They rode beside it for a long time until a narrow path appeared, leading down into the secluded gulley.

The rock along the creek bed was multicolored, a unique striation of geological layers that had been formed over millions of years. The Chinook wind didn't reach the sheltered canyon, and the creek meandered through, unhurried on this lazy autumn day.

Coop halted his horse at a particularly wide spot and dismounted, letting Sergeant walk forward to get a drink from the cool creek. Mel followed suit, her hand loosely on the reins as Misty dipped her nose in the water. Instead of mounting up again, Coop grabbed Sergeant's reins and started walking, leading him along the creek.

They kept on, silent, until they reached a small stand of trees just barely hanging on to their bright yellow leaves. Coop looped the reins around a branch and then secured Misty as well. Then he held out his hand to Melissa and said simply, "Walk with me."

She hesitated. Coop's hand was still there, waiting for her to take it, and she wanted to and was afraid to all at once. Didn't he realize he was playing with her feelings here? And yet…it was only holding hands, and she was twenty-seven years old. Maybe she was making far too much of things.

She put her palm against his and his fingers tightened around hers.

They didn't go far, just ambled up the creek a little. The stream burbled and whispered over rocks strewn on the bottom, and Coop's steps were slow and lazy. When Mel felt they had to say something or she would surely burst, he paused, turned to face her and said, "I'm sorry, Mel. I can't wait to do this any longer."

Her lips were still open with surprise when his mouth came crashing down on hers. Oh glory, he tasted good. Like rich coffee and sweet brown sugar and one hundred percent man. Every rational thought she possessed, every rehearsed line she'd practiced in her head, was pushed out by the reality that was Cooper. She did the only thing she could in the moment—she responded. She kissed him back, planting her booted feet in the gravel and gripping the shoulders of his jacket to pull him closer.

He leaned his weight against her, forcing her to take a step backward. She nearly lost her balance when she realized he was guiding her, pushing her step by step to the rock wall that kept them secluded from the rest of the world. The cold, smooth surface touched her shoulder blades, supporting her weight, and still Coop's mouth made its magic against hers. Her eyes were closed and every nerve ending in her body was at full attention. It would be so easy to let go. To lose control. It had been so long....

But Coop's urgency grew tempered and his kiss gentled. Instead of relieving the tension, that magnified it by about a hundred. Now it was slow. Seductive. And very, very deliberate. His touch was full of nuances, from the tiny nudge encouraging her to open her mouth wider, to the brush of his hand over her hip, to the delicious sound of pleasure that rumbled in his throat. Never in her life had Mel completely understood what girls meant when they said they melted into a puddle, but she did now. If not for the rock behind her and Coop's body bracing her against it, she was relatively sure that her boneless body would collapse into a blissful heap of arousal.

"I could do this forever," he murmured against her cheek.

"Oh please, no," she replied breathlessly. "I'm fairly sure I couldn't survive that long."

"Without what?" His teeth nibbled at her ear.

"Without..." She lost her train of thought as he nipped at her neck, then slid his lips back to her mouth, where he kissed the sensitive corner. "Oh *God,* Coop."

"You, too, right?" Somewhere in the last few minutes his hat had come off, and he pressed his forehead to hers. "It's not just me. Say it's not just me."

"It's not just you."

"I don't want to stop. I don't think I can stop touching you."

It had been a very long time since someone had said something like that to her, and meant it. She gloried in the sensation of being wanted and craved. As much as she knew there were other things at stake, she wanted just a few more minutes. She could stop thinking for a few more minutes, right?

His mouth fused with hers again, their bodies so twined together that there came a point where they had to either start removing clothing or step away. It was a point of no return, and for the space of a few seconds Mel considered all the possibilities. All of them.

To her surprise, it was Coop who stepped back first. He stopped, looked into her eyes and said something incredibly pithy and profane before turning away. She took it as a very heartfelt compliment. For a woman who'd been made to feel undesirable and inadequate, it was a definite score for her feminine pride.

She waited, trying to rein in her reeling senses. Coop stood on the edge of the creek with his back to her, his shoulders rising and falling as he caught his breath.

Was it really just a week ago he'd offered to help her have a baby?

It was impossible to reconcile the two ideas. Impossible to think of Coop as nothing more than a sperm donor. And impossible to think of making love to him. Oh, she could envision that well enough, but how it would fit into her life didn't compute. She could never just have sex for sex's sake, not with Coop. And she really couldn't comprehend it ever being more than that. It was too big. Too…scary.

They were in such a pickle.

She stepped over the gravel, her boots crunching in the silence. She was nearly to his shoulder when he said, in a low, ominous voice, "The answer was always going to be no, wasn't it?"

It stopped her in her tracks. "I'm afraid so, Coop. I just can't."

She studied his profile. His jaw tightened, and his back was ramrod straight. Without looking at her, he spoke. "I don't suppose I'm ever going to be good enough for you, right?"

"What?" She stepped forward and grabbed his arm. "Where the heck did that come from? I have several reasons for saying no, Coop, but not one of them has anything to do with you being good enough for me! Wow."

"But you'd have some random stranger—or no baby at all, before letting me be the father."

There was such bitterness in his voice, and she wondered where it came from. "Oh, for Pete's sake. You men, it's always about your damned pride, isn't it? You want reasons, Coop?"

She started ticking them off on her fingers. "First of all, you say that this would be my baby, but I know you. You theoretically wouldn't want to be involved, but you wouldn't be able to help yourself. I'm not looking for a parenting partner. Secondly, if I did go ahead with it, knowing this was your baby, how could I possibly deny you access to your child? And before you say it, I know, just as you do, that you want a family and kids of your own. Once he or she was here… Like I said, you wouldn't be able to help yourself."

She touched a third finger. "This is a small town. The secret would get out. Even if we kept it quiet, what if our kid looked like you? Oh, the speculation! The last thing I want is my child being brought up with whis-

pers about whether or not someone local is his real father. I've had my share of whispers behind my back,
believe me."

She lowered her hand. "But more than all of those
reasons, Coop, is this. You and me. This would tie us to
each other forever in ways I'm certainly not prepared
for. We're barely even friends again. Parents? And then
there's…what happened today. Everything is mixed up.
We've got no business bringing a baby into the middle
of that. It's just better if I…if I do this alone."

Today had changed the game, though. Suddenly
"alone" sounded awfully empty. And how would it feel
to carry another man's child, knowing that Coop was
out there, with his great kisses and sexy smile and…

She sighed. And what? Oh, why did he have to come
along and complicate everything?

Coop faced her. "After today, do you think I could
stand to see you carry another man's child? Do you
know what that would do to me?"

Confused, she frowned. "Do to you? It got pretty hot,
pretty fast, but it wasn't more than a couple of kisses,
really. I mean…all our clothes stayed where they belonged."

"You tell yourself that," he said darkly, his eyes glittering. "But a minute more and those clothes would have
been on the ground, and you know it."

Charged silence hummed between them.

"You don't own me," she warned quietly. "You don't
have any say. Any right…"

"No? Well, maybe I want to," he answered.

Coop hadn't planned to say it just like that, but he
hadn't planned on kissing her again, either. Kissing,
hell. They'd been doing a foreplay dance and they both

knew it. One taste of her and everything had exploded, just like the last time, only today she wasn't in such an emotionally fragile state.

And he'd admit to himself that he'd been a little edgy. He'd known since he'd opened the door and seen the up-tight turn of her lips that she was going to say no. On the one hand he was relieved. Especially now, because he couldn't stop thinking about her. The truly crappy thing was that he actually agreed with her. They couldn't do this thing and go their separate ways. Not after today. He could hardly keep his hands off her.

Ironic, considering he'd been doing a great job of that for years now.

"You want to what?" she asked slowly, and he could hear the underlying threat.

"Have a right. Be important to you. Maybe I don't want to be the best friend who hears all your troubles. Maybe I don't want to be the guy who brings you a beer and makes you laugh, but doesn't get to go home with you at the end of the night. I've been doing that for years, Melissa, and I'm tired of it."

"What the…" She stepped back, her face white. "What are you saying, Coop? Years? Are you serious? Because I had the biggest crush on you when we were kids, and you were always so determined to stay friends. You weren't interested in me that way. We were bud-dies, remember?"

"Yeah, and I was an idiot. And by the time I realized it you'd had your cherry popped by my best friend."

She turned away as if slapped. He regretted his choice of words; they'd been harsh and indicative of his frustration. He closed his eyes and tried again. "I'm sorry, Mel. I shouldn't have put it that way."

"No," she said quietly, speaking to the water, "that was pretty clear and to the point."

"It's not your fault, okay? I'm frustrated. I didn't realize how I felt until you were with someone else. We were so young. I thought if I just waited it out, maybe I'd get another chance. And then you married him. What was I supposed to do?"

"You want me to feel bad for you?" She spread her arms wide. "I wasted years on that guy!"

"Why did you?" Coop asked. "I mean, no one forced you to marry him. People kept expecting you to break up. Most high school couples do, you know. So what did the great Scott have that made him such a prize?"

Her eyes blazed at him. "Don't even, Coop."

"Why? Because it's making you take a long hard look at your marriage? Was it his good looks? His charm? Money? What was it?"

"It was everything," she yelled. "It was everything, okay? He was there. He was in it and he asked. And you know what? I genuinely thought I loved him. It's not like I didn't care about him or he didn't care about me. Marrying him made sense, all right?"

"Except it was missing something."

"Yeah, well, we were trying to start a family, remember?"

Coop didn't know how she could be so blind. Did she really think her marriage had failed because of an infidelity? That was the easy and short answer, but he knew it was a lot more complicated than that. He knew more than he cared to, because he'd been caught right smack in the middle.

"I'm not talking about a family. I'm talking about love. I'm talking about soul mates. I'm talking about marrying the one person who gets you. The person people talk about when they say The One. And don't kid yourself. Scott knew he was somebody, but he also knew he wasn't The One."

"Don't be ridiculous."

But her eyes skittered away. He had hit on a nerve and he knew it.

"I'm sorry, Mel. I truly am."

She looked up. "He told you that?"

Coop nodded. "You've got to understand, I was friends with both of you. Guys don't unload like women, but sometimes things get said over a beer or two, especially when a man's troubled. He didn't know how to make you happy, and he could tell that you weren't. I told him he couldn't make you happy if he wasn't happy. Then he laughed. And said that you'd married too young."

"We were twenty…"

Coop shoved his hands into his pockets. He wanted to reach out to her. She looked so forlorn, so alone. But it was time, wasn't it? Time she learned the whole truth.

"He knew you wanted a family, so he agreed to try, remember? I told him that kids wouldn't fix things. That was the first time he ever accused me of trying to push my own agenda. He said I didn't want you to have kids because that would complicate things when I made my move."

"Oh, Coop…" Her eyes widened. She came a little closer, hugging her arms around herself as if she was cold, even though the day was still mild. "Was it true?"

He swallowed against the pain that still managed to rear its head when he thought of those last six months before hell broke loose. "I would *never* have tried to break you up. But understand this, Mel—I knew you weren't happy, and it was killing me. We all still did things together, and we smiled and laughed a lot, and it was all churning around like acid in my stomach. And then I saw him one day, when I was on my way back from Edmonton. He was coming out of that motel—you know, the little one out by the highway? With her. At first I couldn't believe it was him, and that there must be a good explanation. And then he opened her car door and kissed her before she got in."

Silence followed his words. Not once had he shared the details of how he'd found out about Scott's affair. Coop had apologized, but until recently she'd never accepted his apology. He'd tried to explain and had always been cut short. He gave her time now to digest the truth.

She picked up a stone and tossed it into the creek. They both watched the splash and then it was gone.

"You asked him about it."

Her voice was hoarse and tired. He wondered how much more he should say, but then considered where they were and what they'd been doing, and knew he couldn't keep things hanging between them any longer. Not if they were going to move forward.

"I told him I saw him there. I expected him to deny it, but he didn't. He just shrugged and said, 'So what?' I told him that he had to put an end to it. And he asked why. Said that he was twenty-four years old, and did I really think he was going to sleep with the same woman for the rest of his life? When he said that, I lost it, Mel. Things got heated. I said something about how he shouldn't have married you in the first place."

And Scott had been cunning and very astute. Coop could remember clearly the sneer on his friend's face as he turned into someone Coop didn't know. *That would clear the way for you,* Scott had said. *I see the way you look at her.* It had ripped his guts out, hearing that, because Scott was throwing away the one thing Coop would have given anything to have.

And his loyalty to Scott had died a very quick death.

He inhaled deeply, suddenly realizing he'd been silent for several seconds and that Mel was watching him curiously.

"Does it hurt to remember?" she asked quietly.

He nodded. "I demanded that he end it or I would tell you. And he laughed at me, Mel. He said that if I told you, he'd deny it. And he said you'd believe him, especially when he told you that I was in love with you and was making up stories to try to ruin your marriage."

She lifted her chin. "My God. And he thought I'd seriously believe him?"

"Wouldn't you? I'm pretty sure he could have given you a list of times I'd done or said something that was maybe a little too personal for a simple friend. At least enough to make you doubt. And let's face it. You would want to believe him because otherwise the truth meant…"

She heaved out a breath. "The truth would mean exactly what it meant in the end."

"I wanted to tell you so bad. As a friend, I owed that to you. But it was impossible, don't you see? All that would happen was that Scott would go on cheating, and you would hate me and we'd no longer be friends. I thought at least this way maybe you'd find out on your own, eventually, and…"

Her gaze was keen. "And you could be there to help me pick up the pieces?"

He hung his head. That sounded terrible. As if he was just waiting for his opportunity to move in. "Something like that," he admitted. "Please believe me, Mel, that my motives weren't opportunistic. I knew that you'd need a friend, someone to support you."

"Except when I found out, Scott told me that you already knew."

"He turned out to be not a very nice person when he was cornered," Coop said. "I couldn't be friends with him any longer. We had stopped hanging out…."

"You'd started dating Sharla someone from Ponoka."

"Yeah." And before that it had been Christine, and Kirsten, and a bunch of others he hadn't cared for much, but who helped him pass the time. He always broke it off before things got heavy, or if he got the sense they were getting too close. He always tried the parting-as-friends thing before it got too intense.

"He hated you that much?"

Coop raised his shoulders and lowered them again. "He saw what you couldn't. That I cared for you too much. Add in the fact that he was well aware you were both unhappy…"

"And the past three years?"

The wind plus their kissing had taken her neat hairdo and shredded it. He thought it looked beautiful, all wispy around her face. He loved how she never shied away, but looked him dead in the eye, ready to face whatever was coming her way. She'd maybe been a little sweeter when she'd been a teenager, but Melissa was way stronger now, and he loved that about her.

"You told me you hated me. That you didn't want to speak to me ever again. It wasn't really the best time for me to tell you how I felt. Besides, you were right. I had let you down. I didn't like myself for what I'd done. For a while I was angry with you, too, for not seeing how I had been put in an impossible position. I stayed away because I had to find a way to let you go."

"Except here we are."

"Yes," he said, "here we are. Apparently that plan didn't work so well."

And he still loved her. He was as sure of that today as he'd been three, five, seven years ago. And he was equally sure that if he said so, she'd run back to Misty, jump in the saddle and be gone in the space of a heartbeat.

"I need to think about all of this." Mel unlocked her arms and pushed her hair back from her face. "It changes things."

"It doesn't, not really."

Her expression twisted with consternation. "Yeah, it does. Especially when you consider how…what we…" She frowned deeply. "This complicates everything, Coop. And more than ever, I'm positive that the last thing I should do is take you up on your offer. There's just too much history and too much drama. We could never be objective about it."

"I'm sorry, Mel. It seemed like a way to help you, that's all. To make up for all the crap that you've had to deal with. But you're right. I couldn't stand by and watch you carry my baby and stay on the sidelines. It's probably best."

It would also kill him to watch her carry someone else's child, but he couldn't have it both ways. Unless by some miracle she gave up on the idea…

"Can we go back now, please? It's getting late. We're going to lose the light before much longer."

"Sure."

He needed to give her time. Time to digest all she'd learned and time to think about what had happened between them today. It was important. It wasn't going away. It would probably happen again. He knew it, and he was pretty sure she knew it, too.

He untied Sergeant while she put her foot in the stirrup and swung onto Misty's back. She didn't wait, but set off ahead of him, as familiar with the way back as he was.

There was history that she couldn't deny. There was something new she couldn't deny, either. And he knew how to be patient.

But not too patient. Not now that he'd had a taste of her and knew for sure what he'd always suspected. There were fireworks between them—on both sides. She could deny it for only so long. For the first time, he actually felt as if they might have a future.

And yet one question still nagged at the back of his mind. The one thing Mel wanted more than anything was a child. Were her feelings for him genuine, or were they a means to an end? The last thing he wanted was for Mel to be more in love with the idea of having his baby than with him. A relationship with that as its foundation would be doomed to failure, and there was too much at stake.

Once again, his heart was on the line. But this time he was prepared to risk it.

# CHAPTER NINE

THE STRETCH OF WARM weather continued, making October feel more like early September. Mel worked in a T-shirt and her apron most days, finding long sleeves too warm. Amy came down with the flu that had been going around, and Melissa put in long, hard hours trying to keep up.

It was good to keep busy. After leaving Coop at the creek, she'd made good time getting back to the Double C barn, Coop and Sergeant following right behind. Bob had been at the barn already, talking to a man with a huge horse trailer and bigger truck. The rancher from Montana had arrived early, despite it being a holiday. Mel was saved from a long or awkward goodbye as Bob took care of Misty and Coop looked after business.

She was still trying to come to terms with everything she'd learned.

Coop had been in love with her when she was married to Scott. Looking back now, perhaps there had been signs, but she'd been so caught up in herself and trying to make her marriage work that she'd missed them. She believed Coop now, though, when he said he'd wanted to tell her about Scott's indiscretion. It had been in the anguished tone of his voice, the way his eyes were wide and earnest as he explained.

But more troublesome than either of those things were the two truths she had to face.

One, Scott hadn't been the only party to blame in the failure of their marriage. Granted, he'd been utterly wrong to cheat. But they'd been in trouble for some time.

And two, Cooper Ford had the ability to make her feel as if she were going to fire off like a Roman candle.

She couldn't do a thing about the first now. But the second…what was she going to do about Coop?

She didn't have an answer for that, so she avoided him. Religiously. As long as he didn't venture into the flower shop, it was pretty safe. Right now it seemed as if all she did was work and sleep.

Her parents returned from their New England trip and invited her over for dinner. When questioned, she admitted she'd spent the holiday with the Ford family. Her mother and father were surprised and shared a significant look between them, but let the matter drop.

But after dinner, when her father had gone to watch his favorite game show, Mel and her mother were alone in the kitchen washing dishes. "So you and Cooper are on speaking terms," Roseanne said. "That's a surprise."

"It was time to let go of being mad. It doesn't matter anymore, right? Coop explained some of what was going on at the time. He was in a tough position. And honestly, Mom, my marriage wasn't what it should have been."

Rose set down the plate she was drying and put her hand on Mel's arm. "You've never admitted that before."

Melissa focused on the casserole dish she was scrubbing. "I didn't want to face how I'd messed up, too. It was easier to blame everyone else."

Rose withdrew her hand. "So you and Cooper…"

Mel shook her head. "Speaking terms. You said it yourself." She kept scrubbing. If Mel looked at her mother, Rose would see the lie.

"Hmm. I suppose this doesn't change your plans for...the other."

This was the problem. It had been so clear only a few weeks ago. She wanted a baby. She was going through steps to have a baby. Now she had to decide whether or not to try again, or try adopting, or... There shouldn't actually be another choice. She was still not interested in getting married. That hadn't changed. And yet she hadn't contacted the clinic, nor had she taken steps to sign up at the adoption registry.

"You're worried about what people will think," she said to Rose. "I get it. You know, I worried about that when it came to my marriage, and made sure all the outward appearances were beyond reproach. Inside we were a mess. I find I worry less about appearances these days, Mom."

Rose sighed. "I can deal with appearances. Honey, I worry about you. Being a parent isn't easy even at the best of times. I can't tell you how great it is to know that at the end of the day there's someone there. Just... there to share the load. So you're not alone."

Her words sent an ache through Mel. "To be honest, I've been too busy lately to worry about it much."

The conversation changed after that, but Mel knew very well that her mother would think it wonderful if she dropped the single-mom idea altogether. Later that night, lying in the dark, she told herself that she needed to refocus and get back to her plan. Maybe it wasn't ideal, but Mel had learned ages ago that any situation was what a person made of it.

But when she closed her eyes, it was Coop she saw

behind her eyelids. Coop, with his faded jeans and bed-room eyes and slightly crooked grin. Steady, reliable Coop, shaking a rancher's hand with a firm grip and a smile, wielding a hammer for a neighbor, stroking the mane of a fuzzy colt on a warm afternoon.

Coop.

The following Sunday Mel dressed in her favorite plum knit dress and black heeled boots and went to church, something she usually only did on special occasions and holidays, much to her mother's chagrin. She'd stopped going each week when the gossip about her divorce had reached a fever pitch, and she'd never gotten into the habit again. There was only so much she could face down with dignity. But today was special—the bap-tism of Callum and Avery's daughter, Nell. Melissa had been personally invited to the service and to lunch at the Shepard house afterward, and she couldn't say no.

She liked Avery. The pretty blonde had opened up her cupcake shop down the street and had fit into Ca-dence Creek society as if she'd always lived here. And Callum had come out of hiding, smiling and being a proud papa. When they'd stopped in at the shop asking if she'd do a few special arrangements for the church, she'd agreed without a moment's hesitation.

The church was packed. She spotted her parents half-way up on the left, but their pew was full. She waggled her fingers at them and scanned the sanctuary for a free space. A pair of fingers waggled back at her—Jean Ford. Was there really nowhere else to sit? But Mel didn't see any sign of Coop, so it was probably safe. She walked up the aisle and slid into the seat. "Thanks," she said to Jean. "It's full up today."

"Baptisms usually are," Jean remarked. "And everyone is so taken with Callum and Avery and that little Nell. She's such a doll. Callum's family even came up from the lower mainland."

Mel stretched her neck to peer at the front of the church. Sure enough, in the front pew with Callum and Avery was another couple—Callum's parents, she guessed—and a younger man and woman, who each bore a striking resemblance to Callum. "Brother and sister?"

"Yes. Apparently she's some big event planner in Vancouver and is going to help Avery with the wedding. They're getting married at Christmas, you know."

"I hadn't heard. Last I spoke to Callum, he was buying flowers and an engagement ring."

"Fancy meeting you here."

Tingles shivered up her spine as a warm hip nudged against hers on her left. Everyone scootched over a bit, but it was still rather cozy when Cooper slid in beside her.

"I didn't think you were coming," Melissa whispered.

"Or you would have sat somewhere else?"

"Something like that."

He chuckled, the sound low and intimate. "It's church. I think you're pretty safe."

Except that this was a small town and they were two people of the same age sitting together at a church service. That was tantamount to an announcement.

The service started and Cooper of course hadn't grabbed a bulletin, so Mel was forced to share hers as they went through the opening prayers and announcements. They stood up to sing the first hymn and she was ultra-aware of him. He'd left off the jeans today and wore dress pants and shoes along with a striped shirt and tie. And he smelled good—as if he'd just gotten out of the shower and dashed on some übermasculine cologne loaded with pheromones or something. He sang on key but quietly, and once, when she turned the page of the hymnbook, he slid his finger over to brace the spine, and his skin brushed against hers.

This was church. There should not be butterflies winging their way through her stomach at a simple touch of finger to wrist. Or, as they sat down, at the pressure of his hip pressed against hers.

She definitely should be listening to the scripture rather than remembering being kissed beside the creek.

Coop was a mighty distraction through most of the service, but after the sermon came the baptism. Callum and Avery rose and went to the front, Nell cradled in Avery's arms, dressed in a flowing white christening gown. A lump formed in Mel's throat as she watched the proceedings. Callum's hand was along the small of Avery's back and they were both smiling. The minister reached for Nell and went through the ritual, saying the words and making the sign of the cross on her forehead with the water. It was so beautiful, watching them as a family. This was what Mel wanted so badly. They looked so close, like a real unit up there. She knew she could still go through with it all and do it alone, but she finally acknowledged that a small part of her longed for the total package: husband, wife, family.

And that scared her to death.

Nell started to fuss and the minister handed her over to Callum. The baby looked so small and fragile and white in Callum's big, broad arms. She cried for a moment, but Callum nestled her in the crook of his elbow and she settled.

Coop reached over and, between their thighs, cupped Melissa's hand in his.

That one, innocent touch took her reinforced, guarded heart and put a crack right down the center of it.

He squeezed her fingers as the baptism ended, and she squeezed back. He knew. He understood. More than anyone else had or would, he knew what she was feeling in this moment.

When she had been fourteen, Coop had been the guy who had just *got* her. Even if they'd argued, there'd been no drama as there was with girlfriends. The next day it was like nothing had happened. It had been so easy with him. The only thing she'd wanted was for him to look at her like she was a girl.

He was surely looking at her that way now. But she wasn't the same girl she'd been. Back then she'd had an open heart. He could have had it for the asking. Now she didn't trust so easily.

She hoped nobody could see them holding hands, but she didn't pull out of his grasp. It felt too good. Like an anchor in a day that would otherwise make her think and feel a little too much about all that was missing from her life.

He released her fingers when the last hymn was announced, sharing the hymnbook once more and putting it away during the benediction.

When everyone filtered out of the church, Mel took care to slide over next to her parents and walk out with them rather than remain paired up with Cooper. But outside they went their separate ways; Melissa had brought her own car in anticipation of driving out to Callum's, and her parents hadn't been invited to the lunch. Likewise, Bob and Jean left while Coop remained in the middle of the throng in the sunshine, talking and laughing with Ty and Sam Diamond while their wives, Clara and Angela, buttoned their kids' jackets.

Coop caught Mel's eye, and without breaking the link, put a hand on Sam's arm and excused himself.

She really, really wished he wasn't so good-looking. Wished that she could stop thinking of him in more-than-friendly ways. Wished they had less history, less baggage, so she could explore the attraction burning between them. But of anyone in this town, Cooper was the one man with whom she could not play games. He was too important.

"Hey," he said, coming to stand in front of her. "I didn't have a chance to say it before, but you look pretty today."

"Thanks." She chanced a look into his eyes and her whole body seemed to warm beneath the appraising glow.

"You going out to the lunch? I hear Martha Bullock is putting on the spread."

Martha was the best cook in Cadence Creek and the owner of the Wagon Wheel diner, not to mention the mother of their friend Rhys. "I was invited, yes."

"Want to drive out there together?"

Mel scanned the parking lot, and there was no denying that at least some members of the throng were curious. "I don't think so, but thanks. I'll take my own car."

"Screw gossip," he said easily.

Her gaze flickered to his and she kept a smile pasted on. "Easy for you to say."

A shadow passed over his face, just a little one, but she noticed it. Lately she seemed to notice everything. "It was really bad, wasn't it?" he asked.

"Yes. The worst was the pity. Poor Melissa, hadn't

had a clue what was going on right under her nose. But I don't like being the topic of the week under any circumstances. I'll see you out there, okay?"

"Fair enough."

But before he left, he gave her arm a squeeze. She felt the heat of it through the knitted sleeve and bit down on her lip. Cooper wasn't giving up. And knowing what she did now about his feelings and how deep they went, she felt a strange pressure to equal his devotion or just let him go. The worst thing was, she didn't quite know how to do either.

He was just going to have to be patient, she thought as she got into her car. He'd have to wait until she thought things through.

Cars and trucks lined one side of Callum's gravel driveway, parked on the grass. The beautiful fall weather meant that the party was set up outside. People brought their own lawn chairs, but the food was organized on tables beneath a collapsible gazebo. Mel opened the trunk and took out her foldable chair, and then made her way to where people were gathered. After depositing her chair, she went to offer her congratulations to Callum and Avery.

"Thanks for inviting me," she said, giving Avery a quick hug. "It was a beautiful service."

"The flowers were so pretty," Avery declared. "You'll do the ones for our wedding, won't you?"

Mel's heart warmed. "Of course I will. And look at this christening gown." Callum still held Nell in his arms and Mel touched the lace edge of the hem. "Where did you ever find it?"

Callum smiled. "My mom and dad bought it. The

one they used for us was too small. Nell's six months old now."

Avery touched Callum's arm. "Be right back, okay?" She scooted off to greet the minister and his wife as they arrived.

"She's precious," Mel said. "And looks just like you, Callum."

"Poor girl. Would you hold her for a moment? I'm going to grab a few extra chairs. I don't think the minister brought any."

"Sure."

What else could she say? Mel's heart thrummed heavily as she reached out and took the baby in her arms. The satin-and-lace dress was silky against her skin and Nell smelled like baby lotion. "Hello there," Melissa said quietly, unable to stop the smile from spreading across her face. "Look at you, gorgeous girl."

Blue eyes stared up at her from beneath long, dark lashes, and Mel pressed a kiss to the soft, fine hair. "Oh my," she whispered, and by simple instinct rocked her hips back and forth a little. To her surprise, Nell, who'd been the center of attention for quite a while, tucked her head into the curve of Mel's neck. Mel felt a tiny wet spot of baby drool just above the collar of her dress. It was a wonderful feeling. She'd be a good mother, she just knew it. And then her little house wouldn't seem quite so lonely.

She turned around and found Cooper watching them.

Her heart squeezed. He was standing with Rhys Bullock, but his gaze was locked on her and his dark eyes fairly glowed with what looked like appreciation and possession.

"Excuse me, you're Melissa, right?"

Mel broke her gaze away from Coop and turned to

the voice on her left. The woman wasn't from Cadence Creek. While Mel had felt quite dressed up in her dress and boots, this woman made her feel slightly dowdy. It wasn't that she was heart-stoppingly gorgeous, not in the strictest sense of the word. But she had an aura of worldliness and capability that Mel envied—and all that from a simple greeting.

"Yes, I'm Melissa."

The woman held out her hand and smiled. "Hi. I'm Taylor Shepard, Callum's sister."

"The one from Vancouver. The event planner."

"That's me."

The woman practically oozed sophistication. Her dress was simply cut and color blocked with red, black and tan, and her designer shoes were black but with impossibly high heels showcasing perfect legs. Her dark hair was pulled back and braided on an angle so the tail fell over one shoulder.

Mel shook Taylor's hand quickly, then shifted Nell's weight on her arm. Taylor smiled. "She's something, isn't she? I still can't believe my big brother's a dad."

That statement helped make Mel feel slightly less inadequate. "She really is," Mel replied. "Callum's a completely different person since the two of them came into his life."

"Oh, he's not, not really. He's just back to the man we all knew and loved. Anyway, I'm going to be around a bit, helping Avery plan the wedding. Sort of my wedding gift to them. She told me you did the flowers for today and I wanted to touch base and introduce myself. I'm sure we're going to be seeing more of each other."

"And your other brother's here, too, right?"

"Yeah, Jack's here for another few days. Said he wants to explore the area. He's the sporty one in our family, so all this open space and proximity to the mountains has him pretty jazzed. Speaking of, I'd better get back. I told Martha Bullock that I'd help and I'm over here socializing instead. Nice to meet you, Melissa."

"Just call me Mel. Everyone else does."

Taylor smiled, stroked Nell's cheek lightly. "You've got the touch," she said softly. "She's asleep."

Melissa angled her head to look down at the baby as Taylor walked away, perfectly balanced on her stilettos. She was right. Nell had drifted off, completely relaxed in Mel's arms.

"Looks good on you," Coop said, from just behind her. His voice was soft and low and sent shivers down her spine.

"You have to stop sneaking up on me," she replied. She kept one hand on Nell's back, lightly rubbing.

"I do?"

"Coop."

She said it with such meaning that he laughed.

She sighed. "I thought after the other day…"

"That I'd give up?" He shook his head. "You needed time to think. I got that. I backed off. I didn't go away."

"I sort of wish you would."

"You don't mean that."

She wished she did. She wanted to mean it. It would make things so much simpler.

"You are seriously messing with my plans," she murmured. "It was easier when I was mad at you and not…"

She didn't finish the sentence, but Coop did it for her. "Not thinking about kissing me all the time?"

"I'm not thinking that!" She said it a little louder, and Nell shifted in her arms. "I'm not," she said quietly, frowning at him.

"You are such a liar," he replied easily.

"Coop…"

"See? You can't even come up with a good argument other than I'm messing around with your plans. Why does everything have to be planned out, anyway?"

"Less chance of disappointment," she answered promptly.

"Ah, says the voice of the disappointed," he replied. The truth stung a bit and she lifted her chin.

"Oh, now don't get all like that," he cautioned. "I know I dumped a lot of information on you the other day and I know you've had a lot to think about. But you think too much. The truth of it is, you had a crush on me when I was too stupid to realize it, and I had a thing for you when you weren't available. Now we're both here and we're both available and all I'm suggesting is that we see where things go. Nothing heavy."

"Things are heavy with you by definition, Cooper. Because of our history."

"Forget history," he replied, coming a step closer. "I'm tired of the past getting in my way, aren't you? Let's forget about Scott and everything else and just focus on the present."

It sounded so tempting. "I know I've let him influence my life far too much." She had. She told herself and everyone else that he had no effect on her life, but that wasn't true. His affair and their divorce had changed everything, and colored every part of her life even now. She didn't like it, but she'd learned lessons that she didn't ever want to forget.

"You have a chance to start over," Coop said, his voice persuasive. "Go out on a date with me."

"A date?"

"You do remember what those are, right? I pick you

up and we go somewhere like dinner or a movie. Then I drive you home."

"You're seriously asking me out on a date?"

"Yes. A real date. Not meeting up at some town get-together or hanging out at my parents' place."

She shouldn't say yes. Coop was so complicated, but the idea of truly shedding the past and having an actual date sounded heavenly. When had she last done that? When she was about nineteen. Then she'd been married, and date night wasn't quite the same. Then even those had stopped—and there'd been none since. Good Lord. She was twenty-seven and she hadn't been on a date in years.

"Where would we go?"

He grinned. "You let me take care of that. You're saying yes?"

"I'm saying yes. To one date."

"I'll pick you up Saturday night at seven. That gives you enough time to get ready after closing, right?"

She nodded, excitement building in her chest. She was going out and didn't know where. What should she wear?

Neither of them noticed Avery approach until she spoke. "Mel, your arms must be ready to fall off. Thanks for watching Nell for so long. Callum went for chairs and I got sidetracked…"

"It was no trouble." She shifted her arms and slid the sleeping baby into her mother's embrace.

"Oh, she's left a drool spot on your dress," Avery said apologetically.

Mel looked down at the damp circle and gave a soft smile. "Don't worry," she answered. "I love babies. It was a real treat to have her so relaxed. Besides, this gets tossed right in the washing machine."

"Well, you two should get some food. Martha's put on a great spread."

"Thanks."

When she was gone, the silence got a little awkward. "Listen," Coop said, "I'm going to talk to Ty about a mare he's just bought, but I'll see you Saturday, right?"

"Saturday," she echoed.

He smiled, then let his gaze drift down her body. "Oh, and Mel?" He winked before he turned away. "Wear those boots."

She watched him walk off, admiring the view. After thinking of him as a friend for so long, and then as an enemy, it was quite shocking to realize that she was now thinking about him in a totally different manner altogether. One that made her temperature rise considerably.

He wanted to put the past behind them, forget it existed. That sounded good in theory, but there was just one problem. It was impossible, because the past gave them context. And it was impossible because he was making her feel fifteen again, young and nervous and craving a kiss from him. Just like then, she thought about him *all the time*. And that didn't fit anywhere in her formerly well-ordered plans.

# CHAPTER TEN

SHE IGNORED THE ORDER to wear the boots. Instead Mel went shopping. The first "first date" in years deserved a new outfit, and she rarely spent money on herself anymore. Wednesday, after the store closed for the day, she drove to the West Edmonton Mall, determined to find something new and pretty. She liked the result as she stood in front of her bedroom mirror. The black pencil skirt hugged her hips like a dream, and the ivory blouse with its black collar and cuffs made her feel feminine and pretty. Best of all, though, were the shoes. The heels were higher than she normally wore, but manageable due to the platforms in the toe, and they did magical things for her calves.

He would be here at any moment....

Her doorbell rang and she jumped, stared at her wide eyes and pressed a finger to her freshly lipsticked lips. He was here. Coop. As a date. A new beginning for both of them.

Her heels clattered as she crossed the hardwood floor to the front door. Taking a breath and hoping she wasn't blushing, she opened it.

Coop was on the step and he held out a bouquet of flowers. "I know it's weird giving a florist flowers, but..."

He'd brought her three roses, red ones, wrapped up with baby's breath. She didn't even care if they were a cliché and from the grocery store—it was too special. "Not at all," she said, hoping he didn't hear the nervous tremor in her voice. "Come on in while I put these in some water."

He waited just inside the door as she escaped to the kitchen, her heart hammering against her ribs. When she returned she nearly swallowed her tongue, he looked so delicious. Once again he'd left the cowboy hat at home, but he'd kept the jeans—dressier ones—with spit-shined boots, a white shirt with the top button undone and a caramel-colored sport coat.

"You look amazing," he said, pushing the panels of his coat back and hooking his thumbs in his pockets. "Really...amazing."

"I went shopping," she explained, belatedly realizing he'd know she went especially for tonight. She hid her face inside the closet as she reached for her coat.

He took it from her and helped her put it on. When he smoothed it over her shoulders, his hands paused. He was standing close behind her, the air between them filled with silent possibility. "We'd better go," he said roughly. "Or we're not going to get there at all."

Funny how one little sentence could nearly send her into complete meltdown. She prayed her knees would hold out as she reached for her purse and stepped away from the warmth of his body. Coop moved aside and held open the door, letting her out into the cool autumn air.

It helped, getting outside. Coop caught up to her at the bottom of the steps. "I borrowed Mom's car. I thought it might be nicer than going in a huge pickup."

Once more he held the door for Mel, closing it behind her when she'd slid into the car.

During the drive into the city Coop thankfully kept the conversation neutral, chatting about town events and what was going on at the Double C. But the whole time Mel was thinking about what would happen when he drove her home; not if he would walk her to the door, but if she would ask him in.

Coop tried to talk about every possible subject during the drive to the restaurant. Anything to distract him from the way Mel looked tonight.

She'd dressed up. For him. The tidy little skirt illuminated every curve, and the blouse she was wearing made her look a little like a librarian fantasy. All she was missing was the glasses. And he was glad she hadn't taken his suggestion of the heeled boots, because seeing her in those shoes...

His first impulse was to not even leave her house.

But he'd promised a first date, and a first date she was going to get. So he'd held her coat and the door, and tried to think of other things besides getting her out of that killer outfit piece by piece.

They had reservations at an Italian place in downtown Edmonton. Once they were seated, they each ordered a glass of wine and scanned the menu. He was nervous. He was with a woman he'd known most of his life and he was suddenly unsure of what to say or do. When their drinks came and they'd ordered, it was Mel who held up her glass and offered a toast. "To starting over," she said.

"To new beginnings," he echoed, clinking the rim to hers. He watched her lips touch the glass as she drank, and he took a bigger gulp than he intended.

They kept the conversation neutral as they dug into their antipasti and then main courses—he had a spicy pappardelle and Mel had a truffle ravioli that looked delicious, along with a second glass of wine. She made him laugh as she told him about how someone's dog had got loose, run in the store, investigated every corner and then, to everyone's horror, lifted his leg on Amy's expensive handbag—clearly not as funny for Amy as it was for Mel. He talked to her about his plans for the ranch, the new stud stallion he was buying and how he was asked to speak at a conference coming up in Colorado. It was the strangest, best first date he'd ever had—getting to know someone he'd known all his life. New and yet familiar. And exciting. Oh yes, exciting. He didn't want the evening to end, but he couldn't wait, either.

They lingered over dessert, ordering coffee and a rich chocolate *torta* laced with hazelnuts. Somehow they ended up missing a spoon, and Mel had used hers to add cream to her coffee. Coop spooned up a little of the *torta* and held it out for her to taste.

"Coop…" she chided, raising one eyebrow. But he saw the longing in her eyes and waited, holding her gaze. Watching it heat as the moment drew out.

She leaned forward and took the dessert from the spoon. Closed her eyes and sighed. "Oh, that's good."

He wasn't sure how he was going to be able to drive the forty minutes back to her house.

He tasted the chocolate confection and agreed it was delicious. But he derived far more enjoyment from feeding it to her from the spoon. The fact that she accepted it without argument took things a step further with them tonight. This was going somewhere. Where, he wasn't exactly sure. But he was looking forward to finding out.

The drive back to Cadence Creek was quiet, the car filled with delicious tension. He reached over once and held her hand, driving with his left. Her fingers twined with his and she looked at him and smiled lazily. "Sorry I'm not such a good conversationalist," she said, leaning her head back on the seat. "A long day, full stomach and two glasses of wine have made me sleepy."

Disappointment threaded through him, but he smiled back anyway. "It was a good night."

"As first dates go, it was top-notch."

He hit the exit for Cadence Creek and started down the secondary highway that led to town.

It was after ten o'clock and Mel's quiet street was mostly dark, save a few lights over front doors. "Not much happening here on a Saturday night," Coop commented, pulling into her driveway.

"You know how it is," she said with a smile. "If you want to get into some trouble, you do it outside town limits."

He was thinking he could get into a fair bit of trouble inside town limits without much effort. "Hang on," he commanded, and got out of the car, jogged around the front and opened her door.

She pivoted and put her legs out first before reaching for the door frame and boosting herself up.

"Mel, if I can just say one thing…damn, you've got the greatest legs."

She blushed. Even in the dim glow of her porch light he could see the color touch her cheeks. He shut the door and walked her to the steps, but before she could put her foot on the first one he grabbed her hand and pulled her back.

"I want to do this and I don't want to do it in the

light," he whispered, and then he finally—finally—kissed her.

He took his time. He wasn't some callow teenager in a hormonal hurry to get to the end zone. He pulled her close, twined his fingers into her hair and explored her mouth as if he had all the time in the world.

Just like before, passion exploded between them. It was thrilling, knowing that it wasn't just an emotionally heightened situation causing things to run hot, but actual chemistry. Her heels put her eyes on a level with his nose, so that he had to tip her head only the slightest bit to have full access to her mouth. He fumbled with the large buttons on her wool coat, opening it and slipping his arms inside, pulling her flush against his body.

"Mmm," she said into his mouth, a little impatient sound as she pushed away. But she only did it to spread his sport coat wide as well, so that they were pressed together, cotton shirt to flimsy blouse, with all their body heat between them.

Kissing was all well and good, but eventually it did have to lead somewhere, and right now all Cooper could think of was making love to her. "Invite me inside," he said against her lips.

She didn't answer, just ran her fingers through his hair, pulling his head down so she could kiss him again. What else could he do but oblige?

But after a few minutes more, with their breathing heavier and his hands roaming farther than he'd planned—especially while still in her front yard—he put his palm along the side of her face and forced her to look at him. "Invite me in," he commanded again.

"I…I can't," she stuttered, her breath coming in short gasps.

"Sure you can," he replied smoothly. "You say, Coop, would you like to come inside?"

She shook her head. "If we go inside, we're going to…you're going to…"

"With any luck," he answered. And he'd thought ahead. Inside his coat pocket was a condom. For a second he paused, wondering how she'd react to the insistence for birth control. But he had to know she was with him for him, and not for his genetic material.

He pushed the thought away. Mel wouldn't do such a thing; he knew her better than that. And he wanted her more than he could remember ever wanting a woman before. To help convince her, he ran his hand beneath the flap of her coat, down her shoulder and over one tightly peaked breast. She shuddered.

"Coop?"

"Yes, honey?"

She grabbed his wrists and stepped back a little. "I am not the kind of girl who puts out on the first date."

Dammit. "Are you sure?"

"I'm very, very sure." She blinked at him. She meant it, the sassy thing. And he'd better get control of himself in a hurry if he had any hope of leaving this situation gracefully. And possibly making her regret her decision. Because if they kept on this way, it was going to happen sooner or later. Given how he was feeling right now, he prayed it was sooner.

"You realize you're killing me here."

She nodded slowly.

He sighed. "Damn you, Melissa, for making me behave."

She laughed at him. "You know the show biz motto, Always Leave Them Wanting More?"

He couldn't help it; she looked so impish and sexy

and wonderful that he chuckled. It might be killing him, but he'd wait. It would be worth it.

He was in love with her. Any doubts about that had fled at Thanksgiving. How she'd held his hand at the baptism, the date tonight—it all told him he had a chance if he played his cards right. At this moment that meant stepping back and giving her time.

"Okay." He gave in, releasing her completely. "You win."

"Thank you for a wonderful evening, though."

He put his hand in his pocket. "You up for a second date?"

"Even though I'm sending you away…unsatisfied?"

"I thought you said you were leaving me wanting more. I want more."

The air sizzled between them. "We're going to do this, then?" she asked quietly.

"I want to. I want to see where it leads. Don't you? It doesn't have to be any heavier than that. Let's just see where it takes us, Mel."

"And what if it doesn't work?"

The smile slid from his face as the tone suddenly turned serious. "Then we can say we tried. And no matter what, we stay friends. No more going back to the way things were, I promise."

"I promise, too. I didn't really enjoy hating you all that much."

"When can I see you again?" He didn't want to wait a week. Or even days. He wanted to see her as often as he could. Every minute.

"I suppose Tuesday-night bingo at the community center doesn't float your boat."

"I could live through it if you were there."

She laughed then, a light, musical laugh that he

hadn't heard in years. "I won't make you do that," she replied. "Let's just meet up for dinner at the diner, then go for a walk or something."

It sounded perfectly boring. "If that's what you want."

"I'll meet you there at six, right after the store closes. How does that sound?"

He'd rather she asked him here for a private dinner for two, but she was bent on taking it slow. His head told him that was the right move, no matter what his libido was screaming right now.

"Perfect."

"Coop?"

"Hmm?"

"Kiss me once more before you go?"

Kissing her was the easy part of the request. The just once part? He was going to have trouble with that.

For two weeks Mel let herself be wooed into Coop's definition of dating. They went to the diner on Tuesday and decided on burgers and fries and milkshakes as a throwback to high school days, then took a long walk along the creek in the dark. He stopped by the shop once with a bag lunch and convinced her to eat with him on a bench along Main Street, soaking up the sun. On Saturday they drove to Edmonton for a movie, sat near the back of the theater and held hands. The next week they took a short drive to the coffee shop out on the highway for dessert, and she took a precious few hours one afternoon to go riding out at the Double C.

There were kisses, but Coop was on his best behavior, with no more suggestions to take things further. Which was a shame, because being kissed at the door was leaving her distinctly unsatisfied. If he was trying to leave *her* wanting more, he was definitely succeeding.

They made plans to eat at the diner again, and Melissa told herself that tonight she was going to ask him to her place for their next date. She could cook and they could share a meal without being so incredibly visible to the town. Besides, she had a very nice sofa in her living room and she wouldn't mind more than a few stolen kisses outside the circle of her porch light.

She dressed for their date when she went to work, as she'd head to the Wagon Wheel as soon as she turned over the Closed sign. Mel wore the boots he'd admired that Sunday at Callum's. She chose them because he liked them, and it meant she could wear one of her favorite outfits—snug denim leggings and a scoop-neck tee with her sweater-coat overtop. It was casual but fun, and she put her hair up. Maybe when Coop walked her home, he'd take the clip out and run his hands through her hair the way he seemed to enjoy....

Tuesdays weren't the busiest night at the Wagon Wheel, and when she walked in the atmosphere was relaxed and friendly. A few tables were occupied, a gray-haired man was putting quarters into the genuine jukebox, and the twang of a country classic filled the air. Off to one side she saw Coop. He was early and was talking to Clara and Ty Diamond. Melissa took a minute to simply stare at him and appreciate the scenery. Mercy, he was good-looking. No one could wear a pair of jeans like Coop. The denim was wearing around the pockets, the faded spots strategically placed for her viewing pleasure.

Beside him, Clara was in maternity clothing, and as she was reaching into a diaper bag, her one-year-old daughter, Susanna, made a wobbly dash down the

aisle between booths. With a laugh Coop reached out
and snagged her midstride, scooping her into his arms.

Instead of fussing or squirming, the little girl gig-
gled, reached out and patted his face. He said something and then tapped his cheek with his finger. Susanna
leaned forward and delivered one sloppy wet baby kiss
there. Mel was dangerously close to melting. Then
Coop's eyes closed—just for a second—and he gave
the baby a tender kiss on the head before handing her
to her father.

It was a strange moment for Mel to realize that she
was in love with him. Not just sentimentally affected, or
that she *could* love him, but that she *did*—a bone-deep,
right-to-the-center-of-her-soul kind of love. So much for
taking it slow and seeing where it went. Or being in any
way casual about what was happening between them.

She loved him. She loved him so much that it was
freaking her out right now. So much that it was suddenly
hard to breathe and she could feel the beginnings of an
anxiety attack. This wasn't supposed to happen. They
were supposed to be casually dating. Exploring. Not…
Oh God. Not this. She couldn't do *this*.

She slipped out the door before he could see that
she'd arrived and jogged away from the diner, trying
to put some distance between them. Her breath came in
shallow gasps. When she turned the corner, she stopped
and pressed her hand to her chest, trying to steady her
breathing. He was going to be expecting her at any moment, but she couldn't go back there. Couldn't go in
and have supper and act as if everything was all right.
It wasn't. She didn't know what to do with the sudden
rush of feeling.

For the longest time she hadn't been sure she was
even capable of being in love. She'd thought she was

before, but recognized now that she'd been far more enamored with the idea of love than actually in it up to her eyeballs. But here it was, and it honestly felt as if the earth had fallen away beneath her feet.

She pulled her cell phone from her purse and sent him a quick text message, saying she wasn't feeling well and needed to take a rain check, and that she'd call him later.

Once at home she changed into fleecy pajamas and shoved her hair into a ponytail. What was she going to do? She wasn't ready for this, and she certainly wasn't ready to tell Coop how she felt. She was smart enough to know that the reason she'd been so very angry with Coop all this time was because she'd felt betrayed and abandoned, and it had damn near killed her. It had been the darkest period in her life—realizing that her husband didn't love her, and losing her best friend. She'd understood then that she was an easy woman to leave. And she'd promised never to let herself be that emotionally vulnerable again.

And here she was. She'd let down her guard, agreed to make amends, and found herself in a worse predicament than she could ever imagine. She loved him. Something he'd said that day at the creek echoed in her head: *I'm not sure you ever get over someone you really love.* It was time she faced the worst truth of all. The greatest loss from the breakup of her marriage wasn't her husband, but her best friend. *He* was the one she couldn't get over. And if they took this thing all the way and it didn't work out…

It would be ten times worse. A hundred. She would be…empty.

She reached for the tissues. This had truly gone beyond taking it easy and enjoying each other's company, beyond seeing where it would lead. This was the real deal. She knew, because it had never hurt to love this way before. It had never caused this paralyzing fear.

The third tissue was balled up and thrown on the floor when there was a knock on her door. She knew without asking that it was Coop. She should have known that a text message wouldn't keep him away.

"Mel? Open up."

She wiped her eyes and went to the door, knowing he'd knock until she opened it. Hopefully, she didn't look too bad; at least with the runny nose she might be able to fake it. There was no way she was going to let on the real reason she had red eyes and was in her pj's. She had to sort through her feelings before she could have this conversation with Coop.

"Just a sec," she called, deliberately making her voice sound stuffy. She took a deep breath and opened the door.

"Dear God, you look awful."

He, on the other hand, looked amazing. He always did. The jean jacket was back and so was the plaid shirt, only it was clean for their "date." His hat was perched on his head, throwing his face half in shadow. It was dead sexy, and she felt her resolve weaken.

"I don't know if it's allergies or a fall cold, but my head is plugged," she lied.

"Allergies? But you're a florist."

Damn. She was so off her game. She forced a shrug. "Fall cold then. Sorry, Coop."

He bent his knees a bit so that he was on eye level with her. She stayed still beneath his scrutiny.

Coop rose up again and held out a paper bag. "Martha put together a container of chicken soup for you."

Her throat clogged again. Of course. She'd said she

wasn't feeling well and Coop had decided to make her feel better. As if she needed one more reason to love him.

"That's so sweet." She reached out and took the bag.

"You sure you're okay? Do you need anything?" A wrinkle formed between his eyebrows.

She hated lying. She was certain he could see right through it. But how could she possibly come right out and say what was going on? Considering what he'd told her about his own feelings, she wasn't ready to be that open. That honest. That…intense. That was it. Things would get really intense, and right now just realizing that she even had these feelings was overwhelming. She needed time. Time to decide what to do. What she wanted. Time to simply get used to the idea.

Not just that. She was in love with her best friend. Perhaps they'd taken a hiatus, but she knew deep down that was what Coop was. He'd been her best friend, and the last two weeks had shown her how close they still could be. There was something so very heavy about having this many feelings for one person. So much potential for things to go wrong.

So much to lose.

"I'm going to be fine, really," she assured him. "I'm going to eat my soup and go to bed, and I know I'll be much better tomorrow."

He looked disappointed that she didn't ask him in, just stood in the doorway to her house, shutting him out. "If you're sure…"

"I am. But thank you, Coop. For the soup. And sorry about tonight."

"It's no biggie. We'll do it another time." He stepped ahead and planted a gentle kiss on her forehead. "Feel better."

He went back to his truck and she shut the door.

What on earth was she going to do now? She couldn't avoid him forever. Nor did she want to.

She just needed time to think. To sort things out. And to make a plan.

# CHAPTER ELEVEN

COOP KNEW DAMNED WELL that whatever had made Mel's eyes puffy and red, it was no allergic reaction or fall cold. That kind of look only came from hard crying. She could sound as congested as she wanted, but he knew. She'd blown off their date and she'd been home crying, and whatever had gotten her upset, she'd been so determined to keep it from him that she'd lied about it. The last time she'd had a hard cry, she'd gotten her period. Though he hated it, a little voice inside him asked what else she might have lied about. They'd never talked about her giving up her plans for IUI. He'd just assumed, when they started seeing each other...

He watched one of the hands bring a dun-colored stallion named Crapshoot back to the stable. Standing at over sixteen hands, he was a big, beautifully muscled animal whose strong hindquarters could turn on a dime. He'd bring a pretty penny, but Coop was tempted to keep him for himself.

Tonight, though, he wasn't in the mood to spend longer in the stables. He was restless. It was clear to him that Mel was avoiding his calls, and in the ones she did take she said things like it was really busy at the store, or she was on her way out the door. It annoyed the hell out of him. Almost as much as it hurt. He hadn't expected her to blow him off. Not like this.

Then again, he always did make a habit of expecting more from Mel than she delivered.

A small voice inside told him that wasn't fair, but he was mad enough that he didn't listen. Not just mad. Afraid. Being with her these last few weeks had taken all the feelings he'd tamped down and given them the opportunity to run free. He'd stopped imagining what it would be like to hold her in his arms because she'd actually been there. He knew what she tasted like, the way she melted against him, the sound of her voice on the phone late at night. He'd given himself permission to love her again. And boy, did it hurt.

Enough was enough. If this wasn't going to work, he had to know. Playing games, not being honest—they couldn't maintain a friendship that way. And even though the very idea tasted like ashes in his mouth, he knew that was what he'd promised. Friendship.

It was full-on dark by the time he'd showered and got up the gumption to drive over to her house. Light glowed from the front window—her living room—and it flickered, letting him know she had the television on. A week ago they would have been out together, having coffee or looking at the stars or just talking on the phone. Not now. Something drastic had changed, and he wanted to know what.

He knocked on the door.

It took a minute, but finally the dead bolt clicked back and she opened it. "Hey," she said.

"You look like you're feeling better."

She smiled softly and it damn near broke his heart. "I am, thank you."

"Can I come in, Mel?"

His gaze caught hers. Her eyes were wide and soft and he lost himself there for a moment. Then she lowered her lashes and stepped back. "Of course. Come on in. I'm just switching some laundry over, but I'll be right back. Make yourself at home."

The television was turned on to a popular crime drama and there was a cup of tea, half-gone, on the end table next to the sofa. He took off his hat and put it on the back of a chair, then ambled through to her kitchen. It was cozy and warm, painted a soft cream with dark red accents. The oak table had a red plaid place mat in the middle and there was a small bouquet of flowers, too.

It was strange that he'd never seen her kitchen before, but she'd always made sure they went somewhere else on their dates. The closest he'd ever come to inside was helping her with her coat the night they'd first gone to dinner.

By keeping him out of her house she was always able to keep him at arm's length. Never let him too close. He got it now, and felt just a little bit like a fool.

He heard the beep of the washing machine somewhere in the hall behind the garage. Absently, he picked up a stack of adverts from the mail that was strewn on the counter, flipping through flyers and coupons. A slip of paper fell to the floor. He picked it up and saw the scribbled appointment in Mel's delicate handwriting. The appointment had been for two days ago. His heart tumbled down to his toes. He should have listened to the warnings in his head.

She came back from the laundry room and stopped short at the sight of him in the kitchen. "Oh," she said, then gave a small smile. "Can I get you something to drink, Coop? I was having tea, but I've got other stuff in the..."

"Cut the small talk, Mel. I don't have the stomach for it."

Her eyes widened and her cheeks paled at his sharp tone. "Okay, let's cut to the chase then. Why are you here?"

"To find out why you've suddenly started blowing me off. Looks like your cold is all better, by the way."

He heard the sarcasm in his voice and exhaled. This wasn't how he'd planned on talking. He wanted to be reasonable. Calm. But the paper he held in his hand had taken those intentions and blown them sky-high. It certainly told him where he ranked on her priority list.

"I never had a cold," she admitted.

"I know. I can tell a virus from a bout of crying. You've been avoiding me ever since."

"I can explain that. Please, why don't we go in and sit down. Let me get you a drink and—"

"Does it have anything to do with this?" he asked, holding up the paper.

Her eyes lit on the note in his hand, then slid over to meet his gaze. "Where did you get that?"

"Off your counter." He swallowed tightly. "Were you going to tell me, Mel? Have you already done it?"

She frowned. "Done what?"

He shook the note, hurt, angry, unsure of what to call the other emotions rattling through him right now. "This is the clinic, right?"

She nodded. "Yes, but—"

"And even after last time, after you turned down my offer, after we started seeing each other, for God's sake, you still went ahead? Again?" He shook his head. "I trusted you. I thought we had...that we were..."

He loved her. He'd offered to father the child she wanted so badly. He'd wooed her, for the love of Mike. And she'd left him out, shut him out, gone ahead with her original plan as if he was nothing. As if what they had meant nothing. As if they had absolutely no future together, but she hadn't felt it necessary to tell him.

He tossed the paper on the table and walked out of the kitchen.

"Hold on a minute, Coop." Her command stopped him halfway to her front door. "How dare you! How dare you come in here and make assumptions and proclamations. What exactly are you accusing me of?"

He turned back around. "Did you or did you not have an appointment at the clinic in Edmonton?"

She put her hands on her hips. "I did."

He let out a sound of frustration. "You're still bent on this asinine idea of using a sperm donor! Have you been planning this all along? Just amusing yourself with me? Heck, let's go out with Coop and have some good times, but it's never going anywhere because I have my own plans. Never let anyone too close! And whatever you do, never trust anyone again. You went ahead with another treatment like what we had meant nothing!"

"Wow." She looked at him, but she'd masked her emotions so completely that he couldn't tell what she was thinking or feeling. "Now I know exactly what you think of me, Coop. What was your plan, to come in here and fix me and solve all my problems? News flash. I can solve my own problems. I've been doing just fine on my own."

"Oh, no doubt," he answered. The TV chattered in the background, the sound rasping on his already frayed nerves. "You're one hundred percent capable, you are. It's all about you now. No one is ever going to hurt you again because you won't let them. You're so bent on control that heaven forbid there's a father in your child's life. Someone to love it and you, right? I can't live like that, Mel. I can't. I can love for only so long without getting anything back."

He grabbed his hat from the back of the chair and put it on his head. "I deserve better."

He paused in the doorway. "You could have at least been honest with me instead of playing games."

The door was just starting to swing shut again when she came through it. "Playing games? Believe me, Cooper Ford, this has been anything but a game!"

"Keep your voice down. The neighbors will hear you."

She scoffed. "Oh, like you've ever given a good damn about that."

He stood on her front step. "Let's just leave it, before we say something we'll both regret."

"Oh, you mean leave it now that you've had your say and I don't get mine? How convenient for you. You don't want to hear how you got it all wrong, do you? Let me tell you something, Coop. Being with you—taking a chance—came with a whole lot of built-in pressure. It's pretty hard to be breezy about a relationship when the other person confesses to being in love with you half your life. There's no halfway in. It's all the way or no way. The only choice I had was taking it slow."

"Funny, because you always seemed to have one foot out the door."

"That's right," she admitted. "I did. Because being with you was the single most terrifying thing to happen to me since walking in on my husband in bed with another woman."

"Great. I'm so glad that we're equating dating me

to the horror that was the end of your marriage. That tells me a lot."

"You're deliberately misinterpreting. What are you so afraid of?"

"Me?" Their voices were raised now, and he knew he should lower his, but couldn't seem to find the ability. "That's your thing, not mine."

She came all the way out onto the porch. "I moved on when we were kids, and I never looked back, right? And now you're so afraid of not holding on to every piece of me that you're pushing me away. Finding something to blame. Mainly me. After all, if you leave me first, I don't get the chance to leave you."

He shook his head. "This is ridiculous. You're the one who blew me off. You were the one who refused to take a next step with us, who backed away from intimacy, who started making bogus excuses when I called. You're doing all the pushing away. You don't think I see? You're lonely, Mel. And if you have a baby you won't be lonely anymore, and won't have to risk your heart, either. Win-win for you."

Her face paled as his words struck their mark, and he almost wished he could take them back. Almost. For the sake of total honesty he was glad he'd put into words something that had been bothering him for some time now.

She pressed a hand to her chest as if wounded. "That's a terrible burden to put on a child."

"Yes," he said quietly. "It is."

"Look, let's leave the baby thing out of this for a moment. You're right. I took a step back. To think. To make some plans. But tonight? You're so scared this is the end that you're making sure it is. You're making sure you can walk away from here absolutely certain that it's my fault."

"I don't see how it can be anyone else's," he answered. "That paper…"

"You didn't even ask what that paper was about. You saw what you wanted to see, Coop."

"If it's not that, what the hell is it?"

She shook her head and suddenly looked very sad. "No. Not tonight. Not now. Maybe not ever. But definitely not now. I'm too damned angry with you."

"I don't understand." She was talking in riddles.

"Because you never asked! Please leave, Coop. I don't know what to think right now and I don't want us to say more that we can't take back."

He looked at her and realized that it was really over. He'd just been fooling himself, seeing what he wanted to see because he'd loved her for so long. But he needed more. He needed someone who loved him as much as he loved her. He couldn't live his life waiting for crumbs of affection. She had to be all-in, meet him in the middle. Maybe he'd been right the day he'd sat outside her shop with a container full of cookies. Maybe what he really needed was to let her go. Maybe they had to go through all of this so he could finally let the dream of her go and move on with his life.

"Just answer me this." He had to know. It was the one question that burned, the one he couldn't come up with an answer to no matter how he turned it over in his mind. "What changed? One day we were planning to grab a bite at the diner and the next you're home in your pajamas crying and refusing to see me again."

She was quiet for such a long time that he felt the traitorous stirrings of hope in his chest. Her eyes glistened as she shook her head. "No. I'm sorry. I can't talk about this now."

He'd bided his time, done everything slowly and the way she wanted, but this time it was truly, truly over. He didn't want to be bitter, but bitterness blackened his heart, anyway. "I was right," he murmured. "I do deserve better. I can't go on giving all of myself and getting nothing back in return. I'm not your fallback when things don't work out, Melissa. It's not fair to either one of us, so maybe it's better for us both to leave it here."

He walked out to the truck on wooden legs, got in, turned the key, put the vehicle in gear and backed out of the drive as if he was on automatic pilot.

It was time he faced the truth. He couldn't carry their relationship all on his own. He needed a partner. And Melissa, with all her plans and lists, needed guarantees and absolutes before she'd risk her heart.

The trouble was, no one could offer guarantees, and he knew for sure that whoever did was a liar. Life didn't work that way. It took a little faith. He could try to make her happy, but unless she gave up this crazy idea of relying only on herself, they didn't stand a chance.

And maybe what hurt the most was realizing how little faith she actually had in him.

Melissa waited a few days. She needed that time to let the dust settle. To stop being angry at Coop's erroneous assumptions. To put what had happened in perspective, and to get up the nerve to go to see him.

She was terrified. The only thing to do now was bare her soul and tell him everything, if they were going to have a chance to be together. She'd spent a very long time feeling "leavable" and never wanted to put herself in that position again. But Coop had walked away anyway. And she could be hurt and she could be angry, but she'd spent too much time on those sorts of feelings. He had jumped to conclusions, but she understood why. He was right. She had always kept one foot out the door because she was scared. Just as she knew he'd lashed out because *he* was scared.

They could either leave things as they were or she could take the first step toward repairing the damage. There really was no choice. She was miserable without him. Everything had changed. Loving him would be a risk, but for the first time in her life, it was worth the potential consequences. She had to at least try.

And that first step was telling him the truth about her appointment in Edmonton.

She waited until a weeknight, when he was most likely to be at home at the Double C, and drove out there in the dark. Her fingers drummed on the steering wheel as she forced herself to observe the speed limit even though the short drive seemed to take forever. The pounding of her pulse intensified as she turned in the lane and saw his truck parked in front of his house. The porch light was on and as she pulled up next to his half-ton she noticed potted mums on his front step. She inhaled deeply and breathed out slowly. This was so Coop. He was so settled, so sure of himself. He knew what he wanted and where he belonged. Except when it came to her. She knew he wasn't sure of her at all, because she'd never given him a reason to be. It was time she finally set things right.

The slam of her car door sounded terribly loud in the quiet night. She stopped for a moment, gathering her wits, staring up at the stars. Even though it was long past twilight, she focused on one twinkling pinpoint of light and closed her eyes. *Please let him be the one,* she wished. It was nearly the same wish she'd had the night on the swings. But then she'd wished for a baby, and tonight she was wishing for something else entirely, something that had somehow become more important to her—a future. Tonight was all about Coop and trying to repair the damage to their relationship. *And please,* she added, *let me find the right words to fix this.*

When Coop answered the door, she lost her train of thought. All her practiced introductions flew clean out of her head now that he was before her. She just stood there, looking up at him, loving him so hard, scared to death and without any idea where to begin.

"Mel," he said quietly.

"Can we talk?" She managed that much without stuttering.

He shrugged. A barrier fell over his eyes, shutting her out, but he stepped aside. Knees shaking, she moved past him into the foyer of his house.

She lost her breath momentarily. His place was beautiful. It was all creamy walls and high ceilings and gleaming hardwood. Ahead of her, white-painted railings wound around a circular staircase leading to the second floor. She'd expected a smaller version of the main house, but she hadn't expected it to be this fancy. Not for a bachelor. How lonely this huge house must be for one person.

"You want a glass of wine?"

"If you have it, that would be nice." Maybe it would steady her shaky nerves. It would at least give her something to occupy her hands.

She followed him into the kitchen, still bundled in her wool jacket. It was only when he turned around with the glass of wine in his hand that he noticed. "Oh. Let me take your coat."

She shrugged it off and handed it to him, exchanging the coat for the glass. As they traded, his fingers brushed against hers. Sparks jolted up her arm at the very touch, and their eyes clashed. *Thank God,* she thought. Some things hadn't changed. It gave her hope.

Melissa had just spent days avoiding him, sorting through feelings, wanting to work through what was in her head. Ironically, the one person she'd wanted to talk to most to work things through was the one person she couldn't ask—him.

But he was here now, and all she wanted was to draw from his strength. To feel safe. She put her glass down, stepped forward and wound her arms around his ribs.

She needed to feel close to him. Needed nothing more complicated than a hug right now from the one person who always seemed to make things better. She closed her eyes and pressed the side of her face against the solid wall of his chest while his arms cautiously came around her, still holding her coat. "Hold me," she murmured into the soft cotton of his shirt. "Just for a minute."

His arms tightened and he rested his chin on top of her head.

A lump formed in her throat. It was going to be okay. It had to be. She would find the right words somehow, and he'd understand. It couldn't be too late.

But there was so much to say that she truly didn't know where to begin.

"Why'd you come here?" he asked.

She spread her hands over the warmth of his back. He felt so good. So right. She tilted her head just a bit and replied, "I needed my best friend. I've needed him for a very long time, but I shut him out."

Coop backed out of her embrace. "You know how I feel, Mel. I don't want to be just friends."

"That's not what I want, either. But right now I need my friend Cooper to listen to what I have to say. It's important."

"You're asking too much." He put her coat over a chair and then rested his hands on top of it. His face was all hard lines and uncompromising angles. "Mel, if you're coming to say you're pregnant…"

He looked so tortured that she instantly took pity on him. "I'm not pregnant," she said clearly. "That would be impossible."

His eyes met hers, the barrier stripped away for a moment as he latched on to that one very significant word. "Impossible?"

She nodded. "Can we go sit down somewhere? This could take a while and right now it feels like we're in a standoff."

And down came the shutters again. "Of course. Let's go into the living room."

She grabbed her glass of wine and took a healthy sip before following him there. The room, vaulted with cathedral ceilings, featured a surprisingly large angled window that faced north. During the day there was surely a gorgeous view of the Double C pastures. A fire snapped and popped in a fireplace complete with stone flue. It was like something out of a magazine. Mel had known that the Double C was doing well. She'd had no idea it was this prosperous.

She sank into the cushions of the soft leather sofa and toyed with the bowl of her wineglass for a moment. Then she put it down and shifted so she was facing him. "When you found my appointment card, you thought I'd gone for another fertility treatment, didn't you?"

"You mean you didn't?"

She shook her head. "No. I didn't."

"But…"

She reached out and put her hand on his forearm. "What bothers me most about that moment was that I realized you really don't trust me. You honestly thought I would go ahead and do that even though we'd started seeing each other."

"It was a pretty strong statement about where you thought our future was going," he remarked, pulling his arm away. "Nowhere. If you saw a future with me, you wouldn't be looking to be carrying someone else's child. You had to know that I…"

"That you what?"

He looked away. "That I'd find that impossible to live with."

She'd hurt him. Badly. She got what he was saying. She'd given him hope and then, in his eyes, stripped it away. She knew how cruel it was to have hopes crushed. Even though she really hadn't, and certainly hadn't meant to, she knew the fault was partly hers, because she hadn't wanted to say the words in the middle of an argument. She'd wanted everything to be perfect…and because of it she'd ruined everything.

"I backed away from us without telling you why, so I can't blame you for making the wrong assumption. I wasn't ready to explain and I certainly didn't want to do it when we were arguing. So I waited a few days. Thought a lot."

"Planned it? Like you plan everything?"

She nodded. "I do plan things. It comes from being surprised and blindsided and never wanting that to happen again. And this time it also comes from being scared and not wanting to mess up the most important relationship in my life."

She sighed, gathering strength. "Coop, when everything went wrong with my marriage, the one person I wanted to turn to was you. You had always, always been there for me, only this time you weren't. I think you probably would have been if I'd asked, but I couldn't. You hurt me, you see. I felt so foolish that I hadn't seen what was right in front of my face. I even felt foolish in front of you. It seemed everyone knew what was going on but me. Poor innocent Melissa. I decided then and there that I wasn't going to rely on anyone again. Especially not you—even though I missed you like crazy. Coop, we've always had a special bond, even when I was married to someone else. I made so many mistakes. When you said you deserved better? Well, if I'm being completely honest, we all did. I know that Scott and I should never have married in the first place. I'm partly to blame. We didn't have the kind of marriage we should have, and when that happens, people stray."

"People should get out first and not cheat."

"Agreed. But I can't help but wonder if Scott wasn't a bit jealous of our friendship."

Coop nodded. "I know he was. He threw it in my face when I threatened to tell you."

"It was all wrong," she said quietly, "but the one thing we can't do is turn back the clock and fix our mistakes. Which brings me to a few days ago."

She reached out again and took his hand in hers. "I know what scared looks like, Coop. I know because I've been terrified of my feelings for you. Ever since we made peace you've been everywhere I go. First the housing project, then Thanksgiving, at church, in my life. Not only that, but I had to get used to the idea of what you said that day by the creek."

She gave her head a little shake. "When I was fifteen you were all I thought about. I tried not to pressure you, because we were friends, but I wanted so much more. It finally got to a point where I just had to let go. I valued your friendship too much to push you away by demanding something you didn't want. So finding out over ten years later that you finally felt the same way... This all could have ended so differently. Sometimes that's made me a bit angry, to be honest. So much pain could have been avoided. But then I tell myself that maybe we weren't ready then. Maybe we were too young. Maybe we had things to learn before we could be together. The last thing I wanted to do was play with your feelings. I know what it's like to love someone who doesn't love you back. That's why I wanted to take it slow. I was unsure, and I didn't want either of us to get hurt."

"I tried to give you space...."

His voice was hoarse and she blinked against the stinging at the backs of her eyes. "You did. You did every single thing I asked. And I had so much thinking to do. I wasn't as sure as you. I'd been going in one direction with a goal in sight and suddenly the road map changed. I'd been thinking about trying to have a baby for so long that it felt scary and strange to put it on hold while we explored this thing. But that's what I did, Coop. I put it on hold. The appointment at the clinic was not to give it another try. And I'm also to blame for you thinking that. I pulled away from you without an explanation. It's not surprising that you jumped to the conclusion you did."

Coop's brows knitted together. "If things were going so great, then why did you pull away?"

Here it was, the moment of truth. "This is so hard,"

she whispered. Once it was out she couldn't take it back. Things would change forever.

"Is there someone else, Mel?"

Her heart lurched as he asked it quietly, cautiously, as if preparing himself for the worst.

"No," she whispered, sliding over and lifting her other hand to his cheek. "No, Coop. There's no one but you, I promise."

*No one but you.*

And with her next words she was going to hand him so much power it was staggering.

"That night at the diner, when we were supposed to meet? I showed up," she began. "You were there, talking to Ty and Clara and there was a moment where you caught Susanna and lifted her in your arms. This little curly-haired doll in your big strong arms, Coop. She kissed your cheek and you kissed her hair. And that was the moment. It was like the world tilted and suddenly there was a brand-new reality in front of me. It wasn't just us seeing where things were going anymore. It hit me so hard. I love you, Coop."

"You love me."

She nodded, felt one tear slip down her cheek. Why did his voice sound so tight rather than happy? Why wasn't he pulling her into his arms and telling her it was okay? Panic started to slither through her veins, making her chest tight as she hurried to explain. "I realized I was in love with you, and I didn't know what to do with everything I was feeling. I had to make sense of it all. It scared me so much. I never wanted to care for someone that much. I've let go of you twice already, don't you see? And it hurt so badly both times. The idea of having to do that again someday—after sharing a life with you, after knowing what it is to have you—I'm not sure my heart could survive that. So I backed away, tried to make sense of my feelings. To decide what to do."

"And the appointment?"

He was still fixated on the clinic appointment. This wasn't going at all as she'd hoped. She'd thought she would say the words and it would make everything all right. That he'd confess his love, too, and she'd be in his arms by now. But Coop seemed more distant than ever. Maybe if he understood the reason behind the appointment he'd see the same future she envisioned in her heart.

"I've done a few treatments now and it hasn't worked. I was going for further testing to make sure there's not a fertility issue. For us. Just in case…"

Coop got up from the sofa and went to the window. What was his problem? She'd explained the appointment and just told him she loved him, and he was cold as ice!

"What's wrong?" she asked. "I thought once I explained the appointment, once I told you how I was feeling, you'd…"

"I'd what? Throw myself in your arms?"

Confused and afraid, she gave a quick nod. "Well… yes, something like that. Isn't that what you wanted?"

He cursed and ran his hand through his hair as he turned back to face her. "Yes, it's what I wanted! But it's not that easy. When your marriage broke up, the one thing you were trying to do was start a family. It's so important to you that you were prepared to make it happen all on your lonesome. Then I jump in and complicate the whole thing—especially when I made that stupid offer to help you. Oh, I wish I'd never done that…."

He started pacing in front of the fireplace. "Now you come to me and say you love me after…" He heaved a breath and stopped, facing her directly. "After you see me holding some kid, and decide I'd make perfect father material?"

"Don't you want children?" she asked, feeling desperately as if she was losing him, and not understanding why. "You'd be such a good father...."

"What I want," he said significantly, "is a woman who loves me for me and not my DNA."

She sat back on the sofa, her mouth hanging slightly open. Was that how he saw her? That she was so fixated on having a baby she couldn't tell the difference between love and a means to an end? Was he so unsure of her that he'd think she'd use him that way?

"What do you want me to say?" Mel asked weakly. "I can't lie and say I don't want children, because I do. Can you stand there and say you don't want a family, too? That doesn't mean I don't love you, Coop. I'm just not sure how to prove it to you."

"I'm not sure you can." His voice was flat and resigned.

There was a long pause where the only sound was the fire crackling. Finally Coop looked down at her. "I thought I knew what I wanted. I thought by telling you about my feelings at Thanksgiving, it would somehow work out. Believe me, no one is more surprised than me at what I'm saying right now. Everything I wanted is right in front of me and I'm not reaching out to take it."

"Why?"

"Because a part of me would always wonder if you were with me for me, or if I was just part of a plan you had for the perfect life."

She got up from the sofa. "I had a plan like that once. It didn't turn out so well. I try not to repeat the same mistakes. I thought that was why I was here. I don't know which is worse—the idea that you don't have faith in me to love you or the lack of faith you have in yourself to be able to hold me."

The future was slowly slipping out of her fingers, but she was glad she had come. She'd said the words and she'd meant them. She'd meant every syllable. She went to him and lifted her hand, brushed his hair back by his ear with her fingertips. "You're breaking my heart right now," she murmured.

"I can't be someone who is just *enough,*" he replied, stopping her hand by circling her wrist with strong fingers. "I can't be second best or an alternate choice. If we do this, I have to be *everything.*"

"You are everything," she replied, gazing deeply into his eyes. "That's what I'm offering, Coop. I love you. If you send me away tonight, that won't change. I was afraid of falling in love. Afraid to give anyone that much control over my life, because when you're in love you put that other person ahead of yourself." She moved closer so that their clothing brushed. "Loving you means handing you my heart for safekeeping. I get that now, because seeing you that night, I realized my heart was no longer mine to give."

She stood on tiptoe and touched his cheek with her lips. "It's you, Coop. It's always been you. And nothing you say or do will change that."

"What if your test results say you can't have children? What if, by some crazy circumstance, I can't? What then?"

She put her hand over his heart, feeling the strong beat against her palm. "I would be upset and disappointed. And I would hope that we would face it together. The day you made your offer to help, I told you that I didn't believe in marrying someone just to have a baby. I meant that with all my heart. I don't want your DNA, Coop. I want a *partner.* Someone who loves me for me and someone I adore in return. Someone I can talk to about anything and trust with my life. I want to put aside my dreams and replace them with *our* dreams. I can't imagine being with anyone but you."

"You really mean that, don't you?" he asked, and she saw a tiny crack in the wall he'd built around himself. He put his hand over hers, his strong fingers circling her wrist once more.

She nodded. "I do," she confirmed. "The night you came to see me, you asked me what had changed. My whole world changed that night. Everything I thought I knew no longer existed. And if I needed time to plan, it's because the one thing I didn't want was to screw this up. So please, please. Trust me. Love me. Let this be everything."

For a long moment silence hummed between them. Coop seemed to struggle, and she thought that her one last effort to reach him was a failure. Then he loosened his grip on her wrist and his Adam's apple bobbed as he swallowed. "I'm so afraid," he admitted. "I thought I couldn't love you more than I already did, and then there you were, and it was more than I ever imagined. You have the power to hurt me, Mel. And I got so scared, because if love just gets bigger, then losing you would destroy me, and I could feel you slipping away."

"Then don't lose me," she replied. "I'm not going anywhere. I promise."

His dark eyes shone in the firelight. "Then stay," he commanded. "Stay with me tonight. We've wasted so much time already."

She knew what he was asking. There would be no turning back after this. And for the first time in years, there was no hesitation, no insecurity, no fear in not knowing exactly what the future would bring. Instead there was relief and happiness and a strange but welcome sense that everything in her life was finally right where it was meant to be. In this moment.

"Let's not waste any more," she replied.

# CHAPTER TWELVE

GRILLING WAS COOP'S specialty, and despite the brisk day and snow clouds building to the west, he had a roaster full of ribs ready to slap on the barbecue. The playoffs had started and dinner was at his place today, and Mel had agreed to come over and help with the meal.

He came back in from the deck, where he'd turned on the barbecue to heat, and saw her standing at the threshold to the kitchen. The pregame was on the television and the announcers' voices were muffled. She looked beautiful in faded jeans and his Eskimos jersey, which was about two sizes too big. Beautiful and adorable and his.

"You're early."

"Mmm-hmm." She put grocery bags down on the counter and walked over to him in stocking feet. "I wanted to get here before your parents."

"Really. And why is that?"

A slow smile curved her lips. "So I could do this without an audience."

She wrapped her arms around his neck and pressed her mouth to his. With a chuckle he blindly put the lighter on the counter and pulled her closer, cupping one hand around her neck as they kissed fully, completely.

"I don't suppose we have time…" she murmured, slightly out of breath.

"Why, Miss Stone," he teased. "Are you suggesting…"

She grinned. "Yeah, like you're surprised."

Being with Mel was more than Coop had ever dreamed. She was beautiful, responsive, loving. They'd been using protection at her insistence, so that he'd be absolutely sure of her and her motives. They needed to do this right and with total honesty, and when the time came…

Which was why he put his hands on her arms and pushed her away gently. Today he was going to be as honest as it was possible to be.

"I have something for you," he said, stepping aside and opening a drawer. He took out a flat, rectangular box that was wrapped in blue foil with a silver ribbon.

Her eyes lit up. "A present?"

He handed it over, hoping to God his fingers weren't shaking. "Open it."

It seemed to take forever for her to get through the ribbon and wrapping. She was very precise, careful not to rip anything, which was starting to drive him a little crazy. His parents would be here at any moment and he wanted her to himself just a little bit longer.…

Her laugh bubbled out as she lifted the lid to the box. "Oh!" she exclaimed, reaching in. "Coop, this is so funny!"

She held up the canvas apron and slid the loop over her neck, laughing as she read the front. "'Keep Calm and Cowgirl Up.' Cute."

"I thought that if you're going to be hanging out with us Fords and helping with the cooking, you need your own apron."

"Thank you, Coop. I love it." She secured the ties around her waist and spun in a circle. "Now, about my first proposition…"

She wound her arms around him again and whispered a suggestion in his ear that made him go hot all over.

"Wait," he said hoarsely. As much as seeing her in that apron—and only that apron—was an intriguing idea, there was something more important that came first. "I noticed that your work apron at the shop has lots of pockets to keep stuff in."

With an impatient sigh she admitted, "I do love my pockets. They're very handy."

"This apron has pockets."

"So I see."

It was hard to think with her pressed so tightly against him. "Mel," he insisted, closing his eyes. "Maybe you should check the pockets."

He didn't know if it was something in his voice that did the trick, or the words themselves, but Mel stood back and met his gaze with wide eyes. And held it as she dipped her fingers into the wide pockets of the cobbler's apron.

He knew when she found the ring, because her eyes widened even further and started to glisten. She slowly took it out of the pocket and held it between two fingers. "Coop…"

He went to her and took the ring from her hand. "I love you, Mel. I've loved you for so long that it's hard to remember a time when I didn't. I tried, God knows I tried, when I thought there would never be a chance for us, but no one ever measured up to you. Now that you're mine I want to keep it that way. Forever."

She sniffled, and his chest expanded with emotion

and possibility and hope and fear and a million other emotions.

"I want you to marry me. I want to make a life with you, and see you every morning when I wake up, and hold you close every night when I go to sleep. I know you're scared and you want guarantees. Some guarantees are impossible to give because we don't know what life holds for us. But I can promise you this—I will love you until my dying breath. I will always be there for you. I want to have a family with you. I want everything from you and I'll give you everything I have in return. Will you marry me?"

Her lip quivered. "I love you, Coop. Yes, I'll marry you. Yes, yes, yes!"

It felt as if his heart was exploding with relief and happiness, even though it still beat along in his chest, perhaps just a tiny bit faster than normal. As she sniffled again, he held up her hand and slid the ring over her knuckle. The simple square-cut diamond caught the light and sparkled as he squeezed her fingers. He'd never thought this day would actually come. That she'd say yes. That he'd have everything he'd ever dreamed of having.

The front door opened, bringing a gust of wind tunneling through the foyer and into the kitchen. "Hello!" called Jean. "We're here!"

Coop cupped his hands around Mel's face and gave her a quick kiss during their last few moments of privacy. "I'll take a rain check on that other offer," he murmured with a secret smile.

When his parents entered the kitchen, Mel and Coop broke apart. She stayed in the shelter of his arms, though, wanting to remain close. They were going to do it. They were getting married. And one day they'd start a family together. It surprised her to realize she didn't want that to happen right away. She wanted a little time for just the two of them first.

"I see we're interrupting," Jean said, her eyes twinkling as she set a casserole dish on the countertop. Mel grinned at the approving note in her voice, and the sound of Bob's dry chuckle behind her.

"Not at all," Melissa replied, dropping her arms.

"Oh, look at you!" Jean laughed. "Nice apron."

"I figured if everyone else in the family had one, then Mel should, too," Coop said. "Especially since…"

He looked down at her and his dark eyes were filled with love and hope and happiness. "Especially since I asked her to join the family about five minutes ago."

Jean hurried around the corner of the counter. "You asked her to marry you?" To Mel's delight, Coop's mother grabbed her hand and lifted it to see the evidence. "Oh, Bob! Look! She has a ring and everything!"

"It's about time," was all Bob said, coming forward to clap Coop on the arm. Then he stopped to fold Mel into a hug. "Welcome home," he said softly, making more tears prick the backs of her eyes. "We've been hoping for this for a very long time."

She squeezed him back.

Jean interrupted the moment with a question. "Do your parents know?"

"Of course not. It just happened." Mel laughed. "But they're going to be very happy." She didn't mention their displeasure with her other recent decisions, but knew for sure that the news that she was marrying again— and marrying Coop—would be cause for celebration in the Stone household.

"Then get on the phone, girl! Invite them over. There's plenty of food and this deserves a party."

Bob went to work putting beer in the fridge, while Jean bustled around, taking stock of food supplies. Mel took advantage of the chaotic moment to snuggle close to Coop. "Sorry about the hoopla," she murmured. "Looks like that private celebration will have to wait."

"It's okay," he answered, dropping a sweet kiss on her forehead. "We've got all the time in the world. We've got forever."

\* \* \* \* \*

**"You look beautiful."** And that was an understatement. She took his breath away. The more he'd thought about it in the past twenty-four hours, the more he really wanted her to say yes to his idea.

Ben backed the SUV out of the space and headed for the exit that would take them to downtown Blackwater Lake.

"Is there a reason we're not going to Fireside here at the lodge?" she asked.

He glanced over at her and smiled at her expression. "Yes. My criteria for tonight is a locals favorite because it's always busy."

"I haven't agreed to this insane charade yet."

"I'm aware of that. But I think I can win you over."

"Pretty confident, aren't you?"

"Power of positive thinking." He grinned at her. "Plus whatever your decision, being seen together will keep everyone off balance and that can't hurt."

"By 'everyone' you mean women."

"Men talk, too." He parked and shut off the ignition, then got out and walked around to open the passenger door.

# THE DOCTOR'S
# DATING BARGAIN

BY
TERESA SOUTHWICK

First published in Great Britain 2013
by Mills & Boon, an imprint of Harlequin (UK) Limited,
Eton House, 18-24 Paradise Road, Richmond, Surrey TW9 1SR

© Teresa Southwick 2013

ISBN: 978 0 263 90134 4
ebook ISBN: 978 1 472 00518 2

23-0813

Harlequin (UK) policy is to use papers that are natural, renewable and recyclable products and made from wood grown in sustainable forests. The logging and manufacturing processes conform to the legal environmental regulations of the country of origin.

Printed and bound in Spain
by Blackprint CPI, Barcelona

**Teresa Southwick** lives with her husband in Las Vegas, the city that reinvents itself every day. An avid fan of romance novels, she is delighted to be living out her dream of writing for Mills & Boon.

To Maureen Child, Kate Carlisle, Christine Rimmer
and Susan Mallery, the best plot group ever!
Thanks for the friendship. And the fun. (Wine, too.)

# Chapter One

"I'm in so much trouble."

Ben McKnight sat in the twilight shadows on the rear second-story deck of Blackwater Lake Lodge. The angry blonde who'd just stomped up the wooden stairs from the lush grounds below obviously was too caught up in her snit to notice him. She continued to mumble to herself as she paced back and forth in front of the redwood railing.

"Is it me?" she grumbled. "Do I attract trouble like black pants pick up pet hair? Or lint? Or fuzzballs? What is my problem?"

Then she lashed out with her foot and connected with one of the sturdy, upright posts anchoring the railing. It was a solid kick and after a few seconds the message traveled to her brain. When it got there, she blurted out, "Damn it! Now my foot's broken."

Beautiful, angry women who talked to themselves were not in Ben's wheelhouse, but broken bones he knew something about. He stood and walked out of the shadows into the circle of light cast by the property's perimeter lights.

"Maybe I can help."

She turned and gasped. "Good Lord, you startled me. Where the heck did you come from? I didn't know anyone was here."

"I figured that. The talking to yourself sort of gave it away."

"That happens when you don't want to talk to anyone else." She limped closer. "Who are you?"

"Ben McKnight. *Doctor* McKnight. I'm an orthopedic specialist at Mercy Medical Clinic."

"Call me crazy, but I didn't think it was in a doctor's job description to scare a person to death."

"True. *Do no harm* is the cornerstone of the Hippocratic Oath."

She pressed a hand to her chest and took a deep breath. "Then your bedside manner could use a little work, Doctor."

"Sorry." He watched her put weight on the foot and wince. "For the record, I don't recommend kicking things as a communication technique. Especially when you're wearing four-inch heels. Next time I'd use my words if I were you."

"What am I? Five?" The tone was full of irritation that seemed completely self-directed. "Okay. That was childish."

"Would you like me to take a look at the foot?"

"No. I'm fine. Completely over it. I'm calm and tranquil."

"I could tell," he said dryly. "All the pacing, stomping and trash talk were a clear indication that you're totally in your Zen place."

"I didn't mean for anyone to see that. It's been a bad

day and when that happens, I come up here to decompress. Pretty much every night. My serenity spot isn't normally occupied."

"Since I'm trespassing, the least I can do is listen." It would give him a chance to look at her mouth.

"Thanks, but I really have nothing to say."

"All evidence to the contrary. Look, whether or not you feel like talking, you should probably sit for a few minutes and elevate the foot. There could be swelling."

"Did you learn that in medical school?" She limped toward the two chairs nestled in the shadow of the lodge.

Ben put his hand under her elbow, mostly to help take some of her weight, but partly to touch her. "Actually, that's basic first aid. Every coach of every team I've been on since I was five has preached ice and heat for an injury."

"How many teams have you been on?"

She lowered herself into the Adirondack chair and leaned back with a sigh. There was a matching natural-wood ottoman and he cupped her ankle in his hand, then lifted it, resting it on the flat surface before slipping off her high-heeled shoe.

"A lot." Ben sat on the ottoman beside hers.

"What sports did you play?"

"Soccer. Basketball. Football. My senior year I was on the Blackwater Lake High School team that won state about fifteen years ago."

"So you're a local boy?"

"Yes."

"How come I haven't seen you around?" she asked.

"I just got back."

"Do you have family in Blackwater Lake?"

"Father. Older brother, younger sister."

"That qualifies." She thought for a moment. "So, I can't help being curious. You have family close by, which makes me wonder why you're sitting in the shadows on the deck all by yourself. Did you have a dinner date here at the lodge and she left in a huff? Are you a guest here at the hotel? Or just stalking someone who is a guest?"

He laughed. "I'm a guest. Staying here while I'm having a house built."

"Too old to live at home?"

"Something like that," he said.

The clouds drifted away from the moon and the deck was bathed in silver light, giving Ben a better view of the blonde. She was prettier than he'd thought, with a small face and deep dimples. Her eyes looked blue, although he couldn't tell the shade, and tilted up slightly at the corners. Her hair was straight, and cut in layers that framed her face and fell past her shoulders. Her arm through the light sweater she wore had felt delicate and small-boned. Although the heels gave the impression of height, she barely came up to his shoulder, which made her not so tall.

Suddenly he wondered who he was talking to. He didn't even know her name. On top of that, she was the one asking all the questions. "Are you sure you don't want to tell me why you're so ticked off?"

"There's nothing to say."

"For starters you could define the mess you're in."

"I was hoping you didn't hear that," she said.

"Nope. Sorry. Every word. And let me quote here, 'I'm in so much trouble.' Should I be afraid to get too close? Are you at the top of an assassination list? On the run from law enforcement? A CIA spy doing covert surveillance?"

"Right, because so much happens in Blackwater Lake that the government needs to surveil." There was a suggestion of sarcasm and the barest hint of mockery in her tone.

"You don't like it here?"

She met his gaze. "Let's just say it's not New York or L.A."

"So define trouble. You could be pregnant," he pointed out.

"You have quite the imagination." Her lips turned up at the corners in a brief show of amusement. She had an awfully spectacular mouth when it wasn't all pinched and tight. "And that would be a miracle since I haven't had sex in—"

"Yes?" He looked at her and waited.

"That's really none of your business."

"Maybe not, but now I'm awfully curious."

"Be that as it may," she said, "you're a stranger and I'm not in the habit of sharing personal information with someone I've barely met, Dr. McKnight."

"At least you know my name. That's more than I can say about you."

"Camille Halliday." She looked at him expectantly, as if waiting for recognition. Actually more like bracing for it, as if the information would be unpleasant.

The name did sound familiar, but he couldn't place it. "It's nice to meet you, Miss Halliday."

"Likewise, Dr. McKnight. Now, I really should be going." She slid the punting foot off the ottoman and gingerly tested it on the deck.

"How does it feel?"

"Several of my toes hurt," she admitted.

"Can you walk on it?"

"I have to. Work to do."

"At the hotel?"

"Yes."

"In what capacity?" he wanted to know.

"I run the place."

That's when her last name clicked. Her family had made

a fortune in the hotel and hospitality industry. "You're one of the Halliday hotel chain family."

"Among other things," she said a little mysteriously. After sliding her other leg off the ottoman, she moved forward in the chair and tested more weight on the foot. Drawing in a breath she said, "That smarts a little."

Ben realized he didn't want her to leave yet. "I'd be happy to look at it for you. Sometimes taping a couple toes together helps."

"Thanks for the tip. Taping a toe I can handle." Her words implied there was a whole lot more she couldn't handle.

"Okay. But if you don't want me to examine it, at least sit for a few more minutes and take the pressure off."

She sighed, then nodded. "I can sit, but that won't relieve any pressure."

"You're not talking about the foot now, are you?"

"No." She caught the corner of her bottom lip between her top teeth as she stared out over the back grass and the thick evergreen trees beyond.

"What's wrong? Might help to get it off your chest."

"It might, but I can't. One of the first things I learned getting a master's degree in hotel management was never unburden yourself to a guest."

"I'm not really a guest," he said. "It's more like a lease until my house is ready."

"Why didn't you do that?" she asked. "Rent a place, I mean?"

"Oh, so you get to ask questions but I don't? How about a quid pro quo?" He met her gaze. "You tell me about your trouble and I'll spill about my living arrangements. What can it hurt?"

She stared at him for several moments, then nodded. "It's pretty common knowledge that this property in the hotel chain isn't doing well financially. My father gave me six months to stop Blackwater Lake Lodge from hemorrhaging money or he'll close it down."

"I see. So you have half a year."

"Not anymore." She blew out a breath. "I've been here two and a half months. The employees are intractable and do their own thing. Personnel turnover is too high and we bleed money in training until a new hire is competent enough to pull their own weight. I think someone is skimming money from the books, but I'm so busy putting out fires that I can't get to the bottom of it. And I'm running out of time."

"Do you have a personal attachment to this property?"

"I'd never seen it until January." She sighed. "But my father is testing me. If I can pull this off, I'll get a choice assignment somewhere that's not in the wilderness of Montana."

"Ah." Making the lodge successful was her ticket out of here.

Ben could understand. Once upon a time he couldn't wait to shake the dirt, mud and mountain air off, but he didn't feel that way now.

"So, why are you back here?" she asked.

"To build a house and put down roots. Blackwater Lake is a great place to live." When she stood, he did, too. "Can't see renting something, settling in, then moving again. I'm focused on expanding Mercy Medical Clinic and providing quality health care for the town and the tourists who come here to visit."

"It's a really noble goal." She touched his arm to steady herself while slipping her shoe back on, then limped toward the stairs. At the top she turned and said, "Good luck with that, Doctor. Now I really have to say good-night."

After she disappeared from sight, he heard her uneven step as she walked down the stairs.

Ben found her intriguing and was sorry she'd had to leave. Still, the quid pro quo had put everything in perspective. He was staying and her objective was to get out of town as fast as possible.

That was too bad.

Until last night Camille hadn't known Ben McKnight existed and now she wondered how he could have been staying in her hotel without her being aware. He was tall, funny and as good-looking as any man she'd met in L.A. or New York, and she'd met a lot of men, according to every rag sheet tabloid paper on the planet.

Now Dr. Ben McKnight was having dinner in the Blackwater Lake Lodge restaurant where she was filling in as hostess. The last one had quit and it was hard to run a five-star establishment without a greeter and seater. Hopefully the interviews she had tomorrow would be productive. Fortunately it was Sunday and not busy. At least it hadn't been until Doctor Do-Good had arrived and asked for a table by himself.

Since then at least four women, two from the lodge staff and two civilians, had come in, sat with him, written something down on a small piece of paper, then handed it to him. Since they were small scraps of paper, she was pretty sure the information wasn't their medical history.

At the moment he was sitting by himself and the place was practically empty except for a couple lingering over coffee and dessert at their table near the stone fireplace.

Cam just couldn't stop herself. She strolled over to where she'd seated him a little while ago and smiled. "Did you enjoy your dinner, Doctor?"

Ben nodded. "I did. The food here is excellent."

"Amanda will appreciate hearing that. She's the chef." And someone Cam had coaxed here from New York. The plan was to prove herself in six months and the two of them would get their pick of prime assignments in one of the Halliday Hospitality Corporation's other properties. "Can I get you something from the bar?"

"No, thanks. I'm on call for the clinic."

"Are you expecting broken bones tonight?"

"Mercy Medical Clinic docs rotate the responsibility of being available to triage emergency calls."

"Excuse me?"

"We take information and decide if the patient on the phone needs to see a doctor and which one could best take care of them. If it's an orthopedic problem, I'm their guy. Otherwise Adam Stone, the family practice specialist, is up."

Cam was "up" all day and night here at the lodge. It wasn't the same as life and death, but she had to be available to deal with any crisis situation. Her performance was being evaluated, and Dean Halliday, her father and president of Halliday Hospitality, didn't grade on a curve.

"Maybe dessert and coffee?" she suggested. "I happen to know the chef makes the best seven-layer chocolate cake in Montana."

"Is that a fact?" Dark brown eyes teased and taunted.

"Slight exaggeration. But if it's not the best you've tasted in Blackwater Lake, this meal is on the house."

"Can you afford to take the chance, what with losing money and all? Or," he added, "I could lie just to get the meal comped."

"You could."

It wouldn't be the first time a man had lied and taken advantage of her, but she'd been younger then. Naive. Vulnerable. All of that was a pretty way of saying she'd been stupid and her judgment about men sucked. But she was going to prove herself here in this little backwater town or die trying.

She gave him her best smile, the one that showed off her dimples. "But if you don't tell the truth, we'll both know."

"You're on." He laughed and showed off his own considerable charms.

His teeth were very white and practically perfect. The pretty people she'd once counted as her closest friends all had cosmetic work to make their smiles perfect, but Ben's looked like nothing more than good genes. There were streaks in his brown hair that came from the sun and not a bottle at the salon and the bump in his nose kept him from being too pretty. He had a natural ruggedness about him that had nothing to do with acting technique and everything to do with being a manly man. Again with the good genes.

Cam had promised herself after a teenage run-in with police that she'd never again do anything she'd regret. Last night she broke that pledge. She regretted not letting Dr. Ben McKnight examine her foot. Not because she needed anything more medical than an aspirin and a bag of frozen peas for swelling, but simply to feel his big, competent hands on her leg.

Focus, she told herself. Glancing around, she saw Jenny, the lone waitress tonight, and signaled her over. The server shot her a dirty look, then moved to the table and smiled warmly at the doctor.

"What can I get you, Dr. McKnight?"

"Miss Halliday has talked me into a cup of coffee and a piece of Montana's best chocolate cake."

"Excellent choice," Jen said. "I'll bring it right out."

"I should walk back and get it myself," he said. "It's going to add an extra mile to my run in the morning."

"You look fine to me." Jenny smiled and there was definite flirtatious eyelash-batting going on.

Cam held in a sigh and made a mental note to add an item to the staff meeting agenda. Friendly, but not too friendly. It was a fine line.

She looked down at the customer and gave him her professional, but not too friendly smile. "You may have to run an extra mile, but I promise the cake will be worth it." Then she turned away.

"You're leaving?"

"I have work to do."

"Is the place that busy? Can you keep me company?"

"From what I saw you had plenty of company during dinner, Doctor."

He shrugged. "People in Blackwater Lake are friendly."

"Is it just me or merely a coincidence that all those friendly Blackwater Lake people were of the female persuasion?"

"Are you jealous, Miss Halliday?"

"What if I were, Dr. McKnight?"

"I'd be flattered," he said.

"And I'd have a target on my back. Enjoy your dessert," she said, turning away.

"Whoa, not so fast, Cam. Do you mind if I call you that?" Without waiting for an answer he pointed to the chair at a right angle to his. "It's just plain mean to make a cryptic remark like that, then walk away."

"I have no reason to stay."

"Aren't you supposed to be friendly to your guests?" he asked.

"The first rule of hospitality," she confirmed. "And I have been. But there's a line that shouldn't be crossed."

"Isn't the customer always right?"

"Yes, but—"

"So, sit. Take a load off that foot." He looked down at her legs in four-inch heels. "Nice shoes. How is the foot, by the way?"

"Fine." She didn't take him up on the offer to sit because that wasn't professional. But she didn't leave, either.

"Tell me about the target on your back."

"Obviously you were smart enough to pass medical school. Do you really not get it?" That was tough to believe. A man as good-looking as he had to have had opportunities. He'd probably left this small town for college a naive guy of eighteen, but surely he'd been around the block a time or two since then. "You're quite a catch."

"What am I? A fish?" The twinkle in his eyes said he knew where this was going and wasn't the least offended.

That was fortunate because in the hospitality game one always aimed to please. "You're a doctor and not hard on the eyes—"

"Did you just say I'm cute?"

"I said the women in this tiny little town might perceive you that way and you probably make a decent living as a doctor."

"Are you asking?" He rested his forearms on the white-cloth-covered table.

"I'm not interested. But clearly a number of women are. A single guy—" She stopped as a thought struck her. "You aren't married, are you?"

"Nope."

"Divorced?"

"One would have to have been married for that to be the case."

"So you've never been married."

Before Camille could continue the line of questioning, Jenny brought over his cake and the assistant waiter delivered a saucer and cup, then filled it with coffee.

"Anything else I can do for you?" Jenny asked.

"No. But thanks." Ben gave her a smile.

The waitress returned it and moved behind him where she leveled Cam with a look that if it could kill would render her a rust-colored stain on the floor.

Ben forked off a piece of cake then put it in his mouth, his eyes never leaving hers. After chewing and swallowing, the sound of pleasure he made was almost sexual. Since her January arrival in this state that was so close to Canada, she'd never once been too warm. Not until now. And she very much wanted to fan herself.

*Steady, girl.* What were they talking about? Oh, right. He'd never been married.

"What's wrong with you?" she asked.

"Excuse me? I believe I just proved your point about this being the best cake in Montana."

"I'm not talking cake." She folded her arms over her chest. "You're handsome, smart, a doctor who returned to his hometown to practice medicine. Approximately thirty-five—"

"Close," he confirmed. "Thirty-four."

"Apparently I'm out of practice. And don't interrupt me. I'm on a roll. You're thirty-four, not married and never been married. What's wrong with you?"

"Am I gay, you mean?"

"That's not what I asked, but—"

"No. I'm not."

"That's a relief." She realized that thought hadn't stayed in her head and added, "I mean, for the single women in Blackwater Lake who went to all the trouble of giving you their phone numbers."

"How do you know that?"

"I've been watching them hand you slips of paper too

small to be a résumé or autobiographical novel. And I did catch a glimpse of numbers."

"You're very observant."

"Attention to detail is the hallmark of the hospitality business," she said, irritated at how much she sounded like her father. "So, how does someone who looks so good on paper escape personal entanglements unscathed?"

The twinkle in his eyes vanished and the warm cocoa color turned almost black. "Who says I did?"

"So you have a story." It wasn't a question.

"Doesn't everyone? You go first."

"Nice try." She shook her head.

If he was curious he could just Google her. There was plenty documented on the internet that she'd never live down no matter how hard she tried. Or he could ask the hotel staff. They'd be happy to share.

And judge. The employees had made up their minds about her based on tabloid stories and entertainment gossip. They'd decided she was too shallow, too spoiled, too short and too blonde to be taken seriously.

Why should Ben McKnight be any different?

## Chapter Two

"I don't think it's broken, but I'll know for sure after I look at the X-ray."

"The garage is really busy right now so I'm holding you to that not-broken thing."

Ben hadn't expected to start the week treating anyone in his family, but he had been wrong. Sydney McKnight sat on the paper-covered exam table cradling her right hand. His little sister was a pretty, brown-eyed brunette who loved fixing cars as much as he liked fixing people. As a little girl she'd followed their father around McKnight's Automotive and learned from the best mechanic in Montana.

"You know," he said, "if you wanted some big brother time, we could have done lunch. It would have been a lot less painful for you."

"Not if you made me buy." She winced as he probed the swelling. "In my opinion, what this clinic really needs is a neurologist. You need to have your head examined, find out why it's so big."

"Seriously, Syd. This is nasty. What happened?"

"An accident at the garage." She shrugged. "There was a wrench involved. My hand slipped. Occupational hazard."

"And aren't you lucky big brother the doctor is back to take care of you?"

"We've done all right."

Without you, he thought. Ben knew she hadn't meant to make him feel guilty for leaving, but he did anyway. His father had encouraged him to do what was necessary for his future the same way he'd nurtured Sydney's love affair with cars. Eventually Ben had gone, but now he was back. Where he wanted to be.

The exam room door opened and nurse Ginny Irwin walked in. She was in her late fifties and had blue eyes that missed nothing. Her silver hair was cut in a short, no-fuss style. It suited her no-nonsense attitude.

"Hey, Syd," she said.

"Hi, Ginny." His sister started to lift her hand in greeting, then winced and lowered it.

"I've emailed the X-rays to the radiologist at the hospital and it will be a while before we get the report. But here are the films, Ben." Ginny had known him since he was a kid and didn't feel the need to address him as *Doctor*.

He liked that. Adding *Doctor* to his name didn't make him a better medical practitioner. No polite protocols or assembly-line medicine, just solid personal care to, sometimes literally, get people back on their feet.

"Let's take a look." He put the films on the lighted view box. He wasn't a radiologist, but in his expert opinion there was no break, although he took his time studying all the small bones, just to be sure.

"Don't keep me in suspense," Syd said.

"I have to look at the full range of densities. It can go from white to black and I need to evaluate the contrast ratio for a diagnosis."

"Please don't go all medical techno-speak on me," Sydney begged.

"It's not broken."

"Good." Ginny almost smiled, then looked sternly at the patient. "I don't want to see you back in here, Sydney Marie."

"Yes, ma'am. I'd salute, but this Pillsbury Doughboy hand would just punish me."

"In so many ways. Take care," Ginny said, just before slipping out the door.

"She scares me," his sister said. "So I'll ask you. Can I go back to work?"

"Really?" He folded his arms over his chest. "I'm the weak link? Do we need to get Ginny back in here to keep you in line, Sydney Marie?"

"I'm happy to stay in line if you'll just tell me what I have to do so I can get back to work."

"Take the rest of the day off. Use ice and over-the-counter pain meds. When the swelling goes down you can work."

"That's it? You're not going to do anything? No quick fix? What kind of doctor are you?"

"The kind who replaces hips and fixes broken bones, sometimes with surgery. I have a piece of paper that says it's okay for me to do that."

"Just asking. I guess you'll come in handy for water- and snow-skiing seasons." She settled her injured hand on her thigh. "Speaking of that…how do you like living at Blackwater Lake Lodge?"

The mention of his living arrangement turned his thoughts to the lady who was in charge of the place where he lived. This wasn't the first time she'd crossed his mind and every time it happened, the thought was followed by a vague regret that she wouldn't be around very long.

"Did I say something wrong?" Syd's eyes narrowed.

"What? No. Why?"

"You look funny."

"Define funny," he said.

"I don't know. Sort of goofy. Sappy. Like you walked down the hall at Blackwater Lake High and saw the girl you had a crush on."

"Interesting diagnosis, Doctor."

"Am I right about a woman being involved?" she persisted.

"Yes."

"I'd clap my hands in excitement, but…" She looked ruefully at the puffy extremity. "Who is she? Anyone I know?"

"Do you know Camille Halliday?"

"Everyone knows her." Syd's expression said it wasn't in a good way. "She's the hotel heiress."

"I know. Met her Saturday." And he'd seen her again at dinner last night. He wondered if she was having another bad day.

"Are you aware that she has a certain reputation?"

"What kind of rep?"

"Partying. Hanging with a wild crowd. Name always in the paper and not for sending mosquito nets to Africa to wipe out malaria. She even went to jail. Although they let her out early."

"Good behavior?"

"Overcrowding," Syd answered. "You didn't know about this stuff?"

"No."

"Have you been living under a rock?"

Sort of. "Las Vegas is surrounded by rocky mountains and rocks are frequently used for landscaping, what with water being scarce in the desert. But none of that qualifies as living under one."

Unless you counted working too hard to think about anything else. Now he had time to wonder about Camille Halliday. What his sister just said didn't fit the ambitious, hardworking woman he'd met. "Was this jail thing recent?"

"No. She was in her teens."

Ah. "And where did you get all this unimpeachable information?"

"The tabloids." Syd grinned shamelessly. "I love to read them. A guilty pleasure."

"Then here's a headline for you. Don't believe everything you read." He slid his fingers into the pockets of his white lab coat. "I found Cam to be bright, funny, focused and a serious businesswoman. Sexy, too."

His sister's eyes narrowed. "Do you have the hots for her?"

No. Maybe. Irrelevant. "She's got her sights set on bigger and better things. Blackwater Lake Lodge is where she's proving herself. She can't wait to move up the career ladder, preferably to a city with a more impressive population."

Syd's dark eyes gleamed with plans he knew he wouldn't like. "That's a relief."

"Why?"

"Here's the thing. You're not getting any younger, Ben."

"Yeah. I think they taught us that in med school," he said dryly.

"No. Seriously. You should think about settling down."

"I'm building a house. Doesn't that count?"

"Good start." She shifted her tush on the table and the

disposable paper rustled. "You should think about a woman to go along with it. And I just happen to have some suggestions."

His sister and every other female in this town had ideas. There'd been matchmaking vibes since he'd touched down. Even Cam had noticed women giving him their phone numbers. "Why am I not surprised?"

Syd ignored his sarcasm. "Annie Higgins is pretty and fun."

"Isn't she divorced with three kids?"

"So?" His sister obviously saw the negative in his expression because she moved on. "Okay. Darlene Litsey has never been married. She has a great personality."

"Personality? Isn't that code for a deal-breaking flaw?"

"Maybe she's a little controlling," Syd admitted. "Okay. I've got the perfect woman for you."

A vision of Cam Halliday flashed into his mind. Specifically her expression when he'd eaten the sinfully good cake. He'd have sworn it was a look of pure lust, but that could just be wishful thinking.

"Are you paying attention?" Syd demanded.

"I'm all ears."

She eyed him critically. "They are a little big. I wasn't going to say anything…but you're a doctor. Surely there's something you can do to fix them."

"Very funny. Now that I think about it, what woman would want to go out with Dumbo?"

"Don't sell yourself short. You've got a lot to offer." She did that critical appraisal thing again. "Handsome, in spite of the ears. Funny, except to me. And you're a doctor."

Cam had said almost the same thing last night. "So?"

"A woman wants to be taken care of. Goes back to caveman days. Picking the biggest, strongest Neanderthal/

Cro-Magnon who can hunt, gather and beat the crap out of anyone who tries to take what's his."

"None of that pertains to me," he protested.

"Sure it does. Modern man just pays people to do all of the above and you can pay better than most. I happen to know you got a couple of bucks when you sold your practice in Las Vegas."

"You could say that."

When he finished medical training, Ben had researched areas of the country for a place to practice medicine. Las Vegas was booming and there was a scarcity of doctors in his field. He set up an office, built a solid reputation all over the valley, hired more doctors to make the business end of it more lucrative, then sold it to the partners. The deal made him a millionaire and wise investments had more than doubled his net worth. He never had to work again if he didn't want to.

Except he loved what he did. Long hours and hard work had earned him the freedom to use his knowledge to help people without having to practice cookie-cutter medicine. He could take his time and give patients the personal attention he wanted to.

"Ben, Emily Decatur is really nice."

"I remember her from high school. She works at the Lodge."

"Right. And you live there. It's a sign. It's convenient."

Cam Halliday worked where he lived, too, and somehow that seemed more convenient to him. "I'm sure Emily is great, but there's no spark."

"Three strikes and you're out. I just provided you with a list of perfectly lovely women and you found something wrong with every one." Syd's frustration was showing. "If you don't want a woman, why did you come home?"

"I'm not sure those two statements actually go together."

"They do in my mind. Las Vegas has a bigger dating pool than Blackwater Lake, so why are you here?"

"Believe it or not, dating isn't my reason for coming back."

"I get it." She was angry and frustrated in equal parts. "You're not looking at all. This is about Judy Coulter, isn't it?"

"My main squeeze in high school and college." After that not so much.

"Yeah. The same one who strung you along for years then married some ski bum she'd only known a month. And moved back East with."

All of that was true and it hurt at the time. But he'd gotten over her a long time ago. "She did me a favor, Syd."

"She broke your heart. How is that a good thing?"

"She didn't break my heart. When I started med school there were no distractions. I put all my energy into school and becoming the best doctor possible."

"You are pretty good," she grudgingly admitted.

"I thank Judy for that."

His sister frowned. "If you were really the best, you'd make my hand better right now."

"Only time can do that," he said gently.

"Speaking of time and healing, I just thought of someone else for the dating list—"

"Stop. I've barely unpacked."

"Oh, pooh," she scoffed. "It's been a couple weeks. You have a duty to date someone."

Now he was getting frustrated. "Right back at you, sis. Who are you going out with? Do I know the guy?"

"I'm taking a break from men."

"Why?"

"I don't want to talk about it."

There was a story. Ben saw it in her eyes, but wouldn't

push. If he set a good example, maybe she'd back off, too. "Okay. So you understand where I'm coming from."

"Not really. You've had a very long break," she started.

He barely held back a groan. She was like a bulldog with a favorite bone. How long would it take before she decided to let this go? He wasn't opposed to dating, just wanted to do it in his own time, his own way.

He would go out when he met someone who intrigued him as much as Camille Halliday.

With a four-inch heel in each hand, Cam walked out of the bedroom into her suite's sitting area. All the bigger, more expensive lodge rooms were on the top floor and she liked living here a lot. It was big, a convenient distance to work and the mattress was soft and comfy. Love seats covered in earth-tone stripes faced each other in front of the fireplace. There was a small kitchen and a cherrywood table in the dining area.

She stopped in front of the mirror over a small table in the entryway for a last check on her appearance before starting the day.

"Hair?" She nodded with satisfaction. "Check."

Something about the water here in Montana brought out the best in her shoulder-length layered style.

"Makeup? Check." It was flawless. She had the money to buy good skin care products and cosmetics and had paid big bucks for a professional makeup artist to teach her the techniques for perfect application.

"Clothes? Dressed for success." She loved this lavender suit with the pencil skirt and fitted matching jacket. The heels matched perfectly.

"It's Tuesday," she reminded herself. "Maybe today I'll get staff cooperation. And maybe I'll flap my arms and fly to the moon."

All those power of positive thinking seminars had been a waste of time for this exile in Blackwater Lake. So far the information and methods hadn't achieved any measurable real-life results.

She was about to slip her heels on when shouting in the hallway shattered the silence in her room. "It's too early for this," she groaned. "Rocky and Apollo Creed couldn't make it just one day without going a couple of rounds?"

Cam opened her door and hurried into the carpeted hall barefoot. Patty Evans and Crystal Ames, a housekeeping team on the staff, stood two inches apart, shouting into each other's faces. They were in their early thirties and about the same height, which made them quite a bit taller than Cam, but she couldn't spare the time for her shoes.

She tried to get between them, but they pretty much ignored her. "Ladies, this is unprofessional."

"Stop flirting with him." Patty's hair curved under in a brown bob. She wore the black pants and gray, fitted smock shirt that was the department uniform.

A honey blonde, Crystal had her hair held back with a big clip. "I wasn't flirting. Just being friendly. You're paranoid." She waved her index finger in the other woman's direction. "And you need your head examined."

"There's nothing wrong with my head," Patty retorted. "I know what I saw. You always want what's mine."

"You're imagining things." Crystal moved even closer.

Patty lifted her chin defensively. "Stay away from Scooter."

Someone named Scooter was worth coming to blows? Cam had to break this up. The most expensive lodge rooms were nearby. Unprofessional behavior like this was inappropriate anywhere, but especially here. Social media being what it was, negative information could go viral on the internet and she had enough problems without that.

"Ladies—" She put a hand on each of their shoulders and used gentle pressure to move them back an inch or two. "That will be enough."

Patty's blue eyes blazed. "It's not nearly enough. Not until she backs off my boyfriend."

"How many times do I have to say this? I'm not coming on to him." Crystal jammed her hands on her hips. "You've got quite an imagination. Get over it."

"Stop it." Cam raised her voice which she hated to do, but a sharp slap to snap them out of it wasn't an option. "This is unacceptable—"

A door opened behind them. "Hi."

Cam held in a groan. It was only one word, but she knew that deep voice. Before she could turn and respond, the two housekeepers relaxed their combative body language.

"Hey, Ben." Patty smiled. "I heard you were back in town and staying here."

"It's been a while." Ben was wearing surgical scrub pants with a long-sleeved white shirt beneath the matching shapeless blue top. "How are you, Patty? Crystal?"

The blonde flashed him a flirty smile. "Fine. How've you been?"

"Good. It's great to be back."

"We should get together for a drink and catch up."

He nodded. "After work some time."

"Sounds good." Patty looked at her partner. "Speaking of that, we've got to get busy."

"Right. Catch you later, Ben."

"Have a good one." He returned their wave before the two women moved down the hall to where the housekeeping cart was pushed against the wall.

"I'm sorry you had to see that," Cam said.

"I actually didn't see anything. Hearing is a different

story." He leaned a shoulder against the doorjamb that was right next to hers. "Are you still in trouble?"

"Tip of the iceberg. Those two are on a very long list of employees who do their own thing."

"So, that's a yes to trouble?" His dark eyes sparkled with humor, no doubt the memory of the other night on the deck.

"It is," she admitted.

"Are you going to kick something?" When he looked down at her bare feet, his gaze turned decidedly, intensely sexy and suggestive.

"No. It was a lesson. I'll use my words. Right after I get my shoes." Every time she saw him it felt like a power struggle and she didn't like feeling at a disadvantage. She also didn't like the little shimmy in her heart when his eyes went all hot and smoldery. That couldn't be good. "I have to get to work."

"Don't let me keep you."

She nodded, then looked up. "And Ben?"

"Hm?"

"I'd consider it a personal favor if you forgot about the little disagreement. I really am sorry you had to see that and I intend to talk to them." For the umpteenth time. If only she could promise him it wouldn't happen again.

Ben glanced down the empty hall where the two women had been. "I take it Patty and Crystal don't get along?"

There was no point in denying what he'd just witnessed for himself. "I referee practically on a daily basis." Then his words sank in. "You know their names."

"We went to high school together."

"I see." Small-town life, she reminded herself. "They're good at their jobs. When not arguing."

"Those two haven't gotten along since Crystal stole

Patty's boyfriend before prom and she missed the highlight of high school."

Cam wouldn't know. Her teen years had been erratic
and traditional school wasn't in her frame of reference.
"That's good information."

"I've noticed that housekeepers here at the lodge work
in teams."

"It's efficient."

He nodded. "I know what you said about personnel
turnover and the cost of training. Obviously you feel it's
important to retain those two. So it might be a good idea
to split them up."

"It crossed my mind, but I've been working in—what
did you call it? Triage? Dealing with the most important
things first. Operating in crisis mode."

The longer Cam stood looking up at him, the more she
noticed how handsome he was. How easy he was to talk
to. How good he smelled. How safe he made her feel.

That was something she hadn't felt since losing her big
brother when he was only nineteen. Since then men had
come on to her, using her to get their name in the paper.
Famous by association. But there was something trustworthy about Ben.

He folded his arms over his chest. "You should be used
to crisis mode."

His voice was pleasant and teasing, but her stomach
dropped at the words. It had been too much to hope for.
"Why?"

"Your tabloid history is pretty colorful."

"So you know about that."

"I Googled you."

"That's a lot of information to wade through." Disappointment sat like a stone in her gut.

"Not so much after you went to jail."

It was hard, but she managed not to wince. She would never be able to erase her infamous past and the lies that were part of it. She knew the truth and could set the record straight, but she couldn't make him believe it.

"Being in a cell, even segregated from the general population, was more scary than I can tell you. I was grateful for early release and determined not to go back. Ever. I returned to college."

"Coincidentally, that was about the time all the stories dried up."

"Photographers still stalked me, waiting for a screwup to document and sell papers. But I was more determined to get an education and have a career. Accomplish something. Do more than be famous for being famous."

"Good for you."

Right. The words sounded supportive, but she knew better. Everyone wanted something.

"I really have to get to work," she said.

"Me, too." He straightened and looked down at her. "I'd like to see you later."

"That's not a good idea." The door to her suite was right next to his and she headed for it now. Over her shoulder she said, "Have a wonderful day."

In her room she leaned against the closed door and dragged in air. Since college the nice guys had shunned her. Classes, studying and getting exemplary grades were all she had. The loneliness and isolation hurt deeply, but she'd learned valuable lessons. She needed a solid, successful career because that would be all she had, all she could count on.

It was time to focus on that career. Making Blackwater Lake Lodge into a lucrative property in the family hotel chain was her ticket out of this town. It would get her away from the handsome, sexy doctor who was nothing more than another nice guy who wouldn't want to bring her home to meet his family.

## *Chapter Three*

Ben McKnight had never pictured himself as a Chamber of Commerce sort of guy, but here he was at the monthly Blackwater Lake meeting. He'd been interested in hearing Mayor Loretta Goodson's plans for growing the community, expanding Mercy Medical Clinic and eventually building a hospital here in town. Being in on that project from the beginning was one of the reasons he'd come back. Blending the best and newest medicine with a small-town, hands-on approach was exciting and rewarding.

Apparently he wasn't the only one interested in long-term planning. It was a standing-room-only crowd in the council chamber here at City Hall.

"I think we've thoroughly covered all the information about the architect hired to draw up the plans for the Mercy Medical Clinic expansion. The town council and I liked the work she showed us, but she also has the lowest fee. McKnight Construction will be doing the building. Is there any further business or questions?" The mayor, an attractive woman who looked thirty but was probably ten years older, glanced around the room. Her shoulder-length, layered brown hair caught the overhead light as she turned her head. She smiled, but it didn't quite reach her gray eyes. "All right, seeing no raised hands, that concludes the meeting. There are refreshments in the back. Thank you for coming, everyone."

Almost instantly chair legs scraped and talking commenced as people stood and filed out of the room or to the table filled with coffee and dessert.

Ben had been at the clinic late setting a patient's broken arm and barely made it to the meeting. With no time to eat, he was starving. After grabbing a couple cookies and a brownie, he looked around. Against the wall he noticed Cabot Dixon, an old high school friend, talking to the pretty redhead who owned the marina store on the lake and was engaged to Adam Stone, the family-practice doctor at the clinic. He moved toward them and Cabot grinned.

"I heard you were back in town, Ben."

"Good to see you, Cab." He set his coffee on the seat of a chair and shook the other man's hand.

"Do you know Jill Beck?"

"I do. How's that little guy of yours?" Ben had met them at the clinic when they visited Adam at work.

"C.J. is great." Her blue eyes glowed with pride and pleasure. "Adam is keeping an eye on him tonight. Tyler's there, too."

"How old is that boy of yours, Cab?"

"Seven. Can't believe it. I remember when he was hardly bigger than my hand and I was trying to figure out which end to put the diaper on and which one to feed."

"You've done a great job," Jill said, "because he's healthy and happy."

"It was one day at a time, one crisis at a time." He shook his head at the memories. "Seems like yesterday he was a toddler."

"I look forward to seeing him. Preferably not at the clinic."

"From your mouth to God's ear," the man said fervently.

Ben knew Cabot had been married and his wife took off right after the baby's birth. Apparently, in addition to a husband and newborn son, small-town life wasn't her thing. And speaking of that... In his peripheral vision he noticed a flash of red. Camille Halliday was a few feet away from the refreshment table, by herself and holding a cup of coffee. She stood out like a fly in milk.

The people in this room were dressed in denim and flannel. Mayor Goodson had on a navy blue blazer with her jeans to negotiate the line between casual and professional. There was an occasional pair of khakis, and Ben was in scrubs, but that was as formal as anyone got.

Cam was wearing a stylishly short, snug skirt and fitted red jacket with a ruffle at the waist. Her four-inch red come-and-get-me heels made her legs look longer than he thought they were and shapely enough to make his fingers tingle to know for sure.

Jill must have noticed where he was looking. "Camille Halliday is prettier in person that she is in photographs."

"I'll have to take your word." Ben forced himself to look away. He took a chocolate chip cookie from his plate and bit into it. After chewing and swallowing he said, "I've never seen pictures of her."

"Really?" The redhead looked surprised. "She's been all over magazines and tabloid news."

"I've been busy." He shrugged. "Barely put it together when I met her at the lodge. I'm staying there until I build my house."

"I'd steer clear of her." Cabot's eyes were dark with suspicion.

"Have you met her?"

"No. And that's fine with me."

"I can't help wondering what she's doing in Blackwater Lake." Jill sipped her coffee. "It's painfully obvious that she doesn't fit in here."

Ben noticed that people were looking curiously at her, but no one ventured over. She looked a little lost and the stubborn lift of her chin said she was trying not to be.

"I'm going to talk to her," he said.

"Bad idea." Cabot shook his head in warning.

"Why?"

"She's way out of your league."

"That would be a problem if I were looking for something serious." He already knew that was a waste of time, because the lady had her sights set on bigger and more high-profile than here. "But there's no harm in being friendly."

"Yes, there is." His friend looked like he'd rather take a sharp stick in the eye.

"I'd go with you and introduce myself," Jill said, "but I have to get home. Although I'm sure Adam has everything under control."

"And I have to pick up Ty and get him home. It's a school night. And I'm your ride," Cabot reminded her.

"That, too."

"Okay, then. I'll see you guys later."

Cabot's expression was filled with fraternal sympathy. "You're a braver man than I am."

Ben laughed and said his goodbyes, then picked up his coffee and dropped his empty dessert plate in the trash before heading in Cam's direction.

There was relief in her eyes when he stopped in front of her. "Hi, Ben."

"Cam." He sipped cold coffee. "How are you?"

"Fine."

He hadn't seen her since yesterday morning when she'd broken up the housekeeping hostilities. "Is there a cease-fire at the lodge?"

"For Crystal and Patty there is." That implied not so much with the rest of the staff. "I paired them with other people. They weren't happy, but I pulled rank."

"I think it was General Colin Powell who said that to be an effective leader, sometimes you have to tick people off."

"I'd just settle for a little respect," she said ruefully.

Ben wondered at the twinge of protectiveness he felt. This big-city girl was more than capable of looking after herself. Rich, beautiful and experienced, according to the press. But there was a look in her eyes, an expression that said she was a little out of her depth.

"So, what are you doing here?" he asked.

"I already told you—making the lodge profitable."

"No, I meant why did you come to the Chamber of Commerce meeting?"

"Oh." She shrugged and what that small movement did to her breasts in that tight-fitting jacket should be illegal. "I thought it couldn't hurt to be here to see other business owners in action. Maybe it would spark marketing ideas in the mountain milieu. Promotion strategies for increasing spring and summer bookings. And get a jump on fall and holiday reservations."

"Throw everything at the wall and see what sticks," he agreed.

"Pretty much." She tossed her half-empty cup in the trash beside the table. "I like Mayor Goodson. She's smart to open up some of the town's property for sale and development."

"Maybe. It's going to be a juggling act, though. Growing, but not so fast that we lose the qualities that make life here special."

"Bigger means more people can enjoy special."

"Not always," he disagreed.

"For the sake of argument… Didn't the mayor say that as far as health care escalation goes, right now a grant for the money to add on to Mercy Medical Clinic is the best she can do? An actual hospital needs enough of a population to support it. Bigger would be better for everyone."

"That's true. As much as I'd like to see it built, going too big too fast makes for a weak foundation that won't support the existing residents. Everything collapses."

She opened her mouth to say something, but before any words came out the lights went off and on. He looked around and noticed there were only a few people left in the room.

"I think they're throwing us out," he said.

"Looks that way." She took a cell phone from the small purse hanging by a handle from her wrist. "I need to call a cab."

"You don't have a car?"

"Not one with four working tires. I had a flat. The good news is I noticed before leaving the lodge parking lot."

That meant she took a cab here. "I'm surprised you went to the trouble of showing up."

"I didn't want to miss the meeting."

Anything and everything possible to get the job done and move on, he thought. He'd moved on, made his mark, and when he did it felt as if something was missing. They said you could find anything in Las Vegas, but that wasn't true for him. Contentment couldn't be bought at a high-end store on the Strip. But clearly Cam had things to do, places to go. Except right now she didn't have the wheels to get there.

She started to press numbers on her phone. To call a cab.

"I'll drive you back to the lodge," he said.

"I can't ask you to do that."

"There was no asking involved. I offered. Seems silly to pay for a ride when we're both going to the same place."

She smiled for the first time and it was like sunshine. "I'd appreciate that very much. Thanks."

"Okay." He pointed to the rear exit. "I'm in the back lot."

They walked side by side through the room and outside. His Mercedes SUV was one of the last cars there. He pressed the button on his keys to unlock the doors and the lights flashed.

"Nice car," she said.

"Thanks. I like it." He opened the passenger door for her.

She hesitated, obviously wondering how to get in without flashing the goods. He was going to hell but couldn't stop the anticipation coiling inside while he waited for her to maneuver up and in with that short skirt.

"Thank goodness for running boards," she said.

Lifting one foot, she stepped on it and took the hand hold just inside, then settled her butt on the seat. She swung her legs in and reached for the seat belt.

Ben hadn't seen much more than everyone at the Chamber of Commerce meeting. Maybe a couple extra inches of bare thigh, but that was it. Disappointment snaked through him along with a growing desire to see what she looked like out of that chic suit clinging to every curve. That wasn't likely and it was the kind of regret a guy would carry for a long time.

"Nicely done, Miss Halliday."

"Thank you, Dr. McKnight."

He shut the door and walked around to the driver's side, then got in and started the car. A few minutes later he parked at the lodge and they walked into the lobby with its big stone fireplace, cushy leather couch and chairs and the reception desk off to one side. When he started for the elevator, he assumed she'd be coming, too. Their rooms were side by side.

"This is where I say good-night."

"You're not going up?" he asked.

"Later. Work to do."

When she shrugged, he felt a stab of desire shoot straight through him. "It's late."

"I know." She smiled and it was a little tattered around the edges. "But thanks to you, I'm back earlier than expected. I appreciate the lift. Good night, Ben."

"Sweet dreams." He watched the unconsciously sensuous sway of her hips and heard the click of her heels as she walked away and knew his dreams would be anything *but* sweet. Then he thought of something. "Cam?"

She turned. "Yes?"

"My father owns an automotive repair shop in town and my sister works there. I'll have her check out your tire."

"That would be great. My Mercedes is in the employee lot, and probably the only car there with a flat tire. Just have her let me know the cost."

"Will do. Don't work too late," he cautioned.

"Okay." She walked into her office behind the registration desk and shut the door.

The two of them couldn't be more different, but that didn't stop Ben from wanting her. It seemed to get more intense every time he saw her and she worked where he lived. She'd spend the night right next door. It was just a damn shame that she wouldn't be in his bed.

\* \* \*

"Hello?"

Cam looked up from the spreadsheet on her computer monitor when the voice from the registration desk outside the office door drifted to her. In a perfect world there would be a front-desk clerk on duty, but her world wasn't perfect. She was getting used to that particular customer tone, a combination of surprise and annoyance that they'd been waiting longer than necessary for someone to check them into the hotel.

"Damn it, Mary Jane—" Cam had been through this too many times not to know the woman had abandoned her post yet again.

She hurried out and plastered a big friendly smile on her face. A man was standing there and did a slight double take.

"Hi, there," she said. "I hope you haven't been waiting too long."

"A few minutes." He was alone, in his early forties, balding and twenty pounds overweight. He didn't look irritated, which was a good thing.

Cam's motto was never give the customer a reason not to come back. "How can I help you?"

"I'd like to check in."

"Of course. What's the name?"

"Stan Overton."

She pulled up the reservations screen on the computer. "Here you are. Three nights?"

"That's right." He wasn't much taller than she. "Would there be a problem extending my stay?"

If only, she thought. "Not at all. We'd be happy to take care of that for you."

"Great." He glanced around the lobby. "I've never been

to Montana before and I might want to hang around longer."

"I'm sure you're going to love it here." She pressed some keys and pulled up his information. "What brings you to Blackwater Lake?"

"A combination of business and pleasure," he said vaguely.

"Did you want to use the same credit card?"

"Yes." He pulled out his wallet and handed it over. "Have you been in town long?"

It felt like forever. But she wondered why he would ask. Was "greenhorn" tattooed on her forehead? "Long enough to appreciate how special it is."

"What's your favorite restaurant?"

"I could be prejudiced, but the best place in town is the five-star restaurant right here at the lodge. The chef is from New York."

The man leaned an elbow on the high desk that separated them. "What do you like to do here? On your day off, I mean?"

"What's a day off?" She hoped he would take the remark in a teasing way, but it wasn't a joke.

"I know what you mean." He laughed. "But what I'm asking is if you only had a short amount of time here, what would you see?"

"The lake is beautiful. I'm told the fishing is good." She printed out a summary of the hotel's daily room rate and policies. "I'll need your signature and if you could initial the places I indicated…"

"Sure thing." He scrawled an indecipherable name. "I did some research on the Net and what I found said there are hiking trails and places to camp. Is there any place you would go? Somewhere not to be missed?"

Now she was starting to get irritated. Was he just

friendly or hitting on her? That was just... Ew. Or maybe he didn't get out much. The worst thing anyone in hospitality could do was to show impatience.

"To be honest, I can't recommend any outdoor activities from personal experience. But we have a variety of brochures and the concierge desk is right across the lobby. Dustin would be happy to help you. One key or two?"

"One."

She put it in a folder and handed over the packet and receipt. "Third floor. The elevators are right around the corner." Forcing a charm into her smile that she didn't feel, she said, "If there's anything the staff can do to make your stay more pleasant, don't hesitate to ask."

"Thanks. It's starting out great." He nodded and walked away.

Cam let out a breath and saw Mary Jane Baxter rush around the corner. She stopped short for a second, then just looked guilty.

"I just left for a minute, Miss Halliday. I didn't think I'd be missed."

"You never do."

"I'm sorry."

That statement should have been followed by something along the lines of it would never happen again. Cam was just about to the point of making sure it didn't. "Mr. Overton just checked in. Would you please finish up the paperwork?"

"Of course."

The woman handled people and paperwork flawlessly—when she was there. The disappearing without a word was a chronic problem and needed to be managed, but not when Cam was this angry.

"Are you going to be here for a while?"

"I—" She nodded.

"Good. I'm going to take a fifteen-minute break."

Cam turned on her heel and headed for the exit and the rear of the property. Breathing deeply of the clean, fresh air, she climbed the wooden stairs up to the second-floor deck. Her serenity spot. She looked down at the green grass and beautiful flowering plants in the fast-growing shadows. It was six o'clock and the sun had disappeared behind the mountains, taking the warmth with it, and that was just as well. She needed to cool off.

Just as the irritation started to dissolve, she heard the sound of footsteps, heavy ones. A man's walk. There was someone behind her.

"You look ready for a knock-down, drag-out with that railing, but I don't recommend it."

Ben. The corners of her mouth turned up, which was a minor miracle. She turned. "And yet again you're trespassing."

"I saw you at the registration desk, but you were gone before I could flag you down."

"So… Stalking?" She lifted one eyebrow.

"More of a house call. Someone to use your words with."

"McKnight in shining armor strikes again."

"You look like someone broke the heel off your favorite shoe. What's up?"

"Same old thing. Personnel insubordination." She leaned an elbow on the railing. "My clerk at the registration desk disappeared again."

"Again?"

"I know employees are entitled to breaks. That's not a problem; someone is assigned to cover the desk for a scheduled break. But with her it's chronic, unscheduled disappearances. Every two hours she's gone without a word. It's flaky and irresponsible. And I might have to let her go."

"That doesn't sound like Mary Jane Baxter."

"You know her?" She should stop being surprised by that.

"From high school. The blessing and curse of a small town." He shrugged. "She was student body president. Smart, efficient. Every two hours?"

"Like clockwork," she confirmed.

He looked thoughtful. "Now that you mention it, I recall that she's hypoglycemic."

"Can you dumb that down for those of us who didn't go to med school?"

"Her blood sugar dips and she needs to eat regularly."

"So it's a recognized medical condition?"

"Yeah."

"I'm not a monster who'd keep her chained to her post until she passes out. I can be fair, but only if I know what the problem is." Cam threw up her hands in exasperation. "Why didn't she say something?"

"Maybe it's famous heiress intimidation syndrome. All the symptoms are there."

"I'm a very nice person," she defended.

"Then try talking to her like one."

Cam thought about it and nodded. "Can't hurt. Thanks for the suggestion."

"You're welcome."

Now that she was calmer, she remembered that he'd planned to flag her down. "Was there something you wanted?"

"Yeah." For just an instant intensity darkened his eyes and then disappeared. "My sister checked out your tires."

"And?"

"They're practically new and she couldn't find any damage. No evidence of puncture, but the cap was missing.

Syd's guess is that someone deliberately let the air out." He frowned. "Probably a prank."

"Is it still considered a prank when a disgruntled employee does it?" Her sigh had an awful lot of defeat in it.

Obviously Ben noticed because he slung an arm across her shoulders. "They'll come around. Give it time."

She leaned into him for a moment, soaking up the comfort he offered. Again he made her feel safe, made her miss her big brother. He'd taken care of her in a way her father never had and she missed him every single day. But Ben wasn't her brother and a hum of awareness vibrated through her that suddenly didn't feel safe at all.

She pulled away from him. "It's been almost three months and things here at the lodge are worse than ever. In my experience, people either don't like me or they pretend to be my friend in order to get something from me."

"Betrayal leaves a mark."

She wasn't going to confirm or deny. "What do I owe your sister?"

"Nothing. She took it to the shop and put air in the tire then brought it back."

"A house call?"

He shrugged. "Call it public relations. If anyone here at the lodge needs a good mechanic, put in a good word."

"Okay. Please give her my thanks and tell her that I appreciate what she did very much." She started toward the stairs. "My break is over."

She didn't want it to be over because being with Ben felt like a sanctuary.

"I'll see you around," he said.

Not really a good idea. He was right about betrayal. The mark it left on her was about not being able to trust anyone. Ever. That wasn't much of a problem here, since everyone fell in the hating her camp. So that made her wonder why the hometown hero was the only one in town being nice to her.

# Chapter Four

"I put a patient in exam room one. And I use the term *patient* loosely, if you know what I mean."

Ben looked at the disgusted expression on nurse Ginny's face and was afraid he did know what she meant. It was another single woman faking a sprained ankle or wrist or something else as an excuse to put the moves on him.

"Does she have a casserole?"

Ginny grinned, a sign she was enjoying this way too much. "Yes."

"Okay. Is there a chart?"

"Uh-huh." She handed it over. "The home phone number is highlighted and underlined and asterisked."

He looked at the paperwork inside the manila folder. Cherri Lyn Hoffman. Twenty-five. Worked in accounting at the Blackwater Lake power company. Single. Discomfort in right ankle. "Well, I guess we should see what's wrong with her."

"Or not." Ginny headed down the hall to the break room. "Aren't you coming with me?"

"You're a big boy. I think you can handle this." She kept walking, then turned into the last room and disappeared.

Ben sighed as he knocked once on the exam room door. "Miss Hoffman?"

"Come in."

He did. In this Victorian house donated to the town and turned into a clinic, the rooms were bigger. There was a sink in the corner and walls filled with charts and posters. One for nutrition, with portions of fruit and vegetables dominating. Another was a skeleton with bones labeled.

The patient was sitting on the paper-covered exam table with her legs dangling. Brown hair fell to her shoulders and teased the tight white T-shirt. Some shiny stuff sparkled on the front of it. A denim skirt the size of a postage stamp hit her just below the curve of her thigh and barely covered her…assets.

He left the door open, then went to the sink to wash his hands. "Hi, Miss Hoffman. I'm Dr. McKnight."

"Please, call me Cherri."

*And you can call me Dr. McKnight,* he thought, but couldn't say it. "What seems to be the problem?"

"I think I twisted my ankle."

"Let me take a look." He sat on the rolling stool and moved toward her, and the very high heels she was wearing. That was the first clue she was faking. He looked at both legs. "Which one hurts?"

"The left."

He looked in the chart where Ginny had noted that, per the patient, the injury was to the right ankle. "I don't see any swelling or trauma."

Cherri stuck her leg out. "Maybe you can feel something."

He could feel it was a sham without touching her or looking at an X-ray. "Why don't you walk across the room for me?"

"All right."

She slid to the step at the end of the table, then stepped to the floor with an exaggerated wince as her right leg took her weight. Turning toward the doorway, she limped on the right leg. After a pivot she came back and favored the opposite side before stopping at the exam table next to him.

She blinked her big blue eyes. "What do you think, Doctor?"

God, he hated this. Several times a week this happened. He wanted to tell her not to waste his time. This wasn't a game and he wouldn't order needless diagnostic tests or prescribe medication for a nonexistent condition. But he was a professional and couldn't say any of that.

"I don't think it's serious." He kept his tone neutral with an effort. "When it bothers you, take over-the-counter medication for pain. Elevate it and alternate cold and heat."

"Thank you. I'm so relieved it's nothing serious."

It *was* serious, but not in a way she would understand. He stood and headed for the door. "All right, then. Have a good day."

"Wait." She moved quickly to stop him. "Don't I need to see you again? Another appointment? Or something?"

"No. I'm sure you'll be fine."

She lifted a covered casserole dish from the chair next to the door beside her purse. "This is for you. I thought you being a bachelor and a busy doctor that you might like something home-cooked."

"Thank you." He took it but couldn't manage a smile. "Goodbye."

"Are you going to call me? To see how I'm doing?"

"I'm sure you're fine."

Before she could stop him again, he walked out, down the hall to the break room. Once safely inside, he shut the door. There was a refrigerator on the wall beside it and he opened the freezer, then shoved the food in with the five or six others there. The fridge was running out of room.

Ginny was sitting at the oak table having a cup of coffee. "We usually leave that door open."

"I know." If only it had a lock.

"Are you hiding?"

"Damn straight," he said.

"How'd it go with Cherri Lyn?"

"Same as always. Couldn't keep the limp consistent." He leaned back against the counter. "That's actually a good thing, because otherwise it would have been tempting to order unnecessary X-rays just to be sure."

Ginny's blue eyes sparked with mischief. "So, are you going to call her?"

"Of course not. What she did is inherently dishonest. You can never trust someone like that."

Talking about trust made him think of Cam, who clearly had issues with it. As far as he could tell her checkered past was isolated in her rebellious youth. Anyone should get a pass on that. Now she seemed straightforward and sincere. He couldn't picture her faking a medical problem. In fact, he'd seen her do a number on her foot and refuse to let him look it over. He wouldn't mind seeing her any time, for any reason. Or no reason.

He looked at Ginny. "I'm losing my patience."

"From where I'm sitting, patients of the female persuasion are on the rise here at Mercy Medical Clinic."

"You know what I mean." He snapped out the words, then drew in a deep cleansing breath. "Sorry. But I'm really frustrated with this situation. This is a medical facility, not a speed-dating event. I have a professional reputation to maintain."

"You've got a reputation, and being a doctor is only part of it. The other part is bachelor."

"You're enjoying this, aren't you?"

"Yes." She grinned.

"Well, that makes one of us. The thing is, it could be dangerous. What if I blow someone off who really has a medical issue because of all the women who are faking it?"

"They shouldn't have to fake it if you're doing it right."

"Ginny—" he warned.

"All right." She held up her hands in surrender. "This is the thing. It's your own fault."

"Mine?" That hit a nerve. "What did I do?"

"How can I put this delicately?" She thought for several moments. "Tough love time. And I do love you. A doctor who isn't married and doesn't have a girlfriend is fair game for every marriage-minded woman or matchmaking mother within a five-hundred-mile radius of Blackwater Lake."

"God help me." He shook his head. "And there's no immunization?"

"Nope."

"So, you're saying I need a wife?"

"Or steady girlfriend."

"That's just wrong," he said.

"Are you gay?"

"No."

"Confirmed bachelor?" she persisted.

"Not exactly."

"Then, what exactly are you?"

"Just a guy who wants this to stop."

"Then you need to hook up with someone so the women will leave you alone."

"I haven't met anyone to go out with." No one except Cam Halliday and she'd only be around another few months. She was leaving town.

And just like that he realized she would be perfect. It wouldn't exactly be faking it, not if she knew exactly what was going on.

The best part was that no one would get hurt.

*Try talking to her like a very nice person.* Cam recalled Ben's advice as she waited for the employee in question. When she heard the knock on her office door, she swiveled her chair away from the computer and called out, "Come in."

She hoped Ben was right about this, because so far nothing had worked. Her role model had taught her the scare-the-crap-out-of-employees style of management. Her father had managed family the same way.

The door opened and Mary Jane Baxter took a hesitant step forward. She was a very attractive blonde in her early thirties, with blue eyes and square black glasses. "You wanted to see me, Ms. Halliday?"

"Yes. Thanks for coming, Mary Jane." She folded her hands on her desk. "There's something I'd like to talk to you about."

"All right."

"Please shut the door. And have a seat," she added.

The woman's expression said she was terrified, but she did as instructed and they faced each other across the desk. But Mary Jane's leg was moving nervously and she looked everywhere but at Cam.

What would Ben do to put her at ease? Probably ask a personal question.

"How long have you worked here at Blackwater Lake Lodge?"

"Almost eight months."

"Are you married?"

"Yes."

"Children?"

"Yes." Mary Jane almost smiled. "A girl and a boy."

"That's really nice. Are they in school?"

"When the youngest, my daughter, started first grade, I decided to go back to work."

The woman still looked tense enough to snap in two. What else could she try? Mary Jane was already scared, so maybe it would be effective to do the exact opposite of her father. Take down the barriers.

Cam stood, rounded the desk and sat in the other chair beside her employee. *And stop keeping her in suspense.* "I might as well come to the point. We need to talk about your unscheduled breaks from the registration desk. Because that's the first place our guests see, there really needs to be someone behind it at all times to greet and take care of the customer."

"I know." Mary Jane twisted her fingers together in her lap. "My husband was laid off recently. I really need this job."

"You're good at it. When you're there, your performance is exemplary. Efficient. Friendly. And you have a fantastic way of calming down the most irate customer. My issue is with you disappearing."

"It won't happen again. Really, Ms. Halliday—"

Cam held up a hand. "The thing is, I was talking to Ben McKnight and he mentioned that you need to eat every two hours for health reasons."

"I can't believe he remembers that." Her leg stopped moving. "It's true. I get lightheaded if I don't have something regularly."

"Is there a reason you don't keep snacks at the desk?"

For just a second there was a wry look in her blue eyes. "There's a company rule against it."

"A stupid rule. Fortunately I can do something about that." Cam tapped her lip thoughtfully. "Keep whatever you need in a drawer. Obviously if a customer is there, don't grab a handful of cheese puffs, but you already know that. In a discreet way, do what you need to do to take care of yourself. I can't afford to lose you."

"Really?"

"I wouldn't say it if I didn't mean it." Cam figured she had nothing to lose by putting it all out there. Again, the opposite of Dean Halliday Senior. "This hotel is in financial trouble."

"There were rumors," the other woman admitted.

"I'm here to turn things around. Part of that hinges on employee retention. Training is expensive and time-consuming. If I can't do what I'm supposed to, the property will be closed down or sold. A lot of jobs will be in jeopardy. Maybe I shouldn't say anything, but the situation is serious."

Mary Jane nodded. "Not knowing what's going on is the worst. Thanks for being honest. I appreciate it."

"So, we're okay and on the same page? Just to make it clear, if you need to leave the desk, for any reason, just let me or someone else know to cover you."

"Of course. Thanks, Ms. Halliday—"

"Please call me Cam."

"Okay. Cam. And I'm M.J." She smiled, a genuinely warm look.

It was the first friendly expression she'd seen in Blackwater Lake from anyone other than Ben. This talking like a nice person was working for her. And that made Cam wonder.

"Can I ask you, M.J., why you didn't just come and talk to me about this?"

"I was intimidated. You're the Halliday Hospitality heiress. Famous. And I'm just—me." She pushed her black glasses up more firmly on her nose. "I didn't want to ask for special treatment."

Cam smiled at the fact that Ben was right. "It's not special treatment from my point of view. Frankly, I'd rather have you on your feet than passed out behind the desk. Just be healthy. That's an order."

"Yes, ma'am." She saluted smartly.

Cam laughed. Since a fragile connection had been established, this might be her only chance to find out a little about her McKnight in shining armor. "Ben said he knew you in high school."

M.J. nodded. "And we went to college together. He could have gone out of state anywhere because his grades were scary good. But he didn't."

"Why?"

"Didn't want to leave his girlfriend. Judy Coulter." There was a sharp edge in her voice when she said the name. "For a smart guy, he was really stupid over her."

"Oh?"

"He'd been accepted to medical school in California and proposed to her so they could go together. She turned him down. Said she wasn't ready yet. Six months later she met a ski bum. Arrogant jerk talked about the Olympic team as if he'd made it. Said he was going to be a star and make a fortune in endorsements. She married *him*."

"Ouch." Poor Ben. What kind of idiot would turn her back on a man like him? "Did he take it hard?"

"I heard he nearly flunked out of med school." She shrugged. "But he didn't. And he got the last laugh."

"How's that?"

"The bum didn't make the Olympic team and Ben made a bundle on his medical practice in Las Vegas. He sold it before moving back here." M.J. smiled. "He really dodged a bullet."

"Sounds like it."

Cam couldn't help wondering if he felt that way. There was something about that first love. Not in her case, because no one had ever loved her for herself. It was the Halliday name and wealth that were the draw.

But that was old news. The good thing was she was doing girl talk and employee bonding. It felt good, really good. And she had Ben to thank for it. And she would.

"She moved back to Blackwater Lake a few months ago," M.J. added.

"His old girlfriend is here in town, too?"

The other woman nodded. "I haven't heard that they've seen each other, but it makes you wonder."

Yes, it did. But Cam couldn't afford to get sidetracked by stuff like that.

"I'm really glad we cleared the air, M.J." She stood and started for the door.

"Me, too."

"There's something I think you should know."

"What is it?" Cam met her gaze.

"The guest that you checked in. Mr. Overton. He's been asking the staff a lot of questions."

"Has he been inappropriate with them?" That's the last thing she needed.

M.J. shook her head. "Mostly he's been curious about you and your family."

"Most people are," Cam said. "But we're just people who put their pants on one leg at a time. Like everyone else."

"I just thought you should know. I have to get back."

She smiled at her employee. "Keep up the good work."

"Thanks, Cam."

After dinner in her suite, Cam was too excited to stay put and decided to get some air. She grabbed a sweater and went out in the hall, her gaze drawn to Ben's door. It was tempting to knock, but he was a paying customer and disturbing a guest's privacy was something a Halliday would never do.

She left the lodge by a rear entrance and walked up the back steps to her serenity spot. It was the first time since coming to Blackwater Lake that she'd come here when she didn't need to find her serenity. She was in the best mood and realized it was about possibilities. There were still mountains to climb and hurdles to get over, but those were for another day. This was a time to savor even minuscule progress.

At the top of the stairs, she automatically looked around for Ben. The last two times she'd been up here it was to get her temper under control when she'd had a bad day and he'd helped her do that. Today was a good day and things continued to go her way when she saw him in the same place he'd been the night he startled her.

"Hi," she said.

"Hey." There was no automatic grin or welcoming smile.

"I was hoping I'd see you." She walked closer.

"Oh?"

"Yes." She sat in the Adirondack chair beside his. The spotlight illuminated his expression and it wasn't happy. He looked a little broody. "What's wrong?"

"I'm trespassing. This time I've got a reason. I'm borrowing your serenity. I hope you don't need it tonight."

"I don't, actually. Bad day?" she asked.

"You could say that."

"Want to talk about it?"

He shook his head. "Not when you look like that."

"Like what?"

"Like you're *not* dying to kick the snot out of something." He settled his linked hands over his flat abdomen. "I was hoping I'd see you, too. There's something I'd like to talk to you about."

"What?"

"You first. Tell me why you're smiling from ear to ear."

"I took your advice," she said.

"Good for you. I'm glad it worked out. What advice would that be?"

"I talked to Mary Jane—M.J."

"What happened?"

"You were right. She was disappearing to eat because she couldn't have food at her desk. There's a company rule against doing that, so I made a unilateral decision to change the rule. Now she's going to keep snacks with her. The conversation went really well. You were right about something else, too. She *was* intimidated by me, but I think she's reassured now."

"I'm glad." He didn't sound glad. He sounded crabby.

Maybe she could cheer him up. "It's all because of you that we're okay now. Thanks for the suggestion. I owe you one."

"Funny you should say that." He looked at her and there was a spark in his eyes. "I have a favor to ask you."

"I'm in a really good mood. Ask away."

"I'd like you to be my pretend girlfriend."

## *Chapter Five*

Cam stared at him for several moments. Surely she must have heard wrong. "Did you just say you want me to be your *pretend* girlfriend?"

"Yes. What do you think?"

It was a good thing she was already sitting down. "I think I'll pretend you didn't just ask me that."

"Why?" He sat forward, all semblance of relaxation disappearing. Tension rolled off him in waves. "You said I was cute. And a good catch because I'm a doctor. Is there something wrong with me?"

"Not on the outside, but I'm thinking a psych evaluation might not be a bad idea."

"That's harsh. It's not like I asked you to run away and get married."

"For reasons I can't even begin to explain, that would be less shocking." She stared at him, waiting for the easy smile. Disturbing though it was, she would even prefer that hot, smoldery look in his eyes that made her a little weak in the knees. She didn't see either, just the frown indicating something was bothering him. "Tell me what's going on. You don't look like yourself, Ben."

"If only that were true."

"Stop being cryptic and—dare I say it?—a little sulky, a tad pouty. Tell me what the problem is."

"Okay." He met her gaze. "Women won't leave me alone."

She waited for more explanation or a punch line indicating that he was joking. Neither happened and she couldn't help it. She started laughing. When his expression grew more intense she said, "You can't be serious."

"Why not?"

"Because most men would give anything to have a problem like that."

"I'm not most men." Now he looked downright glum.

"Sorry." She got a grip on her grin and did her best to be as solemn as he was. "I agree that you're not most men."

"Why do you think so?" He gave her a sideways glance, a flicker of interest breaking up the gloom.

"For one thing, you're the only man in town who's even friendly to me."

"What else?"

"Talking to you about my problems actually made me feel better. And you had helpful, commonsense advice that was useful."

"It's not that big a deal." He shrugged it off.

"It is to me. Nothing about my childhood, family or internship for my father was normal, so practical is a new experience."

Dean Halliday Senior didn't understand a pragmatic, down-to-earth style of management because he'd never lived in that world. And neither had Cam until arriving in Blackwater Lake, Montana.

Ben rested his elbows on his knees. "Good to know."

"Okay. So. Now that I've boosted your ego to the breaking point, tell me what this is all about. Why is it a problem for you that women won't leave you alone?"

"If I was at The Watering Hole—"

"The what?"

"It's the local bar on Arrowhead Way and Buffalo Boulevard."

"Ah." She nodded. "I don't get out much, what with working all the time. You were saying?"

"If I was sitting at the bar and a woman started a conversation, I'd happily participate. It's public. It's expected. It's honest. It's a way to meet people."

The Fireside restaurant here at the lodge was public. Maybe it was just that all her life she'd endured photographers ambushing her wherever she went, whatever she was doing, because she'd been concerned that his privacy was violated when he'd been eating alone.

"So you didn't mind that strangers walked over while you were having dinner the other night and handed you their phone numbers?"

"No. I was fair game."

"So call one of them to be your pretend girlfriend. Or, and here's a novel suggestion, maybe a real girlfriend."

"Not a good idea."

"None of this is," she pointed out. "Seriously, Ben, this is like a wacky sitcom episode."

"I'm desperate." He looked it. "Women show up at the clinic with phony ankle injuries or holding their wrists. They're not particularly good at faking it and can't remember which limb is injured."

"Wow. What's the world coming to. No pride in lying anymore."

"Go ahead. Kick a guy when he's down." There was a flash of heat in his eyes but it wasn't lust. More like anger. He stood up. "I guess it was unrealistic to think you'd understand and take this seriously."

"Ben, think about it—"

"For what it's worth, walking in the other guy's shoes is good training when you're developing a management style."

When he started to walk away she surged to her feet and put a hand on his arm. "Don't go. Help me understand. Take me for a walk in your shoes. I'll be good." She held up her hand, palm out. "I swear."

He dragged his fingers through his hair. "Every woman in this town has a mother, grandmother, daughter, niece or friend of a friend and knows of someone I should meet."

"They're just looking out for you."

"More like marriage on their minds. It's like I have a duty to pick one. Even my sister is trying to fix me up."

"So let her." Cam wasn't a good candidate for this. She was damaged goods, so wrong for the hometown hero.

"Maybe I'm old-fashioned, but I want to be the one asking for a phone number when I'm ready."

To her it sounded more like he wanted to control the situation and that could have something to do with the high school sweetheart who threw him over for a ski bum. She could see where he'd be cautious, but that was a long time ago. He was too well-adjusted and normal now. Not to mention too smart and sophisticated not to have gotten over it. Maybe he was the stubborn kind who just didn't want to be told what to do, and wanted to make things happen in his own time, his own way.

"I get that. But—"

"Wait. There's more and it's what's really important."
His mouth pulled tight. "When someone comes in to the
clinic, I'm obligated to help. I've sworn an oath and this
ongoing scenario could potentially affect my ability to do
no harm."

"How?"

"These women are taking up appointment time, faking an orthopedic problem to get my attention. And they
bring food."

"The way to a man's heart—" She saw the warning look
and said, "Sorry. Go on."

"The situation is creating an atmosphere of doubt, for
me and the staff. If there's any question in my mind, I'm
bound by that oath to order diagnostic tests. X-rays. CAT
scan. MRI—magnetic resonance imaging. They're expensive and possibly unnecessary. Exposing someone to
needless radiation. Also, there's a very real possibility that
under these conditions a real medical condition could be
missed."

"Sort of like the boy who cried wolf so often, eventually no one listens."

"Exactly." He rested his hands on his hips. "On top of
that, it's disrespectful to the clinic, to me and to patients
who need my help."

"So say something to them."

He shook his head. "I will if necessary, but it's awkward. Especially if I'm wrong. I'm concerned about my
career. You can't understand what it's like to be a doctor,
but I know we share a common interest in doing the best
job possible."

He had her there. She'd told him about her ambitions
and what the stakes were for her. But that brought another
question to mind. One she'd sort of asked already.

"Okay, I see your dilemma." She recognized skepticism

in his expression and added, "Really. But why not ask one of the women who gave you a phone number? Why me?"

"Because they all live here in town and you're leaving."

Any flattery she might have felt at being asked just evaporated. *Be still my heart,* she thought. "I'm not sure what difference that makes."

"This is a small town. You can't keep up a pretense for long. The truth would come out and spread like the flu on crack."

"Secrets do have a way of not staying secret. What makes you so sure that would be any different with me?"

"Like I said—you're leaving. We both know that so neither of us would have unrealistic expectations. All the cards on the table. No one gets hurt."

"Okay. All sensible reasons. But here's a thought. When I'm gone, what are you going to do? When the whole thing starts all over again?"

"Good question." He nodded thoughtfully, as if that hadn't crossed his mind. "I could claim you broke my heart. Spread the word that I need space and a very long time to get over you."

"That could just throw kerosene on the fire. Women are nurturing by nature and would be absolutely convinced that they're the one who could take away your pain and rabid to do just that." She met his gaze and shrugged. "Just saying."

"I'm the new guy in town. A novelty. If I'm off the market for a while, maybe this intense interest will die down. An affair would take me off the radar."

Her heartbeat stuttered. "Since when did it become an affair?"

"Bad choice of words. I meant girlfriend."

"Title only?"

"As God is my witness." He blew out a breath. "Basically it will buy me time. If I'm wrong and things get out of hand after you're gone, I'll come up with a plan B."

If she agreed to this screwy dating bargain, the deck was stacked in his favor. He would get everything and she got nothing. Unless they really did have an affair. At least then they would have sex. It had been an awfully long time since she'd had sex. She couldn't speak for him, but a man as handsome as Ben probably hadn't gone without.

"So far this is all about you," she said. They were standing close together and she looked up at him. Way up. "Not to be too selfish, but what's in it for me?"

"Unfettered access to practical solutions to your personnel problems."

"And this is valuable to me—why?"

"Because I know these people. I grew up here. I can help you build a bridge over troubled waters."

"You've already done that out of the goodness of your own heart."

"I could clam up next time you seek out my advice." He shrugged. "A man's gotta do what a man's gotta do."

So he wasn't a true friend. He wanted something from the Halliday Hospitality heiress after all. Just like everyone else. Granted, his motive was more noble than most, and she suspected deep down this was partly about the woman who'd tossed him aside for a jerk. But still he wanted something. Except she'd sort of grown accustomed to talking with him and didn't want to slam the door on that. Another three months without a friendly face was an incredibly lonely proposition.

"You know this is completely nuts."

He looked surprised. "Does that mean you'll do it?"

"It means I'll think about it."

"Thank you."

He pulled her close for what she'd thought would be a

thank-you hug, but it wasn't. He kissed her. His lips were soft, warm, appealing. The touch lasted a shade longer than simple gratitude warranted and then he pulled away just before she melted against him.

"Have dinner with me tomorrow night and give me your answer." His voice sounded a little raspy, a little husky. "What do you say?"

"Okay, I guess."

But she would be crazy to agree to this. Ditto on looking forward to it.

At promptly six-thirty the next night, Ben left his suite at the Blackwater Lake Lodge and walked next door. He knocked and Cam opened up almost immediately, as if she'd been waiting.

"Hi."

"Are you ready?" he asked.

"As I'll ever be." There was a distinct wariness in her voice. Cam looked at his jeans, white shirt and sport coat. "Where are you taking me?"

"Don't make it sound so ominous. There's a nice little place in town called the Grizzly Bear Diner."

"Sounds kind of ominous to me. Am I overdressed?"

"You look beautiful." And that was an understatement. She took his breath away, which made no sense since she was wearing what she always did to work—a suit. The narrow skirt was lavender with a matching fitted jacket and she had on beige patent high heels. Her makeup was impeccable. There was nothing out of the ordinary in her appearance, so the shift in his awareness level must be coming from him. The more he'd thought about it in the last twenty-four hours, the more he really wanted her to say yes to his idea.

"Okay. Let's do this," he said.

She nodded, but he was pretty sure someone being led to the guillotine would look happier than she did.

They walked to his car in the parking garage and he handed her inside, then walked around to the driver's side and slid in behind the wheel. Ben backed the SUV out of the space and headed for the exit that would take them to downtown Blackwater Lake.

"Is there a reason we're not going to Fireside here at the lodge?" she asked.

He glanced over at her and smiled at her expression. "Yes."

When he didn't elaborate she said, "I'm guessing the food's not better. Best seven-layer chocolate cake in Montana. Just saying."

"It's not fine dining, if that's what you're asking. My criteria for tonight is a locals' favorite because it's always busy."

"I haven't agreed to this insane charade yet."

"I'm aware of that. But I think I can win you over."

"Pretty confident, aren't you?"

"Power of positive thinking." He grinned at her. "Plus, whatever your decision, being seen there together will keep everyone off balance, and that can't hurt."

"By 'everyone' you mean women."

"Men talk, too."

The signal light at the intersection of Main Street and Pine Way changed to green and Ben turned left into the parking lot. The diner was on the corner and the whole block was lined with businesses—Potter's Ice Cream Parlor, Tanya's Treasures, Al's Dry Cleaning. He parked and shut off the ignition, then got out and walked around to open the passenger door. Cam was just sliding out.

"You should know that I always open the door for a lady."

"Even a pretend girlfriend?"

"No exceptions." He thought for a moment and added, "Well, my sister."

"Because she works on cars?"

"No. She's my sister and that would just be weird."

Instead of the expected laugh, her forehead creased in a frown. "I wouldn't know."

"You don't have siblings?"

"Actually, I have a sister. My older brother died when he was nineteen."

"I'm sorry."

"Me, too."

He settled his palm at the small of her back and guided her to the front entrance of the Grizzly Bear Diner. It was Friday night and the place was packed.

They stopped at the podium displaying a sign that said "Please Wait to Be Seated." There was a young woman wearing a green collared shirt with a grizzly bear on the pocket. Her name tag said *Bev* and she was probably somewhere in her twenties. She looked Cam up and down but said nothing to her.

"Party of two?" she asked him.

"Yes."

Bev checked her clipboard. "It'll be about fifteen minutes."

"That's fine."

When he started to give his name Bev interrupted. "I know who you are, Dr. McKnight."

"Okay. This is Camille Halliday."

"I know who she is, too. But I didn't know you knew her. Go figure." But this time she nodded politely and said, "Nice to meet you, Miss Halliday."

"It's Cam." She slid him a glance and said, "Thanks. You, too."

People were waiting behind them, so they moved aside to clear the area. "So what do you think of the place?"

"The decoration clearly incorporates the diner's name and establishes a brand."

Ben glanced at the bear wallpaper, the laminated menus with grizzlies on the front and grizzlies tucked on the side of the greeter's podium. There was even a glass case with plastic bear toys and logo T-shirts and hats.

The bell over the door rang and a middle-aged man with a beer belly walked in. Cam smiled and nodded at him.

"Friend of yours?" he asked her.

"Stan Overton. He's a guest at the hotel. He's never been to Blackwater Lake before and was asking me about the sights."

"What did you tell him?"

"That I haven't been here long enough to see the sights," she said wryly.

"I'm guessing you didn't add that you don't intend to be here long enough."

She smiled up at him. "I kept that to myself."

The bell over the door rang again and Adam Stone walked in with a pretty redhead. He spotted his clinic coworker and smiled. "Hey, Ben." The family practice doctor did a double take when he noticed Ben was with Cam. Clearly he knew who she was. "You've met my fiancée, Jill."

"Nice to see you." Jill had grown up in Blackwater Lake but was younger and their paths hadn't crossed then.

"This is Camille Halliday."

"I didn't know you knew each other." Jill looked from Ben to her and smiled. "So, you're the competition."

Cam shook her hand. "Sorry?"

"I'm sort of in the hospitality business. I rent out the apartment above my house. Adam was my tenant when he first came to town last year. It's how we met." She looked a little self-conscious in the presence of the Halliday Hospitality heiress. "Bad comparison. No way I'd put you out of business."

"I'm relieved to hear that."

Cam flashed a charming smile that would fool the general public but Ben knew better. Jill's rental apartment wasn't really competition, but Cam was concerned about the property's future in a less than robust economy.

"Do you two want to join us?" Adam asked.

Ben met Cam's gaze and shook his head. "Thanks, but we have some things to talk about."

"Another time," Jill said, holding her fiancé's hand. They wanted to be alone, too, but probably not for the same reason.

"Dr. McKnight?" Bev walked over to them with two menus in her hand. "If you'll follow me, I'll show you to your table."

"Thanks." Again he settled his hand on her back. Partly it was being a gentleman, but mostly he just wanted to touch her. He liked touching her and not just her back. A blast of pure yearning poured through him when he thought about touching her everywhere.

The path to their table took them past the counter with swivel stools, then all the way to the back of the diner. He felt Cam's body tighten with tension as people stopped talking to look first at her, then him.

He leaned down and whispered, "Everything will be fine. You gotta have faith in me."

"Words that strike fear in a woman's heart," she said under her breath.

So the lady had trust issues. He could win her over. His plan was foolproof.

She looked relieved when they were finally seated at

a table across from each other. After unrolling her paper napkin from around the silverware, she put it in her lap.

"Smells good in here," she admitted. "I'm hungry."

"Me, too." He looked at her lips, full, defined and incredibly kissable. The lust not only hadn't subsided, it compounded. "I think you'll like—"

"Ben?" A woman passed the table, then backed up a step. "Ben McKnight?"

He recognized the brunette. "Hey, Tanya. How are you?"

"Fine. I heard you were back in town." She looked at Cam, speculation in her green eyes.

"This is Camille Halliday. Tanya Smithson. We went to high school together," he explained.

"Nice to meet you." Cam's eyes were cool as she looked at the other woman.

"I didn't know you knew our Ben," Tanya said.

"We met at the lodge. How's your store doing?" he asked, wondering when he'd become "our Ben."

"Hanging in there. I own the gift store next door. Tanya's Treasures."

"Right," Cam said. "I saw you at the Chamber of Commerce meeting."

"That's why you look familiar." There was a hint of nerves and a suggestion of guilt in her voice. "I didn't know you and Ben were acquainted."

Cam slid him a flirtatious smile. "We've become good friends."

"Really?" She glanced at her watch. "Unfortunately I have to run. Just took a quick break for a bite to eat." She smiled at Cam. "I hope you'll drop by the gift shop and say hello."

"I'll do that." When the woman was out of earshot, Cam's eyes narrowed. "That was quite an about-face. She went out of her way to ignore me at that Chamber of Commerce meeting. She had to walk around me to get to the refreshment table and didn't bother to introduce herself. Whatever happened to courtesy and old-fashioned friendliness?"

"Like I told you. There's the heiress intimidation factor." He grinned. "And you weren't with me."

"If I hadn't seen it with my own eyes, I'd never have believed it."

"What's that?" he asked.

"I've been here for weeks and no one smiled at me. But with you it's like something shifted in the universe. Attitudes altered. You're the cool guy. The hometown hero."

"Stick with me, kid. You'll see that we can really help each other out."

She nodded thoughtfully. "If you can work that kind of magic at the lodge... I mean, change attitudes and rally cooperation just by being my pretend boyfriend, I just might be able to pull off salvaging that property."

"Does that mean what I think it does?"

"Before I give you an answer, you need to know that this isn't a joke to me."

"I never—"

She held up her hand. "My brother was the Hallidays' young prince. He was being groomed from birth to take over running the corporation. When he died, the job fell in my lap and I didn't want it. After that I made choices and they weren't good ones. But now I'm all grown up and it's important to me to step up. For my family. For my brother."

"I understand. And I'm sure you'll do a terrific job."

"Maybe." She folded her hands and set them on the table's paper placemat. "I don't know how to do it right. Dean Junior would have aced being the boss. He'd have made our father proud if he'd lived. I can't do it as well as my brother, but I'll do my best. And if that means winning hearts and minds in Blackwater Lake by pretending to be your girlfriend, then that's what I'll do."

"Let's shake on it." He held his hand out across the table.

She put her fingers into his palm and her eyes widened. Clearly she felt the sparks, too. She was more fascinating every time he talked to her and talking wasn't the only thing on his mind.

He was sick and tired of all the women throwing themselves at him, but this woman could come on to him any time she wanted. He would be very willing to oblige.

## *Chapter Six*

At the Grizzly Bear Diner cash register, Cam stood beside Ben while he paid for dinner. Later she would settle with him for her half of the meal, which had been delicious, and worth being here for more than just the food. She couldn't swear to it, but her impression was that the friendliness quotient from people in the diner had gone up by a lot since she'd walked in beside the handsome doctor. With luck this—*liaison* was the best word she could come up with—would thaw out her stubborn, opinionated employees and convince them to help her save their jobs here in town and get her a better one somewhere else.

After signing the credit card receipt, he took her elbow and ushered her out the door. Spring was on the way, but the air was still cool and she shivered.

"Are you cold?"

"Just for a second." And thanks to him not as much as she'd been since coming here. "The fresh air feels good."

"Would you like to walk a little? I can give you a guided tour of downtown Blackwater Lake."

"I've seen it. But walking sounds good. I'm so full."

They strolled past Potter's Ice Cream Parlor and its brightly lit interior. There were little round tables with chair backs shaped like hearts. Colorful prints of sprinkles, cones and scoops were scattered on the walls. A glass case was filled with different flavors of ice cream.

"So I guess you don't want dessert," Ben said.

"Not even the best seven-layer chocolate cake in Montana." She groaned. "I can't believe I ate the whole Mama Bear burger."

"I can't believe you ordered it." He slid his fingers into the pockets of his jeans. "I have to admit I misjudged you."

"How so?"

"I figured you for a gourmet greens and goat cheese kind of girl. That hearty appetite of yours was a pleasant shocker."

"Why pleasant?"

"Because there will be more dinners and I'm not a fan of eating with someone who takes one bite and pushes the rest of the food around the plate."

Cam liked to eat. She liked good food. But she tried to make sensible choices, not deprive herself. She was glad he favored a normal, not stick-thin type. But what pulled her up short was the mention of more dinners.

As they walked she glanced up at him. "I don't understand. Why do we need to go out to dinner again? We've been spotted. As the cops on all those TV shows say, we've been made."

"And we'll need to build on that—otherwise the plan won't work. It's what a dating couple does."

Cam realized she hadn't thought this through. She'd been so caught up in the power of his aura and how just walking in it gave her Blackwater Lake street cred. That's what had convinced her to agree to the bargain. So far it was working, but she hadn't considered what came after.

"Hm." She caught her heel in a sidewalk crack and stumbled a little. His steadying hand was warm, strong and masculine, and desire knotted in her belly. He was the kind of guy a woman could count on. Heck, the town counted on him. "Our Ben," they'd said. But she wasn't the kind of woman a hometown hero like him made promises to. "Maybe we should figure out exactly how this is going to work."

"We're dating," he said. "Don't tell me a girl like you has never dated before."

"Of course. But it was spontaneous. Not calculated."

She glanced into the big picture window of Tanya's Treasures. Ornate silver picture frames, collectible figurines, crocheted tablecloths and delicate crystal lamps decorated the window. It looked like a charming place. The owner was behind the register counting bills.

"What are we going to *do?*" she asked.

"This isn't rocket science. We'll just do the things a man and woman do when they date."

Her insides quivered at the thought of that. It was the whole sexy gray area of this bargain. Men and women did a lot of very physical things when they dated. But she wasn't going there. Keep this conversation generic.

"I know what people do in New York and Los Angeles. What is there to do here in Montana?"

"Same things. Dinner. Movies. Watching movies at each other's houses."

"We don't have houses," she reminded him.

"You have no imagination," he scoffed. "Your house is right next to mine. It's handy."

That fact was beginning to concern her the most. "But

sneaking back and forth between rooms won't get us seen by the gossip-loving people in town."

"That's true. But it would be fun."

"This is *pretend* dating," she pointed out. "We're not supposed to have fun."

"That's too bad." He grinned. "Because I'm having a great time."

So was Cam. That was the other problem. Too much fun in the past always bit her in the backside. "Let me re-phrase. The whole point of pretend dating is to be seen in public doing public things."

At the end of the block instead of crossing the street, by mutual unspoken agreement, they turned and started back toward the diner.

"I think we should hold hands," he said.

Really? Because shaking on their bargain and feeling the heat of his touch sizzle all the way to her toes wasn't enough fun for him?

"No one is watching us," she protested.

"You never know." His voice was solemn, but laced with teasing.

"There's no one around."

"But the night has a thousand eyes."

"That's just creepy. And Blackwater Lake may be many things, but *creepy* isn't an adjective I'd use to describe it."

He laughed and slipped her hand into his, linking their fingers. They were strolling past the gift shop again. "Think of this as good practice. A chance to get used to each other. Make it look more real—"

Cam was just beginning to relax with the touch when she felt him tense. "What's wrong?"

"I can't believe it." He was staring down the street at a woman waiting for the signal light at Main Street and Pine. "Of all people—"

"Who?"

Cam followed his gaze and saw the light turn green. The woman, tall and slender with dark hair, crossed the street. She passed the diner and glanced in the window as she walked.

Ben leaned down and whispered into her ear. "It's time to kick this bargain into high gear."

"What?"

He stopped dead in his tracks, right under a streetlight, and pulled Cam into his arms. "This is another public thing dating people do all the time."

In the next instant his lips were touching hers. Even if her mouth hadn't been otherwise occupied, she wasn't sure forming a protest was possible. His fingers tunneled into her hair as he cupped her face in his palm and brushed his thumb tenderly over her cheek.

His body felt solid and strong and wonderful pressed against hers. Her heart started a weird thumping as he nibbled quick little kisses over her mouth and jaw, inching toward her neck. His breath tickled her ear and raised tingles that raced over her shoulders and down her arms, settling in her belly. A moan built inside her, but the click of a woman's heels on the sidewalk beside them trapped the sound in her throat.

Ben lifted his head and stared at her as he drew in a breath. Deep down she felt a small flicker of satisfaction that she wasn't the only one feeling *something*. It was a really good kiss. Unfortunately it didn't last nearly long enough.

The footsteps stopped. "Ben? Is that you?"

He straightened and looked at the woman. "Judy Coulter?"

His ex-girlfriend. The one M.J. had told her about. Cam stared up at him as the realization hit her that he'd recognized this woman before the kiss and that's why he'd pulled her into his arms.

"Ben McKnight." She smiled up at him. Darn it, she had a beautiful smile. "It's been a long time."

"So you're back in Blackwater Lake?"

"Yeah. And so are you. How long has it been?"

"I'd have to do the math." He laughed.

"You were always good at it." She finally tore her gaze from his and gave Cam a look she was all too familiar with. It said you're the airheaded infamous heiress, the one whose only talent is turning outrageous antics into outrageous stories for the tabloids.

Ben looked between them and slid his arm around Cam's waist, intimately nestling her to his side. "Judy, this is Camille Halliday. She's working at the lodge."

"I know who she is." Unlike at the diner, this woman's attitude didn't warm up. That changed when she looked up at Ben. She was very warm to him. "Now that I see you, it seems like yesterday that we were prom king and queen."

"High school was a lot of years ago," he said.

"We used to date," Judy informed Cam.

*And you're the moron who threw him over for a ski bum,* Cam thought. It might be a long time ago for Ben, but it was new to her and she wanted to get even on his behalf. She wanted to tell the witch what she could do with this walk down memory lane. She wanted to protect him.

She snuggled against him and gazed adoringly into his eyes, seeing the amusement there. "Ben and I are dating now."

"Really?" Large, dark eyes glittered with dislike until she looked at Ben. "I didn't realize that spoiled heiresses were your type."

When he started to say something, Cam put her hand on his chest to stop him. "I've got this."

"Oh?" Judy gave her a dismissive stare.

"Yeah." Cam gave it back to her. "If you were his type, honey, you wouldn't be his *ex*."

"It's getting late, sweetie," Ben said to her. "We have work tomorrow. See you around, Judy."

They walked away and she knew the ex-girlfriend was watching because it was several moments before she heard the clicking sound of high heels on the sidewalk behind them. Cam was angry and upset, but mostly with herself. She wasn't sure where the inclination to protect him had come from. He was nothing if not a nice guy, and a woman like Judy was a cobra. Still, he was a big boy and didn't need Cam coming to his defense. He'd only kissed her to get his how-do-you-like-me-now? moment.

He'd used her. At least it was for revenge, a cause she could get behind, but being used was never fun. Especially for someone like her, who'd been manipulated and tossed aside too many times to count.

But not again. This time she was using him right back and would get something out of the bargain, too.

After clinic hours on Friday, Ben pulled his SUV into McKnight Automotive and stopped beneath the covered area connecting the office to the work bays with hydraulic lifts. That part of the business was shut down for the day with chains across the opening to keep cars out. It was ghostly quiet since all the employees had gone home. He planned to leave his car for servicing in the morning and get his sister to drop him off at the lodge on her way home.

He opened the heavy glass door and walked into the office. There was a high counter where several computer monitors sat. On the wall was a Peg-Board with hooks to hold customers' keys, numbered to link them with the correct vehicle. To the right there was a lounge with chairs and a TV. A side counter held a coffeemaker and a refrigerator underneath it was stocked with water and soda. A vending machine had candy, chips and nuts. It was a comfortable place to wait while your car was being worked on.

"Hi, guys."

Tom McKnight looked up from his paperwork, and immediately grinned, obviously happy to see him. Syd's expression was guarded, which meant happy to see him, something on her mind.

"Hi, son." His dad turned off his computer and slid off the high stool in front of it. He held out his hand and after grabbing it, he pulled Ben into a quick hug. "Good to see you."

His father had just turned sixty, still a handsome man with brown hair that was liberally sprinkled with silver. There were crinkle lines at the corners of light blue eyes that would always show the shadow of sadness from losing his wife too soon. She'd died from complications of childbirth after Syd was born. As the face of McKnight Automotive, he dressed professionally in a long-sleeved yellow shirt, coordinating striped tie and sharply pressed khakis.

"What can I do for you?" he asked.

"The SUV needs an oil change and tire rotation. Can you do it first thing in the morning if I leave it overnight?"

"Sure. Can you spare it?"

"I'm not on call, so if Syd will give me a lift to the lodge…"

"I'm happy to." She looked up from the computer, clearly having listened to the conversation. "But why can't your main squeeze come and get you?"

Ben met his father's gaze and saw the question reflected there, too. Main squeeze? What was she talking… Oh. Right. Cam. So they'd heard about the diner. He'd forgotten how fast word spread in Blackwater Lake, even though that's what he'd been counting on. Apparently the plan was working even better than he'd hoped.

"Cam has her hands full at work and I don't want to bother her." The first part was true or she wouldn't have agreed to the bargain. As far as bothering her? He hoped that kiss was bothering her as much as it was him. He looked at his sister. "Besides, you go right past the lodge on your way home."

That was also true.

"What makes you think I don't have plans? A date?"

"You told me you were taking a break," he reminded her. "Speaking of that, how's the hand?"

She flexed her fingers. "Good as new. You were right about giving it time."

"Glad to hear that."

"Bev Thompson from the diner was in today." His father gave him the what-the-hell-are-you-doing? look. "I didn't know you were going out with that hotel woman."

Hotel woman? That made Cam sound like a room-by-the-hour girl and Ben felt a quick spurt of anger. "When I lived in Las Vegas it wasn't my habit to run past you every woman I went out with."

"You're not in Vegas anymore." His father loosened his tie. "This is where you grew up."

Ben decided not to debate the point. "Cam is a dedicated businesswoman. Ambitious, conscientious and smart."

Syd's eyes widened a little at his sharp tone. "Looks like you hit a nerve, Dad."

"I didn't think taking her to dinner was breaking news or that you guys needed advance notice. It's my private life."

"In Blackwater Lake nothing stays private," his father said, stating the obvious.

Ben knew that but hadn't been prepared for the part of

the plan where his family would find out. As fast as word got out about them dating, it could get out about them being a phony couple. He had to play this just right. Best to stick with the truth wherever possible.

"Things with Cam and me happened pretty fast."

That was true. He hadn't planned to kiss her, but when Judy appeared out of nowhere it had seemed like an excellent idea. After the fact he wasn't so sure, because the taste of her had made him burn for more.

Tom McKnight looked at him long and hard, then nodded. "You're a grown man and I guess you know what you're doing. But I can't help worrying about you. It's what a father does."

"There's no need, Dad. But I appreciate it."

"Comes with the territory, son."

Ben looked at Syd. "About that ride home…"

"Let me change and I'll be right with you." She headed out of the office toward the employee area.

"Why is Syd taking a break from men?" he asked when his sister was out of earshot.

"Beats me." Tom shrugged. "You'd think in a place that can't keep a secret someone would know. If they do I haven't heard."

"I guess she'll talk when she's ready." Speaking of ready… Ben could barely recall the time before Syd was born when his mother had been with them. To his knowledge, his father had been alone ever since she died. "How are you, Dad? Anyone *you* want to tell me about? Are you seeing anyone?"

"I have friends and some of them are of the female persuasion. But your mother was the only one for me." He smiled, but it didn't fool either of them. Tom McKnight was the kind of man who loved fiercely and only once.

Ben wondered if that was a quality he'd inherited, but

seeing Judy again went a long way toward answering part of that question. He felt absolutely nothing for her and wondered now why it had hurt so much when he'd heard she married someone else.

"Your ride is here and it's leaving." Syd had changed out of her overalls into snug jeans, a camisole top and red blazer. She'd transformed from a scrappy little mechanic into a beautiful, sophisticated woman. They said clothes didn't make the man or woman and that was true as far as character, but the change in his sister was truly amazing.

He slid his arm across her shoulders and resisted the familiar urge to rub his knuckles across the top of her head. There would be hell to pay now if he messed up her hair. "You're a very stylish grease monkey."

"I'm sure there's a compliment in there somewhere, but I'll have to dig it out later." Her eyes twinkled when she looked up at him. "Are you ready to go?"

"Whenever you are. I'll see you tomorrow, Dad."

"Since I'm holding your car hostage, I'll look forward to it." He lifted a hand in a goodbye gesture.

Ben followed his sister to the parking lot and got in the passenger side of her sporty red compact. He moved the seat back for more leg room and noticed how close Syd was to the steering wheel. She was a small woman, like their mother.

She fastened her seat belt and turned on the ignition. Before they reached the exit, the doors automatically locked. "Now I've got you where I want you."

"Should I be afraid?"

"A smart man would be. I want to know what's really going on with you and that woman. Consider yourself lucky that I didn't push this in front of Dad."

"Her name is Camille and we're friends who enjoy each other's company."

"Trying to decide whether or not to take it to the next level?"

"Exactly," he agreed.

"Is she seeing anyone else?"

"No." He hadn't actually thought to ask her that question.

"Are you?"

"No." That he was sure about.

Syd shook her head and tightened her hands on the steering wheel. "I don't buy it. She's not your type."

That's what Judy had said. And how did they figure that? "What *is* my type?"

"Not a hotel heiress who went to the slammer, I can tell you that."

The slammer was a long time ago and everyone was entitled to a second chance. Cam had definitely made the most of hers. "Have you been talking to Judy Coulter?"

"I wouldn't waste my breath on that…witch." She glanced over at him. "Why?"

"Cam and I ran into her."

Syd glanced at him. "You're trying to change the subject, but it won't work."

"What exactly is the subject?"

"Your personal life. I have questions. Starting with: For a guy who's been avoiding a serious relationship for a very long time, you picked the wrong woman to break the dating fast."

"That's not a question, it's a statement," he pointed out.

"The question is implied," she shot back.

"How do you know I haven't dated?"

The question *was* a diversion to get her off the scent. When had his sister become so perceptive? Ben hadn't counted on that either.

"I listen. You should try it sometime." She flashed him

a grin. "The thing is, I tuck away information. And women just know this stuff. There hasn't been anyone serious for you, not since college. Now the first one you pick is the type to get her name in the papers for all the wrong reasons?"

"For the record, I don't have a type."

"And it has to be said, that's all the debate strategy you've got?"

"Yes." The less he said, the better. "No type."

"Baloney. You have one and Cam Halliday isn't it. There's something fishy going on here."

"To quote you, baloney. There's nothing fishy about an attraction to a beautiful, brainy woman with a terrific sense of humor," he defended. And a body that makes a man's palms sweat.

What else could he do? If this ruse was going to work, everyone had to believe they were a couple. When the message spread and sank in, women would back off and leave him alone. He'd get peace and quiet at work. Was that really too much to ask?

"She is pretty," Syd conceded. "And a great dresser. I'd give almost anything to have a shoe wardrobe like hers. But I'll have to reluctantly take your word for the rest."

The rest was a petite package who'd kissed him back. A kiss that packed a punch and he hoped she'd "hit" him with it again. The fact that she turned him on would make it really easy to play the part of her boyfriend.

"It sounds like you're smitten."

"I definitely am," he agreed.

"Then you should bring her to dinner Sunday night. It's family night. We'd all like to get to know her." She pulled the car into the Blackwater Lake Lodge and braked to a stop by the front door.

Ben released his seat belt and tried to think of a way out

of this one. It would be easy to play his part with people who didn't know him, but him and Cam spending time with his family was a recipe for disaster. If he put up a protest the way he wanted to right now, it would be like pouring kerosene on the flames of his sister's curiosity. She was already suspicious and would want to know why he was hiding Cam from them.

He hoped he didn't regret this. "That sounds great. What time and what can we bring?"

"Dad's barbecuing and we'll eat around six. Why don't you bring that seven-layer chocolate cake from the lodge restaurant that everyone in town is raving about?"

"I can tell you from personal experience that it's fantastic. We'll be there at five-thirty."

"Great." Syd smiled with a satisfaction that was unnerving. "We'll see you then. Can't wait."

"Me either. Thanks for the ride."

"Any time, big brother."

Any time little sister had an ulterior motive, was more like it, he thought, watching the taillights on her car move out of sight. He blew out a breath. It was put up or shut up time. He was going to take his fake relationship out for a spin with his father, older brother and baby sister—the three people on the planet who knew him best. If they weren't fooled it was game over.

Now all he had to do was talk Cam into it.

## Chapter Seven

Late Sunday afternoon Cam was sitting in the passenger seat of Ben's car and not a particularly happy camper. Even though he'd said something about more dinners, she'd been hoping that no further action would be required from her for this bargain. Was it too much to ask that gossip from the diner sighting of them together would hold everyone for a while? At least long enough for her to get over that kiss?

"Tell me again why I have to meet your family and eat Sunday dinner at your dad's?"

Ben glanced over at her, then settled his gaze back on the road. His dad lived just outside of town, not too far from the lake, and the way was winding. "Red flags will be raised if anyone asks about us and my family hasn't met you. It's what a normal couple would do."

"Is it what you and Judy did?" There was just the tiniest bit of shrew in her tone and that wasn't a particularly good thing. Was it jealousy? Or annoyance that he'd only kissed her to make some kind of statement to his ex-girlfriend?

"Judy and I were just kids." Was it imagination or did his jaw just clench? Did he still have scars from what happened? "Now, a few pointers about the McKnights."

Ah. He didn't want to talk about the ex. Cam wasn't sure what that meant, but was happy to change the subject.

"Anything you can tell me will help," she said.

"Remember, this is just a low-key dinner. All very normal."

"I wouldn't know about normal. Nothing about my life ever was. Especially after my brother died."

He shook his head in sympathy. "As annoying as they can get at times, I can't imagine losing one of my siblings. That must have been hard."

"It was." Her heart caught as an image of Dean Junior's handsome, teasing face flashed into her mind. "But before I'd even dealt with the loss, the burden of responsibility that he was supposed to carry shifted to me. In the blink of an eye I was the oldest child of Dean Halliday. As such, I was expected to take over the reins of Halliday Hospitality Inc. someday." She gripped her hands in her lap. "I rebelled."

"All kids do."

"But I elevated it to an art form. Sneaking out of the house in the middle of the night to party with friends I knew my parents didn't like." She cringed, remembering the chances she'd taken. "That resulted in more than one ultimatum."

"They were worried about you."

"No. They worried that company stock prices would drop. I didn't care about anyone but myself then. All I could see was that the kids I thought were cool wanted to hang out with me."

"Every kid goes through that stage."

"I bet you didn't."

"Sure I did." He glanced over and met her gaze. "To me that all sounds pretty normal."

"Not when the police get involved. There were brushes with the law. Then I was in the wrong place, wrong time, at the wheel without a driver's license and someone in the car had drugs. The judge didn't believe I didn't know. And my last name is Halliday. He decided to make an example of me."

"That was a long time ago."

"Yeah." She looked out the window, at the scenery going by. The trees were green and serene and when he drove around the lake, the sight of sunlight turning the surface of the water to shimmering blue took her breath away. "I grew up and discovered I have a head for business."

She glanced over at him and lost her breath again for a different reason. Ben McKnight was an incredibly good-looking man. He would turn women's heads in Hollywood or New York, cities that had some of the most handsome, sophisticated men in the world. As far as her head was concerned, she was having trouble keeping it on business because of him.

"Cut yourself some slack," he suggested. "You turned your attention to school and proving yourself to the corporation. That means you're focused. And you're going to need to be for the McKnights."

"Now you're scaring me."

"My family has to believe we're a couple or no one else in town will buy the act." He glanced at her. "No pressure."

And if the act was outed, any strides she'd made with the employees at the lodge would disappear. Any career ambitions she'd had would go up in smoke because she would fail the test her father had given her.

She nodded emphatically. "Okay. We're a couple. Got it."

"You should also know that my sister is already suspicious."

"Great."

"We're almost there."

"And the hits just keep on coming," she mumbled.

He turned off the main road into a tract of homes. After following the road around a curve, he stopped the car at the curb of a small house with gray siding and white trim. The tops of the pine trees behind it were visible over the roof. In the front a large expanse of grass was green and manicured. There were three vehicles in the driveway—a small, sporty red compact, a big black truck and a silver Cadillac sedan.

Ben met her gaze. "Here we go."

"I can hardly wait," she muttered.

After exiting the car, he took the boxed seven-layer cake, then put his hand at her waist, guiding her up the drive to the covered porch. Cam could feel the heat of his fingers through her wool blazer and satin blouse. The touch skewered rational thought just when she needed it the most. He knocked on the door and it was opened almost immediately.

A beautiful, brown-eyed brunette stood there. "Hi. Glad you guys could make it."

"Me, too." Ben put his free arm around Cam's shoulders. "Syd, this Camille Halliday. Cam, my sister, Sydney."

"It's nice to meet you." This is the one who was suspicious. Cam smiled and held out her hand. "Thanks for fixing my flat."

"You're welcome." The other woman shook it as she looked over her outfit, including the black silk-blend slacks and Jimmy Choo heels. An expression somewhere between admiration and envy slid over her face. Sydney was wearing jeans tucked into brown calf boots and a long-sleeved yellow T-shirt.

Two men came up behind her. One was a handsome, slightly older version of Ben and the other a good-looking guy who had a strong resemblance to his sons. Both wore jeans, boots and T-shirts. Ben wore essentially the same outfit, which should have been a clue that Cam was severely overdressed. Her heart sank because you didn't win hearts and minds by not fitting in.

She shook hands with both of them. "It's a pleasure."

"All mine," Alex said, smiling. He was a local building contractor. "I can't imagine what a woman like you is doing with my brother."

What gave her away? She hadn't really done anything yet and the jig was up. Then she realized the two men were grinning at each other so she deduced that his comment wasn't about their charade but simple good-natured sibling teasing.

Obviously feeling her tension, Ben tightened the arm he still had around her shoulders. "Don't mind Alex. He's okay when you get to know him."

"Don't keep her out here on the porch, Ben." His father smiled. "Come on in, you two."

"Thank you, Mr. McKnight."

"Call me Tom." He stepped aside as they walked in. "What would you like to drink? Beer? Wine? Soft drink? Iced tea?"

"I'd love a glass of white wine if you've got it."

"Chardonnay?" Sydney asked.

"Perfect."

As they followed the other three McKnights into the kitchen, Ben took her hand. It felt weird and wrong and fake and wonderful. She really liked the strength of his fingers, the warmth and the tingles. The you-and-me-against-the-world touch took a little energy out of her nerves.

Alex pulled a bottle of wine out of the refrigerator and expertly used a foil cutter and corkscrew to open it. Like his brother, he was an extraordinarily good-looking man. Like most women would, Cam glanced at his left ring finger, which was bare. He was probably single and she made a mental note to find out from Ben if Alex was having the same problem with women throwing themselves at him.

"Here you go," Alex said, handing her a glass of wine.

"Thanks." Their fingers brushed and she felt no tingles or anything out of the ordinary. It was a totally different and distinct experience from when she touched Ben and that shouldn't be. The terms of their bargain didn't allow for heat and tingles when touching.

Finally everyone had a drink and Tom said, "Let's go outside."

"Sounds good, Dad." After setting the cake on the counter, Ben slung his arm across her shoulders again, as if they'd been going together for years instead of days.

He was surprisingly good at this pretending thing.

The rear yard was just as beautiful as the front. It felt like a park, with an expanse of grass surrounded by shrubs and flowers. The wooden fence held back a forest of pine trees.

On the covered back porch there were two wrought-iron love seats covered with pads and a couple of matching chairs. Cam and Ben sat side by side, thighs touching and sparks flying. The closeness caused a hitch in her breathing and she sipped her wine to cover it. Alex took one of the single chairs closest to her and Tom sat with his daughter across from them.

"So, Cam, how do you like Blackwater Lake?" Alex

took a drink from his longneck beer. The label read Moose Drool. Ew.

"It's a beautiful place." She glanced at Ben. The twinkle in his eyes told her he knew she was lying. That wasn't fair. The town *was* beautiful; it just wasn't New York or L.A. "We drove past the lake and with the sun shining, the surface looked like glittering diamonds."

Sydney's smile was supposed to look friendly and to her family it probably did. But a woman could see the cynicism around the edges. "Diamonds are a girl's best friend."

"I couldn't agree more." Cam met her gaze. "A girl who doesn't like jewelry is a quart low on estrogen. Call me shallow, but I can't be friends with someone like that."

"Well put," Sydney agreed, grudging respect in her eyes as a smile turned up the corners of her full lips.

"I know my sister is outnumbered by the boys and taking advantage of having another woman around," Alex said. "But please tell me we're not going to discuss the latest feminine hygiene product."

"I think he just challenged us," Cam said. "Sydney, do you want to start or should I get the ball rolling with what's new in shapewear these days?"

That got an actual laugh from the McKnights' lone female. "High five, Cam."

"Well, well…" Alex glanced between the two women. "That sounds a lot like a seal of approval from my little sister, and I agree. Camille, a lady as pretty as you should feel right at home in a place as beautiful as Blackwater Lake."

"Thank you." If he talked like that to all the girls, they'd be lining up to contract his house-building services and a whole lot of things that had nothing to do with construction.

"Hands off, bro. I saw her first." Ben threaded his fingers through hers and settled their linked hands on his muscular thigh.

The resulting wave of heat almost kept her from noticing the slightest edge to his voice and the possessiveness of the gesture. Was this real jealousy, or was he pretending? It was the sort of thing an actual boyfriend might do and felt very real. So real she had to remind herself that this was just make-believe.

Sydney's gaze narrowed as she studied them. "Is anyone else starving? I think it's time to cook the steaks, Dad."

"Okay. I'll fire up the barbecue."

"I'll take care of everything inside." She stood. "Do you want to give me a hand, Cam?"

This was a test, Cam thought. "Of course."

"Me, too," Ben said.

The three of them went into the kitchen where Syd pulled an already-put-together salad from the refrigerator. "Why don't you two set the table?"

"Okay." Ben turned toward the cupboard nearest the natural pine table in the kitchen's eating nook. "I'll show you where everything is, sweetie."

"Thanks."

Was she supposed to add an endearing nickname, too? This phony-girlfriend thing was harder than she'd thought. Play-acting for his family was a lot of pressure, but if they passed this test, fooling the rest of Blackwater Lake should be easier. But the McKnights seemed like a wonderful family. There was a part of her that wished this wasn't an act and normal could be hers.

"So, Cam," Syd said, setting a bowl of potato salad on the table. "Do you like the outdoors?"

Was this a trick question? "I love the fresh air here in the mountains. But work keeps me pretty busy. I don't get out much."

"So you haven't been camping yet?"

"No." That was the truth. Not once ever in her life had she slept without four walls surrounding her that included a bathroom with running water and electricity. She looked at Ben for guidance, but he was just taking plates down from a shelf and the rattling kept him from hearing the question. "Like I said, there hasn't been much time off since I got here."

The look in her brown eyes said Syd was just getting started. "Ben loves backpacking, fishing and camping, don't you, big brother?"

He set the five plates on the table, which was big enough for six people, and put one in front of each chair. "Yeah. I've missed doing that."

"Isn't that one of the reasons you moved back here?" his sister persisted. "Camping, fishing, being outdoors?"

"It is," he agreed.

"Have you ever camped out, Cam?"

She looked at Ben again, unsure how far this pretense should go. It was all a big lie, but lacing everything with some truth would make the ruse easier to pull off. "Since my family owns a hotel chain, the only camping out we did had room service. But it's something I've always wanted to try."

A little truth followed closely by a whopper of a lie.

Ben moved close and settled his arm around her waist. Tension was evident in his body. "As a matter of fact, I'm taking Cam backpacking next weekend, right, sweetie?"

Cam's gaze snapped to his. This was not what she'd signed up for, and definitely not spelled out in their verbal agreement. It did, however, fall into the category of convincing his family. If they were convinced, people in town would be, too.

"Right," she said, shooting him a glare.

Syd pulled a platter of raw steaks from the refrigerator. "Ben, would you take this out to Dad?"

"Yeah." He took it and opened the door. "Be right back."

Then Cam was alone with the suspicious sister. Ben's dad had seemed happy that his son was happy. His brother appeared to approve of her. Sydney McKnight was the lone family holdout and kept staring as if she expected an alien to pop out of Cam's chest.

"There's something fishy going on," she said.

"I guess that happens when camping and fishing are involved." Cam winced at the stupid joke.

The serious expression on Syd's face didn't change. "Just so we're clear, if you break my brother's heart…"

"What if he breaks mine?" That was an automatic response, but for the first time Cam realized it was a possibility.

She liked Ben more every time they were together. That was potentially a problem, because the longer she had to keep up the pretense of being his girlfriend, the more she could see herself falling for him, for real. And now they'd been maneuvered into a weekend trip.

Maybe they could just pretend to go camping.

Cam was standing at the front desk with M.J. and Glen Larson, the general manager. He was tall, dark and nice-looking, in his early twenties and a recent college grad with a brand-spanking-new business degree. The three of them were looking over upcoming bookings. Summer was only a couple months away and she'd feel a lot better if reservations increased.

Shaking her head Cam said, "I have to figure out a way to pitch the positives of Blackwater Lake Lodge to travel professionals and online sites."

"I can help with that," Glen offered. "I've got some experience in web marketing. There's a way to make sure this town and the lodge come up first in the search engine when someone is looking for information on Montana."

"That would be great." She smiled at him, his earnestness and willingness to help. Cooperation was a nice change and there was little doubt that she had Ben McKnight to thank for it. "If you need extra time to work on it, let me know. I can handle some of your management responsibilities. And if necessary and you're okay with it, I can authorize limited overtime."

"Thanks, boss." His surprised tone said he hadn't fully expected teamwork or support from her.

"Okay, now for the employee appreciation dinner next week. We need—"

Her two employees smiled at someone behind her; she'd been concentrating so hard she hadn't heard anyone approach. Then strong hands on her shoulders gently turned her and she saw Ben standing there. Her heart did a little skip and shimmy when he smiled.

"Hey, beautiful." He was looking at her mouth.

"Hi." She blinked up at him, wondering if the glow growing inside her was visible to the naked eye. "It has to be said that there are rules against non-employees being behind this desk."

"Rules were meant to be broken." He took her hand and settled it in the bend of his elbow. "But I respect you and your work so I'll just have to lure you out into the neutral zone and away from all this."

"Good luck with that, Doc." Glen slid his hands into the pockets of his charcoal slacks. "M.J. and I have been trying to get her to go home for an hour."

"He's right. She works too hard. All work and no play…" M.J. lifted one eyebrow to make her point.

"I love what I do and it doesn't feel like work," Cam protested.

"Still—" Ben gently tugged her around the desk to the lobby side. "I've got you now, my pretty. And we have shopping to do."

"Shoes?" she asked hopefully.

"Yes." His eyes twinkled. "Hiking boots."

"What did I ever do to deserve this?"

"She's a wilderness virgin and needs stuff. I'm taking her camping," he explained.

Because his family, specifically his sister, was torturing her. "Lucky me."

"Sounds like fun." M.J. walked into the office behind the desk and returned with Cam's purse and handed it over. "Go. Work will still be here in the morning."

How many mornings after that would it be here if business didn't pick up?

"Okay." She started to turn away, then thought of something. "Wait. One more thing. What's happening with the employee dinner? I know the restaurant chef is handling all the food. Do we know—"

"Today is the deadline for RSVPs," M.J. said. "I'll get the head count to Amanda. I formed a volunteer committee to decorate the conference room. We'll keep it simple. It's being handled. Go. Fly. Be free."

"Thanks." She saluted. "See you guys in the morning."

Ben walked her out the front door to where he'd parked his car, then handed her inside. He went around to the driver's side and got in. "This will be fun. Trust me. Don't look like the Olympic rifle team is going to use your designer shoes for target practice."

"It feels that way."

"You're such a glass-half-empty person. Where's that stiff upper lip?"

"There's not enough Botox or filler on the planet for that when you're talking boondocks and backpacks."

He laughed, which meant one of them was having a good time. Actually, she was, too. Who'd have thought?

Ben drove into town and pulled into the parking lot behind the large sporting-goods store. After getting out of the car, they headed for the rear entrance, where he held the door for her to precede him inside. Straight ahead was a locked glass case displaying rifles, pistols and some lethal-looking hunting knives.

Cam stared at the weapons, then up at her pretend boyfriend. "About that whole execution thing? Are you sure camping isn't like that?"

"You'll be completely safe," he assured her.

She shook her head. "I think we need to renegotiate the terms of this bargain."

Ben glanced around to see if anyone had heard the incriminating statement, then took her elbow and led her to a secluded corner behind a rack of quilted down vests and cargo pants.

"The agreement is perfectly clear," he said calmly. "There's not really anything to define. We're making it up as we go along, but everyone needs to believe you're my girlfriend."

"And two nights of sleeping on the ground is going to convince them?"

"Yes."

"Can't we go to a hotel in a big city far from here and just tell everyone we backpacked into the mountains?"

"You mean lie?"

"We're already doing that," she pointed out. "After the first whopper it gets easier."

"My sister isn't completely buying us as a couple. She knows I like the outdoors and anyone I go out with would have to be willing to try it. And the trying it part has to be convincing. A lie only works if you wrap it in enough of the truth."

"So, I need snake bites, scratches and dirt under my fingernails so she'll believe?"

"Yeah." He shrugged. "Either that or things go back to the way they were."

That meant a return to uncooperative lodge employees and the cold shoulder from the rest of the town. She shuddered. Things had been noticeably better since she'd "been with" Ben. There was an actual *volunteer* committee, for goodness' sake. She was beginning to have a glimmer of hope for upward mobility in her career.

And that was just her. If the deal fell apart, women would start throwing themselves at Ben again. Now there was a thought that she wasn't crazy about. Oddly enough, she liked it a lot less than being able to bring only what she could carry on her back for a whole weekend in the mountains. If she didn't know better, she'd call what she was feeling jealousy. But that wasn't part of the bargain.

"Wow, I think all the fresh air here in Blackwater Lake is beginning to affect my reasoning ability."

He looked amused. "Why?"

"Because I, Camille Halliday, am going to buy camping stuff. The world has gone mad."

He grinned. "Let's do this."

About an hour later, they had backpacks, sleeping bags, a lightweight tent and the sturdiest and chicest hiking boots money could buy. The wiry, gray-haired man at the cash register put the newsmagazine he was reading down on the counter. He must have been the owner, because he was practically quivering with excitement at all the stuff they piled up.

"This be all for you, Doc?" He looked at Ben, then her.

"I think so, Mr. Daly."

"Got your sunscreen and mosquito repellant?"

"Do you have anything that will discourage snakes?" Cam asked.

The owner laughed. "She's a pistol. Got a great sense of humor."

"Yes, she does." Ben put his arm around her shoulders and squeezed.

Cam was getting far too used to that. She liked feeling his strength and that big, warm body close to hers.

"So what's the damage, Mr. Daly?"

The man gave them a very impressive total and Cam started to pull a credit card out.

Ben stopped her and said, "I've got this."

"We'll settle up later." She had skin in this, too, and couldn't let him do that.

He shook his head. "It's settled now."

Unsettled was more like it, Cam thought when her heart started beating erratically. But it was stupid to do that. This was just him playing a part, showing people that he wasn't Mr. Camille Halliday, but a man with deep pockets of pride who paid his own way and hers. Wouldn't it be nice if it weren't an act at all? Talk about make-believe.

The man put the smaller items into bags and slid them across the counter. The newsmagazine caught underneath the plastic bag and fell on the floor at her feet.

"I'll get that." Cam picked up the paper, absently looking at the front as she handed it back. Her hand froze as something caught her attention. She read the headline and her stomach knotted until losing her lunch along with her sense of humor was a real possibility.

There was a picture of Ben kissing her outside the Grizzly Bear Diner and the headline screamed, "Halliday heiress hot for hug-a-licious hunk."

## Chapter Eight

Ben wanted to put his fist through a wall when he saw the headline and Cam's stricken look, but she was upset enough for the both of them. He decided to try and keep it light. "Good alliteration."

"I'm so sorry." She glanced at him, then skimmed the article some more. "I was so sure that I was off the ragsheet radar. This is awful. M.J. even warned me that the guy was asking questions."

"What guy?" Anger curled through him.

"Stan Overton, the sleazy guy we saw at the diner that night. Obviously he was following me and snapped this picture. I was so sure it was all behind me. If I'd thought for a second you'd be involved, I'd never have—"

Ben touched a finger to her lips. Partly because he hated to see her so upset about this trash, but also to keep her from revealing their secret. Mr. Daly was watching intently.

"Let's go put all this stuff in the car," Ben suggested.

She looked at him, then the man, and comprehension flared in her eyes. "Okay."

Together they carried all the bags to his SUV and stowed them in the back. Then he put her in the passenger seat and jogged around to get behind the wheel.

"I'm so sorry, Ben. I should have known better than to get you mixed up in this."

"It was my idea, remember?" He was angry, but not with Cam. It was with the bottom-feeders who victimized someone like her. She'd been through the devastating loss of her brother and hadn't been allowed to act out without every move ending up on the front page. If her family hadn't had money, no one would have cared. "You've got to shake this off. Don't let them get to you."

"I'm not worried about me. Although when my father sees this, and he will, my odds of getting a better assignment at a bigger property are about as good as managing a motel on the moon." She met his gaze. "You need to find someone else to run interference for you."

He didn't want someone else. "Don't be hasty."

"Seriously. Associating with me could jeopardize your credibility at the clinic. I couldn't stand being responsible for that."

"You underestimate the people of Blackwater Lake. They can separate personal from professional."

The outside parking lot lights illuminated the shadow of betrayal in her eyes and Ben badly wanted to make it go away. If they hadn't been sitting in the car, he would have taken her in his arms, so it was probably a good thing they were here.

She shook her head. "This is a lousy situation without recourse. The public believes that someone with monetary resources is fair game for their entertainment. In their minds the question becomes: Is the crown too tight? Are the jewels too heavy?" She sighed. "So I just have to suck it up. If it ruins my life, there's not much I can do. But I won't let them take you down, too. You need to distance yourself from me—"

"No."

She blinked at him. "What?"

"You don't need to protect me. I can take care of myself."

Distance was the last thing he wanted. Taking care of her was the first order of business. This protective instinct was usually reserved for his patients. He channeled it into his profession. With Cam it was personal, more than he'd expected.

"I'm sure you can protect yourself, but dealing with negative tabloid publicity isn't something they taught you in medical school." She wadded up the newsmagazine. "They twist the truth or print outright lies. I'm a demanding diva who cracks the whip. I broke up a perfectly good housekeeping team because they talk too much."

"Yeah," he agreed. "They talk at the top of their lungs."

"That part was conveniently left out because it doesn't sell papers. I've dealt with it all my life. But they'll try to dig up dirt on you, too. It's best if we don't see each other and cancel the camping—"

"Let me stop you right there." He took her hand and the delicacy of her fingers and wrist twisted him up inside. "A backpacking trip is just what the doctor ordered. We'll get away. Let the dust settle. By the time we get back, the whole thing will have blown over."

"That would be running away, and Hallidays don't do that."

"Neither do McKnights."

She was quiet as she studied him, but didn't pull away

when he linked his fingers with hers. "Don't be a martyr, Ben."

"The thought never crossed my mind." He laughed, then turned serious. "Don't let them win, Cam. It's an opportunity. I can show you how beautiful Blackwater Lake is so you can pass it on to guests at the lodge. First-person experience."

"You're saying this is all about business?"

"Exactly." Sort of. Although it was feeling a little more personal than he'd expected.

"Okay, then. Let's go backpacking."

"I must have been high on clean air when I let you talk me into this." Cam walked the uneven trail beside Ben.

There was a slight grade and that took them steadily uphill. Fortunately gym workouts and stair-stepper sessions had kept her in good enough shape so as not to be embarrassed. But at the fitness center you didn't have to carry on your back all the stuff you needed for one night and two days in the mountains. Ben had shown her how to attach her sleeping bag to the lightweight frame.

"You're going to love this," he predicted.

"Wouldn't it be easier to be airlifted in by helicopter?"

"Of course. But there are several problems with that scenario. First and most important, the trees are too thick for a chopper to get through." He looked down at her. "Second, while hiking you get to appreciate the beauty and awesomeness of these spectacular mountains. And—"

"There's more?"

"No pain, no gain. You'll appreciate it a lot more where we're going if it's not easy to get there."

"So it's like banging your head against the wall? Feels good when you stop?"

"Something like that." His gaze was assessing as he

looked her over, checking for fatigue. "Are you sorry yet about insisting on bringing the wine?"

"Never." She shook her head emphatically. "Just because this is the wilderness doesn't mean we have to be uncivilized."

"Unlike the offensive bottom-feeders who write stories for the rag sheets."

"Yeah. Like them." She brushed the back of her hand across the perspiration on her forehead. Wearing a baseball cap, she'd pulled her hair through the opening at the back, getting it off her neck. "That still makes me mad enough to spit."

"Self-control," he warned. "You don't want to dehydrate."

"Gotta love the great outdoors. And, speaking of that, it seems pointless to put myself through this when there's a very good chance that tabloid story will put an end to my career before it even gets started."

Ben handed her one of the refillable water bottles that was strapped to his pack. The plan was to refill them at the stream where they'd set up camp. "I disagree about your downward career trajectory."

"This will not endear me to employees who already think I'm a privileged, ditzy diva. And you don't know my father."

"Then he doesn't know marketing strategy. You're famous. Any publicity will be good for the lodge and the town, too. Local businesses will be grateful for all the customers you bring in and you didn't have to pay for it."

"Not out of pocket, but there's still a price." Self-esteem. Reputation. Dignity. Respect.

"The people who know you won't believe that trash. And everyone else doesn't matter."

"It's easy for you to say that because your life has never

been turned upside down by someone who stalks you with a camera then writes lies about the pictures that are flashed all over the world."

"Speaking of that…" He pulled out his digital pocket camera. "Everyone in town is expecting pictures of us."

She snorted. "We could stage them. Photoshop everything. Paparazzi do it all the time."

"I'm not an underhanded reporter trying to make a buck by slandering a celebrity. And it's the most natural thing in the world for us to take photos on a camping trip. We're supposed to be a couple."

"About that…" She took a drink of water, then looked up, but couldn't see his eyes behind the aviator sunglasses. "I wouldn't blame you if you changed your mind about the bargain. It's not easy being my boyfriend."

"So far it's been pretty stress-free."

"Because we're pretending. What happens because of that picture of you kissing me will be very real. Now you're a target, too. If there's anything to find they'll drag your name through the mud." She handed back the water bottle. "I'd like to apologize in advance for that."

"You have nothing to be sorry for." He hooked the bottle on his backpack. "And don't worry about me. I'm a big boy. I know what I'm getting into."

"No offense, but you really don't. They'll say that you're only with me to kick-start your medical practice in backwoodsville. Or you came back to a small town because you weren't good enough to make it in the big city. Possibly that a love affair gone bad turned you into Grizzly Adams, a recluse who can't hack it anywhere else. They make stuff up. That's what they do and it's the reason I've been single so long."

"Because of unscrupulous reporters?"

"Yeah." She glanced up at him as her boots scraped

across the dirt trail. "They make up front-page lies and the truthful retraction is buried on the second-to-last page days later. But trash sells. Some guys wanted to be with me to get their name in the paper, to get noticed by producers, directors, people who could fast-track a career." She shrugged. "Other guys didn't want anything to do with me because the circus that is my life could spill over into theirs. I've found it's just easier to be on my own."

"Again, I need to remind you that this bargain was my idea."

"Only because you didn't fully understand what dating me would entail."

"There's some truth to that." He nodded. "But we've spelled out the rules and both of us know why we're doing this. I *am* using you for my career—to keep women from turning my medical practice into a farce."

"And I'm using you to rehabilitate my image with everyone in Blackwater Lake. As far as I can see that tabloid story makes us zero for two."

"I think you're wrong." He glanced down. "The goal was to spread the news that I'm not available. One picture is worth a thousand words."

"I hope you still see it that way after you fully experience the fallout from this. Believe me, you're going to be relieved that this relationship is fake."

Cam looked up when he didn't respond to that statement and realized that part of her wanted him to refute what she'd just said. Part of her wanted him to say that so far it had been fun playing out their secret arrangement. But she didn't get that vibe from what she could see of his face.

There was an intensity tightening his jaw and with the stubble darkening it, he looked decidedly uncivilized—in the sexiest possible way. Her heart stuttered and her stomach shimmied in a way that had become unfamiliar, a way she'd put aside because that was easier than giving her heart to a man only to be disappointed yet again. She was attracted to Ben McKnight and it had nothing to do with the agreement they'd made.

Wanting him wasn't part of the bargain, but that didn't stop it from being true.

"Are you warm enough?" Squatting by the campfire, Ben put more kindling and wood on the glowing embers.

"Yes."

The fire was lovely, but Cam was plenty warm admiring how the glow of the sparks highlighted the lean, rugged angles of his face and broad, muscular shoulders. She was warm from the tips of her toes to the top of her head from watching the competent way he'd set up the tent and arranged the sleeping bags inside while she'd gathered rocks and arranged them in a circle for the fire. They'd refilled water bottles, then Ben had fished in the stream, eventually catching the trout that he'd cooked.

"That fish you made was as good as anything I've eaten at the lodge's five-star restaurant."

"Too bad we don't have Montana's best seven-layer chocolate cake for dessert."

He looked over his shoulder and grinned before standing, looking all masculine mountain man. In two steps he was beside her, then lowered all that lean strength to a sitting position next to her, so close that his shoulder brushed hers. Sparks from the friction felt as real as the ones she'd seen when he stirred up the campfire.

"At least there's wine." She sighed and it had nothing to do with the absence of cake and everything to do with the presence of this sexy, competent doctor.

He made her feel safe and she hadn't thought any man could make that happen. They were sitting on a blanket with their backs braced against a fallen log, legs stretched out in front of them, holding plastic wine glasses.

"If I'd known fish was the main course, I'd have brought a nice white instead of Pinot Noir. But when you're rough-ing it in the godforsaken wilderness, beggars can't be choosers."

"Has anyone ever told you that you have a finely tuned flair for the dramatic?" He shook his head. "We're a couple hours' hike from town, not on an expedition to the waste-land of the North Pole."

"Still…" She finished the wine in her glass and refilled it from the bottle beside her. When she held it out to him, he shook his head.

"What do you think of camping so far?" he asked.

"It's not hideous."

He laughed. "Wow. I'm not sure the Blackwater Lake Chamber of Commerce and Visitor Guide is going to want that as a slogan for their advertising campaign. I can see it now—'Come to Montana. It's not hideous.'"

She laughed, too. "Let me frame that comment better so you'll understand where it came from."

"I can hardly wait to see how you can spin it to reha-bilitate that remark."

"It's about me, and I don't mean that in a self-centered way." She took a sip of wine even as the relaxation from the first glass slid through her. "I wasn't sure how I'd hold up just getting here. Would I collapse in a heap on the trail? Break a leg? Snake bite?"

"I can't believe how optimistic you are."

"Seriously. I didn't know if I had the stamina and in-testinal fortitude. Heck, I had no idea if I was in good enough shape."

He let his gaze trail over her hiking boots, past the jeans on her legs and long-sleeved T-shirt. His eyes narrowed and filled with naked intensity. "Your shape looks pretty good to me."

*Oh, my...* Her heartbeat went all weird and thumpy. "Thanks, but I wasn't looking for a compliment, just explaining that I'm happy I made it and proud, too. You know?"

"Yeah."

"I'm more relaxed than I've been in a long time." If the paparazzi could follow her here, then more power to them. She took another sip of wine. "The campsite is cozy. Food was delicious."

"Always is in the fresh air."

"It's so clean and pure. Beautiful here." She dragged in a deep breath, then wiggled to get comfortable. "Although I can't say this log is especially comfy."

"Lean forward." When she obeyed, he put his arm behind her as a cushion, then pulled her against him.

"Much better. Thanks." She automatically curled into him as if she'd been doing it for years, and that was a different kind of danger from navigating the great outdoors. But at this particular moment she was too comfortable and content to worry about danger.

She leaned her head against his shoulder and stared at the sky. The beauty was breathtaking. "I don't think I've ever seen so many stars in my life."

He looked down at her and their mouths were only inches apart. When he spoke his voice was a little deeper, a lot huskier. "That's probably because there's too much nuisance light in L.A. or New York."

"But not here," she said reverently.

"No, not here." He gently put his fingers on her chin and held it at just the right angle for their mouths to meet. Searching her gaze he said, "I'd really like to kiss you."

*Me, too,* she wanted to say but barely managed to hold back the words. "That isn't part of the bargain."

"It should be." There was a hint of irritated frustration in his voice.

"Why?"

He thought for a moment. "Couples kiss openly all the time."

"PDA."

"Excuse me?"

"Public display of affection," she explained.

"Right."

"The thing is, we did that and ended up on the cover of a nationally syndicated magazine." Funny, she thought, right here and now with a sky full of glitter and the scent of pine surrounding her, the bad stuff just didn't seem to matter as much.

"To convince the skeptics, we need to do it again and make it look good, like it happens all the time in private."

She blinked up at him. "You're saying that we have to practice kissing?"

He nodded. "What do you think?"

That this is trouble, she thought. Trouble she could enthusiastically get behind. "I think if you think practicing is a good idea, then it's probably okay."

"That's not exactly wholehearted agreement." He glanced up at the sky. "Can you think of a better place?"

It was the most romantic spot she'd ever been in her entire life. "No," she whispered. "This is perfect."

"Okay then. Practice makes perfect, too." He shifted his shoulders toward her, getting ready to move in. "This first one we'll need around town. The playful peck on the cheek."

"You name kisses?"

"Don't you?"

It had been so long she couldn't remember. "Not really."

He brushed his thumb over her chin. "Now stop talking and concentrate."

"Okay." She realized she'd spoken and said, "Sorry." She shrugged.

"Here goes." He dipped his head and gave her a quick kiss just in front of her ear.

She felt his breath stir her hair and that raised tingles on her arms. "M-my family does that, but it's an air kiss."

He nodded. "Next up is the haven't-seen-you-all-day. This will come in handy at the lodge if you happen to be at the registration desk when I get back from the clinic."

"Definitely important to practice that one," she agreed, anticipation trickling through her.

"I'm glad you comprehend the full magnitude of the situation." He started to lower his head, then stopped and said, "Keep in mind we'll be standing up for this one."

"Got it."

She closed her eyes and lifted her chin just as his mouth met hers, lips slightly apart. Before she was ready to let go, he pulled back.

His chest was rising and falling quickly. "That was pretty good."

"Thanks." She stared into his eyes and asked breathlessly, "What else have you got?"

He touched his mouth to her cheek and nibbled his way to her neck. "I call that the wait-until-I-get-you-alone."

She didn't have to wait; they were alone.

"Very nice." She swallowed hard. "That's an impressive repertoire. I think that covers just about everything we should need—"

"There's one more we might have to pull off."

She settled her palm on his chest and felt his heart pounding. "Does it have a name?"

"I call it get-a-room."

"Oh, my—"

He called it right, she thought when he touched his mouth to hers. At the same time he pulled her tightly against him and wrapped her in his arms. Heat devoured her when he traced the seam of her lips with his tongue. She opened for him and he willingly took what she offered.

He stroked her and she let him, loving the feeling of being held and stroked. But it was more than that. It was the fact that *this* man was doing the holding making all the difference. She wanted this; she wanted him.

"Oh, Ben, this is so—"

"If you say it's not right, then I'm doing something wrong."

"No. Everything is perfect. Get-a-room delivers in a big way, and—"

He pulled back to look at her and seemed to know what she was thinking. "We don't have a room, but the tent is handy."

It had been so long for her and he felt so good that she just couldn't find the will to say this wasn't a good idea. At this moment it seemed like the best idea she'd ever heard.

"I'll race you."

Ben surged to his feet and pulled her up with him. He tugged her to the dome tent at the edge of the clearing, then led her inside and zipped the entrance closed after them. Cam dropped to the sleeping bag and pulled off her hiking boots. He did the same.

The sound of their rapid breathing filled the tiny space as they yanked at buttons, shirts and jeans. Clothes were gone in what was possibly a land speed record and she was naked in the sleeping bag with an equally naked Ben.

He settled his hand on her breast and brushed his thumb across the peak. The sensation started a throbbing between her legs and she moaned with need. She put her hand on his chest, letting the dusting of hair tickle her palm, and her touch made him groan.

He kissed her over and over until she could hardly draw enough air into her lungs. When he pulled back she nearly whimpered with disappointment.

"What do you call that one?" she asked, cupping his lean cheek in her palm.

"The I-need-you-now." Just enough glow from the fire penetrated the tent to see the primal intensity in his eyes.

She nodded wordlessly and tried to pull him down.

"Hold that thought." He fumbled through the tangle of clothes beside them and finally found his jeans. After pulling something from his wallet, he was back. "Condom."

Cam didn't ask why he'd brought it; she was only grateful that he was prepared. When he'd put it on, he settled on top of her and she wrapped her legs around his waist as he entered her.

He was still for a moment, letting her get used to the feel of him. Then he started to move and in seconds she caught his rhythm, as if this weren't their first time together. He stroked her over and over, then slid an arm beneath her and rolled until she was straddling him.

"What do you call that move?" she asked, gently biting his earlobe.

He sucked in a breath and said, "I've got you right where I want you." His voice was a sexy growl that scraped over her bare skin.

Then he cupped her breasts in his hands and groaned as she arched her hips and lifted them up and down. He reached between their bodies and rubbed his thumb over the bundle of nerve endings between her thighs. Instantly pleasure exploded through her and she collapsed on top of him. He held her until the shudders subsided, then gently rolled her to her back.

He moved inside her once, twice. The third time he groaned and his body went still as he found his release. Cam held him the same way he'd held her. She held him until he relaxed in her arms. It seemed as if they stayed that way for hours but probably was only minutes.

Ben lifted his weight onto his elbows and said, "We better put clothes on. It's going to get cold."

It wasn't the mountain air, but his words and tone that chilled Cam. Holy cow, she thought, sex wasn't even on the list of rules they'd discussed. But now that they'd done the deed, talking was probably mandatory.

When she was dressed and in her sleeping bag, she glanced at Ben. Their shoulders almost touched, but his face was in shadow and she couldn't see his expression.

"Are you awake?" she asked.

"Yeah." His tone somehow said that sleep was the last thing on his mind.

"So that probably wasn't the wisest thing we could have done."

"Fun though," he said.

She smiled in the dark. "It was fun. But this doesn't change anything."

"I know." There was a restless rustling as he shifted in the sleeping bag. "I'm not looking for a relationship."

"Right," she agreed.

"And you're not staying in Blackwater Lake, no matter what happens to the lodge."

"Right again. If it turns around financially, I'm gone. If not—same thing."

"So we're on the same page. Good, that's settled. We should probably get some sleep." He rolled onto his side, away from her. "'Night, Cam."

"Good night."

But there was nothing good about this night, and things *had* changed, no matter what he said. After what they'd done, the reasons for the bargain were less about practicality and logic. Just like that, there was an unforeseen personal investment, at least on her part. Suddenly the "no one gets hurt" clause of the agreement turned into gray area and she had to find a way to shift it back to black and white.

## *Chapter Nine*

**B**right and early Monday morning Cam walked out of her suite and came face-to-face with Ben, who was just coming out of his. She hadn't seen him since returning to town exhausted yesterday afternoon. They'd both worked very hard to pretend sex hadn't happened.

"Good morning."

"Hi," she said, brightly, still working to forget.

He fell into step beside her on the way to the elevator at the end of the hall. "Apparently a weekend in the mountains agrees with you."

"Oh? How can you tell?"

"Because you're looking particularly lovely this morning. And relaxed."

That just meant she was a good actress. "Thanks."

If he wasn't simply being charming, that was just proof of how good cosmetics could be. She wanted to say that he was looking particularly good, too, but she preferred the sexy, scruffy, hair sticking up first thing in the morning look. And she'd never have experienced it if they hadn't gone camping. Though their rooms were side by side, there seemed to be an invisible line neither of them was willing to cross here in the civilized world.

A lot of things had changed because she'd gone away with him. For the first time since he'd invaded her serenity spot here in the civilized world she didn't know what to say to him. Finally she came up with, "I miss trout for breakfast."

He grinned. "That's the nicest thing you've ever said to me."

"I was talking about fish. That has nothing to do with you."

"Sure it does." At the end of the corridor he pressed the elevator's down button. "I caught it, cleaned it, cooked it. I feel a deep, personal satisfaction at having introduced you to the great outdoors."

He'd introduced her to more than that, but it was best not to go there. "I'll admit to doubts about hiking into the mountains."

"Doubts? You were looking for an exit strategy until we set up camp."

"You're not going to let up, are you?"

"That's not my current plan, no."

"Okay. I was wrong." Best to keep things light, she decided. "There, I said it."

"You're a big person," he said, looking down at her.

Two dings behind them indicated the elevator had arrived and when the doors opened they got in.

"What's on your agenda for today?" she asked, moving away from him. As much as she liked breathing in the scent of his skin, it was best to keep her distance.

"Patient appointments this morning, then a trek to the hospital for a hip replacement."

"That's close to a hundred miles away, isn't it?"

He nodded. "Plans are moving forward for the Mercy Medical Clinic expansion and part of that is an outpatient surgery center. That will make a huge difference to people here in town."

"And to you."

"Yup." They arrived on the first floor. "What's up for you today?"

"Battle damage assessment."

"Excuse me?" He took her elbow as they rounded the corner to the lodge lobby.

"That article wasn't especially flattering to me and I've been unavailable for the last couple of days since it hit."

"You're welcome for that." He wore a smug expression, but on him it looked good. Better than good.

"Your humility brings a tear to my eye." She shook her head. "Anyway, I need to evaluate the fallout and hope that it hasn't set me back in my quest to win the hearts and minds of the lodge staff."

"I think you'll be pleasantly surprised." He stopped by the corner of the registration desk. "People in Blackwater Lake can be stubborn, but if they decide you're a friend, you'll be one forever. They're incredibly loyal. Don't forget you started to break down the walls and show them the real Camille Halliday, not the one created by the media to sell newspapers and magazines."

"I'm not sure that will be enough." She glanced over to where M.J. talked to the night manager to coordinate any unresolved issues at the change of shift. "It could be back to them calling me Ms. Halliday, or better yet, the rich witch."

"Then maybe it's time for a couple refresher course."

He moved closer and his eyes went dark, the way they had by the campfire just before he took her into the tent. "I call this one the it-will-have-to-hold-you-until-later kiss."

Cam's heart started thumping wildly as he cupped her cheek in his hand, then lowered his mouth to hers. It wasn't a playful peck on the cheek, just a quick touch that left her wanting so much more.

He stared into her eyes and gently brushed his thumb over her jaw. "Have a good day."

This was a really good start. Dangerous, but good. "You, too. Drive carefully."

"Will do." He moved toward the front door and waved at M.J. before walking out.

Cam watched through the floor-to-ceiling windows until he disappeared. Then she took a deep breath and braced for a bad day. After pasting a big, everything's peachy smile on her face, she rounded the high registration desk.

"Hi, M.J."

The blonde looked up from the computer monitor, then pushed her square black glasses more firmly up on her nose. "Hi, Cam. How was your weekend? Did you and Ben have a good time?"

She wasn't getting any unpleasant vibes, at least not yet. "It was my first time. Camping," she added. To distinguish the outdoor experience from her first time with Ben, which had been pretty awesome. "As you can see I survived."

"When they do Survivor: Blackwater Lake, the celebrity season, you'll have to try out." Her smile said she didn't mean that in a bad way. "Seriously, I'd expect nothing less of Ben McKnight. There was no doubt that he'd take good care of you."

"He certainly did." And then some. A blush crept up her neck and she hoped her face didn't look as red from the outside as it felt on the inside. "The mountains are so beautiful. I can't even put it into words. Everything took my breath away."

That was the honest truth in every single aspect.

M.J. smiled. "I'm glad."

"The next time a guest asks me what to do while they're here, I can recommend hiking and camping without hesitation." The other woman looked at her like a proud mother, as if Cam had somehow passed a test. "How was everything here at the lodge while I was gone?"

"No more scum-sucking journalists asking questions, I can tell you that."

"Good to know."

"Otherwise, it was busy. Really busy." She clicked her mouse and pulled up a computer screen. "Remember how sparse the reservations looked last time you checked?"

"Unfortunately, yes." Cam scrolled through, studying the information. "Is this a mistake?"

"No. The phone's been practically ringing off the hook. The summer is filling up nicely." What looked like teasing stole into M.J.'s blue eyes.

Cam was afraid to trust both the woman's expression and the explosion of business. "This is on the level?"

"I think it's a direct result of the public finally discovering the whereabouts of the notorious Halliday heiress and her hunky boyfriend. Because curious people want to know."

This *was* teasing. A normal give-and-take between friends. And Cam liked it a lot. "You know, I still hate that story, but if it helped put Blackwater Lake Lodge on the map, then I'll gladly take one for the team."

"I didn't believe any of that stuff written about you. The jerk put the worst possible spin on it."

"Thanks for saying so." Cam meant that from the bottom of her heart.

"It's just wrong for someone to invade your privacy like that and imply what he did in that article. Anyone can see by the way you look at Ben McKnight that you've got genuine feelings for the man." She sighed. "Just the way he kisses you goodbye…"

"Oh?"

"Who's kissing?" Jenny the hostile waitress from Fireside walked up and rested her forearms on the high desk in front of them. "Hi, M.J. Hey, Cam."

"Good morning." Her good feeling disappeared and she tensed for the worst. It was best to ignore the kissing question. "What's up?"

"Amanda sent me to ask if you're still having lunch with her today. She said to tell you before you asked that she's too busy cooking to call or come herself."

"That sounds like her." Cam laughed. "Yes, I'm planning on it."

"Good." Jenny hesitated for a second, then said, "She also wants to hear all about your weekend with Dr. McKnight." She shrugged. "And she's not the only one. I'm curious, too. So shoot me. Did you have fun?"

"I had a great time. I'm no longer a wilderness virgin." The two women laughed as she'd hoped. "And the scenery is spectacular."

"A boyfriend like Dr. M doesn't hurt either." Jenny was just stating a fact and seemed genuinely interested.

"That man can definitely hold his own with Mother Nature and enhance any setting." Again that was the truth.

"Amen. Glad you had a good weekend. I have to get back before I get in trouble with the boss." Jenny winked. "I'll let Amanda know about lunch."

"Thanks."

Cam was truly amazed, and the feeling continued for the rest of the day. Dustin from the concierge desk strolled over to find out if she'd had a good time. Then someone from housekeeping stopped by to see how the weekend had gone. She felt as if they'd accepted her, as if she was one of their own.

The good news was that so far they all seemed to be talking to her. The bad was that they really believed she and Ben were a romantic couple. More astonishing was that the staff seemed to be in favor of the relationship, which made Cam feel like a fraud for deceiving everyone.

But worst of all, she couldn't stop thinking about her hunky wilderness guide. Cam wished she could tell Amanda everything and talk this through, but that was impossible. If she let the truth slip to anyone at the lodge, everything could blow up in her face.

Her only other real friend was Ben, and she couldn't discuss him with him? The bargain seemed to be working, but sometimes it was inconvenient when a plan came together.

Ben was glad he hadn't scheduled appointments until later in the morning and had taken his time getting to the clinic. It had been a late night at the hospital when the patient had a complication from surgery. She came through fine, but then there was the long drive home. He'd hung around the lodge longer because of that; at least that's what he'd told himself.

But if he was being completely honest, it was more about hoping to catch a glimpse of Cam. He hadn't. Now he wasn't sure if his bad mood was a reflection of that or simply fatigue. If he had to guess, it would be the former. Yesterday, kissing her goodbye before heading off to work had been the best part of his day.

Camping with her had been such a good time, and not

only because of the sex—although he couldn't deny that was a highlight. But seeing through her eyes the beauty of the mountains, streams and big blue sky he loved and had missed so much had been satisfying in a way he'd never experienced before. She could have been a whining, complaining diva, but that wasn't how it went down. The awe she'd felt was as clear as the blue of her eyes and she'd been a terrific sport.

Seeing her in the morning had been pretty amazing, too. All that tousled blond hair, messed up because he'd run his fingers through it the night before, was flat-out the sexiest thing he'd ever experienced. Even now the memory shot pure lust straight to his groin. Really inconvenient, since he'd just pulled into the clinic parking lot.

His office was on the second floor of the Victorian mansion donated to the town and turned into a medical facility. The first floor had exam rooms and reception and waiting areas. There was a lab for simple tests, nothing sophisticated since there wasn't the equipment or personnel for that. Anything complex went to the hospital. His footsteps sounded on the wooden floor after he walked in the back door and down the hall to the stairway.

After climbing it, he passed the first door, where Adam Stone's office was located. The other doctor was there talking to their nurse, Ginny Irwin.

"So—Bermuda, Tahiti or Fiji?"

Ben stopped and poked his head in. "Are those the only countries in the world without an extradition treaty with the United States? Is there something you want to share?"

Adam grinned. "Very funny. In case you were wondering, we had some patients cancel this morning, so I'm taking a minute to look through these travel brochures." He pointed to the oblong pamphlets spread out across his desk. "Those are the three places I've narrowed down for

a honeymoon destination after I marry the love of my life."
A satisfied expression settled in his brown eyes. "Jill's
going to be one knockout of a June bride."

It was obvious that the man was actually looking forward to committing. Ben could see happiness written all
over his face. But tying the knot didn't guarantee a happy-
ever-after. His parents were proof of that. When the love
of your life dies in childbirth leaving you with three small
children and a business to run in order to support the family, it's not especially idyllic. And his father had never gotten over the loss of his wife.

Ben pushed the dark thoughts away. "So, I take it that
Jill wants to go somewhere with a beach?"

"I plan to surprise her."

"She hasn't had a lot of good surprises in her life."
Ginny looked at Adam with an expression telling him that
this honeymoon better be a good one. "If you can pull this
off, you're a better man than I thought."

"Wow, that gave me a warm fuzzy. Feel the love." Adam
glanced down at the ads for the beaches. "I just want it to
be perfect for her. And I want to see my bride in a bikini
for a week. I don't think that's too much to ask."

"And there it is." Ben leaned a shoulder against the
doorjamb. "Ulterior motive."

"Do you blame me?"

"Absolutely not." He remembered the erotic sight of
Cam's naked body silhouetted inside the tent by the fire
just outside. Every single cell in his body ached to see her
that way again.

"Before Jill's mom died, I promised her I'd look out for
her daughter and grandson. She was my best friend since
grade school," the nurse explained to Ben, then leaned
over to study the brochures. She picked up the one from
Tahiti. "So keep this in mind about your bikini-wearing

bride. That girl's never been farther from home than Helena." She looked at Adam. "For the greenhorn who needs a geography lesson, that's the capital of Montana."

Ben reminded himself not to get on this woman's bad side. "I think I know where you're going with this."

Ginny grinned. "Take her to whichever one of these places is the farthest from Blackwater Lake. She'd be happy if you pitched a tent in the backyard so long as you're there with her."

"And she's with me. God, I love that woman," Adam said cheerfully.

"Good enough." Ginny patted his shoulder. "Then my work here is done."

"Speaking of work," Ben said, "I'll just go stash my briefcase and get downstairs—"

"Not so fast, buster. The patients can wait a few more minutes." Ginny put her hands on her hips and drilled him with a look. "You were in and out of here so fast yesterday we barely saw you. Let alone get a chance to grill you about your weekend. What happened with Miss Halliday hotel heiress?"

"We hiked up to that stream a couple miles above the lake." He shrugged, hoping to leave it right there. "So, it's time to get to work—"

"And you spent the night?" Ginny asked, not in the least sidetracked or discouraged.

"Yes."

Ben glanced at the other doctor, shooting him a help-a-brother-out look. Adam Stone might be a hyper-observant family practice doctor, but he was a crappy wingman. The grin on his face said he was enjoying this and had no intention of intervening on a brother's behalf.

"How did she handle that? It's hard to picture Miss Four-inch Heels and Short Skirts getting her hands dirty."

"She was a real trouper. Pulled her weight and didn't complain. She actually seemed to take to the whole outdoor experience." Including the kiss practicing and everything that came after. Don't think about it now, he cautioned himself. "She even tried fishing but swore if a miracle happened and she caught anything she'd throw it back. No one was going to accuse her of finding and filleting Nemo."

Ginny smiled. "Sounds like she's got a good sense of humor."

"That she does," he agreed, remembering her insisting on having wine in the wilderness. "I have to admit that I wasn't sure what to expect." He smiled as her words went through his mind. "To quote her: It wasn't hideous."

"So, her not liking that sort of thing would be a deal-breaker for you?" Ginny asked. "If she didn't take to the outdoors you'd be outta there?"

Ben couldn't tell her he had no "there" to be out of. The lying to everyone part of this bargain hadn't really become real until he'd started. With his family and everyone else. He'd been on the receiving end of being strung along and didn't like it. He wasn't that kind of person. In the end, he just told the truth without answering the question asked.

"Spending time in the outdoors is very important to me."

"Not hideous," Adam mused. "I'm hoping for a more enthusiastic reaction when I take Jill to Tahiti."

Ginny clapped her hands together. "And we have a winner."

"Yes." Adam gave her a warning look. "Keep it to yourself."

"I won't breathe a word." She looked at her watch. "The patients will be here for their appointments now. I'll get them in the exam rooms for you. We've got a full day, Doctors."

"Thanks, Ginny. Don't know what we'd do without you," Adam said.

"It's my job." The tone was matter-of-fact, but there was a smile on her face when she walked out the door.

"I guess we better get down there, too," Ben said.

"Just a second." Adam stood and walked around the desk. He was wearing the usual green scrubs and white lab coat. "Can we talk?"

"Sure." But Ben knew those words were never good. "Is something wrong?"

"No." The other man looked thoughtful. "Just something I thought you should know."

"Okay. What's up?"

"I guess you're aware of that article that came out in *The Rumor Report*."

"Yeah. Cam was really upset about it."

Adam nodded. "I can imagine. It was pretty unflattering to her."

"You read it?"

"Someone left it in the waiting room. You were on the cover. Kissing a woman." He shrugged. "I was curious."

"It's not true." Ben folded his arms over his chest.

"So, you're not going out with Camille Halliday?"

Not the way everyone thought, but he couldn't say that. "Yes, we're going out. What I meant was the unflattering stuff that was printed about her. It was blown out of proportion and laid out in a way that would make her look bad. Their goal isn't to tell the truth."

Adam studied him. "You look like you want to punch someone."

"I'm a supportive boyfriend." If you took the "boy" part out that statement was true. He was her friend. "So are we done here? Is that it?"

"Actually, no. I haven't gotten to that part yet."

"Okay. What?"

"Almost every patient I've seen in the last two days has asked about you and Ms. Halliday."

"In what way?"

"They're speculating that you're after her money—"

That had been implied in the article and he had to admit it ticked him off. "I don't need hers. I've got plenty of my own."

"I'm just saying. Don't kill the messenger." Adam held up his hands in a simmer-down gesture. "The other theory is that she's paying you to rehabilitate her bad-girl image."

"No to that, too. Trust me on this. No money is being exchanged."

"I wouldn't care if there was," Adam said. "It makes no difference to me. You're a good doctor and we work well together. I just wanted you to know that the patients you see are probably going to ask."

"I appreciate the warning." And he really did.

Ben wished he could tell his friend the truth, that what he had with Cam was a deal to keep the clinic from becoming a circus because of him. But living with this bargain was different from what he'd expected. People in town obviously had questions about him and Cam. They would be shocked to find out that he had some of his own about the two of them but had no answers. All he knew was that he liked her. Liked her a lot.

Everything was supposed to be casual, but he hadn't taken sex into account. Actually, he'd thought about it almost from the first time he'd seen Cam in the moonlight, but he hadn't thought to include rules about it in the bargain negotiations.

This whole deal had been about getting what each of them wanted. A win/win where no one gets hurt. From where he was standing, it didn't feel like anyone was winning.

## Chapter Ten

"Welcome to the first annual Blackwater Lake Lodge employee appreciation dinner."

Cam stood at the head table during the applause that followed her opening remarks and looked around the small conference room. There were about twenty people in attendance, a better turnout than she'd expected.

Actually, since her disastrous track record after arriving, she'd tried to set a low bar for expectations, because the disappointment was easier to bear.

"Did everyone enjoy dinner?" she asked and barely got the words out before the eruption of applause, whistles and woo-hoos. "I'm glad. I'll be sure to pass that on to the chef. And, by the way, everyone who volunteered to serve your coworkers tonight will receive dinner on the house at Fireside. Just a special thanks for your loyalty and spirit of cooperation."

She waited while there was more clapping and a few

whistles. When it died down she continued. "I'll keep this short. I don't want anyone getting indigestion." There was a laugh as she'd hoped. "It's my goal to make the lodge successful and I can't do that alone. Reservations are increasing—"

"Thanks to you getting your name in the paper." The comment came from one of the guys in the back.

"I'm happy to do my part." Cam didn't mind the good-natured teasing. Now that she knew it *was* good-natured. More than one person in Blackwater Lake had told her they'd gotten a glimpse into her world from that tabloid story and seen the ugly side of fame, and she had their sympathy. It was new and different and wonderful. The comment just now had no animosity behind it. "And I just want to thank every one of you for your hard work every day. Without you, there wouldn't be a Blackwater Lake Lodge. Lately I have reason to be cautiously optimistic about the future of this property. If everyone continues pulling together, jobs will be preserved and we may be able to do more hiring soon."

Someone, again probably the guy in the back, started chanting, "Hall-i-day!"

Everyone in the room picked up on it and for a few moments Cam couldn't say anything. And not just because it was too noisy. There was a lump in her throat. She'd never felt accepted anywhere the way she did now. This group had given her a chance, thanks to Ben, but she wanted to believe that she'd won them over because of her fair management style and willingness to work harder than anyone.

Except somewhere along the way she'd started to care about these people, and if the enthusiastic clapping and chanting was any indication, the feeling was mutual. In that moment she realized the effort and hard work she'd put in wasn't just about her career anymore.

"Thanks, everyone." She held up her hands for quiet. "That means more to me than I can put into words. Now I just have one more thing to say. Dessert."

And the crowd went wild as servers brought out the seven-layer chocolate cake.

"How do you think it went?" She sat down and whispered to M.J. on her right.

"Really well. Everyone likes to be appreciated for their efforts and you did that."

"It was short and sweet." Jenny was on her left. She took a bite of her cake. "Speaking of sweet, I never get tired of this."

"It is pretty wonderful," Cam agreed.

"Speaking of wonderful…" M.J. looked around. "Where's Ben tonight?"

That was a good question, but Cam couldn't very well say that she had no legitimate right to have an answer. "He understands that tonight isn't about significant others or a plus-one."

"Somehow he seems like so much more than a plus-one." Jenny sighed dramatically. "Can I be honest with you, boss?"

Cam studied the pretty, heart-shaped face with the dark hair pulled back into a ponytail. There was no hostility in her brown eyes now, just new frankness and authenticity. That was to be encouraged.

And a little levity couldn't hurt. "Should I be afraid?"

Jenny laughed. "A couple months ago maybe, but not now."

"Okay, then. I much prefer candor."

"I'm pretty envious of you. Being with Dr. McKnight. I tried really hard to get him to notice me when he moved back here. And I'm not the only one. Patty and Crystal did, too." She glanced at the two women who were seated to her left.

"I completely understand," Cam told her with absolute sincerity. "And the truth is, I can hardly believe this relationship myself."

"All the single women in town are envious of you. At first no one could understand what he saw in you," Jenny shared. "No offense."

"None taken."

"It's just that he's a great guy and we all had you pegged as a stuck-up, rich, self-centered heiress."

"Don't sugarcoat it, Jen. Tell me how you really feel."

The waitress laughed. "The thing is, you're not at all what we thought. In fact, the unofficial word-of-mouth poll is that the two of you make a great couple. So it's all good."

"That's nice to hear." And the guilt just kept on coming.

"I'm actually glad to see him with someone," M.J. said.

That made Cam curious, and a lot of questions popped into her mind. But it was important to set just the right tone, keep this casual. Too much prying would show insecurity and weakness and make them wonder why she didn't know. Not enough could imply she didn't care and that wasn't the vibe she wanted to project.

"Why are you glad?" she finally asked M.J. Jenny was talking to Crystal and Patty on her other side.

"I guess because Ben came back to Blackwater Lake still single and not in a relationship."

His status hadn't changed, although no one knew, but that still didn't answer Cam's question. "I'm not sure what you mean."

"Me either, to be honest. It's just that I was surprised to find out he'd never been married." She shrugged. "It crossed my mind that what Judy did might have turned him against commitment."

"He's too well-adjusted for that. He's sexy, funny, flirty and gorgeous. And he's a doctor."

"I know. It seems silly to even say it. I'm sure he has his reasons for waiting and that's fine. As long as it's not Judy who's keeping him from being happy."

"I don't think he gives her much thought," Cam said. And she truly believed that. Still, he was the kind of man that most women—not her, but the average female—would give almost anything to be with. "I know he's not gay."

M.J. grinned. "And just how would you know that?"

"I asked. He told me."

"And you believe him?"

"Yes." That and he'd made pretty amazing love to her in the mountains. Memories of that had heat creeping up her neck and into her cheeks. "Any theories about why he's not married?"

M.J. shrugged. "Since we agree he's emotionally stable, one would have to assume he's been busy. After medical school he started a practice in Las Vegas. That probably took a lot of time and dedication. The opposite sex can be a distraction when one is trying to focus on a career."

No kidding. But this conversation was hitting far too close to things she didn't want to get into. Too many questions could imply that she wasn't talking to her boyfriend, which was true. Time to change the subject. "So, how are the kids?"

"Great." A soft expression slid into M.J.'s eyes. "They're looking forward to the end of the school year."

A strategic question here and there had the other woman talking about all the activities available to children during the summer months in Montana. Cam put on an interested face and she truly was. But there was a part of her mind occupied with questions about Ben. Questions she hadn't thought about until M.J. said it out loud.

Why had he never been married? And was their fake romance really about what he'd claimed or something more?

"There's someone here to see you."

M.J. stood in Cam's office doorway smiling a sappy smile. The one every woman wore when she thought romance had come calling.

"Ben's out there, isn't he?"

"Yes—"

"I'm actually in here," he said, moving around M.J.

"I'll just leave you two alone." She walked out and closed the door.

Cam almost told her to leave the thing open. It wasn't like they were going to have sex. Their suites were side by side upstairs and neither had trespassed on the other's territory, although she'd been sorely tempted. But she was waiting for him.

"What are you doing here?" She looked at her watch, which said it was after noon. "No wonder I'm hungry."

"That's why I'm here. To take you out and feed you."

"I have a lot of work. My plan was to grab something quick at my desk and—"

"No."

She looked up and met his gaze. "Excuse me?"

"You're not going to eat at your desk, and I don't care if it's a seven-course meal that takes hours." He came around the desk and gently tugged her to her feet. "I'm taking you away from all this."

"But—"

He touched a finger to her lips, putting a stop to the protest. Her mouth tingled from his touch and she wished he'd kissed her instead. That would have worked really well for her.

"No excuses," he said. "Come with me."

"Where?"

"You'll see."

"Don't you have patients?"

"Not for a couple of hours. There's time." He smiled mysteriously.

"Can I have a hint where we're going?" Passing the registration desk, she waved goodbye to M.J. The sappy smile just got sappier.

His SUV was parked near the front of the lodge and he opened the passenger door for her. She got in and fastened her seat belt, which suddenly seemed an apt metaphor for her life. After he got in the driver's seat, it occurred to her that was another appropriate metaphor for them. He always seemed to be plotting the course. Of course it was working for her professionally. And yes, darn it, she was more personally involved than she'd expected.

"So," he said, "you want a hint about where we're going."

"That would be nice, yes."

"Okay. It's not in town."

"I don't understand." She looked at the smug expression on his face. "We're always in town. That's the point. So everyone can see us together. To keep up the charade."

"M.J. saw us. She'll spread the word that we're inseparable."

For now. But they'd be separating soon. If the upward trend continued, she'd be lobbying her father for a more high-profile position at a Halliday Hospitality Inc. property in a city far away from Blackwater Lake. The thought made her stomach feel empty and that had nothing to do with being hungry. She would miss Ben and that wasn't supposed to happen.

He drove out of town as promised and headed north on Lake View Drive. Trees lined both sides of the road and the sky overhead was big and blue. Big sky country. Words couldn't describe how beautiful this place was. It was something a person had to experience firsthand. Oddly enough, she could feel the tension easing out of her.

"Okay. We're out of town. I need another hint. Is it bigger than a breadbox?"

"Yes. And it has great views." He glanced over, mischief in his eyes.

"Just so you know, I'm not dressed for camping and hiking."

He laughed. "Me either."

The mountain-man look on their weekend trip had been rugged and appealing, but she kind of liked him in the long-sleeved white cotton shirt and khaki pants he was wearing now. In fact, he didn't seem to have an unappealing look. She liked him in anything. Or nothing.

"Are you okay?"

"Dandy." She looked out the window so he couldn't see the heat in her cheeks.

He made a right turn onto a road that went uphill. At the top there was a lot littered with construction materials and in the center there was the shell of a structure going up.

"We're there." He put the car in Park and turned off the ignition.

"Is this your house?" she asked.

"Yes." He reached into the backseat. "I brought water and sandwiches from the diner."

"Good. Because I'm too hungry to wait for you to catch, clean and cook a fish." She opened her door and slid down. "It's like a picnic."

"Watch your step," he warned. "The ground is uneven and there's trash around."

And fresh air. "The breeze up here is wonderful."

He took her elbow in his free hand and guided her over

the uneven ground to where the solid foundation stood and the scent of sawdust tickled her nose. The framing was complete with wooden stairs up to the second floor, but no solid walls separated out the rooms. There was a lot of space.

Ben pretended to open the front door and let her precede him. "This is the entryway and leads all the way to the family room. To the left there will be a formal dining room and the living room is on the right."

"Formal dining?"

He shrugged. "Family dinner on Sunday night."

She walked to the back of the house and looked around. "Is this going to be all windows?"

"Yeah."

"Good. It would be a crime to block a view this spectacular."

"I couldn't agree more." Hands on hips, he stared at the view of the mountains, which was breathtaking. Then he pointed to a spot in the kitchen. "The sink is going there. You can see the lake while doing dishes."

She knew he meant that as a generic "you," not as in *she* would be around to see the lake or do dishes. On the cement floor there was writing that looked like measurements. "Is this going to be an island?"

"Yes. Big enough to land a jet and space for lots of cupboards underneath." He pointed to the corner. "Over there is a large, walk-in pantry. Beside it will be two built-in ovens and a microwave. A cooktop just there and room for a Sub-Zero refrigerator."

"Nice. Really nice. Can I see the upstairs?"

He grinned at her enthusiasm. "Follow me."

She held on to the wooden railing and at the top of the stairs he led her through what would be the double-door entry to the huge master suite, with a large dressing area with his and hers closets. He took her through four more bedrooms, two baths and a big game room.

"How many square feet is this going to be?" she asked.

"Five thousand—give or take."

"Wow." She wandered back to the master bedroom with him behind her.

"Right there," he said indicating a corner, "there's going to be a fireplace."

"Nice." What she wanted to say was *almost as romantic as the stars in the mountains,* but she stopped herself just in time.

He pointed up. "I'm putting in skylights to bring in light for a dreary winter day."

"This is going to be wonderful," she said, filled with a longing she didn't understand. "Who's the builder?"

"My brother. This is the first of a development of custom homes in this area. I bought the lot from him. I'm the guinea pig, I guess. It will be sort of a model for buyers looking in this neighborhood."

"Willing to spend the big bucks," she guessed.

"Alex is looking at a tidy profit margin." He walked over to the wooden window seat, took a napkin out of the bag and brushed it off. "Your table."

"Thanks." She sat and took the club sandwich he held out.

Ben sat next to her with his own. "Bon appétit."

They ate in silence for a few minutes and the breeze drifting around them carried the fragrance of pine and spring wildflowers.

"This is a beautiful spot. And that doesn't even do it justice." She looked at him. "There are a lot of bedrooms in this house. You must be planning to have kids to fill them up."

"I hadn't really thought about it. It's big and that's good for resale."

"So you didn't factor in a wife and children when you had the plans drawn up?"

He shrugged. "Maybe someday."

She studied him, looking for signs of—something. She didn't see shadows or sadness in his expression. "Are you dragging your feet on marriage for any particular reason?"

"Are you psychoanalyzing me?" He chewed a bite of sandwich and there was nothing but amusement in his eyes.

"You can call it that if you want. Or it could come under the heading of making conversation. But pretty much I'm just being nosy."

He laughed. "I don't think I'm a marrying kind of guy—"

She wanted to leave it hanging there, but just couldn't. "Are you avoiding a commitment because of Judy?"

"What do you know about her?" *Now* he looked annoyed.

"She was your high school girlfriend. You gave up a prestigious college in the east to go to school close by because you didn't want to leave her. After graduation you proposed so you could take your wife to med school, but she wasn't ready to leave. You were willing to do the long-distance relationship thing and she agreed. Six months after you left she married a ski bum and moved to New York." She looked at him and shrugged. "People talk."

"Remind me to have a word with M.J." He scowled.

"Did I get it right?"

"Pretty much."

"Does it still bother you?" She watched his expression carefully.

"I hadn't thought about her for years. Not until we ran into her on the street."

The night he'd kissed her. Studying him, she saw no evidence in his expression that he still had feelings for the woman. "Have you had a significant relationship since?"

"I'm feeling a cross-examination vibe," he said, eyes narrowing.

"This is a great house. It would be a wonderful place to raise a family. We're putting on a show for Blackwater Lake, but I feel as if we've gotten to be friends." And lovers, even if it was only one time. Intensity shadowed his eyes and she'd bet he was remembering that night in the tent, too. "I'm trying to figure out why you're building a family house without thinking about a family to fill it."

He shrugged. "I dated in Las Vegas. But I was pretty busy growing my medical practice. There wasn't a lot of time to build a relationship. Women tend to lose interest if they get bumped for a medical emergency too many times." He finished his sandwich and wadded up the paper.

That confirmed what M.J. suspected. "So after Judy you didn't meet anyone who made you want to take a chance on marriage?"

"No. What about you? Anyone special?"

"I thought so once or twice, but they had another agenda. Now it's all about my career."

That was his way of changing the subject, because she'd already told him why she had good reasons not to trust. Once a Halliday, always a Halliday. Her last name would always be well-known and she'd never know whether a man wanted her or the recognition that went with her. But building a career was something she could trust.

"So, I'm curious. Why did you bring me here?" Certainly not for her approval. And he didn't seem like the kind of man who was a show-off.

"This is sort of taking our relationship to the next level."

"I don't understand," she said. "We don't have a relationship."

"Really? You said we were friends."

"Well, yes. But that's a one-level sort of thing. How is this taking it up?"

"My brother, Alex, was wondering if you'd seen this place yet."

"Ah. It would be a logical next step if we were actually dating." She should have known. It was all part of the act.

"Right. So, if you happen to see him, or any other members of my family, you don't have to pretend."

Like she was pretending to care about him. Except it was feeling less and less like pretending.

She'd never met a man who had the capacity to care as much as Ben did. She liked him a lot. She found herself wanting what they had to be more. And now she'd seen where he planned to live. It was a wonderful place to raise a family and the idea of that started a yearning deep inside her for the family she'd always wanted and stopped believing she'd ever have.

She couldn't help thinking what a waste it was that a family wasn't in his plans. That was silly, really, because it wasn't her plan either. But this bargain had become way more complicated than she'd expected and she was beginning to regret making it.

The only thing she regretted more was that she wouldn't be around to see Ben's house finished.

## Chapter Eleven

Ben was beginning to regret the bargain he'd made with Cam Halliday.

After seeing his last patient of the day at the clinic, he drove back out to his house under construction. He walked through the opening where the front door would eventually be and swore he could still smell the fragrance of her perfume. In the big open room where the cement foundation was marked off for the kitchen island and cupboards, he could still see her looking out at the mountains, fascinated by the majestic sight. She'd picked up on the fact that it would be criminal to put in any walls and obstruct that view.

He climbed up the crude staircase and remembered the sensuous sway of her hips as she'd moved to the second floor. It had taken every ounce of his willpower to keep from scooping her into his arms and sweeping her the rest of the way up. Unfortunately that romantic gesture would have been wasted since there was no big fluffy bed to put her on.

Then again, maybe that wasn't such a bad thing. It was the only reason he hadn't kissed the daylights out of her before loving the daylights out of her. He'd badly wanted to.

He wanted her so much it hurt.

In the master bedroom he stared at the window seat where they'd sat and the empty bag from lunch. It wasn't littering. Not really. This was his house. Eventually he would move in here. Alone.

Ben remembered Cam's words and the wistful look on her face when she'd said this would be a good place to raise a family. He could picture her here, putting her touch on everything, infusing her classiness into the decorating, adding a lot of color to the landscaping. And that gave him a bad feeling.

Inserting her personality into his life wasn't supposed to be part of this bargain.

It was so quiet out here he heard the sound of a car coming up the hill, then pull onto his lot. In one of the unfinished front bedrooms he looked out the window and saw his brother's black truck. Alex was just getting out.

"Thank God." He needed a distraction. Anything to keep him from thinking about Cam.

Ben jogged downstairs to the kitchen. His brother was carefully looking over the framing and whatever else a building contractor inspected. Alex was really good at what he did. He'd started McKnight Construction in California, then opened a branch here in Blackwater Lake when he brought his pregnant wife here to live. But she'd had secrets and Alex's family had unraveled. Ben wasn't sure his brother would ever get over that.

"Hi," he said.

Alex dragged his gaze away from the heavy-duty metal

floor brackets that held the weight-bearing beams in place. "Hey, little brother. What do you think of the place so far?"

"I think that everything you talked me into is perfect. So far."

"Good." He settled his hands on lean hips. "Like what?"

"The walk-in pantry." Cam's eyes had glowed with approval.

"What else?"

"The window seat in the master bedroom." Ben could still see her brushing her hand over it as if she was deciding on fabric for the cushion. With an effort he pulled his thoughts back to the here and now.

It was amazing how Alex managed to look confident and professional in jeans, boots, T-shirt and baseball hat sporting the McKnight Construction logo. But he carried it off beautifully. "And?"

"What?"

"Isn't there something else I was right about?"

His brother had suggested the corner fireplace in the master bedroom. Ben had pictured himself in a big, fluffy, king-size bed with a fire going and Cam in his arms after making love. It was romantic crap with zero chance of happening.

"I'm not feeding your Montana-size ego anymore."

Alex's eyes narrowed on him. "Bad day at the clinic?"

"No." Work wasn't the problem. Lunch had unsettled him.

"Has Cam seen the house?"

"Why would you ask that?" Ben demanded.

"Gosh, I don't know. Maybe because the two of you are always together." Alex shrugged. "Just seems to me you'd want her opinion on this place."

"I'm building it for me."

Could have been the words or the tone, but something

about that statement had his brother's eyes narrowing. "Is everything all right with the two of you?"

"Of course." Ben's voice was sharper and more defensive than he'd intended.

"That doesn't sound good at all." Alex moved closer, studying him. "Want to talk about it?"

"There's nothing to say."

"You're not a very good liar, little brother."

"What makes you think I'm not telling the truth? That there's nothing wrong?"

"Because you look like someone cut the ears off your favorite stethoscope. What's her name?"

"What makes you think it's a her?"

"Come on, Ben. Tell me what's going on."

"I could. But then I'd have to kill you." He was going for humor, but his brother's expression didn't lighten up.

"Seriously?" Alex shook his head. "This is me. No way I'm going down."

Ben figured he was probably right about that. The guy worked with his hands, swung tools, carried heavy building materials and was in really good shape. Ben ran and lifted weights, but that wouldn't tip the scales in his favor during a physical confrontation with his older brother.

"I was kidding. Just drop it, okay?"

Alex shook his head. "Not when you look like that. Spill it, bro."

Ben wondered when he'd become so easy to read. He really needed to talk to someone, because this bargain was dishonest and so not like him. Realistically, he didn't have much to lose if word got out about it. Cam would be leaving soon and he didn't have a plan B for when she was gone. So what if he confided in Alex, who then spilled the beans? It would be a relief to tell the truth. Maybe when word spread, and it would, women would get the message that he wanted to be left alone.

He took a deep breath, then said, "Cam and I aren't really dating."

Alex stared at him for several moments. "That's funny, because the two of you have been spotted all over town together. And there was that backpacking trip. Your rooms at the lodge are right next door to each other, which makes things pretty convenient."

More like pretty tempting. Ben spent a lot of sleepless nights thinking about her on the other side of the wall. There was nothing convenient about it.

"All the dinners and hanging out? It's not real."

"It looked real. And what about that camping trip three or four weeks ago? Did you, or did you not, take her into the mountains?" Alex asked.

"I did. Just to further the pretense." Sex hadn't been a part of the charade. It had been real, and awesome. Unfortunately, having her had twisted everything up. "This whole dating thing is staged."

"Doesn't look that way. People all over town have betting pools going."

"Betting on what?" Ben demanded.

"When you're going to pop the question. Wedding dates. All kinds of stuff."

"People all over town need to get a life," Ben said. "I'm telling you it's all an act."

"I can't speak for the lady because I don't know her that well. But you're not that good an actor, bro. No offense."

"Cam and I made a bargain. My idea." He didn't want anyone to get the wrong impression about Cam. She wasn't dishonest, just the opposite. And funny, sweet, vulnerable, beautiful. Damn it. Even in his own head he was sticking up for her. "I talked her into pretending to be my girlfriend so everyone would think I was off the dating market."

"The brilliance of that bachelor strategy makes me proud to be your brother." Alex shook his head with amazement. "But how did you get her to go along with it?"

"She was having trouble with the staff at the lodge. I gave her practical advice on how to handle different situations. Because I know most of the key players." He shrugged. "Women left me alone at the clinic. And everything at the lodge is running more efficiently."

"I see." His brother walked over to the doorway and leaned a shoulder against the exposed wood. "So you don't have romantic feelings for her?"

"No." Unless that included sleeping with her that one time. He wasn't sure where romantic feelings fit into wanting to sleep with her again. And just plain wanting to be with her.

"You're just friends," Alex persisted.

"Yeah." Ben knew this man. These weren't just idle questions. Something was on his mind and it wasn't good. "You could say that. Why?"

"Just wondering. I guess you wouldn't mind if I asked her out, then."

An image of Cam with his brother flashed through Ben's mind and white-hot anger roared in his head. No way, he thought. He didn't care if Alex could take him.

He moved a step closer and his hands curled into fists. "Don't go there, Alex. You stay away from her. I'm warning you—"

"Gotcha." The other man grinned. "You're too easy."

It took a couple seconds for anger to fade and reality to sink in. He'd been had, set up. Alex was right. He was easy. "I should pop you one for that."

"Gotta watch those surgeon's hands. Besides, you could

make more work for yourself. On the off chance you did me some damage, you'd just have to patch me up. I'm sorry about that." His brother didn't look sorry at all. "I thought you were feeling more than friendly toward the pretty lady and you just proved my point. I did it because someone had to make you see the truth."

Ben stared at his brother as thoughts raced through his mind, his conversation with Cam earlier. She'd asked about Judy, whether or not he was avoiding commitment because of her, and he hadn't lied. He'd been the one to leave and Judy had refused to go with him. Obviously she hadn't loved him, so he'd dodged a bullet. Eventually he'd realized that a long-distance relationship probably wouldn't have worked either.

His feelings for Cam were threatening to spill over the friendship limitation he'd put on them. And *she* was leaving. He'd suggested this bargain, but she'd agreed because she wanted to go somewhere else. He'd made a deliberate career choice to come back. And no one was supposed to get hurt.

Things were not going as originally planned.

Now Alex had just punked him by bluffing about asking Cam out. He'd done it to make a point. Ben asked, "What truth are you trying to make me see?"

"You've got to nip those feelings in the bud, Bud." Alex nodded emphatically. "If you don't, you're going to be in a lot of trouble."

Ben blew out a long breath. "Tell me something I don't know."

"I really feel awful," Cam said into the phone. Normally she was at work by now, but she was moving slowly. She leaned against the counter in her small kitchen. "I just wanted you to know that I'm going to be a little late today."

"What's wrong?" M.J. asked.

"Same as the last couple days. I'm nauseous and tired. I'll work here in my suite until I can shake it off. Then I'll come down to the office in a while."

"Cam, I'm coming up there," M.J. said.

"That's so nice of you, but really not necessary." She walked out into the living room because the smell of freshly brewed coffee turned her stomach. "It will pass soon."

"That's what you said yesterday. And the day before that. And the day before that."

"I'm okay. Room service is bringing ginger ale and crackers."

"Oh, my—"

Cam couldn't see M.J.'s face, but the tone of voice didn't sound good. "What's wrong?"

"I'll be right there. Glen's going to man the desk for me. Sit tight." There was a click on the line indicating she'd hung up.

Cam sat on the overstuffed sofa and leaned back, closing her eyes. If she could stay like this and not move, everything would be just fine. It was when she sat up or walked around that her stomach turned on her.

She thought about mentioning it to Ben but decided against that. She hadn't seen him for a few days, since he'd taken her to the construction site for his house. On the drive back to Blackwater Lake he'd given off a weird vibe. Probably she shouldn't have asked about Judy, but she couldn't help herself. It would be too sad if that's what was keeping him from being happy. He'd denied it and she believed him, but there was something standing in his way.

Her life hadn't been anywhere close to normal, but even she wondered about building a house big enough for a family when he didn't seem to want one. He might have thought her questions were a hint, that she was trying to change the rules of their agreement on him. She wouldn't do that, but it had gotten her thinking.

There was a knock on her door, which was either room service or M.J. She could take on one or the other but not both at the same time. She managed to stand, walk to the door and open it, all the while keeping her rebellious stomach under control.

Peg Simmons wheeled in the room service cart. She was in her fifties and had more energy than a lot of people twenty years younger. Silver was liberally streaked in her short, dark hair and her brown eyes were warm. And concerned.

"Here you go, Cam." She looked uneasy. "You might want to try and get in some protein. I can go back downstairs and have them fix you an egg and toast—"

"No." She pressed a hand to her stomach. Just the thought of it was unpleasant. "Thanks, but this will be fine—"

M.J. appeared in the doorway. "How's our girl?"

If Cam had felt better the words would have produced a warm glow, but the nausea had put that reflex out of commission along with the rest of her.

She looked from one woman to the other, so grateful that they were on her side now. "I'll be fine," she told them.

"She's not eating," Peg said to the other woman. "Ginger ale and crackers isn't a well-balanced breakfast and this is the fourth morning in a row you've ordered this."

"Have you talked to Ben about not feeling well?" M.J. asked. There was edginess on her face, but something else, too, as she exchanged a look with Peg. It was as if the two of them knew a secret that she didn't have a clue about.

"As you both are aware, Ben is an orthopedic specialist. Nausea isn't in his field of expertise."

"Then maybe you should see Adam Stone. He's a *family* practice doctor." Peg nodded emphatically.

"I don't think it's necessary—"

"Peg is right." M.J. exchanged another knowing glance with the other woman. "Just get a checkup. You've been under a lot of stress lately."

"That's true." She chewed on the inside of her cheek. "Maybe this is female-related. My periods aren't regular but I'm a little late—"

Oh, dear God. She was late! She could be…

No way. That wasn't possible. She looked at the two women as panic scratched inside her. "I can't be pregnant."

Peg breathed a sigh of relief. "Oh, thank God. I didn't think you knew."

"You did?" Cam blinked at her.

"I suspected. Nausea and fatigue are classic symptoms, right, M.J.?"

"Hit me hard, both times. Ben will be so pleased. He's really great with kids." M.J.'s smile was happy and excited in that way women get when a female friend is doing the most womanly thing a woman can do.

"It's not true—I can't be pregnant," she said again.

"So you didn't have sex with your boyfriend the doctor?" Peg's look was skeptical.

Cam wasn't thinking rationally enough to lie. "We used protection."

"Sweetie, if you're not on the pill…" Peg's voice trailed off and let the truth hang there.

"I'm not."

Cam hadn't trusted any man enough to let him that close so there was no reason to take an oral contraceptive. She hadn't expected that to change in Blackwater Lake. She hadn't planned to have sex. She hadn't planned on meeting a guy like Ben McKnight.

"Only abstinence is a hundred percent effective," Peg informed her. "And when a couple gets…" She hesitated, searching for the most delicate word. "Athletic, condoms can be tricky. That's why my two oldest kids have a brother six years younger."

Cam waited for her cheeks to get warm at the frank talk. She didn't remember having a discussion this personal with her own mother, but somehow didn't mind it now, with these two women. They were her friends.

"I'm going to take a wild guess here that you haven't said anything about this to Ben." M.J. took her arm and led her to the sofa.

Cam couldn't sit. "No."

Peg took the soft drink can and a glass of ice from the room service cart and poured the carbonated liquid. She handed it to Cam. "It'll be okay, honey. He's a good man."

There would be no argument from her about that. But what a mess. And maybe it wasn't true. She put her drink on the coffee table and looked at them. "Before I tell him, I think it's important to know for sure."

"Pregnancy test," M.J. said, nodding.

"If I go get one at the drugstore it will be all over town." At least here in Blackwater Lake people's behavior was predictable. Her whole life paparazzi had stalked her every move and she never knew when, where or what she'd done that would result in a horrible, incriminating picture on the cover of a magazine. She met M.J.'s gaze. "Can you get one for me?"

"Of course. There will be talk about me, but I can take the heat." Her smile was reassuring. "I'll go on my lunch hour."

"I'll make it up to you—"

"No need. It's what friends do."

"Thank you—" Her voice caught and she pressed her fingers to her lips.

"Getting emotional is another sign," Peg said helpfully.

Cam hugged the older woman, then M.J. "Thank you for being here. Both of you."

"This is just the way folks in Blackwater Lake roll," Peg said with a shrug. She pushed her room service cart to the door and M.J. opened it.

Just after the two women left the suite, the phone on the desk rang. After picking it up she said, "Camille Halliday."

"Hi, Cam. It's Glen at the front desk."

"Hey," she said, trying to sound cool and collected, as if her whole life wasn't coming apart at the seams. "What's up?"

"Your parents are here."

Her heart stopped, then started to pound. "What?"

"Dean and Margaret Halliday just checked in with me here at the desk. You look a lot like your mom," he said cheerfully.

The assumption was that she'd be glad to see them. And she was. But the timing of this surprise visit couldn't be worse.

"Where are they now?" she asked.

"They said to tell you they'll be waiting in your office."

"Understood." Her hand was shaking when she hung up the phone. "I'll be down soon."

Waiting in the office was Halliday Hospitality code for *get your tush down here as soon as possible.* That didn't give her much time to transform herself from looking like something the cat yakked up to the business professional she wanted her father to believe she was.

The thought of facing Dean Halliday Senior made her stomach drop. With the exception of a roller-coaster ride, she couldn't think of any other occasion when that was a good thing. She'd just realized that she might be pregnant.

All things considered, throwing up seemed like the sensible thing to do.

## Chapter Twelve

"Mother. Dad." Cam walked into her office with a bright, phony smile plastered on her face for the parents who were seated in front of her desk. "This is really a surprise."

"I was anxious to see you." Margaret Halliday lifted her cheek for the traditional air kiss. She was blonde, blue-eyed, petite and perfect. Probably there was a resemblance until you got to the perfect part. "You look tired, Camille."

She glanced down at her designer suit and expensive heels, regretting the fact that she'd put herself together in a hurry. She also regretted that there wasn't enough concealer on the planet to hide the dark circles under her eyes. So much for plan A.

"It's been a busy few months. I'm fine." And possibly pregnant, she thought. But that wasn't something she would share until absolutely necessary. "How are you?"

"I'll be better when you give me a report on this property."

Dean Halliday Senior was a handsome man in his late fifties. His hair was dark with the exception of silver at his temples. Stray gray wouldn't dare crop up on his head to make him look anything but distinguished. If Hollywood was casting someone to play the president in a movie, Dean Halliday could be on the short list.

Cam leaned down to kiss his cheek and imagined that it was a lot like touching her lips to one of the Mount Rushmore commanders-in-chief. In all fairness, maybe her attitude toward her parents needed an adjustment. At least they were here. Then she half sat on the corner of her desk and met her father's gaze, bracing for the grilling she knew was coming.

"Things are going really well, Dad. This property could be something very special. A place to get away from it all. *Really* away, if you know what I mean."

"I do." Margaret crossed one slender leg over the other, rustling the silk of her black designer slacks. "The only airport is nearly a hundred miles away."

"Once you get here, the trip is worth it." Cam looked from one to the other. "Towering mountains. Lakes and streams so crystal clear you can see the bottom. Fresh air—"

"You sound like a travel brochure," her father said.

"If only a tri-fold glossy paper with words and pictures could adequately convey the splendor." She straightened away from the desk. "Let me show you. I'll give you a tour of the lodge."

"Lead the way." Her father stood and buttoned his dark suit jacket.

"Follow me." Cam walked out of her office and around to the lobby side of the registration desk, then looked at the blonde wearing square black glasses behind it. "M.J., these are my parents, Dean and Margaret Halliday. This is Mary Jane Baxter, one of the best customer service representatives I've ever worked with."

"It's a pleasure to meet you both." M.J. smiled, but the expression in her eyes was questioning. Did the folks know yet about the suspected pregnancy?

Cam gave a slight shake of her head, then smoothed her hair. "The staff here at Blackwater Lake Lodge is excellent. If you need anything, just let us know and—"

"How are reservations?" her father asked. "Is there an improvement?"

"Up sixty percent from this time last year," Cam said. "We're completely full for the summer and already starting to take reservations for the fall and holidays. There are even a couple of small regional conferences scheduled."

"Hmm." Her father nodded, but there was no way to tell what he was thinking. Turning away, he inspected the furniture grouping in the lobby by the stone-front fireplace. "Rustic."

His tone wasn't necessarily critical or condescending, but Cam found herself wanting to defend the lodge. "This room reflects the mountain milieu. People from New York or Los Angeles don't want the chrome, crystal and marble they see there. Here in Blackwater Lake the wood and stone brings the outdoor magnificence inside."

"Hmm." He nodded. "Let's see the rest."

"Okay. Let's go to the dining room. Amanda will want to say hello."

She led the way to Fireside and through the dining room, which was currently dark and empty of people since it didn't open until five in the evening. All the tables had linens and silverware rolled in cloth napkins. The fireplace was cold now but in a few hours flames would be dancing cheerfully. Through the double doors in the back of the room was the kitchen and that's where they found Amanda Carson.

She was about Cam's height, a beautiful brown-eyed brunette. At work she wore her long hair up in a twist and had on a white chef's coat with a single row of buttons up the front.

"I smell something burning." She sniffed and instantly the sous chef and food preparers were scrambling to find and fix the problem. "That's not the kind of smell that comes out of my kitchen."

Cam's high heels clicked on the tile floor as she walked over to where her friend stood by the long, stainless-steel work area. "Hi, Amanda."

"Cam." The chef turned and smiled. Then she spotted the elder Hallidays and moved to give each of them a hug. "I didn't know you guys were coming."

"That's because we didn't tell anyone. If you really want to know how a place is running, drop in. Advance warning gives people a chance to sweep everything they don't want you to see under the rug." Dean gave her a fond look. "How are you, Amanda?"

"Doing all right here in Mayberry." It's what she'd called the place when Cam first approached her with the deal to parlay six months into a career- and reputation-building job in the city of her choice. "Blackwater Lake is kind of growing on me."

Cam knew what she meant. The people were salt of the earth and the scenery had sort of gotten into her soul. "Tales of her culinary expertise are really bringing customers into the lodge."

"How many people could there possibly be?" Margaret asked. "This is the wilderness. Awfully far from the airport, as I was telling Camille. It took the driver forever to get here."

"It's quiet, for sure, but there's something to be said for that." Amanda warmed to her subject. "The most excitement this town has seen was when that guy checked into the hotel pretending to be—"

"Do you have the profit numbers for the restaurant?" Cam interrupted. She knew where her friend was headed with that and it wouldn't go over well with her parents. She was still trying to live down the days when she was the tabloids' favorite target. The Hallidays would probably never forgive her for that.

"I can show you the spreadsheets." The chef pointed to her glassed-in office in the corner of the kitchen. "Or you can take my word that revenue is way up from this time last year. Your daughter has really turned this place around. The staff adores her."

"It's not a popularity contest," her father said. "Sometimes you have to irritate people to run a business."

"That's the thing," Amanda said. "Cam is great at running the business and doesn't irritate anyone."

Except maybe Ben. If the pregnancy test said what she thought it was going to say, he was going to be plenty irritated. No strings attached in this bargain, he'd said. A baby was kind of a big string.

"Cam?"

"Hmm?" She looked at her friend. "I'm sorry, my mind was wandering. Did you say something?"

"Yes. You look tired."

"That's what I told her," Margaret said.

A gleam stole into Amanda's dark eyes. "Is that dashing doctor keeping you up too late at night?"

"Would that be the doctor you were kissing in the picture on the front of that horrific newspaper?" her mother asked.

Cam's chest felt tight. "I was hoping you hadn't seen that."

"Yes, indeed we did." Dean fixed his blue eyes on her and there was no warmth in them. "How did that happen?"

"I have no idea." She shrugged. "Somehow I was tracked here and the guy checked into the lodge under false pretenses to spy on me. Nothing in that article was the truth."

"What about the man you were kissing?" Margaret asked.

That kiss hadn't been for real, either. Cam hadn't felt this uncomfortable, awkward and guilty since her arrest as a teenager. "That's Ben McKnight. He's a doctor."

"Hometown hero," Amanda added. "Good-looking and smart. He likes my seven-layer chocolate cake."

"Anyone who doesn't like it would be too dense to find their way out of a plastic bag, let alone complete medical school," Dean pointed out.

Cam was pleased that the president and CEO of Halliday Hospitality, Incorporated, liked her friend's cooking, but how she wished her father had a compliment for his own daughter. She knew she'd been a pain in the neck to them for a lot of years after her brother died. She knew she'd never be as good as Dean Junior, or be able to run the business as well as he would have. But she was trying to be a Halliday her father could be proud of. Didn't that count for something?

Her best was better because of Ben, and speaking of the good doctor, she needed to change the subject before Dean and Margaret could ask more questions and trip her up, make her slip and spill the beans about their phony relationship.

"Okay, I have a lot more to show you. We'll see you later for dinner, Amanda."

"You're going to love it," she said to the elder Hallidays. "I recommend the trout. It's going to be awesome."

"You're ever the humble cook," Cam teased.

Amanda grinned. "False humility is a waste of time."

"Well said," Dean commented.

"We look forward to it, dear," her mother added.

Cam showed them every square inch of Blackwater Lake Lodge, from the large suites to the pool and extensive grounds. She saved the second-story deck that overlooked the grass, shrubs, flowers and trees for last. It was nearly noon, but the Adirondack chairs were in the shade and she urged them to sit and soak in the fresh air and view. She was surprised when they actually took her suggestion.

"I love it up here," she told them, leaving out the part where she'd used it to find her serenity when exasperated with staff who didn't take her seriously. She sat on the ottoman by her mother's chair. This was also where she'd found Ben, where he'd proposed the dating bargain. Where she'd accepted, desperate to find a way to be successful and prove to her father that she could be. All she wanted was to make him proud.

She didn't think her getting pregnant was going to achieve that objective.

"This is a very beautiful spot," her mother said.

"It is," her husband agreed. "You've done a good job with this place, Camille."

She wanted to shake her head and make sure her hearing wasn't playing tricks on her. Had the daunting Dean Halliday just given her a compliment? "We have a way to go, but things are looking up. No more hemorrhaging money. Waste has been cut and the budget trimmed in a way guests won't notice. I've hired a trustworthy accountant, who assures me that if things continue as they are, next year we'll be in good shape."

Her father nodded. "The staff looks efficient and it would show in more than the books if that wasn't the case. The grounds and public areas are well-maintained. It's a property that Halliday Hospitality can be proud of."

He'd all but said he was proud of *her*. She wanted to grin from ear to ear and maybe do a little happy dance, but that wasn't what Hallidays did. The thought of dancing made her a little nauseous and all the joy imploded.

"So tell us more about the doctor you're seeing," her mother said. "I didn't read the dreadful article. I do hope there won't be any more of that."

"I'm sure it won't happen again," she assured them.

"We're going to hold you to that." Dean put his feet up on the wooden ottoman. "Now, how did you meet Dr. McKnight?"

And so the third degree began. "We met here. He's staying at the lodge while having a house built in an exclusive luxury development that overlooks Blackwater Lake. His medical specialty is orthopedics. He grew up here in town and came back because he loves it so much."

Everything she'd said was the truth. Her parents had never been overly into her feelings, so maybe facts were enough, because defining her feelings for Ben was difficult. She was grateful for his help. She liked being with him and missed him when they weren't together. He was funny and sexy and made her heart beat faster whenever she saw him. Just thinking about him quickened her pulse. She'd never felt this way about any man. Ever.

"I imagine he'll be pretty busy during ski season." Dean looked at his wife, who nodded. "We'd like to meet him."

Her stomach dropped and when it bounced back up

there was a huge knot in it. "How long are you going to be here?"

"A night. Maybe two," he said.

"I'll notify housekeeping. There's an unoccupied suite."

"We took care of that. Our luggage has already been delivered there," her father said.

"It was a noble attempt to change the subject, though." Strangely enough, there was a twinkle in her mother's eyes. "You're not going to get out of introducing us to your doctor. We promise to be on our best behavior, right, dear?"

"No. I intend to have a word with the man who is interested in my daughter and find out *why* he's interested."

Of course her father thought it was about money, because no man could possibly be interested in her for any other reason. Of course there was a reason, but they'd never guess it. In all fairness, they had as much reason to distrust her suitors as she did. But her deal with Ben was new and different. When she'd agreed, it never occurred to her that they would have to pretend in front of *his* family, which had been hard enough. Now they'd have to do it for *hers*.

"So, will we see him for dinner?" Her mother crossed one leg over the other.

"Yes."

She'd played the part for the McKnights, and now it was his turn. It was incredibly important to keep up the pretense with her parents, especially after hearing that she was doing a good job. Now wasn't the time for how screwed up her personal life was to come out.

There was reason to believe she was pregnant by a man who was building a big house for resale, not a family. And she had taken his help and advice in order to get the career she wanted in a place that was far away from Blackwater Lake. If that wasn't messed up, she didn't know the meaning of the words.

"I'll let Ben know to meet us for dinner here at the lodge. Seven o'clock?"

"Perfect," her mother answered.

She'd do her best to keep her parents from finding out this situation was anything but perfect.

"Do you like that label, Mother?"

Cam sat on the love seat across from her parents in their suite. She'd put her own wineglass down on the coffee table and hoped now wouldn't be the time they actually noticed her. No way she wanted to explain that she wasn't drinking alcohol because she might be pregnant.

Margaret took another sip of the red. "It's quite good, Camille. A wonderful choice."

Her father was having something stronger from the suite's full bar. "This is an excellent Scotch."

"I'm glad." She smiled. "And since there was no advance warning of your visit, you know we didn't get it in just for you. No special treatment. Every guest is treated in the same special way."

"The Halliday Hospitality mission statement." He nodded approvingly. "I propose a toast."

What? she thought. No. Not that. But both of them held out their glasses, so she picked hers up. "What are we drinking to?"

"The hotel business in general, Blackwater Lake in particular. To better times ahead."

Her mother and father clinked glasses, then held theirs out to her. Her crystal wineglass tinkled when she touched theirs, but she only put it to her lips without drinking. She could fake this. It occurred to her that she was getting pretty good at faking life in general. Look at her and

Ben. They'd successfully fooled everyone into believing they were in love.

Being spotted together had required an investment of time in each other's company. She'd begun to look forward to seeing him after a stressful day at work. He actually listened to her troubles, which was better than talking to herself in the serenity place. She enjoyed his sense of humor, his smart and practical approach to problems.

If she were being completely honest, she grew breathless and weak-kneed at the sight of him and ached for him to hold her. Kiss her. Since making love to her in the mountains, he'd only touched her because they were pretending to be in love.

But for Cam it was feeling less and less like a pretense, more and more like...

"Are you all right, Camille?" There was concern in her mother's voice.

"Yes. Why?" *Please don't ask why the level of my wine hasn't gone down.*

"You had the strangest expression on your face. Are you not feeling well?"

"I'm fine," she lied. She should be getting used to it, but deceit didn't come easily to her and never would. "My mind was just wandering. I'm sorry. I was thinking about Ben."

"So, the two of you are getting serious?" There was wariness on her father's face. "I wasn't aware that something like this was part of your career trajectory."

How to answer? Cam wondered. Things were getting serious, but not in the way he was talking about. "I'm enjoying Ben's company. The reality is that I never expected to meet someone like him here in Blackwater Lake, Montana. In fact, nothing about this place is the way I thought it would be. I even went camping."

"With Ben?" her mother asked.

"A Halliday in the wide-open spaces," her father mused. "Not in a hotel."

"I know, right? That's the first time in my life that I didn't have four solid walls around me and a bathroom." But she'd been with Ben and that was enough.

Margaret glanced at the delicate, diamond-trimmed Rolex on her wrist. "Is he as handsome as the photograph on the front page of that horrible newspaper?"

"Better." Cam smiled, picturing his boyish good looks and sigh-worthy grin. "It doesn't do him justice. Pretty soon you can judge for yourself."

"Then I'm even more anxious to meet him. And it's just about time to go downstairs. I think I'll take a few moments to freshen up." She stood and went into the other room.

Moments later there was a knock on the door and her father asked, "Did you order room service?"

"No. Maybe Mother did."

"She would have said something to me."

"I'll see what's going on." She was closest to the door and went to open it.

Mary Jane stood in the hall, twisting her fingers together. "Thank God it's you," she whispered. "Your father scares the crap out of me."

"Join the club. What's up?"

"I need to warn you—"

"About?" Dean Halliday was right behind her. "Ms. Baxter, for many years I have frightened employees and I'm very good at it."

"Yes, sir." Blue eyes behind the black-framed glasses grew wide.

"Now, what is the problem?"

"Mr. Halliday—" M.J. glanced first at him, then Cam.

"There are a bunch of reporters and photographers in the lobby."

"What in the world—"

"They've been badgering the hotel staff, attempting to get quotes. As far as I can tell they're trying to support a story in which Cam—" She hesitated. "I mean Ms. Halliday—that she's in trouble again." Her voice hardened when she met the gaze of the CEO of Halliday Hospitality, Inc. "With her parents."

*No. No. No,* Cam thought. *Not this. Not now. Think. Problem solve.* What would Ben do?

She glanced up at her father. "We don't have to go down to the restaurant for dinner. I'll order something from room service and—"

"Absolutely not." He shook his head. "Thank you, Ms. Baxter. You did the right thing."

"You're welcome."

"And for the record?" he said. "You have nothing to be afraid of on my account."

"Yes, sir. Thank you." She smiled at him, then looked at Cam. "Call me if there's anything I can do."

"I will. Thanks. I owe you."

She closed the door. "Dad, really, I'll call Ben. He can come up the back way and meet us here."

Dean shook his head again. "Hallidays don't sneak around. We face things head-on. We don't avoid even sleazy reporters who are looking to write a sordid story about my family in order to sell newspapers."

"Okay." She decided to share Ben's wisdom after the last paparazzi ambush. "Publicity is good. Even the bad stuff. It's important to get our name out there."

"Not in those sordid papers. Not when the name is Halliday."

"Curiosity can boost reservations." It was worth one more try.

Her father looked grim. "Let's get this ordeal over with. I'll fill your mother in."

Cam watched his back as he left the room and realized that it was a terrible thing when a person lost hope. She'd been so close to getting what she wanted, so close to an assignment in Los Angeles, New York or Phoenix. Now the same seedy reporters who had ruined her life before were sabotaging the career she was moving heaven and earth to resurrect.

And then there was Ben.

He was the one she was most worried about now. This wasn't what he'd signed up for when they made their bargain. She should be glad they weren't a real couple, because it was becoming more apparent that it would really hurt when he dumped her for being constantly pursued by the press. No guy who wasn't in it to get his name in the paper could put up with this.

Now he had to meet her parents with the press photographing everything. At least she could control who else was around when she broke the news to him that he was going to be a father.

## *Chapter Thirteen*

There was something wrong with Cam.

Ben had heard it in her voice when she'd called about having dinner with her parents. He didn't know if it was about them being here or another issue with the press.

He was sitting by the fireplace waiting for the Hallidays in the lodge lobby and it would have been hard to miss the reporters and photographers milling around and grilling the employees for dirt on the family. One of them had said to a colleague that he'd been staking out Cam's parents, just waiting for them to meet her for a face-to-face about the doctor she'd been slumming with in Blackwater Lake, Montana.

Ben had to smile at the reporter's irony. He had a heck of a nerve talking about slumming considering how the guy made his living.

Although Ben had to admit that he was a little nervous about meeting Cam's parents. Considering that their relationship was based on a mutually beneficial bargain, he shouldn't give a rat's behind what her parents thought of him. But he did care.

So far the press hadn't noticed him, but one of the reporters drew his attention. The jerk was badgering M.J. at the registration desk. She was doing her best to ignore the questions fired at her, but apparently she'd lost patience.

She raised her voice and said, "I have only one comment. Camille Halliday is a terrific boss. She's the best one I've ever had and everyone here at Blackwater Lake Lodge feels the same way."

The boss in question was just coming around the corner with a nice-looking older couple. The energy level in the lobby had been hovering in the lower register and shot through the roof when the power family was spotted. Dean and Margaret Halliday were elegant and composed as cameras started flashing and reporters hit them with a barrage of questions.

"Is Cam in a jam again? I can see the headline." The jerk held out a digital recorder.

"What do you think about her and the doctor?" another one asked.

"Is it true she's pregnant?"

"Are you here to break them up?" This guy shoved a microphone at the older man. "Care to comment?"

Ben looked at Cam's face and again knew there was something wrong. He saw shadows in her eyes and a vulnerability that made him want to protect her, to wrap his arms around her and shield her from all this craziness. She'd been putting up with it her whole life and he wondered how she'd managed to stay so sweet and strong.

He stood and pushed his way to her side through the crush of people badgering her. Standing between her and the horde who wanted a piece of her, he forced a smile.

"I'll hold one if you want to kick him."

That got a small smile. "As appealing as that would be, I'd probably just hurt myself. Besides, the assault and battery charges would just be a win for them. And it wouldn't do your career as an orthopedic specialist any good either."

"I'm getting you out of here."

He put his arm around her shoulders and led her out of the lobby. She'd told him dinner would be at Fireside and he led the way. The noise was close behind them a minute later when they arrived at the restaurant doorway.

"Do you want me to call lodge security?" he asked her.

"It's already done."

He nodded. "I went to high school with local law enforcement. Sheriff Marshall probably owes me a favor."

There was humor in her eyes. "Really? Sheriff Marshall?"

"It's catchy," he said with a shrug.

She could smile under this kind of pressure and that took guts. Ben admired the hell out of her.

The hostess was at the podium and immediately said, "Your table is ready. Please follow me."

Dean Halliday said to her, "If anyone intrudes on our privacy, I want you to call the local authorities."

"Yes, sir."

Ben and Cam looked at each other and said at the same time, "Sheriff Marshall."

When they started laughing, her father lobbed a censoring look in her direction. Ben could imagine Cam as a little girl on the receiving end of that disapproving expression for even a small infraction like fidgeting at dinner. But the rigid upbringing hadn't managed to squeeze the spirit out of her. Thank God.

They were seated in a far corner of the sparsely filled dining room, far from prying eyes. Ben held out a chair for

Cam that would put her back to the rest of the room. Even if a nosy reporter managed to get in, she wouldn't have to see and no unflattering photos could be snapped. Her father and mother were barely seated when the waiter arrived.

"Good evening, Mr. and Mrs. Halliday, Ms. Halliday. Dr. McKnight." He looked at everyone. "Welcome to Fireside. What can I get you to drink?"

"A bottle of Jordan Pinot Noir, please, David," Cam said.

"That's an excellent choice," her mother agreed.

"I'd like something stronger," her father ordered. "Scotch."

"The best," Cam added, to the waiter.

"I'd like a beer. Whatever you have on tap is fine," Ben said.

"I'll bring that out right away. Would you like menus now or after drinks?" David was in his thirties, nice-looking and clearly knew how to provide exceptional service.

"After drinks," Cam said and her parents nodded.

Ben had a feeling she had talked to the staff here ahead of time to make sure there were no slipups in service with her parents. Probably even before she knew the press would descend like locusts.

"Well, that was unpleasant." Dean looked at his daughter. "One can never live down the past, it seems."

Ben was watching Cam's face, knew the exact moment when the barb pierced her and burrowed in. Anger instantly ignited inside him and he couldn't let the comment go unchallenged.

"We haven't been formally introduced, Mr. and Mrs. Halliday. I'm Ben McKnight." He held his hand out across the table and one after the other they each took it. "The thing is, that unpleasantness happened because the two of you showed up here." He held up a hand to forestall her father's protest. "Not saying it's your fault, but the Halliday name brings them out no matter who's attached to it. I heard one of those reporters say he'd staked you out, just waiting for you to show up here in Montana."

The older man's eyes narrowed. "Be that as it may, Doctor, if my daughter had kept a low profile in her younger years, no one would care about the comings and goings of her parents."

"Dad, let's not do this now—"

Ben put his hand over hers and squeezed reassuringly. "The thing is that if presidents and movie stars can live down outrageous behavior and rehabilitate their images, a hardworking young woman like your daughter should get a pass on being a kid. Shouldn't there be a statute of limitations on immaturity?"

Dean opened his mouth, but the waiter arrived with their drinks and set the beer and Scotch in front of the men. Then he proceeded to open the wine deftly and pour a small amount for Cam to taste and approve.

She sniffed, then barely touched the glass to her lips. "Excellent."

"I'm glad to hear it." David filled crystal wineglasses for the ladies, then said, "I'll bring menus as soon as you're ready."

When the four of them were alone her father said, "So, tell me, Doctor, what's a guy like you doing in a small town like Blackwater Lake?"

"I grew up here."

"And what? You were homesick?"

Cam looked like she wanted the earth to swallow her whole. "Dad, please—"

"It's a fair question." Ben smiled at her, then met the other man's gaze. "This town has the very best of what the

United States of America is all about. The people take care of each other. You couldn't find a more picturesque place. The mountains offer outdoor opportunities—hiking, skiing, snowboarding. Then there's the lake for fishing and water sports."

"A great vacation spot. But for a career in the medical field, wouldn't your prospects be better in New York, Los Angeles or any other big city?"

Ben understood that this wasn't about his career as much as it was about whether or not he was after Cam's money. It wasn't bragging to let the man know he was just fine in that regard.

"I actually built a medical practice in Las Vegas and sold it for, let's just say, upwards of seven figures. Prudent investments have paid off and I don't have to work at all for the rest of my life."

"But you do. Here," Margaret Halliday interjected.

Cam's mother said "here" as if Blackwater Lake were the swamp planet where Luke Skywalker crash-landed in the second *Star Wars* movie. They would never understand, but he had to say it anyway.

"I love being a doctor and I'm good at what I do. This town and these people are a big part of the reason I've been successful in life. I wanted to give back to the community, but, believe me, I get more than I give. If the tourism industry is going to grow in this town, medical care needs to keep up."

"True enough. Cam tells us you're living at the lodge," her mother continued. The nesting questions.

"I also said you're building a big, beautiful house in an exclusive community on the lake." Cam was defending him, which wasn't necessarily part of their deal.

When Ben had proposed it, he'd never expected or intended for her to invest so much personally. He knew she was going to hear from her family later about what a low bar she'd set and didn't mind for himself. He had no emotional investment in these people, but she cared very much what they thought. He wanted to tell her parents that there was no danger of him becoming part of the family, but that wouldn't help right now. Soon she'd be gone and in her world he'd be nothing more than a blip on the relationship radar.

Oddly enough, he wanted to be more than that to her.

After dinner the Hallidays said good-night and excused themselves from the table, pleading weariness from traveling and an eventful day. Obviously that was a jab at the paparazzi and proved that they couldn't resist one more dig at the prodigal daughter. Cam should have looked relieved when they were alone in the restaurant, but strangely enough she seemed more tense.

"I know what you're thinking," he said.

She seemed momentarily alarmed. "Oh?"

"You want to kick something, and I know just the spot."

"My serenity place." She nodded. "It's been neglected lately because thanks to you, things have been going well." She sighed. "Until today."

"It happens." He held out his hand. "Let's go."

Without a word she put her fingers in his palm, then set her cloth napkin on the table. They stood and walked out of the restaurant and turned right to the exit door on the first floor. The stairway to the upper deck was right there and they took it up.

Cam settled her forearms on the redwood railing and breathed deeply. "This fresh air is just what the doctor ordered."

"Take several deep breaths and call me in the morning." *Or right now,* he thought.

Just like the first time he'd seen her in this very spot he wanted to hold her, kiss her. Now he knew how soft her skin felt, how sweet she tasted, and *perfect* didn't do her justice. Making love with her seemed like a lifetime ago and right this second he couldn't recall why having her again was such a bad idea.

When she looked up at him there was gratitude in her eyes. "Thanks for defending me tonight at dinner."

"No problem. Speaking of dinner, I noticed that you didn't drink your wine." He rested his arms on the railing and stood as close to her as he dared. Their shoulders brushed and they could almost feel the heat of the sparks flickering and flashing, then flying into the night.

She tensed and said, "I needed to keep a clear head. I'm sorry my parents were so hard on you."

"I can take it."

"You shouldn't have to. Why now?" She shook her head. "I can't believe they picked tonight to be involved parents."

"Don't worry about it. Not on my account."

But she kept going as if she hadn't heard. "Although when I think about it, the timing in every other part of my life has been a disaster, so why not this, too?"

"What disaster?" He looked down and saw a troubled look in her eyes. Then he remembered the troubled tone in her voice earlier. "What's wrong?"

She shook her head, a nonanswer. "Between my parents and the paparazzi, you must be relieved that we have a bargain and not a real relationship. The Halliday heiress and her baggage are more challenge than any man should have to take on."

It was a statement, not a question, and he didn't answer. He had a feeling that there was a lot more going on with her that she wasn't telling him. He should ask, but he wasn't sure he wanted to know.

When she'd called earlier, he'd been aware that there was something wrong without even seeing her face. He knew her well enough to tell by the tone of her voice. Knowing a woman that well could change a man forever, and Ben wasn't sure he wanted to change.

She looked up. "I think I'll say good-night. I have some things to do."

"Okay. Sleep well."

He wasn't going to.

Cam looked at the stick from the pregnancy test M.J. had brought her. It said "pregnant."

"There must be some mistake," she whispered to herself. "A false positive. It could happen."

But in her heart she knew there was no mistake, unless she counted the one where she'd slept with a man who only wanted a pretend relationship. The nausea, fatigue and her highly evolved emotional state were all signs pointing to the fact that she was going to have a baby.

Ben's baby.

She'd just left him a little while ago after standing on the deck under the stars. More than anything she wanted to throw herself into his arms and have him assure her that everything was going to be all right. But she'd sensed a distance in him. She wasn't even sure how she knew that, but he'd definitely closed himself off.

None of that changed the fact that she was having a baby. It was surreal and she couldn't wrap her head around what was happening to her.

The doorbell in her suite rang and she jumped at the unexpected sound. Ben. Part of her desperately wanted to see him. Part of her didn't. She hoped it was him come to insist she tell him what was really wrong. Then she forced herself to get real. She hadn't let herself hope for anything good since that awful day when she'd heard that her brother had been in a car accident. She'd prayed and hoped with everything she had that he would be all right, but it hadn't been enough. Dean Junior had died in spite of her hope.

She heard the doorbell again and sighed. Whoever stood there wasn't going away. If it was Ben, this was as good a time as any to give him the big news.

But when she opened the door her father stood there. "Dad. I wasn't expecting you."

"Am I interrupting?" He looked around as if there would be someone else there.

Probably anticipating Ben, since the man lived right next door. Ironically, he'd never come into her place. Neutral ground camping in the mountains was where common sense had gone out the window—and the tent didn't even have windows.

Cam looked down at her socks, sweatpants and matching zip-up cardigan. "I'm alone. Is Mom okay?"

"Fine. She's asleep. May I come in?"

"Sure. Of course. Sorry." Apparently being pregnant affected a woman's manners and basic brain function. She stepped back and pulled the door wider. "Come in."

"Thanks."

"Would you like a drink?" She looked longingly at Ben's door before closing her own. "I don't have anything here, but I can call downstairs if you—"

He held up a hand. "No. I'm fine."

"Okay." She indicated the conversation area in her suite living room. "Have a seat. It's kind of late, so I'm a little curious why you're here."

He nodded, then sat on one of the small sofas. "There's something I'd like to talk to you about."

"I'll take care of whatever it is. If there's a problem that you noticed here at the lodge, just let me know and consider it done. I have a terrific staff and we can make things happen—"

"It's not about trouble," he interrupted. "I just wanted to talk to you."

"About what?"

"I saw your employees in action with those sleazy reporters earlier. Will you give me your secret to securing loyalty like that?"

Ben. He was her secret and her strength. He'd been her conduit, the bridge to winning the hearts and minds of the workers. "The people here in Blackwater Lake are, quite simply, awesome."

"I actually want to talk about one person in particular, but there's something I need to say first." He leaned back into the cushiness of the love seat and crossed one leg over the other. It wasn't the body language of a father getting ready to grill her about the man in her life. "Your mother and I are heading back to Los Angeles in the morning."

Cam sat down across from him. "But I thought you'd be here for another day."

"I changed my mind. It didn't take as long as I'd figured to see everything I needed to see."

Was that a good thing or bad? "The lodge has turned the corner, Dad. It has the potential to be a very successful property for Halliday Hospitality, Inc. Think Vail. Aspen. Park City, Utah. The town council is investing in infrastructure so that more people will come, tourists and permanent residents both. In fact, that's why Mercy Medical Clinic wanted Ben. And they're expanding the existing clinic to provide more services. Eventually there will be a hospital here. The demographic is going to need Ben's particular skills set for the master plan—"

"Whoa." Her father laughed and shook his head. "You

had me at 'the lodge turned a corner.' I can see that from the financial reports. I'm not here to close it down."

"Good. A lot of people would lose their jobs if you did that." She was relieved to hear that was off the table. Also even more curious. "Then what did you want to talk about?"

"You've done everything you promised when you convinced me to give you a chance to prove yourself. I wanted to personally deliver the news that you're being promoted."

"I am?" Another surreal moment. She couldn't quite believe that at least one part of her life had gone according to plan.

"You can have your pick of any Halliday Hospitality property to manage." He grinned. "So, what's it going to be? Los Angeles? New York? San Francisco? Scottsdale, Arizona?"

"I don't want to push anyone out or cause someone to lose their job."

"Don't worry about that. We'll juggle assignments. No one will be out in the cold or demoted. But you've got my attention. You've earned this, Camille."

She nodded, thinking back to employee hostility and no respect when she'd arrived here at Blackwater Lake Lodge. The collective attitude of the staff and townspeople began to change when she started "seeing" Ben. And seeing him had not been a hardship—just the opposite. It had been far too easy to get used to having him in her life. She could get used to it. But now…

It was time for her to move on, just as she'd planned. She'd earned a promotion.

"Camille?" Her father looked puzzled.

"Hmm?"

"Are you all right?"

*Define all right,* she wanted to say. Professionally all was good. Personally? Not so much.

"Yes, I'm fine," she lied.

Dean leaned forward, forearms on knees, blue eyes intent on her. "Then why don't you look happier about this news?"

That was a very good question, because this certainly wasn't the way she'd expected to feel if this moment ever arrived, and she'd had her doubts in the beginning. When she'd talked her way into getting a chance, and that chance meant exile in Blackwater Lake, Montana, she hadn't expected to fall in love. Or get pregnant.

"I'm just really surprised by this," she finally said.

"You shouldn't be. Hard work should be rewarded. And at Halliday we do that."

"I never wanted any special treatment."

"And you didn't get any."

So spoke her boss. "Good, then."

Her father watched her for several moments, then frowned. "What is the nature of your relationship with Dr. McKnight?"

There was a loaded question if she'd ever heard one. She and Ben didn't have a relationship. All they had was a deal. Then they had sex. Now she was pregnant. All of the above would be tricky to explain in a way he would understand.

Finally she said, "Why do you ask?"

"Because I'm your father."

"Since when?"

Cam wasn't sure why she'd said that or why she wasn't horrified that she had. Maybe the baby made her do it. Whatever the reason she'd surprised her father. The expression on his face was one she'd never seen before, which meant Dean Halliday Senior wasn't accustomed to being caught off guard.

"What does that mean?" he asked.

"Tonight Ben stood up for me." And she loved him for that. There, she'd actually formed her feelings into that thought. She loved Ben. "He protected and defended me."

"From what?"

"You," she went on quickly, before rational thought stepped in to make her stop. "The press being here wasn't my fault any more than it was when they stalked me as a teenager. That was all about being the daughter of Dean Halliday, being from a wealthy hotel family." He opened his mouth and she raised her hand to let him know she wasn't finished. "I take responsibility for my bad choices in friends and the things I did. But I'd just lost my brother—"

Sadness and a grief that would never go away darkened his eyes. "I lost my only son."

She refused to back down. "When he died not only did I lose my protector, the guy who ran interference for me, I lost my father, too. You went from parent to boss, training me to be a stand-in for Dean Junior. My only qualification was being the oldest surviving Halliday heir."

"Camille, you don't know—"

"I'm not blaming you, just explaining things from my perspective. I have no idea what it feels like to lose a child." God willing she never would. "It's got to be the worst thing that can happen and I understand that you went through an awful time. But I did, too. I was sinking fast and no one noticed, no one reached out a hand." Not until she got to Blackwater Lake and met Ben. "It's okay, Dad. I finally grew up. And it just has to be said. I'll never be as good as Dean Junior would have been, but I promise to do my best not to let you down ever again."

His head was bowed, elbows resting on his knees with

fingers linked between the wide V of his legs, as if he was praying. "I appreciate that."

"Good."

He sighed and stood up. "So, you'll think about where you'd like to be transferred?"

"Yes." Then she remembered. "And wherever that is, I'm taking Amanda with me. I made her a deal."

He nodded. "A Halliday's word is more than a promise."

"All right. When do you need my decision?"

"As soon as possible." He suddenly looked tired, and a little older than when he'd walked in. "We need time to reassign personnel."

"Okay." They stared at each other for several moments without speaking, because apparently there was nothing more to say if it wasn't about business. "Will I see you and Mother in the morning to say goodbye?"

"An early breakfast?"

"Just let me know what time. I'll be there."

"Very well. Good night, Camille."

"'Night, Dad."

Without another word he left. Cam wasn't sure whether or not she felt better because of unburdening herself. She was only sad that she and her father could never have had this conversation when she needed it most. He would have told her that Hallidays don't make excuses, because they don't make mistakes.

Eventually she would have to confess to them that she'd messed up again and was pregnant. But first she had to break the news to Ben.

## *Chapter Fourteen*

The next evening Cam called Los Angeles to make sure her parents had made it home safely. Her father informed her that the executive manager of the Halliday Hospitality Inn, Scottsdale, Arizona, was retiring and she could have the job if she wanted it. She agreed to think things over and let him know in twenty-four hours. He'd given no hint that there were any hard feelings about what she'd said to him regarding her childhood. Then again, her father was like Teflon. Things were thrown at him, but nothing stuck. Just as well.

But before she could give him an answer about the new job and relocation, she had to tell Ben about the baby. Staring at the single wall that separated their suites, she decided that putting it off any longer was just cowardly. Hallidays weren't gutless.

She was casually dressed in jeans, a T-shirt with the Blackwater Lake Lodge logo on it and sneakers. Briefly she considered putting on a power outfit, then decided against it. She was in this predicament because she'd taken her clothes *off* and no ensemble would make a difference when telling a man who'd successfully avoided commitment that he was going to be a father.

She did, however, check her hair and put on fresh lipstick. In this situation, a girl needed all the confidence she could get. With head held high and shoulders back she left her room and turned right, then knocked on his door.

A few moments later Ben opened it, saw who was there, and a slow grin turned up the corners of his mouth. The warmth moved to his eyes and for just a second there was a flicker of what looked a lot like lust.

He leaned one broad shoulder against the doorjamb in just about the sexiest pose ever. "Hi."

"Hi."

Cam's heart hammered in her chest, partly because of what she had to say, but mostly it was simply her uncontrollable reaction to this man. She lifted her hand in a small wave, then stuck her fingers in her jeans pockets. Apparently her tongue was stuck, too, because she couldn't think what to say next.

"I'm glad you finally came over."

"Oh?" She'd been tempted many times and wondered if the word *finally* meant he had been, too. But his glad reaction wouldn't last very long when she told him. "Why are you glad?"

"Word around the lodge is that your parents are gone and I was wondering how everything is." The pose got even sexier when he folded his arms over his chest. "I was going to call if you hadn't stopped by."

That was something positive, wasn't it? At least he was thinking about her. And he'd stood up to her father last night. No one had ever done that for her, not even the older brother she'd idolized. In spite of her effort to suppress it, she knew hope was hovering.

"Can I come in?" Just about twenty-four hours ago her father had asked her the same thing and she'd wanted to say no. If Ben felt that way...

"Of course." He straightened out of the lazy pose and stepped back from the door to open it wider. "Do you want a beer or glass of wine?"

Her stomach dropped. Last night, out on the deck, he'd commented on the fact that she hadn't had any of her wine at dinner. Now she was here to tell him the real reason. She toyed with the idea of mentioning that he might want a drink before hearing the news, but decided not to. Looking on the bright side, it was possible the information that he was going to be a father might not produce a response that required alcohol.

"No, thanks," she said.

He closed the door and walked over to her. She was standing by the back of the love seat. His suite was a duplicate of hers, the mirror image. As he looked down, Ben curled his fingers into his palms, as if he was fighting the urge to touch her, pull her into his arms. At least she hoped... There was that word again.

The expression in his eyes grew more intense as he stared at her. "Sit. Stay awhile."

"Maybe I will." She'd really like to if this conversation went well.

"Did your folks give you a hard time about last night?" He seemed genuinely concerned. "I didn't mean to cause trouble. But none of what happened was your fault."

"I know. Dad didn't mention it again."

"Good." There was a question in his eyes. "So. I'm curious. To what do I owe the honor of a visit from senior management here at Blackwater Lake Lodge?"

"Well." She blew out a breath. "I have news. And some other news."

"Okay." He settled his hands on lean hips. "Why don't you start with the news first."

"My father is extremely pleased with my work here at the lodge."

"That's good." But the easygoing manner disappeared. "Right?"

She nodded. "He's offered me the top management position at Halliday Hospitality Inn, Scottsdale, Arizona."

"Congratulations." His voice was oddly flat. "Desert. That's different."

And he seemed indifferent to the information that she would be leaving Montana. Cam waited for more, a reaction indicating he cared even a little. It didn't happen. She supposed him asking her not to go had been a stupid fantasy, but it had been there in spite of her warning to herself.

Even so, she had no right to be disappointed. He was sticking to the letter of the agreement. He'd helped her get what she wanted and it wasn't his fault she wanted him now.

"What's the other news?" he finally asked.

It was best to say straight out what she had to say. There were no words that could possibly soften the blow. "I'm pregnant."

He looked at her for several moments, then actually laughed. This wasn't anywhere near the expected response. "You're kidding, right? It was a test. To make sure I was listening?"

She blinked back tears and double-damned the out-of-control hormones that were making her react in this hyperemotional way. When she could speak without a sob sneaking out, she answered.

"No, it's not a joke. I'm going to have a baby. Your baby." Her chin inched up slightly.

He stared at her as if waiting for her to say "gotcha." "I don't understand. How could this have happened?"

"Maybe it's time for a refresher physiology course, one that highlights bodily functions, Doctor. It's called—"

"I know what happened. I was there. We used protection."

"Yes, we did."

She remembered being really grateful that he'd had some, for all the good it had done. She'd known the risk and in the heat of wanting him so badly, she'd been willing to take that chance. She was also a victim of that natural human malady known as the it-won't-happen-to-me syndrome. Now she was just a terrible warning.

"If you recall—" She put as much primness as possible into her voice. "It was very—athletic—when we, you know—"

"Slept together," he finished.

"Yes." Although if they'd actually slept, they wouldn't be in this mess. She wanted to look anywhere except at the grim expression on his face but wouldn't let her gaze wander. "I'm told that under those circumstances condoms can be ineffective."

And that was when she realized her second fantasy of the evening had bitten the dust along with the one where he asked her not to leave. It had crossed her mind that there could be the cliché hug and twirl of happiness when he scooped her up in his arms because he was happy about becoming a father. But there wasn't so much of that reaction, either. There wasn't a speck of joy on his face, just dark looks and frowning.

"Are you sure about this?" he asked.

"I took a pregnancy test. Still have the stick if you want

to see it." She pointed at the wall separating their suites. "I can bring it over."

"Not necessary."

She knew he wanted to ask if the baby was his, but to his credit he held the words back. "Just so you know, I haven't been with anyone else."

"It never crossed my mind." Again to his credit, he sounded sincere.

She nodded. "Thanks for that."

He dragged his fingers through his hair and seemed on the verge of saying something. *Ask me to stay,* she wanted to beg him.

But that wasn't what came out of his mouth. "This is a lot to process."

Oddly enough, those were the words that broke her heart. His voice wasn't unkind and certainly what he said was true. But she'd wanted so much to hear something different.

"I know what you mean. I'm still trying to—process. But we can work something out. Visitation," she said lamely.

"Yeah." He dragged his fingers through his hair.

They stared at each other for several moments, both in shock for different reasons. Finally she realized there was nothing left to say. "I need to go."

"Right. Okay." He went to the door and opened it. "I'll call you. We'll talk."

She nodded, then walked out without another word. There was no way to speak without bursting into tears and she didn't want pity.

She wanted the fairy tale. She wanted him to love her.

Moments later, when the tears started rolling down her cheeks, she was in her own suite where no one could see her break down. Up-and-coming hotel entrepreneur heiresses didn't do this sort of thing in public. Ben hadn't intentionally lied when he'd said the bargain would keep either of them from getting hurt, but that didn't help when the pain overwhelmed her.

In her rebellious stage people had always wanted something from her. She'd thought knowing up front what Ben wanted would insulate her from feeling used. It wasn't fair, and certainly wasn't what had happened, but that didn't make losing the man she loved hurt any less.

When she stopped crying, she'd call her father and tell him Scottsdale near Phoenix was where she wanted to go. She couldn't think of a place that was more different from Blackwater Lake, and maybe a change of scenery would help her forget Ben McKnight.

"What's the holdup with this house, Alex?" Ben stood in his newly wallboarded family room and glared at his brother while their father looked on. Cam had left without a goodbye two weeks ago and every day that went by without her in it shortened his temper. She was going to have a baby. *His* baby. The news had blown his mind.

"There's no delay," Alex answered. "It's all part of the building process."

"You could have built a whole block in the time you've spent on this thing."

Brown eyes a lot like his own stared back at him, but Alex's were brimming with amusement. "Who are you and what have you done with my laid-back little brother? You remember him, right? Doctor. Easygoing. Great sense of humor. The guy who said, 'Take your time. Get everything right.'"

"Now I just want it done."

When Ben had brought Cam here the framing was complete but you could see into everything downstairs, including the garage. Now the wallboard was up, closing things off. Much like himself, he thought. And that made him angry.

The last time he'd seen her standing in his hotel room doorway, lust had hit him like a speeding train. He wanted her in his arms, in his bed, but there was more to it and he didn't think about that. She'd dropped her bombshell, then kept to their bargain and left for a better job. Just as promised, she'd packed up and brushed the mud of Montana from her pumps. And she'd done it without saying goodbye.

Ben dragged his fingers through his hair. "What's the delay?"

"There are building codes." The exaggerated patience in his brother's voice grated on already frayed nerves. "Inspectors need to examine everything to make sure it's built to those codes. After the job is done on each phase, we can't move on to the next until the city inspector signs off on the work. We have to wait."

"So can we buy this guy a drink or something and persuade him to make this place a priority?"

"Are you talking bribe?" One of Alex's dark eyebrows rose questioningly. "Because I'm pretty sure there are laws against that sort of thing."

"Might be worth breaking the law to move this project forward at maybe a pace just a tad faster than a snail's."

Tom McKnight had simply been observing the back and forth between his sons. Until now. "What's your hurry, Ben?"

His hurry was that he wanted out of Blackwater Lake Lodge. He swore his room still held the scent of Cam's skin, but that was impossible because she'd only ever been in it once. Every night of looking at the wall that had separated his room from hers made him sorry for all the missed opportunities. He regretted not going next door and kissing the living daylights out of her when he could have.

The memories were driving him crazy.

"This is about Alex dragging his feet," he said.

Tom shook his head. "Your brother is the best builder around. His reputation in California and Montana is above reproach."

"Thanks, Dad." Alex gave him a "so there" look.

The older man continued, "And you're not acting like yourself, son."

"Who am I acting like?"

"Me." His father's pale blue eyes filled with sadness. "After your mom died."

Ben couldn't believe he'd heard right and glanced at his brother. The shocked expression on Alex's face said he'd heard the same thing.

"I don't understand, Dad."

"Let me spell it out. You're acting like a damn jackass because Camille Halliday is gone." Tom's voice went hard. "The difference between you and me is that you're in a position to do something about her."

"Maybe he shouldn't." Alex was dead serious now.

"Of course he should."

His older brother faced off with their father. "In my opinion Ben dodged a bullet when she left Blackwater Lake."

"She never promised to stay," Ben defended. "It was always her plan to prove herself here then move on to a higher-profile property."

There was no reason for his father to know about the bargain. Obviously he'd pulled off making him believe he cared about her, but somewhere in the pretending he'd begun to actually *care*.

"Women are trouble," Alex continued. "Thank your

lucky stars she's outta here before doing real damage to your impressionable young heart."

Too late, Ben thought. She'd made an impression on his heart that would never go away. He was in love with her. He hadn't seen it coming, hadn't been looking for this to happen, but every night the truth hit him like cold water in the face. She was gone. The worst part was that he missed talking to her. He needed to hold her. Touch her.

"You know, big brother, just because you had a bad experience doesn't mean every woman can't be trusted."

"From what I've seen, your track record with women isn't great." Alex's mouth pulled tight. "Judy dumped you for a ski bum and went back east. Cam headed west. That only leaves ladies from north and south to put you in your place."

"Judy was wrong for him. And Cam isn't like the woman you brought here, Alex." It took some of the sting out of Tom's words when he put his hand on his oldest son's shoulder.

Oddly enough Ben's anger was anesthetized by his brother's bitterness. He'd been deceived and dumped by a woman who took away everything he'd ever wanted, everything he loved. Ben understood where he was coming from, but their father was right. Cam wasn't like that woman. She was straightforward and honest. She'd told him about the baby and he didn't say the right thing, hadn't stepped up. Being in a state of shock was no excuse. Then she'd left without a word. He'd called her, but she was dodging him.

Ben knew he'd go crazy if he didn't talk about it. He looked first at his brother, then his father. "Cam is pregnant with my baby."

"Are you sure it's yours?" Alex's eyes turned dark

and hard. Obviously he was remembering how he'd been lied to.

"I'm sure."

"Damn it, Ben—" His father wasn't in the habit of swearing, so when he did, the McKnight kids listened up. "That's even more reason not to do what I did."

"I'm not sure what you mean, Dad."

"When your mom died after giving birth to Sydney, I was angrier than I'd ever been. Mad at her."

"Why?" Alex stared at him.

"She left me with three small kids to raise all on my own. I didn't know how. She was your mom and I couldn't do it the way she did. I couldn't do it without her."

"At the risk of sounding conceited," Alex said, "you did a great job. The three of us turned out pretty good."

Tom's expression was full of regret when he looked at his oldest son. "You raised your brother and sister when you were just a boy yourself. Because you're like your mother." He sighed. "I couldn't get over her and I didn't want to try. I'm sorry I wasn't there. I'm a one-woman man and Linda was the only woman for me. And take it from me, Alex, that woman you brought here to Blackwater Lake wasn't the one."

"Doesn't matter." Alex shook his head, clearly not open to trying again any more than his father was.

"As for you," Tom said to Ben, "I don't want you to shut down like I did. You're different with Camille. Your spirit is lighter. You were happy—"

"Please don't say she completes me." Ben was going for humor but sounded kind of desperate. Because the truth was that Cam did complete him.

His dad's eyes twinkled. "When a man's been completed, he can see when it's happening to someone else. Especially when that someone is his son."

"Cam is something special," he agreed.

"So what are you going to do about that?"

"Give her time," he said.

"How long has she been gone?"

"Two weeks." It felt like two years.

"Have you talked to her?"

"I've called and left messages because she doesn't pick up. She calls back and leaves voice mail that she's fine." He shook his head. "But—"

"Yeah, but. So you haven't *talked* to her. It's been long enough." Tom's voice was firm. "Don't be stupid, Ben."

"Don't sugarcoat it, Dad. Tell him how you really feel." Alex grinned. "As fun as it is watching you call my little brother names, I've got to go. Work to do."

"What could possibly be more important than my house?" Ben demanded.

"Mercy Medical Clinic. We're finalizing all the details to start the expansion. I have a meeting with the architect. Suellen Hart. From Texas."

"A belle from the Lone Star state." *Payback time, bro,* he thought. "All big hair, sexy Southern drawl and attitude."

"Bite me." Alex scowled, then turned his back and walked away. "I'm so out of here."

Ben watched until his brother's truck peeled out of the lot, the big tires spinning and spraying dirt. He stopped laughing when he saw the determined look on his father's face. "What?"

"I'm serious, son. Camille is good people. Not only that, she's carrying your child. What are you going to do about her?"

He definitely could have handled the situation better when she'd told him about the baby, but the more he thought about it, the more he knew biding just a little time was the right thing. Somehow he had to find the words to explain to his father.

"I know waiting isn't a proactive strategy, but in this case it's the best way. Dad, her family gave her the lodge because to them it was a losing proposition anyway. She was set up for failure."

"They didn't trust her?"

Ben nodded. "She had a rough childhood and made some bad decisions, but she matured and changed. To her the lodge was a way up the success ladder, a way to prove to her family she's not that screwed-up kid anymore. The job in Arizona was her goal all along."

"Goals change. She got the job." His father frowned. "She didn't need to take it."

"Yeah, she did. That's what I'm trying to explain. She needed to know that she could follow her dream if that's what she wanted. She needed to know she was worthy. I had to let her go."

"Is this like that bird analogy? If you let it go and it comes back of its own free will—"

"Yeah. If she does that, then I know I'm her first choice."

"If she doesn't?"

"Then I'd have made her miserable by standing in the way of her trying." Ben blew out a long breath. "I love her too much to do that."

His father nodded. "Have you thought about the baby?"

"Of course. Whatever happens, my child will know me and I'll be a part of his life. Even if I have to leave Blackwater Lake and practice medicine in Scottsdale."

Tom nodded. "Okay, son. That's good enough for me. I trust your judgment."

Ben really hoped that trust was justified. When he'd first discussed the bargain with Cam, she'd wondered what would happen when she left, how he would keep the women away. He'd said he would pretend a broken heart, then come up with plan B.

He'd never dreamed his heart was in real danger, or that Cam *was* his plan B.

## Chapter Fifteen

Cam looked around her new office at the Halliday Hospitality Inn. It was decorated with enlarged photos of the Grand Canyon and beautiful rock formations. The colors were Southwest-inspired—brick red, gold, beige. One wall was windows and gave her a view of Camelback Mountain and the clear blue Arizona sky. She even had a conversation area with a leather couch and chair separated by a coffee table for more informal meetings. It was big, beautiful and her heart ached because it wasn't Blackwater Lake.

There were no trees, towering mountains or grass. That wasn't entirely true, but most of the landscaping was done with rock. Very creative designs, but still hard stone. Never in her life had it occurred to her that she'd look at a pile of rocks and think landscaping. But Scottsdale was in the desert and one couldn't afford to waste water.

"Oh, who am I kidding?" She looked at her cell phone resting on the desk. It was her only connection to Ben. It was where all his texts and messages were stored, where she could hear his voice. "I wouldn't care if peanut shells were used in my yard if Ben wanted me."

A knock sounded on her office door just before it opened. Her father stood there. "Got a minute?"

"Dad. This is unexpected." She stood and moved from behind her desk. "Are you checking up on me? Have I screwed up already?"

"I just want to see if you're settling in all right." Something that looked like regret flashed in his eyes. "And I'm here because I can be. You're only a hop, skip and jump from L.A. now."

As opposed to Blackwater Lake, which wasn't easy to get to. It wasn't an easy place to forget, either.

"Is Mother with you?"

"Yes. The spa at this property is one of her favorites. She's getting some kind of facial, or massage, that involves eggplant and arugula."

She laughed. "It's probably seaweed and cucumber."

"Whatever." He waved his hand dismissively. "I heard her say something about vegetables and tuned out the rest. Don't tell her I said that."

"Mum with Mom. Got it." She tilted her head and stared at him. Who was this funny, playful man and what had he done with her father? He looked the same in his pin-striped navy suit, powder-blue shirt and coordinating tie, but this was a side of him that she didn't know.

"I didn't tune out the part where she wanted me to tell you to clear your schedule for this evening. There's a place we'd like to take you to dinner."

"There's nothing to clear because I don't have any plans." That sounded just too pathetic, but was also the truth.

"That's not good. You need a social life. All work and no play…" He shrugged. "You get my drift."

"I do." M.J. had said the same thing. "But I'm really busy right now. Still doing my homework on this property and getting up to speed. There's a lot to learn, especially before beginning construction on the new tower."

Her father sat on the couch and she settled beside him. "How are things here?" he asked.

"Not bad. Even in this slow economy we have the capital to add rooms." She crossed one leg over the other. "We get a lot of businesspeople and families on vacation. I'm going to check into the marketing campaign to see what we can do about getting more people in the door."

"You should call those friends of yours from the tabloids." He actually winked.

Now she was really weirded out. The same man who'd held her responsible for being stalked by reporters could actually make a joke about it? The world had gone mad, or maybe it was just her.

This was about business. "The employees are on their best behavior, but that's to be expected with a new sheriff in town."

Cam remembered joking with Ben about Blackwater Lake's Sheriff Marshall and then gave herself a mental shake. It was another reminder that she hadn't found the saying "out of sight, out of mind" to be true. She hadn't seen Ben for a few weeks and couldn't stop thinking about him. And the baby.

"So the place is running like a well-oiled machine?"

"Pretty much." If you didn't count the little problem she'd brought with her. Settling her hand protectively over her still-flat abdomen, she gave her father the best carefree smile she could manage.

He looked around the room. "How do you like your office?"

"It's really big." And very far removed from the registration desk. No M.J. right outside her door. Although she had a very efficient assistant, it just wasn't the same.

Dean Halliday nodded his approval. "You're doing a great job, Camille."

And that was another thing. No one here called her "Cam." It was either the full first name or "Ms. Halliday." Maybe it was too soon and she was too impatient, but she missed the personal connection.

"Thanks, Dad."

"I'm really proud of you."

"Probably surprised, too, considering that I didn't set a very high bar in my formative years."

"That's in the past. You've put it behind you and worked incredibly hard. I'm very proud of the woman you've become."

This level of praise was unprecedented and unexpected. When he found out about the baby he'd want those words back. "I appreciate you saying that."

"You've blossomed into an astute businesswoman. If your brother had lived, I don't believe he could have done better. It's important that you know I have every confidence in you to take over for me when I step down."

Cam stared at her father, trying to absorb what he'd said. This was something she'd never thought to hear and, to her horror, she burst into tears and buried her face in her hands.

"What's wrong?" He sounded bewildered and patted her shoulder.

She was just as surprised and wanted the earth to swallow her whole. "S-some b-businesswoman."

"I meant what I said. Never expected tears and I'm getting the feeling they're not happy ones. So let me say this. You don't have to take over for me if you don't want to."

She dropped her hands and stared at him. This time she asked the question out loud. "Who are you and what have you done with my father?"

"I deserve that." He sighed. "After what you said in Blackwater Lake, I've done a lot of soul-searching. Your mother, too."

"You told Mom?"

"Yes. And you're right. We just weren't there for you after your brother died. Stupid, really. We lost one child and instead of focusing on our two surviving girls, it's like we lost them, too." Sadness made the lines by his nose and mouth deeper. "We were devastated and immersed ourselves in work. And I put too much pressure on you. When life is out of control, you control what you can."

"I'm sorry, Dad, about what I put you and Mom through."

"In hindsight I believe you were trying to get our attention. Your mom and I were just too emotionally drained to understand the behavior. I'm the one who's sorry."

"It's okay." She twisted her fingers together.

"It's not." He shook his head. "But I'll do better. And I want you to know I'm incredibly proud of you, Cammie."

The childhood nickname started the tears all over again, and this time her father pulled her into his arms.

"Tell me what's wrong, sweetheart."

"You might want to take back what you just said about being proud. I've messed up again, Dad."

"It can't be that bad."

"It is. I'm pregnant." She lifted her head and met his gaze. "The baby is Ben's, in case you were wondering."

"I wasn't." He tightened his arm around her. "I'm at a loss here. If this were business, I'd know what to do, what to say. But this is you and I've already made so many mistakes."

"You don't have to do or say anything."

"Yes, I do. I'm your father, but this is new territory. Should I ask what his intentions are? Beat him up? Throw vegetables at him?"

"It's my problem." She brushed moisture from her cheeks.

"You're my daughter and that makes it mine." He thought for a moment. "Does Ben know?"

"I told him before I left town."

"And he still let you go?"

"He was in shock."

"I know how he feels, but that's no excuse."

"He's called, but I've been avoiding talking to him."

"You have to sooner or later," he said.

"I know." So much for Halliday backbone.

Her father blew out a breath. "Do you like it here in Scottsdale?"

"Yes," she said automatically.

"Be honest. You can tell me the truth."

"Okay. I miss Blackwater Lake. I miss the town, the wilderness, the people." It was a place where someone noticed you were pregnant and bought you a test to find out for sure.

"I miss Ben."

"Do you love him?"

"Yes." She felt the tears welling again. "I guess I hoped he'd come after me."

"Okay, then. *This* I can help you with."

"What?"

"Don't be a doormat," he said. "Go after what you want."

"I don't think he wants me. Or the baby."

"Did he say that?"

"No." Not exactly, but the house he was building wasn't for a family. "But I didn't give him much chance to say anything." She met his gaze. "The thing is, at first we were just pretending to be a couple."

"What?" He stared at her. "Why?"

"Women were coming on to him. Faking sprained ankles to get his attention. It was disruptive to his medical practice and he felt the need to do something. He figured if word got out that he was dating someone, they'd leave him alone. In return, he helped me connect with the people. He grew up there. He knows the quirks, the personalities, and gave me practical, commonsense advice. More than anything I wanted to be successful there so I could prove to you I could do it. Then I'd get my dream job. So we made a bargain."

Her father thought this over, then nodded. "You wanted it badly enough to make a deal. I think I see what's going on here. Why he didn't come after you."

"Care to share?"

"Unlike me, Dr. McKnight is *not* putting pressure on you. He's giving you space. You have to let him know it's not what you want."

"But what if he doesn't want me? What if he doesn't want the baby?"

"Then he's not the man I think he is and I'll throw more than vegetables at him." His expression was hard. "But I'd bet everything I own that he cares about you very much. Don't forget, I saw him in action." He smiled. "I know it's hard, but you have to try. You might get everything or nothing, but whatever happens, you're not alone."

"Really?"

"You've got your family and we'll be there for you and

the baby." He grinned suddenly. "I'm going to be a grand-father."

"Yeah. How do you think Mom will feel about being a grandmother?"

"Over the moon. She loves babies and she loves you."

"You're going to make me cry again."

"Heaven forbid." His smile turned tender. "But I've got one more thing to say. And this is something I learned the hard way. Life is too short not to grab happiness with both hands. Ben loves you and you'd be a fool to let him get away."

"Don't sugarcoat it, Dad. Tell me how you really feel."

"Damn right." He nodded emphatically. "I haven't always been a good parent, but I'm not in the habit of fathering fools."

"Good to know. And speaking of how you really feel…" She met his gaze. "No matter what happens, I won't be taking over for you."

"It's okay." He kissed her forehead. "I had a feeling. Then I had a long talk with your sister and she'd really like a shot at it."

"Good. Leighton will do a terrific job. Thanks for understanding, Dad."

"Don't mention it. Just take care of my grandchild and go talk to that doctor."

That was her plan.

Cam drove through downtown Blackwater Lake and couldn't look at everything hard enough. Tanya's Treasures. The Grizzly Bear Diner. Al's Dry Cleaning. Even the hardware store was a sight for sore eyes. Finally Blackwater Lake Lodge came into view, with the unbelievably beautiful mountains in the distance. She felt a swelling sensation inside and figured that was just her heart and soul filling up again. After her time away, she'd been several quarts low on scenic beauty and fresh air.

And Ben.

She kept one hand on the wheel and settled the other over her belly. "We're going to see your daddy soon, little one. Hopefully he'll be happy to see us."

It had been a month and he'd continued to text and leave voice mails that had a steadily increasing note of frustration. Once she'd caught him just as he was going into surgery and couldn't talk, but the short back-and-forth made her heart ache.

Except for her parents, no one knew she was coming home to Montana because she wanted to surprise Ben. She turned right into the Mercy Medical Clinic parking lot and noticed piles of lumber and other supplies that indicated construction on the expansion was imminent. Ben would be happy about that.

She pulled her sporty little Mercedes to a stop beside his SUV. Never before had she felt such a rush of anticipation at the sight of a car. After shutting hers off, she grabbed her purse and the small covered dish beside her, then stepped out. Summer was coming and the air was warm and sweet with the scent of pine. A feeling of contentment joined scenic beauty and fresh air in her heart and soul.

Her goal was to top it all off with a healthy dose of love.

Clinic hours were over and since his was the only other vehicle in the lot, it looked like Ben was alone. Walking past his car, Cam glanced into the back and saw his backpack, obviously full. It was the one he'd brought when they camped out. Was he going into the mountains? With another woman? Judy?

Cam's chest squeezed tight as her conviction slipped. What if she was too late? Then she remembered her father's words about fools. If the window of opportunity was that small, she never had a chance in the first place.

Practicing the walk she'd planned to use, she moved to the front door and tried the knob. It was locked, so she rang the bell. She didn't know if he was angry enough to leave *her* out here, but he'd never abandon a patient. Finally the door was opened and he stood there looking too wonderful for words.

"Cam—"

"Hi, Ben."

Surprise was evident in his expression as he studied her from head to toe like he couldn't look hard enough. Then his gaze settled on what she was holding. "What's in the dish?"

"A casserole. Tuna. Cheese. Noodles. A little of this and that."

"Sounds yummy."

"So is it okay if I bring it inside?"

"If you want to." He pulled the door wide and let her pass in front of him.

"Where should I put it?"

"There's a break room in the back. It's past the reception desk. At the waiting area turn right. Go all the way down the hall. Last room on the left before the back door."

Cam had never been this nervous when she was pretending to be his main squeeze. Now she had a lot to lose. She'd missed his smile and the masculine scent of his skin. Her heart was beating so hard it was about to jump out of her chest and her legs were shaking. She wasn't sure she could pull off what she wanted to, but she would give it her best shot.

She moved in front of him and poured on an exaggerated, uneven walk down the long hall, trying to remember how it had felt after she'd kicked the railing on the second floor deck of the lodge.

She turned into the room with a table in the middle and a refrigerator. Holding out the dish she asked, "Where do you want this?"

"In the freezer." There was amusement in his eyes.

She opened the top door and saw quite a few other dishes there. "Wow."

"I'm a popular guy."

"I guess so."

He took the covered dish from her and set it inside, then closed the door and looked down at her. "Are things going well in Scottsdale?"

"Why do you ask?"

"I was sort of hoping you were having problems with the staff and came back for your serenity place."

"Arizona was fine." Her chest was so tight she could hardly talk. "The employees are extraordinarily nice and cooperative."

"Oh." He sounded disappointed.

"Why?"

"Because you're limping."

She searched his eyes for a clue that he cared for her, that she wasn't just a woman he needed a pretend girl-friend to avoid.

"You noticed that. I heard a rumor that there's a very good orthopedic doctor here who can fix what's wrong with me."

"As it happens, I am a really good doctor. Top of my class in med school and a real hotshot during internship and residency." He stared at her. "All that expertise tells me that there's nothing wrong with your leg. In fact you've got great legs and you're using them to get my attention."

"Is it working?"

"Pretty much." His eyes darkened. "Which makes me wonder why you brought food."

"You of all people should know that saying about the way to a man's heart being through his stomach—"

"Not true."

That gave her pause. Maybe she'd been wrong to hope. Maybe the calls and messages while she was away were only because of the baby. Maybe her father was right and she'd need to rely on her family's support after all.

"I noticed the full backpack in your car," she said. "Are you going somewhere?"

"To Scottsdale."

She could hardly believe it. "Really?"

He nodded. "It's been long enough. I gave you space, but I couldn't stand it anymore. I had to see you."

"Really?" Happiness flooded her.

"Yes. And if I couldn't persuade you to come back here, I was fully prepared to move to Arizona and practice medicine there."

"You would give up Blackwater Lake for—" She hesitated, wanting to say for her, but couldn't. "For the baby?"

"I want the baby very much," he said, his voice deep with emotion. "Never, ever doubt that. But I was coming after you."

"I see." She tried to be cool, but the corners of her mouth curved up. "You do realize that I was throwing myself at you just now with the limp and the casserole."

"I got it." He grinned, looking very pleased with himself.

"So I guess I gave up all the power in the relationship."

He took her purse and set it on the table, then pulled her into his arms. "You didn't give up anything because you always had the power and always will. I'm officially giving you notice that I'd like to change the terms of our bargain."

She snuggled into the warmth of him. Scottsdale had been lonely and cold, which was hard to do at this time of year in the desert Southwest. "Okay. I'm willing to negotiate."

"I'd like to propose something more permanent than our previous bargain."

"Oh?"

"Instead of dating, I'd like you to be my wife. My bachelor days are over. All the fun times filled with creative casseroles and phony limps just don't have the appeal they used to."

"I'm very glad to hear that."

"Good, because I'm not pretending. I love you. I think you should marry me and help me fill that big house with a family. Lots of kids and laughter. Make memories with me, Camille Halliday."

"That's the best offer I've ever had." Her eyes filled with tears of happiness. "And that means I'll get to stay in Blackwater Lake, which I've come to love very much."

"What about me?"

Her eyes locked with his and she willed him to see into her soul. "I love you with all my heart. Anywhere you are is home to me."

"Thank God." He pulled her tight against him and let out a long breath that sounded a lot like relief. "I was such an idiot."

"Is that so? What about top of your class in med school?"

"There I was the man. This condition called love is where I exhibited symptoms of stupid. I was so sure that dating you and having a beginning and end all planned out would control pesky emotions."

"You're not the only one. I thought knowing what you wanted up front would protect me." She pulled back a little. "Love is the last thing I expected or wanted."

"And now?"

"I wouldn't have it any other way."

Love and longing slid into his eyes. He lowered his head and whispered against her lips, "This is what I call the will-you-marry-me kiss."

His mouth settled on hers, warm and sweet in the best kiss she'd ever had. It promised love, happiness and the family she'd always longed for.

She smiled. "I would love to marry you."

And she wasn't pretending. The doctor's dating bargain was the best deal she'd ever made.

\* \* \* \* \*

Look out for
**Mills & Boon® TEMPTED™ 2-in-1s,**
from September

*Fresh, contemporary romances
to tempt all lovers of
great stories*

## A sneaky peek at next month…

# Cherish™

**ROMANCE TO MELT THE HEART EVERY TIME**

## *My wish list for next month's titles…*

In stores from 16th August 2013:

❑ A Marriage Made in Italy – Rebecca Winters

& The Cowboy She Couldn't Forget – Patricia Thayer

❑ Miracle in Bellaroo Creek – Barbara Hannay

& Patchwork Family in the Outback – Soraya Lane

In stores from 6th September 2013:

❑ The Maverick & the Manhattanite – Leanne Banks

& A Very Special Delivery – Brenda Harlen

❑ The Courage To Say Yes – Barbara Wallace

& Her McKnight in Shining Armour – Teresa Southwick

Available at WHSmith, Tesco, Asda, Eason, Amazon and Apple

## *Just can't wait?*

**Visit us
Online**

You can buy our books online a month before
they hit the shops! **www.millsandboon.co.uk**

0813/23

# *Special Offers*

Every month we put together collections and longer reads written by your favourite authors.

Here are some of next month's highlights— and don't miss our fabulous discount online!

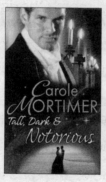

On sale 6th September    On sale 6th September    On sale 16th August

*Save 20%*

*on all Special Releases*

# *Join the Mills & Boon Book Club*

Want to read more **Cherish**™ books?
We're offering you **2 more** absolutely **FREE!**

We'll also treat you to these fabulous extras:

- ❧ Exclusive offers and much more!

- ❧ FREE home delivery

- ❧ FREE books and gifts with our special rewards scheme

*Get your free books now!*

**visit www.millsandboon.co.uk/bookclub**
**or call Customer Relations on 020 8288 2888**

# The World of Mills & Boon®

There's a Mills & Boon® series that's perfect for you. We publish ten series and, with new titles every month, you never have to wait long for your favourite to come along.

**Blaze.**
*Scorching hot, sexy reads*
4 new stories every month

**By Request**
*Relive the romance with the best of the best*
9 new stories every month

**Cherish™**
*Romance to melt the heart every time*
12 new stories every month

**Desire™**
*Passionate and dramatic love stories*
8 new stories every month

# *Mills & Boon® Online*

Discover more romance at
**www.millsandboon.co.uk**

- **FREE** online reads
- **Books** up to one
  month before shops
- **Browse our books**
  before you buy

*…and much more!*

---

**For exclusive competitions and instant updates:**

 Like us on **facebook.com/millsandboon**

 Follow us on **twitter.com/millsandboon**

 Join us on **community.millsandboon.co.uk**

*Visit us Online*  Sign up for our FREE eNewsletter at
**www.millsandboon.co.uk**

WEB/M&B/RTL5